To The Shining Mountains
The Lapoint Series III

by

Wil Michael Peck

Published by Advanced Concept
Lago Vista, Texas

Copyright © 2012 by Wilfred Michael Peck
Published by arrangement with
Advanced Concept Design

Library of Congress Control Number
to be assigned
International Standard Book Number
ISBN 13: 978-0-9826162-5-3
ISBN 10: 0-9826162-5-2

For information, address
rseibert@advancedconceptdesign.com
axlerod@peoplepc.com

First paperback printing October 2012
Printed in the United States of America
derek@kustomkwikprint.com

1ˢᵗ Edition Copy October 2012   10 9 8 7 6 5 4 3 2
Audio published May 19, 2025

LaPoint Series III
To The Shining Mountains

Dedicated to the horses, scouts, and drovers who opened
the southwest to exploration and settlement.
=================================

Much appreciation goes to those who inspired and
encouraged this yarn, beginning with my Grandma Alice
from Plum Creek, who told me my first frontier Texas tales
as a young boy, and continuing through many teachers, to
those who helped edit
To The Shining Mountains

Muchas gracias to Hank Young of Cortijo Jerez, Durango,
Colorado, for introducing me to the Andalusian horse,
and for the cover photo of his stallion
"Escobar"

=================================

What follows is a work of historical fiction,
based on actual events surrounding the
Red River Wars on the Staked Plains,
when the buffalo and Comanche
were replaced by cattle and drovers,
who pushed the ranching culture northwest
through The Dust of Texas
To The Shining Mountains.

Wil Michael Peck

To the Shining Mountains
Wil Michael Peck

Contents

Chapter One: The Shining Mountains

The two dusty horsemen paused on a minor rise north of Bosque Redondo to take in the view and let their Spanish stallions graze. They had traversed a small valley of a side stream of the Pecos River of New Mexico to mount the rise, and the cascading scree had blown dust back and covered them. The shimmering river was to their left a few miles, heading north, while distant blue lines of mountains appeared in the far west and north with the field glasses. The early morning September grass of 1872 was tan and golden browns, with a few scattered cedar and piñon trees and brush in the draws. Recent rains had put water in the creeks.

Josh LaPoint, a slender but muscular and well-tanned man with long blond hair tied back, and a short beard, stood in his stirrups and took in the view with binoculars, slowly sweeping from the Bosque Redondo, four miles to the south, where they had delivered the cattle herd destined for the immense Lucien Maxwell spread, to the distant ridge-lines in the west and north. Both riders wore the latest Remington cartridge revolvers with a hunting knife on the belt, and carried Spencer repeaters and long rifles in saddle scabbards. The horses carried hand tooled Spanish leather tack, the saddles with big ornate horns, the saddlebags covered with floral patterns on the flaps.   A mild norther had pushed through the afternoon before, signaling the end of a scorching summer, as Charles Goodnight had sat astride his favorite horse and made a running count of the cattle herd passing in front of him, never stopping for the windstorm and dust in his eyes.

"Keep them field glasses from flashin', would ya? Keep it in the shade of your big new hat. See any riders?" asked Gabe.

"No. Except for some of the Maxwell drovers moving horses, probably the remuda we sold them, to the south, from Bosque Redondo. Relax for a while. I think I can see the mountains starting up there, far blue ridges in the west, and north too."

"Them's tha Rocky Mountains to the west, started with the Guadalupes, which we first seen when we pointed north inta New Mexico, and goes right on up, between us and the Rio Grande. We'll enter the big shinin' mountains north of Las Vegas, if some Comanchero crew don't spot us first, or Comanches. Then we'll see if these pack horses can climb."

"How far do you figure that is?"

"About a hundred miles or so, five or six days, pretty rough country in parts. Looks like thar's gonna be grass, though."

"Yeah, it does, and fresh water in the creeks from those thunderstorms. No more dusty alkali flats, pulling fractious cattle along."

"Dang right. Did ya ever figure out how far we drove that herd, 'cordin' ta that new map ya got?"

"About four hundred miles from Fort Concho to Bosque Redondo, I figure. Damn I'm glad it worked out so well, and it's over."

"Yeah, yore a top trail boss now, and you got a chance to take a break, get a bird's eye view of yore situation, maybe see some new opportunities. No more nose to the grindstone for a while."

"I heard that. No more running a ranch, chasing mustangs through sticker bushes and rustler bands, nor driving a cattle herd through an alkaline desert. It's a relief, for sure."

"Them cattle had plenty of weight on them, and Goodnight was shore pleased. 'Bout time ya took some time off, I think living near them Helena gun thugs was gettin' ya old 'fore yore time. Anyway, it's good to take a break an access yore situation at around age thirty, I figure, change of scenery, too."

"Yeah, I am about burned out on that running battle with rustlers and gunfighters in south Texas. I'm seeing a whole line of mountains to the west now. So this is what you've been telling me about since I was a kid, eh scout McBride?"

"Yep. Yonder they lay, the shinin' mountains, though we got some rough dry hills and grassland to pass through first," said Gabe.

"How are you feeling, after that long ride across the desert, old timer? Got your water level back up yet?"

"Pert' near, though I'll be glad to be drinkin' some mountain stream water instead of that alkali Pecos River stuff. We got ta pick up some in these canvass bags and boil it at lunchtime. Shore glad to be shed of those baying cattle. Wish we could find a buffalo ta eat."

"You think we'll see any on this route?"

"Ain't likely, but ya never can tell. This fresh grass might draw them over to the front ranges. At least it's quiet now, ain't no bawlin' cattle. I'as about sick ta death of that. Usually I'd be scoutin' far enough ahead of tha herd to miss that, but thar weren't no scoutin' to that hundred mile stretch across the Centralia wash."

"Me too, it was an awful sound when they got to suffering, and being responsible for so many dumb beasts across that waterless stretch was a load on my mind, bigger than a horse wrangling outfit, that's for sure. Glad to have it gone for a while. And you're right, we're due a little break."

"Don't I know it? I was about dried out ta jerky before we got to the Horse-head crossing. If it weren't for Cypress Sally's potion to keep me awake, you might have found me sleeping on the ground in Buck's shadow."

"I know what you mean. When I spotted the Pecos River and realized we had the cattle and drovers across that desert safely, I laid down with a wet hat on my face under a mesquite for shade and fell fast asleep while waiting for the herd. I woke up to Scorpio nuzzling me and hearing Jesse singing and cattle baying thirty yards away. I got up mighty quick when I heard the bell on old Plunger. Jesse laughed his ass off at me."

"Wal, old Plunger woulda stepped right over ya, followed by tha cattle...that'd been a fine sight, trampled by yore own herd after getting' 'em through the desert. Being lucky don't hurt none, huh LaPoint?"

"I know that's right. Having the best old scout and the best point riders, that doesn't hurt any, either. It was a shame to sell old Plunger."

"Don't fret about that, Charlie will take good care of him. He'll be leading herds all up the front range."

"I imagine so. Charlie Goodnight is a determined man. So which way are we heading, exactly?"

3

"Yonder," said Gabe as he pointed northwest, "Keep that peak in front of us for a while. We'll stay to the east side of the Pecos, and follow it on up to Puerto Luna, headin' northwest, generally. Thar will be some side creeks with better water, but it will involve some climbin' like we just done, through dusty draws."

LaPoint slipped his big bandanna over his lower face. "We been through the dust of Texas for over five years, what's a little more dust? Mind if I ride in front for a change?"

"So you don't mind the dust so long as yore in front, huh?

"We'll trade off."

"Alright, lead on, if I get lost I'll just look for that hat. But remember, this is Comanchero country, so don't raise no big dust trail. If the buffalo came over for grass, then the Comanche might be followin' 'em. Keep yore young eyes peeled, and let's don't top no rises that ain't got trees ta hide in. This is the same country where they jumped Oliver Loving."

"How could I forget? Goodnight drilled me about that, and about collecting brands for him, until I was blue in the face. He grabs a hold on a notion like a pit bull and won't let go. Now he's on this cleaning out the Comanchero rustlers notion. And you ex-rangers are not shy about repeating a thing 'til it's ground into the hide."

"Wal watch for dust and movement, or circling birds, with them sharp eyes. And don' top no rises, for they usually got scouts out when they're dealin' with stolen stock," said Gabe. "They will have good rifles, too."

"Yeah," said LaPoint with a little smile. "So did the one chasing you in the dark on the upper Concho River. It made a nice flash so I could shoot him. I have some good rifles too. You ready to move a little faster now?"

"Naw, not yet. Buck is wore down, and we're climbing inta thin air. Keep walkin'. Keep yore eyes peeled."

They rode north at a fast walk, side by side, the proud high heads of their stallions together as the climbed up and down the draws with tiny creeks in them, feeding the salty Pecos. The cattle drive had worn down the stallions, so the two scouts traveled slowly, letting them graze the rich dry grass along the Pecos. Scout McBride, close to sixty years old, still feeling the dehydration, wanted to stop at every mountain

4

stream and collect clear water after weeks of alkali water on the drive for Goodnight. At noon they made a small lunch fire and boiled the fresh water for their canteens. A crow came to their camp and began to repeat a phrase of raucous caws at Gabe. The old scout cocked his head and listened, then spoke.

"Crow says thar ain't no buffalo nor Comanche around. That water's boilin' now, let's get it ta coolin' off and take a rest." Gabe laid under a cedar bush for a siesta, after first rooting around to drive out snakes.

"After telling me to keep my eyes peeled all morning for hostiles, you want to take a nap now?"

"Crow told me that tha range is clear for a while now, and I'm real sleepy."

"So am I, but..."

"Come on, take a rest, that's what folks do when they ain't runnin' an outfit or racin' ta be somewhars," said the scout as he adjusted his felt hat over his face. "Thars no rustlers ta battle, no herd ta watch. Ya ain't seen no buff nor Comanches nor Comancheros in them glasses, let's siesta for a while. Let that water cool 'fore we pour it inta canteens."

Since the old scout was invariably right with his hunches, LaPoint was agreeable to a rest, being concerned for his mentor's condition after the wearisome ride to the horse-head crossing of the Pecos. He was content to move slowly towards the mountains and replenish the stock, letting his older friend recover from the tough non-stop push through the 100 mile dry stretch to the Pecos. Everyone on the drive had suffered intestinal scouring from the alkaline water of that winding river, and all had lost weight and strength, including the horses. After a couple of days of slow travel and grazing near freshwater streams, they all began to recover and to move at a canter, traveling northwesterly along the east side of the Pecos River.

Traveling with two well-selected gelding pack horses, they could go a little faster than with their usual pack mules, who were headed back to their Texas ranches with the rest of the LaPoint outfit. The still-wary scouts tried to pick a trail that raised the least amount of dust, and kept them mostly hidden from long view, while they headed for the mountains.

The countryside of their trek became rougher and more convoluted with mesas, buttes, small hills, and dusty eroded draws as they moved north. Scattered cedar and pinõn clusters began to appear near the watercourses that were running from recent cloudbursts. The friends pushed on at a canter and traveled without pausing except to feed and water. They saw groups of riders twice, but remained out of sight until they passed.

They approached Puerto de Luna at sunset after two days of hard riding that covered about sixty rough miles. The river crossing south of the village was marked with passage of many shod horses, and they crossed easily. The air was dry and cooler than the Texas trail, and the trip was enjoyable for them, without the stink and noise of a bawling cattle herd and without much responsibility for a change. The only difficulty was climbing up and down the rises in the thinner air. Gabe had spent his formative years at high altitude, but that was decades ago, and Josh felt himself drawing deep breaths as well. They kept resting the stock near the side steams and making the adjustment, letting their horses do the same.

"It's best ta climb slow and let yer innards adjust to the thinner air," said Gabe at a water stop on a creek.

"I feel it," replied LaPoint. "I'd about recovered from that desert drive, but now I feel the thinness you're talking about, harder to draw enough breath. Horses feel it too. We'll slow down, take more breaks."

"Yeah, and drink a lot of the boiled water."

The minutes passed into hours of silent plodding with the squeak of saddles and noise of birds they flushed as they rode along the brushy draws. The blue line of mountains to the west was getting closer as they approached the town, with forested peaks of five thousand feet and white clouds hung on their shoulder ridges. Wary of Comancheros, they made a supper camp under a big pinõn pine, with a small fire of dry branches from scrub oak to cook on, ate, then moved their sleeping camp to a hidden arroyo to sleep, surrounded by pinõn pine and big mountain juniper trees with long sweeping lower boughs to hide under. In the evening they heard both coyotes and timber wolves howling when the moon arose, but slept secure with their horses tied close by, and their repeating rifles out and ready.

Awakening before dawn with cold air and dew on their tarps, they had breakfast and went to scout out the herds held

6

north of town, seeing more Texas brands on the horses and cattle there. At sunrise LaPoint had all the brands recorded in his journal, and they headed north towards Anton Chico, located forty miles north in a little grassy valley in the foothills of the rugged southern Rockies. It took them eight hours of steady traveling to arrive near there, on the west side of the Pecos. After swimming a ford they passed with the minor difficulty of slipping in mud on the shore, they followed the east side of the Pecos river as it turned into a mountain river with steeper banks. The grazing was sufficient and they supplemented it with the grain mix they carried on the pack horses. They spotted cattle and horse herds grazing near the river north of town, and LaPoint stopped with binoculars to record the brands.

"Dang, so ya gonna record all the brands you see, like Charlie wanted?"

"I figured I would when I could. He's given me a long list of the brands he's collected powers of attorney for, stolen from the Pecos trail in the last couple of years. I've already recorded a lot of matches. I aim on recording what I see along this whole Comanchero area."

"Is that how come he give ya that big straw hat?"

"He paid me to do it when he gave me that bonus for the outfit. He said he gave me this hat because it had a Loving crease, and he wanted me to have one, in honor of his departed partner, who was shot with arrows around here. You know how he is about old Loving, sort of all misty eyed, so I took the new hat, with the Loving crease. It's an honor, actually, for Charlie to do that."

"Wal, I guess so, and it's dang shore broad enough to make some shade. But that's what I mean about being alert, a renegade party got Loving, just like they got me that time. It's when ya least expect it."

"I'll be as sneaky as a coyote."

"Wal, if ya come racing back, that big flat brim is gonna blow down in yore eyes."

"Naw, I'll tilt my head back and let it blow up if I go that fast. I've been dressing myself for a while now, you know."

"Wal, don't let 'em see tha big white thing neither. Ya ought ta roll that front brim to a point so it don't flop on that fast horse."

7

"Okay ma, and I won't forget my boots neither. Anything else?"

"Keep those field glasses from flashing in tha sun."

"Oh yeah, never thought of that before. Now, which end do I look through? Can I go now?"

"Yeah, go on, I'll keep the stock here in this draw where there's good grazin', and you go look 'em over."

"You're not feeling contrary to it, are you?"

"Naw, long as we don't end up in gun battles with 'em. You gotta stay hidden, and don't let them glasses glint..."

"Yeah, I heard that somewhere. Should be back in an hour," said LaPoint as he nudged his boot toes into his dappled white and gray stallion to walk him towards the river.

"Alright, I'll relax until I hear shootin'."

"They won't see me. I'll be stealthy as a Comanche."

"Watch out for Comanches."

"Cluck, cluck, cluck, you're starting to remind me of Rosita's banty rooster. See you in an hour or so."

LaPoint was gone over an hour, and after he returned with a half-page full of Texas brands, they proceeded to Anton Chico, an adobe village, where they ate chile rellenos at a cantina, on Gabe McBride's hunch that they might hear some worthwhile information. The locals gave them guarded looks and not much information, being willing to talk mostly about the fine Spanish stallions the horsemen rode. After a few drinks of tequila, they decided to move along, heading south out of town, then circling back to the north.

They camped up the valley a few miles without a fire, hidden by a clump of pinõns and mountain junipers, and watched drovers moving small herds in. The mountains were looming close in the west, with their hazy blue mist, but they had another day's ride to the town of Las Vegas, through rough and dry country. Goodnight had warned them of the various Comanchero hideouts and cattle trails near there, and they were wary, traveling where they would not be seen when they could.

They left the Pecos River, cut north and pushed the stock and made the thirty rough miles in one day, camping outside of town under trees near the Gallinas River, a cold clear mountain torrent. They selected a spot that was shielded by a clump of pinõns and mountain juniper trees, on a slight swell above the stream. To the west was a long blue-green mountain ridge rising to 7000 feet or more, and streams from the slope made finding grass and sweet water easy. There were still feedbags of corn and molasses for the horses, and they did well on that and the local grasses, glad to be away from the salty Pecos water. Being near the mountains again made Gabe reminiscent of his trapper days, and he told tale after tale over the campfire as the stars wheeled clear and bright in the mountain air. LaPoint lay back and watched the stars, listening again to tales he had heard in his childhood, but this time with renewed interest. The Robinoix family had been involved in fur trade since shortly after Lewis and Clark's expedition returned, and Josh remembered all the family lore, and the tales of his long missing father in the West.

The next morning they rode back south and saw some drovers running a small herd of cattle in the grassy flats north of the adobe village. LaPoint climbed a pinõn tree with binoculars to spy on them. At the lead of the small herd rode a well-armed ginger-bearded hombre on a black gelding, together with a well-dressed Spanish gentleman on an Andalusian stallion with ornate bridle and saddle. He sat very erect in a light gray riding suit with leather-trimmed short jacket and flashing silver conchos down the pants legs. They were obviously in charge of the rest of the drovers, and sat directing operations as the drovers pushed the stock into corrals outside town. LaPoint and McBride figured these could be the Comanchero raiders that recently struck Charlie Goodnight's herd, as Josh saw Texas brands through the telescope, but seeing over a dozen gunmen drovers, they avoided contact with them and headed into town. LaPoint did take the time to record all the brands he saw, and the exact number of men and location, in a page of his well used journal.

"That list of brands is growing pretty long, Josh. Ya reckon Charlie's gonna find enough drovers that are good gun hands to collect 'em all back?"

"It'll be a chore, Gabe. His chore, not ours. I'm just doing this part for him."

"Alright, just be careful, don't let nobody see you scribbling in that book. Keep it close to your vest when in sight of varmints. Let's find some supplies."

Finding a good general store in an ancient adobe building with walls two feet thick and crumbling whitewashed plaster, they bought more feed-corn, oats, and molasses for the horses, and also heavier wool blankets for their ground tarps. Not having packed for cold mountain weather on the trans-Texas cattle drive, they bought sheepskin coats, knitted wool caps, and wool pants and shirts, as well as provisions for a long trip through the forested Rockies. Gabe bought some fishing line and a variety of hooks as well, and a bottle of brandy. When they left the store they looked less like Texas drovers and more like mountain men. The only thing they could not find was buckskins, but at least they blended in with the local crowd more, and didn't draw as much immediate attention. They could not disguise their fine Andalusian stallions and fancy Spanish tooled-leather saddles though, and they noticed many appraising glances as they rode through.

They stayed for a while in town to rest and relax, sampling the New Mexican cooking at local cafes, savoring the chile rellenos and stacked enchiladas, with different colors of chili sauce, mild red and scorching green. They did some tequila drinking at local cantinas, but the inhabitants eyed them suspiciously, and would not make much conversation, so they learned nothing, other than strangers who could be Texans weren't too popular. They kept camping northwest of town on the clear water stream coming from the nearby hills, acclimatizing themselves and their stock for several days, scouting around to record brands from various herds around town, eventually leaving their final camp there near the beginning of September 1872, with the first traces of yellow appearing in the mountain aspens. The dawn broke with a frost on their tarps and clouds of cold fog rising near the river as they headed up the valley into the blue-green mountains they had been looking at for a while. All week they had been boiling clear river water to prepare for the mountain ascent, and they carried canteens and water-bags full of it.

The air became cooler and thinner while the horses panted more as they headed up the valley, with both horsemen taking deep breaths. They crossed the clear rushing Gallinas River and headed further up the valley into the Rockies, savoring the beauty of the pine covered slopes, the pine scent in the air when the sun heated them. Josh had not seen tall pines since their flight from Louisiana after the war, and felt drawn to

10

the sheltered valley by the embrace of the dark forest around it, after years on the dry prairies.

They took a lot of rest breaks to let the horses blow. Josh hand fed them with grains as Gabe peered around with the binoculars.

"Like old times, huh, scout?" asked Josh.

"Shore 'nuff. I forgot how good the mountains look, and how thin the air is."

"I'm feeling it as we rise, horses too. Let's just keep going slowly, resting a lot. The pack horses are blowing hard."

"Right. They was faster than mules until we get to the climbin' trails, then they ain't as good. Takes some time ta get used to. Leastwise now we're away from them rustlers, I think. And we ain't listening ta no braying mules, even if they do climb better."

"Yeah, right, and we got something done. I have a few pages full of Texas brands and locations for Goodnight. Hell, I didn't see any cattle that wasn't stolen from Texas."

"Lucky they didn't steal our horses, I reckon. They was shore eyeballin' ole Buck back in them towns. They like the lineback duns."

"Buck seems to be taking the climbing better than Scorpio."

"I told ya, line back dun for endurance."

"Yeah, or Scorpio did more running back and forth all through the cattle drive. Well lead on, Old Coon, slow and steady, huh?"

The pervasive fear of Comanche and Comanchero attack slowly left them as they ascended into the mountains, though McBride was still wary, alert for locals who hated Texans for one reason or another. The old mountain man had always gotten along with the mountain Utes, and could speak their language well enough. He had coffee and sugar to trade with them for passing through their country, if they met any. His memories of them were affectionate, more so than with any other tribe of his acquaintance. Many of his trapper scout friends had Utes as trusted traveling companions. It was the Comanchero rustler bands that drew the special ire of the two horse-ranchers and cattle drovers, who had battled them for years across Texas.

11

This whole area along the face of the Rockies had been accused of receiving stolen cattle from Texas for decades, and Texas cattlemen were fed up with it. Charles Goodnight and others had been collecting a long list of cattle stolen on the trail west from Fort Concho, in an attempt to put an end to the constant rustling. With LaPoint filling out the list with the brands of Comanchero herds, the stage was being set for galvanizing action.

The air cooled as they rose in elevation into narrow mountain valleys, the stock panting in the thinning air. The trail was a long rocky switchback up a pine covered steep slope. They all drew long deep breaths to try to stay alert as their bodies adjusted to the elevation change. Gabe cautioned that they should drink lots of boiled water, which they did, to help make the adjustment. They nibbled on buffalo jerky and watercress from the stream as they climbed. They spoke on a switchback as they passed each other in opposite directions, each tugging on his pack animal.

"I reckon ya know we just got a small chance of finding Alex."

"I know," replied Josh. "But I'm enjoying the break and change of scenery. Just getting away from the gun thugs of Helena and Oakville is quite a relief. I never knew when one of them would draw down on me. And being around some greenery is sure nice after that long stretch across the desert. Look back down there, how far we've climbed."

"Yep. A right fur piece. You been pushing non-stop for years, Josh, and I seen ya worn down by it, but ya got the drovers through without losing one, and most of the cattle too. Goodnight was well satisfied. And I'm glad for a trip to the mountains too. Lot's of memories here. Let's keep moving slow, for this air is thin. It ain't like our trip together in '65 when we was on the run from the federals, through them swampy lowlands of south Louisiana."

"Yeah. A lot has changed. Now we make half our living from selling saddle mounts to the federals. But I figure Tom and Pancho and Jesse can handle it until we get back, don't you?"

"Oh yeah, no worries thar. Only worry is not ta let one of these pack horses slip off this steep trail and pull you over. Don't take a wrap around yore hand with the rope, we might

12

have ta let one go, for it gets mighty steep ahead. They ain't surefooted like mules."

"Alright. This is quite a climb, eh?" said Josh as he looked back at the valley below.

"Shore nuff."

They climbed without mishap over the steep sections of the dusty switchback trail, to where if finally leveled into a high green valley. Josh LaPoint was enthralled with the beauty of the pine forested slopes, the cool dry air, so pleasant after the weeks of sweltering across the desert herding thirsty cattle, and the sense of forging into the unknown, country the likes of which he'd never seen before. He'd heard Gabe's mountain tales since childhood, but was still surprised at how tall and steep the slopes were, with the silver streams of fresh clear water tumbling down through the dense forest of evergreens, with the massive craggy peaks rising above timberline with various colors of rock.

McBride seemed off in a highland dream, the sights and smells triggering old memories of his youthful trapper days and putting a smile on his lips. Their pace slowed as they ascended while the pack horses panted and protested, but they made steady progress up the valley with the sparkling river, watching the cutthroat trout hitting at flies in the eddies, clearly visible from horseback as they plodded by, startling mule deer and seeing them bound off with stiff-legged leaps through the fallen timber into the trees.

The scouts came to the valley town of Mora, with high rocky mountains behind it, and stopped at a cantina for lunch while the stock ate from feed bags. After a peppery lunch at the cantina built of adobe walls festooned with scraps of white plaster, they had a chilled beer and it went to their heads.

"Whoa. One beer will be enough for me. I'm dizzy. How high is it here, 'cordin' to that survey map ya got?" asked Gabe.

"Just over seven thousand," said Josh, as he studied the map he had spread on the wooden table.

"You boys feelin' dizzy from the altitude?" asked the bartender in buckskins.

"Shore nuff, this is my first trip back to the mountains in twenty years, takes some getting used to."

"So you was with the old timers then, I thought you had that look. You Scotch Irish?"

13

"Yep."

"Ya like the pipes?"

"Oh hell yes, and now I recognize you. You played the pipes at tha rendezvous a couple of years."

"That's right, piper O'Shaunessy, that's me," said the bartender as he reached under the bar, grabbed his pipes, and blew a highland air for them, which soon had Gabe stamping his boots under the table.

"How's that for old times sake?" he asked when he stopped for some deep breaths.

"Perfect. Reminds me of the old trappin' days. Rendezvous times, gone forever. Here's a toast to them," Gabe said as grabbed the earthenware bottle of rum and took a snort. That'll get that dizzy goin' round tha other way, maybe."

"Was ya with them French trappers in the Sangre de Christos, or the San Juans?"

"Oh yeah, both, mostly Taos and Bent's Fort, thirties and forties."

"Oh yeah? Bent's Fort, eh?"

"I was a meat hunter for 'em, for the wagon trains on tha Sante Fe trail too. Scout and guide too. Did some trappin' for plews."

"Wal, I'll be. Thar's another old timer here you might have known, moved here and opened up a grist mill, selling flour to the army forts and settlers round here. Name of Lorrain St. Cerain, or something like that, French name, never was too good with them. He was in on the Bents Fort setup.."

"Is that right. Ceran St. Vrain?"

"That's it, never could say them French names worth a hoot."

"Ceran is here? I was hoping to find him in Taos."

"Yep, got a mill on the river upstream a couple of miles."

Questioning the bartender, they learned that the old pal of Gabe's had established a grain grinding mill, as he once had in Taos. Of French extraction, with a long history on the frontier, he was a mountain pioneer, scout-hunter, and trader from the early days of exploration. Gabe had known him at Bents fort, where they hunted for fresh meat, played pool, and romanced squaws together, and at Taos in the early days of fur trading. Gabe also had fought with St. Vrain when he led the trappers' forces against the Taos revolt in '47. Later they had worked

14

with Alex Robinoix, Josh's father, in renovating the gristmill at Taos.

So the two scouts decided to pay him a call, and rode to the river after eating. The hacienda was an old style adobe, square with a central courtyard, a dusty beige color, like the dirt. Josh could tell the stucco was made of ashes and sand, and marveled at the thick earthen bricks underneath holding up so well. The gate passed under an overhead room with rifle ports. They dismounted and Josh banged the steel clanger at the gate.

"McBride and LaPoint callin'! We're here to see Ceran," said Gabe to the Navajo woman who opened the massive door after peering out the peephole.

"McBride and LaPoint," said the woman in Spanish-accented English.

"Yes ma'am. Pore favor. Gabe McBride, his old ridin' and huntin' pard, and Josh LaPoint, son of Alex Robinoix."

They waited at the door until they heard someone yell, "McBride!" in a horse and creaky voice. The woman came back and led them into the bedroom where St. Vrain rested. The old frontiersman guide was happy to see Gabe, but was pretty sickly and bedridden, and because of that they decided on a short visit of pleasantries and reminiscences, not wanting to disturb the venerable pioneer. He said he had not seen Alex Robinoix in at least ten years, but that he had only been at Mora a short while, and Alex had been at Taos back then, helping alter Ceran's grist mill with new stones.

"Reasons I ask are for both of us, this here is Josh LaPoint, and he's the only son of Alex."

"I can believe that, looking at him. Same eyes. Proud ta know ya, son. Yore pap was a shore-fire genius at fixin' gristmills. He'd dream about it, then wake up and sketch out a plan that we could make."

"Honored, sir," said Josh as he shook the old mountain man's hand.

"That's a main reason we're taking some time off for a trip to the mountains after over five years of steady horse ranching and cattle droving, to try and find him," said Gabe.

"Alex was supposed to come here and help me set up this mill with new stones and drive shaft, soon after I arrived, like he done for me at Taos back in the old days, but he never showed. I reckoned maybe Comancheros or Apache's got him

15

for his fine Spanish stallion. Later when I was delivering cornmeal to Fort Union, I heard he came in there full of arrows, nearly dead. Then I heard he was with the Colonel at the hot springs, the great Pagosa."

"Ya think he's with ole Albert Pfeiffer, eh? That squat feisty little German drunk doing alright? Is he still agent for the Utes? Did Kit ever get him ta quit drinkin' yet?"

"No, he's not, neither one. Ain't seen Kit in a coon's age, neither. He may be with the army at Fort Garland. Pfeiffer quit tha Ute agency when the war come bustin' in, and has been in bad shape from his wounds and some kind of skin problems, bad rash on his face, probably from poisoned arrows. His eyes are going bad as well. Lost his wife too, captured in an Indian attack and later killed. Both Albert and Kit got into a rough patch after helping on the campaign against the Navajo, bad luck, or a medicine chief put a hex on 'em."

"Aw hell, ya don't say."

"Yeah, they got Albert real bad, wounds won't heal, skin rotting off, eyes gone bad. Snake venom poison, I reckon. He's worn down trying to get his pension from the government, with Kit's help. It's a disgrace the way the government treated him about that, after what he done for them, rounding up those Navajos in those god-awful twisting red sandstone canyons. It was him and his men risked their necks in thar, in the Navajo stronghold, that Canyon de Chelly, whar nobody else would go. Kit didn't even venture in thar, just trailed the poor Navajos that Albert's bunch drug out, all the way down to Bosque Redondo, with over 200 of them keeling over on the march. Now they all walked back."

"We heard about that, for we just delivered a mixed herd of beef down thar, for Goodnight, headed ta tha ranch of Lucien Maxwell, who's turned that old fort into a headquarters down thar. Hell, I knew him when he whar as poor as me! What the hell was that all about? How did he end up buying herds of cattle from Texas?"

"Lucien married inta a huge land grant family, and his wife then died and left it to him. I heard he took over tha fort and all, got a gold mine in the mountains."

"Wal what was the fort thar for anyway? Never offered any protection to trail drives. Warn't no Navajo's thar when we got thar."

"Waugh. Protection my ass. They tried some damn fool scheme of that General Carleton, I recollect his name was, penning them up with Mescaleros down there. Seemed like a good idea to him on paper, I reckon. Utopian pipe dream. Crazy as hell, fell apart 'cause the water was bad and they couldn't grow no corn, not ta mention being traditional enemies for centuries."

"Wal, it shore provided beef contracts for Texas drovers after that. That how Goodnight got the cattle trail established out through west Texas and up the Pecos, those beef contracts for starving Mescaleros and Navajos.'

"You just come from thar? Ya see Lucien?"

"Wal, yeah and naw. We just drove over a thousand head of beef out the Goodnight trail and up the Pecos, to Maxwell's spread. His foreman took delivery at Bosque Redonde, and they paid us at the old fort. Lucien done turned that officer's quarters into a twenty room house. LaPoint here, he headed up the drive, and I did the scoutin', what there was of it. Mostly headin' west on a beaten trail while dreamin' of tha river. Then drinkin' Pecos water and havin' tha scours for weeks. LaPoint here done lost a bunch of weight too, got his cheekbones standin' out like Mr. Alex."

"You shore do favor your father in looks, son. You go by LaPoint, not Robinoix?"

"Yes-sir. I'm an illegitimate son anyway, and I needed a new name after a scrape with the federals."

"LaPoint it is. Suits ya. I see ya got one of Gabe's knives on yore belt, like I carry, when I'm up and about. Did you get hit with rustlers on this cattle drive?"

"No," replied Josh. "But Goodnight had a herd ahead of us that got hit. He's asked me to record the Texas brands I saw out here, and I'm pretty sure I saw his cattle, down at Las Vegas."

"You probably did, with all the raiders around here. It's a plague on folks trying to make an honest living. We have got raiders and rustlers of all sorts. Ranchers around here go broke every time Polonio Ortiza and the Bison fella come through with a herd on the way to Chama."

"I speculate that's that bunch that jumped Goodnight and sent shooters after me in tha dark, when LaPoint here shot 'em dead."

"Well good riddance. All the local stock gets stolen whenever they bring a Texas herd through. Then we got Apache's and Navajos raiding for stock and captives."

"They finally got sick of the Navajo raiding and went in after them, huh?" asked Gabe.

"Yeah they did, they commissioned Kit and Albert to do it. But in the end it was only Pfeiffer's men that entered the canyons."

"Gol-dang, I never thought they'd root them out of those twisting canyons. I guess they wouldn't stop rustling stock from the settlements, huh?"

"Shore, there was that, but... Hell, lots of folks say that the main reason the Navajos had kept on raiding was to recapture their relatives that were being held as slaves and house servants in New Mexico. That Bosque Redondo fiasco was sorta like sendin' 'em ta hell for trying ta protect their kin. Fool idea. Turning raiders inta farmers, with alkali water, eh? Big fiasco. I'm sorry Kit had any part in it, Albert too. Their luck turned bad after that. Real bad, like they was cursed."

"Not the first or the last fool idea from the federals. Glad we never got tangled up in something like that, though the army has badgered us to be scouts for 'em."

"Hit whar a foolish war, and they even had a battle near here, at Glorieta Pass, back in '62. Had thousands of men in tha fight. Albert got right in the thick of that as well. That's whar that damned Chivington rose ta prominence, stealing the Confederates' baggage train. Later he took his volunteers and slaughtered that Cheyenne-Arapaho village at Sand Creek. The lowdown cur."

"We read about that. Sorry affair. But that and Custer's massacre of villagers on the Washita in '68 is part of what got this Quaker peace policy going, and beef and horse contracts for the forts and reserves."

"Wal that's about all they're good for, selling them cornmeal and beef, ain't like these forts provide any protection. They couldn't track one of old Jefferson's camels in a plowed field."

"I know that's right. The federal army in Texas is doing about as poor a job as the Confederates and the republic was, maybe worse, at dealin' with the Comanche and Kiowa. And

18

the Comancheros strike at will on the Goodnight trail, and bring the herds up here ta sell 'em."

"Goodnight trail. Cattle drives now, Gabe? You were a good Comanchero yourself, back in the good old days when it meant peaceful trading with the Comanches. Heard you was horse ranching lately, with this Josh Robinoix LaPoint fella. You keep at it, don't ya?"

"Yep, we done cleaned out most of the good mustangs on the lower San Antonio, all the way to tha Nueces. Been sellin' saddle mounts, trained by LaPoint here, on that little spread that Alex used for gathering herds. Who'd ya hear that from?"

"Britt Jonson, when he come through here a while back. Said LaPoint was a crack shot with a Whitworth rifle, beat him in a shooting match at a thousand yards. Anyway, afore I lose my train o thought, then Albert got shot with arrows at the hot springs, and is still suffering from the wounds, but they won't pension him, last I heard. He's in a bad way. Maybe him and Kit are over at Fort Garland together."

"Ambushed at Pagosa hot springs? I thought he'd be safe thar." said Gabe.

"Naw, though he got in a knife fight thar as well, 'cordin' ta what I heard, with a giant Navajo. This attack was at that hot pool across the Rio Grande Valley from Taos, I reckon it was...lets see now, I think Los Ojos, they call it. Memory all shot to hell though. Seems like he did a knife duel to win possession of the Pagosa hot springs then got attacked, wounded, and lost his wife at the Los Ojos hot springs. He's always in some scrape or another. You'd think he likes fightin' as much as he likes drinkin'."

"Why would the Ute's have a little German do their dueling for them?" asked LaPoint.

"Because Albert was hell with a knife, quicker than a snake, and tight with the Utes, and ya put a jigger of whiskey in him and he'd take on a giant Navajo and half the rest of the tribe ta boot. But he's been laid low by this danged poison rash," said Ceran.

"Well I'll be danged, sorry ta hear they finally caught up with that wily ole fighter. Thought he never let his guard down. Sorry ta hear he's suffering from poisoned arrow wounds."

19

"His face is peeling and his eyes are failing. He wears blue glasses and is losing parts of his face from that poison. Probably a mixture of snake venom and sumac or poison ivy on them arrows, in addition to the lead he's carrying from various fights. Lost his wife ta murdering ambushers, kids sent ta school in Sante Fe."

"That is bad luck. Shore sorry ta hear that, I couldn't help but like that little dynamo. I got some lead in me still, and a need fer hot soaking myself. My head, mainly," said Gabe as he took his knit cap from the scar on his head to show Ceran.

"Your feet too," said LaPoint.

Ceran gave the best laugh he had the whole visit, and reached out and rubbed Gabe's scalping scar with his trembling weathered hand.

"Damnation, they done everything but yank it off. And ya got away.... Waugh! Hell of a scar. Couldn't come no closer ta losing that scalp, eh? It done scared all the red hair from the top of your head and turned the rest mostly gray. I heard they had drained most of yore blood by the time Alex rescued you, and he took you on a travois towards Bent's fort, looking about dead. We all figured you's buried on the Canadian or Cimarron. Alex disappeared like Kit and Albert did. No word. That's the tale the Tonkawas spread, Alex pullin' off your corpse on a travois."

"Alex wouldn't take dead for an answer, and he shot buffalo calves and poured the stomach milk down me for a few days, kept me alive. Horse blood too."

"Yep, I reckon that's what Alex would do, alright. He always said every problem holds a key to its solution. Lucky he found ya. But ya always had good luck, and a sixth sense for directions, and for Indians lurkin' nearby."

"Yas sir, some of us old timers hard ta kill off."

"I'm going under soon, I figure, Gabe, so it's shore good to see you one last time ta say goodbye and thanks for all the good trails we traveled, all the good times in Taos, all them pool games at Bent's fort, all that good meat we brought in, and pelts, and them squaws...that sweet Ute gal of yorn..."

"Shinin' times. Many a fine trail traveled. And we got to be hittin' the trail again."

"Wal, it is sure was good ta see ya with a Robinoix in the mountains again, even though he don't carry tha name, he's his pap's son. Goin' up to pay a visit to Lucien Maxwell now?"

"Probably not this time, going up ta Taos direct, through the mountains. We may head out through the Cimarron Canyon on the way out, and see him then. Goodbye for now, my old friend, may our paths cross again." The two old-timers embraced in a firm lock, shook hands, and the travelers went to load the mules, accepting bags of food from the Navajo cook, and another package as well. Josh could tell how much Gabe hated to see this once-very-strong pioneer-mountain man so sickly. Ceran seemed stirred up and was off his cot, rustling around with the Navajo women inside.

Before they left, Ceran had insisted that they take two buckskin shirts that his Navajo housemaids had sewn of beautiful white deer-hides. The buckskin bag he handed them contained these and tall moccasins for both of them, beaded in the Navajo style. The kindly old mountain man and pioneer said it was for many favors owed to Gabe, and they could not refuse him. With the fringed buckskin worn over layers of cotton and wool, the scouts were well dressed for the mountain travel, with sheepskin vests for the shade and early mornings and evenings.

As they walked towards the door of the old adobe, bearing the last gifts, Ceran rose on his elbows from the cot and in a firm loud voice, a contrast to how he had been speaking, speculated that Alex Robinoix was up at the great Pagosa Hot Springs nursing his wounds with Colonel Pfeiffer, or out on Pfeiffer's ranch on the winding creek west of town, and gave them directions there. While he was telling them this, he seemed to come alive again, like the mountain scout of old, pointing the trail for Fremont out of Bents Fort. Then his eyes clouded and he fell back on the pillows. They bid each other a fond farewell in the cool morning air, and the travelers paced out into the rising valley with refreshed stock.

Gabe shed some tears as they rode away from the grist mill. "Ceran St. Vrain. Ceran. Ceran. Good ole Ceran. I reckon that's the last time I see him in this world. He done a lot to open this country up. Great hunter and scout. Grist mills are mighty important, too. Gonna miss him."

"Yeah, seemed like quite a fella. We can stay longer if you want."

"Waugh! Wouldn't it be nice if thar really was a happy hunting ground, and Ceran and I could ride the trails together again?"

"Yeah, it would. Some folks sure deserve a happy hunting ground. Ought to look like this, with buffalo on the plains nearby, I reckon. You want to stay longer with him?"

"Naw, reckon not. Let's push on ta Taos, pard."

"You don't want to visit this Lucien Maxwell, with the huge ranch, stay at his hacienda for a while?"

"Naw. Taos. Lucien's done struck it rich, but my hunches keep pullin' me to Taos, for some reason. Ceran is goin' under. I could be next to go, and I want ta see Taos once more before I do."

"Yeah, you sure seem stuck on getting there. You think that gal might still be there, the one you were living with when you got caught by the Comanches?"

"Wal, I reckon I'd be lying if I said I hadn't thought of it, 'specially while crossin' that desert. I can't be riding scout forever, ya know. I nearly reached my limit on that danged push across them alkali flats to tha Horse-head crossin'. She whar a good one ta settle down with. Her and that little blacksmith shop I had thar. I still got the papers on it, half and half with Mr. Alex. Hell, he could be thar."

"Well let's go. By the way, the stable boy said the Utes are getting angry because of the miners in the high country. He thought they might try to take our horses."

"Wal, everybody wants our horses. We'll keep an eye out. I'm thinking over Ute phrases as we ride. I got trade goods for 'em."

"Do you reckon I'm going to have to hear your scalping story every time we run into someone you knew?"

"Likely."

"Riding with the legend, blacksmith with cast-iron head, too hard to scalp. At least you gave a short version this time. Let's get to climbing this trail."

The trail into the forested mountains became very steep about seven miles after Mora, and the pace slowed considerably, but the travelers enjoyed the alpine beauty so much they were content to slowly plod along, pausing to rest often, sipping brandy and taking pipe-loads of kinnickinnick at strategic viewing spots. Finally they reached a high valley and rested by a rushing stream before moving on. Gabe's fear of attack by Utes was much less than for Comanches, and they enjoyed riding through the open flowered alpine meadows instead of lurking through the trees. It was in an open meadow that LaPoint saw Scorpio's ears point left and thought he saw riders in the forest. He nudged his stallion to ride up alongside Gabe's.

"I hope you remember the Ute language," said Josh.

"I'm running the words through my mind right now. I ain't too concerned about 'em, truth be told. All my dealin's with them was on the square. Some of my best scoutin' pards were Utes, when I trapped beaver on the upper Rio Grande, and guided the '49ers."

"Well, that's a comfort, because I think I just saw two Indians up on a ridge, watching us, a few minutes back."

"Wal, keep an eye out, but I ain't got no bad premonitions."

"Well that's a change for the better. Your scalping scar isn't itching? Your stick is still floating, your last six hairs on top your head aren't twitching?"

"Dang, yore as bad as hauling mules, just a hee-hawing away since ya got shed of being a trail boss."

"Yeah, I guess so. Been pushing a long time, Gabe, day and night. This is great, being free to see some grand country I've never seen before, without constant readiness for being attacked."

"Wal, I never had a problem with Utes, but don't get too relaxed. Keep them sharp eyes roaming."

They traveled briskly, uphill and down, through stream valleys and back up and over ridge lines again. The forest grew thicker with fir trees on the upper slopes above the orange and black barked pines, and they plodded without worry for hours of silence. Josh found as he relaxed that thoughts of Kathy Hartman filled his head, and were hard to shake. They passed little mountain cabins set on a beautiful stream, and he imagined living with her in one, raising a family, surrounded by the richness of the mountains, bringing in elk meat on his mule, raising horses in the high open meadows. Without steady horse-training or cattle driving work or a challenging goal to bend his mind to, it drifted back to where it wanted to go, to thoughts of the woman he wanted for his wife.

The trail again rose up a steep switchback into a high valley, the slow climb taking all the afternoon hours. They made camp and a fire in the evening, no longer wary of bandits, setting up by a cold tumbling stream. Gabe went off for a walk while Josh cooked rice and beans and relaxed on sips of brandy. He was laying in a mountain meadow, enjoying the smell of the scrub oak fire and the view of the peaks, when Gabe returned from up-stream with five small cutthroat trout, speckled and glistening in the setting sun. The few nips of brandy and smoking his pipe in the thin air had made Gabe a bit tipsy, and he hollered about the trout when he reeled up over the creek edge, waving them in the sun with their skins flashing. The trout had small guts and a lot of meat on them, and they feasted and fell asleep under stars that seemed just five feet above, twinkling and blazing in the cool thin air. They slept in their clothes and sheepskin vests, their ground tarps stuffed with two blankets, for it dropped down to freezing before dawn, leaving their tarps stiff and crinkling with ice.

Mountain scout McBride remembered the trail to Taos like the back of his hand, and they wound their tiny caravan through high mountain valleys that would have stumped LaPoint on directions. Gabe spent time training Josh on how to read directions in the mountains, from moss on the trees and the behavior of animals, and LaPoint quickly comprehended, though he knew a lot of Gabe's success was due to a flawless memory for every trail he had been on, and his uncanny directional instincts. As always, Josh watched the old scout's every move, and recorded it all in his own remarkable memory.

On the second day out, in high alpine meadows with peaks rearing their heads two thousand feet above them, McBride spotted a couple of fat mule deer, young bucks with good sized racks, out grazing up to their hocks in small yellow flowers, surrounded by pine and fir trees. He took one of them down with the Spencer and they spent a day feasting and smoking the meat, as well as more trout Gabe had caught. They used the big antler rack hung from a tall branch to hook the meat on for smoking, the thin strips hanging closely together. The hide was scraped and rolled with salt for further work. After that meat securing effort, they sat back for a smoke and brandy snorts by the fire, feeling full and happy to be re-provisioned. Then Scorpio nickered and pointed with his ears towards a draw coming down the mountain to their south.

A hunting party of Utes with an elk strung over their spare horse came down from the higher country, and signed to them at the edge of the meadow. Gabe signed them into camp, and shared some of the deer loin with them while Josh opened the saddlebags for other gifts for passage through their land. They talked for a while, with a few words and lots of signing, then the three Ute braves rode off to the north, carrying gifts of coffee and tobacco from Gabe.

"They didn't seem hostile at all. So what did you learn from them?" asked LaPoint.

"Wal, they was friendly, but they warn't happy. They say the whites have taken most of their country by treaty recently, and now miners are crowding into the high mountains, the upper Rio Grande and the Animas river valleys, scaring the game, so they hunt down here."

"Miners in the high mountains? We haven't seen any."

"They said the head-water valleys are full of prospectors and miners, scaring the game in the upper Rio Grande and Animus valleys. So they're hunting down south of their normal range. They were up atop this mountain to get that elk. That's the best tasting meat in the mountains, elk."

"This mule deer is pretty good."

"Wait until you taste my elk steaks with mushroom-onion gravy."

"Well, I'm glad they were friendly."

"Yeah. I wonder whatever happened to a Ute squaw I had in the winter of '33."

"Listen, Scorpio hears something again. Over there."

From the woods beyond the creek a large male brown bear wandered up, attracted to the fresh meat, and they had to fire a few pistol shots in the ground at it's feet to run it off. That made him run a few yards, then turn and stand up growling and clawing the air, at which point Gabe grabbed his ground tarp and ran flapping at him, which caused him to bolt and run off into the trees nonstop. LaPoint had drawn his big .44 Remington pistol when Gabe made his run, but did not shoot, as he saw the tactic worked.

"Damn-it, that scared the hell out of me, Gabe, you rushing him like that. Lucky he didn't tear that blanket from your hands and wrap your carcass with it."

"Lucky hell, I run off many a bear with a blanket or pots and pans banging. 'Course, thar's always the one that runs at ya, and needs stickin'. You shoulda had yore bull whip out."

"Well, I hope he doesn't come back. I'm keeping Scorpio right beside me for warning."

"Alright then, lets get some rest, long ride tomorrow into thinner air."

"The air seems pretty thin right now, look at those stars, seem like they're really close."

"Yep. Seem like they're about five feet up thar, don't it?"

They drifted off to sleep under the stars with both stallions tethered close by. A bear returned that night, but Scorpio broke free and attacked him with front and back hoofs. When Josh awoke to the stallion's screams, he saw the enraged horse pounding his front hooves into the bear's chest and knocking him backwards for a loop. Buck had tore loose at that point and went to join him in confronting the bear. LaPoint grabbed his bull whip and pulled his boots on.

As he rushed to help, the brown bear rose up and Scorpio walked on his back legs at it, screaming and flailing his sharp hooves into its face. The bear took a swipe at the horse's legs, but Scorpio jumped back, spun around, and landed a full kick into the bear's belly, causing it's retreat. Buck took the opportunity to land a kick into the bear's ribs with his powerful rear legs. By that time Josh was close enough to pop the bull whip into the bear's face, once, twice, three times, forcing it back each time until it turned tail to run. Scorpio came walking on his hind legs at it again, while Buck reared up beside him. The bear turned towards them, and LaPoint popped it in the nose with the bull whip.

The bear howled in pain as it took to the deep woods of the high slopes surrounding them. Scorpio did a rapid pacing in place, feinting one way and another, as the bear turned towards him near the tree line. Then he raced at the bear, did a rapid spin and another kick as the bear retreated into the trees. Buck was racing back and forth with rapid spins and rear leg kicks. Gabe watched from his bedroll, the covers pulled to his chin.

26

"Gol-dang. Once that horse found out what he could do with them war kicks, thar's not much holdin' him back. Damnest thing I ever seen, horses charging a bear. He even got Buck in on it."

"Yeah, heck of a good camp guard, eh?" LaPoint left Scorpio untied to guard the camp and went back to sleep beside his coiled bull whip. Buck stood nearby, watching where the bear disappeared into the forest, until they fell asleep. LaPoint awoke to the smell of sourdough biscuits and coffee, and found Gabe ready to get to Taos.

They moved slowly up and down the high inclines as their bodies adjusted to the altitude, drank lots of boiled water with lemon juice, and thoroughly enjoyed their several nights of camping in the mountain meadows with stars seeming so close overhead in the clear air. At times in the twilight or early morning they heard the scream of a mountain lion, high on the dark green slopes above them, and it made the horses very nervous.

They arrived at Rancho de Taos in a good mood in mid-afternoon with the sun lighting up the wide valley bordered by tall peaks on the eastern side. To the west the wide expanse of high desert around the Rio Grande opened out. Shepherds in serapes were walking their small goat herds home in the dusty lanes. The town looked to be made of the mud underfoot, stacked in thick bricks, then plastered with the same beige stucco. The high dry air made the shafts of sunlight brilliant as they shone across the wide sky full of golden clouds.

There was still snow on the huge blue-green forested mountain north of Taos, but the semi-arid valley to the west appeared golden and hot, shimmering. They could see the canyon of the Rio Grande, cutting a deep line through the desert southwest of the mud brick town. They pushed their horses into the beige adobe town. Josh noticed wooden lintels over doors and windows, something he would not do in a wetter country. He had fashioned stone lintels for all his openings for the ranch house on the Blanco River in Texas. But with only adobe mud for masonry units, the builders of Taos used what was available, and the dry climate allowed the wooden beams to last through the decades.

McBride was anxious to see his old blacksmith shop in Taos, so they hurried through Rancho de Taos, with it's beautiful old church, towards the main square. The whole place had a sepia tone, the buildings the same color as the narrow dusty streets, the pace unhurried and peaceful. Sheep and milk goats were being herded down the narrow streets, from behind adobe walls out to pastures surrounding the town. Beautiful dark eyed Latina ladies were eying them as they walked up the narrow streets.

LaPoint wanted to ask around if anyone had seen the long lost Alex Robinoix, and McBride figured the old smith shop in an alleyway adjacent the square was as good a place as any to start. Gabe was quiet as they rode through town, taking it all in, peering at the faces of the Spanish people on the streets, hoping to spot a familiar one. Josh kept his eye peeled for an Andalusian stallion, for he knew Alex Robinoix always rode one when he could.

A widely varied bunch of villagers watched them as they passed, native New Mexicans in white cotton, rich looking Spanish in gentleman's dress clothes, lovely senoritas, sheep herders, loafing Indians, potters pinching clay under palapas, weavers with back-strap looms making sashes, jewelers tapping with tiny hammers, cafe proprietors and clients enjoying outside dining, frontiersmen in buckskins haggling over furs, wagons laden with goods, and even federal soldiers. When they got to the smith shop, facing an alley just one street off the square, they found it open and busy, with two wagons in for repair, and the young sturdy smith pounding horseshoes on a good anvil. The smith was a stocky fellow with a good sized chest and belly, and huge arms, with dark olive skin and shining dark eyes, but with copper red hair. He was pounding hot steel, furiously, ringing it like a bell.

"Well, here's one fellow that doesn't seem the sleepy type. Look at him hammering that hot steel, a regular human dynamo, he is!" said LaPoint.

"No kidding. Looks like the shop is in good hands."

"That is one big fellow, look at the power in those arms and shoulders."

"Let's see if he knows anything about Alex," said Gabe.

A sign on the post said in Spanish and English, *Hot Sparks, Stay Back.* The sound of the pounding was furious, the clanging percussion echoing all over the square. The smith had huge chest and shoulders, with a smooth layer of fat over

28

massive muscles, which quivered as he pounded and rang the steel like a bell. Then he quenched it sizzling into a bucket of water and went to the next shoe. Two metal wagon rims were hanging on a peg of the post beside the anvil, and a stack of shoes beside them.

The travelers exchanged glances over that when he quit hammering for a second to take off his cap and wipe his brow. He yelled at them in Spanish-accented English that he was too busy to take on any more work for today, and they rode across the square to check into a small inn, where they had dinner of stacked enchiladas, with beans and fresh corn tortillas. After a meal in relative silence, commenting only on the food and the pretty Latina waitress, Josh spoke up over drinks of clear Taos lightening, after nearby patrons had left them in private.

"Gabe, that smith sure seemed familiar. Sounded familiar too. Had a big nose and red hair like you used to."

"Doan I know it. I'm a sittin' here stumped, wondering if Lupita was pregnant when I left here. If she wasn't, waugh, it warn't for lack o tryin'. I never got back to Taos to tell her what happened, ya know. That smithy could be my son, and it whar danged odd, lookin' at him like seeing myself forty years ago. He looked a powerful lot like me in ways, especially the way he was pounding that shoe." Gabe threw back a shot of Taos corn lightening after that, and poured another.

"My thoughts exactly, ole pard."

"Dang, it whar like lookin' at myself in younger days. How old do you figure he is?"

"Smooth young face, looked un-weathered, maybe early twenties."

"That'd be about right if Lupita was pregnant when I left. It was nigh on twenty years ago."

"Well..could be just coincidence, but..He had a pretty gruff voice like a certain smith I know. Built like him too, with that copper red hair all sprouting out from under his dirty cap. Didn't have any compunctions about yelling at strangers either."

"Yep. Noticed that, I did."

"Sure might be yours."

"Damnation. Do ya reckon I left a son here, abandoned my family? I despise varmints that do such. Josh, hellfire, I never expected this, and it's got me a bit flummoxed and misfired, I admit. My powder is soggy, fer shore. Let's get a good rest go check it out in the morning, give me time to think this through. I never thought I mighta abandoned a family here. This is churning my guts."

"Why? There was nothing you could do, butchered up like you were, hardly a drop of blood left, carried half dead in a wagon to Bent's Fort and then Louisiana. Besides, if it is your son, which I suspect is true, he seems to have done alright, developed into a grouchy blacksmith like his dad. He's a regular hammer-swinger, that guy. Got his own shop. And he hasn't been starving, judging from that belly and those huge arms."

Gabe gave a snort and chuckle. "Gol dang, I like ta pissed when I seen that red hair and seen him hammering just like I do. Lupita was a fine gal; I think I seen her looks in his face."

"Yeah, I noticed you were taken aback. You were looking for a familiar face on the way in, and then saw one a little too familiar, in a way. That's why I suggested coming over here to regroup and consider. What it boils down to is we came up looking for lost family and we might have found some."

"Yeah. Consider what I might have cause to regret. It's a consarnation to me. Lupita and I never got hitched, ya know. We'd just been together for a few months. I regretted leaving her, but I had been with squaws before and parted with 'em."

"I think you left her with something at parting, a little something that grew pretty durned big and resembles you. Looked to me like you taught him to hammer hot steel."

"Might well be likely true, from the looks of it. Yore asayin' what I been thinkin'. I thought we was gonna find yore Pa, instead we find a red-headed young blacksmith that looks like me in darker skin."

"It was a bit of a shock," said Josh, downing another drink, then yawning from the thin air and alcohol.

"In situations such as this, I'm a hog on ice and don't have a clue. Suddenly I'm very tired and ready to sleep in a bed. I can't deal with this tonight. I'm in a fuggin' state of shock at the thought I left that gal pregnant. Wish I'd never left town that day. Just thought I was going out trading for robes, and I never made it back."

"Hell, I imagine you already wished you'd never left town that day, but it's the fault of those renegades that caught and tortured you, not your own."

"I reckon. Still, hit's a shock."

"Alright then, nothing for it now; let it pass. We'll sleep on it and go over in the morning."

The big meal, Taos lightening, and thin air put them to sleep easily in the quiet rooms with their massive thick adobe walls and corner fireplace. Although some senoritas were flirting with Josh as he went through the lobby, he was too exhausted to take one to bed with him, and wrote a letter to Kathy before passing out. It was the first time they had slept under a roof since spring, after months of sleeping on the ground while trailing herds of horses and cattle, then traveling into the mountains.

The next morning Josh awoke to the sound of Gabe sharpening his knife on the green sandstone he carried.

"Why the hell are you grinding your knife before daybreak?"

"Cause I'm usta makin' biscuits this time of tha mornin'," said Gabe. "And I ain't got nothin' ta do."

"But think about talking to that smith today, I imagine."

"Yep."

"So you're ready to go eat and tend to the horses, huh?"

"Yep."

Eating a Spanish breakfast at first light, they fed grain to their mounts, then loosened a shoe on a pack horse and went to the smith shop. The sturdy gelding protested the whole operation, but only had to walk a few yards that way, and Gabe got him settled down outside the shop. They strolled around and went through the shed to an enclosed part in the back to find the stout smith drinking coffee.

"Buenas dias, senors. I'm Roderigo Miguel. Otra vez, back again, eh? Early too, must have pressing business, no? Have some coffee. You both seem familiar, like we've met before maybe. I'm a little late today, getting started. I worked late taking care of that lineup yesterday."

"Thanks for the coffee, and speaking English to us early in the morning, " said LaPoint as he poured some for himself and Gabe, who stood watching the blacksmith.

"No problemo, English, Spanish, Pueblo, Apache, I have a small gift for tongues. You like honey in your coffee? I got honey from my own hives."

"For sure."

31

The heavyset fellow who had seemed so gruff the day before was now gracious and inviting like a Spanish host, and they drank black coffee in blue enameled metal cups. Gabe took his coffee and settled leaning on a bench across from the smith, who eyed him curiously. Josh took his coffee and noticed that the heavy-set smith was eying the knife at Gabe's belt as well as his face, and Josh spoke first.

"Roderigo. I'm Joshua LaPoint, con mucho gusto. We have a loose shoe on our pack horse, and Gabe here says we should put mountain horseshoes on all our stock, with crossbars for climbing steep rocky slopes. Can you do that?"

"Seguro, for sure. I have some shoes with crossbars, but they may not fit, and I might have to custom make you some. Take a while though. You could leave them for a few hours, in the corral out back. You gotta take them over..."

"Around that building next door and around the back to an arched gates" said Gabe.

"You been here before, senor....Gabe? I thought you looked familiar..."

"Familiar, why shore. I'll say it's familiar. Usta be my shop. I'm Gabe McBride, blacksmith."

The smith stood up and put his enameled blue metal coffee cup on the anvil, spilling some as he turned. His blue eyes were wide, and a look of shock was on his big round face.

"Pardon, repete, senor?"

Gabe cleared his throat, a catch in it, took a deep breath, and spoke again, louder.

"I'm Gabe McBride, knife-maker, farrier, smith, of the folded steel blades. This usta be my shop, back in tha old days, thirties, and forties. I partnered with Alex Robinoix in the early thirties to buy this building, then put in the forge and shed and corrals and set up the shop. I black-smithed here off and on for many years, usta make my knives here, folded steel, with the coal forge. Had some big leather bellows back then, not this squirrel cage fan setup, which is better, if ya got a good arm ta crank it."

"Gabe McBride, senor? Verdad? No, si? Did you make that knife on your belt?"

"Right in this shop."

"Could I see it?" Gabe pulled it and handed it with the big antler butt forward.

"Careful, it's sharp."

"For sure, senor." Roderigo took it, stared at it, rubbed the blade across the inside of his finger, then pulled one from his own scabbard on a belt laid across a table. His knife was a smaller match to Gabe's. He tapped the blade and it made a high pitched sound indicating razor sharpness.

"Es verdad. Aaaiee. Gabe McBride. Your name is on the deed to this place, Senor, along with Don Alex Robinoix."

"That's my old pard and his pap."

"Seguro!. My mother spoke of you very highly, with much love and sorrow. She looked for you, always, until she died two years ago. She never believed the Comanches killed you, like she heard from some Comancheros." He handed the big knife back to Gabe, then handed him his own, smaller skinning knife with a mule deer antler for a handle.

"You made mine too, es correcto, verdad? Thees a real McBride, verdad?"

Josh looked at Gabe and said, "It's the real McBride, alright."

Gabe nodded, took the knife, examined it, tested the blade. "Seguro. For sure. My old skinning knife. Lupita used it for a kitchen knife. I kin see her in my mind's eye, choppin' onions and peppers with it in our kitchen. You'd be Lupita's natural son? Born around 18 and 51?"

"Si, Senor McBride. And you were here until..."

"About eight months before then. I reckon I could be yore pa, looking at that red hair and your big Irish lookin' nose with them blue eyes, and the way ya swung that hammer yesterday."

"Aaiiii. Es strange, but I think so too. I always figured you were my blood father, but that you were dead, that my mother was doing the, you know....the wishful thinking, like the church and all that stuff. When I began to work the steel, I used to dream you were my father, for your knives are a legend among smiths and frontiersmen. I remember everything she said about you."

"Oh it's the real McBride alright," said LaPoint, smiling now.

"Senor Gabe McBride, now I know for sure. Con mucho gusto! Where did you go? What happened to you?"

"Captured by Comanches and Kiowa, tortured and half scalped." Gabe took his knitted cap off as he stepped forward with hand outreached towards his son, revealing the big scar and his tangled mass of gray hair streaked with the same copper color of his son. His son gripped his hand with both of his and shook it, his eyes tearing up, his voice choked with emotion at finally meeting his natural father. Gabe put his injured claw of a hand on top of that, squeezing it, then the young smith grabbed in a long abrazos.

"Bienvenidos, welcome back, Gabe McBride. My shop is your shop, Maestro. I am named Roderigo Miguel del Toro Ramirez, but my friends call me Rodney Rojo, or Red Bull, or just Rodney."

"Good ta meet ya. Like I done said. This here is Josh LaPoint, my pard, and the son of Alex Robinoix."

LaPoint shook hands with the young smith, feeling the strength in his grip, enjoying the light in his blue eyes. The big fellow had a thick body that was bigger than Gabe's, covered with massive muscles. Gabe kept speaking, eager to explain his circumstances to his son.

"See this here scalpin' scar across my head, and this claw for a hand?"

"Si. My mother never said nothing about that."

"Here it comes again, keep it short this time, I'm going over to that traders to get a bag of oats for the horses, be back in a few minutes," said Josh with a chuckle as he stepped out the door. Gabe continued with his story, waving Josh on.

"Wal, this is what happened. I went out ta trade on the plains for robes, and got caught by renegades and tortured til I nearly died from loss of blood. A raiding band of Kiowas and Comanches got a hold on me, and they was slow scalping and heaping hot coals on this here mangled left claw I got left and slicing my stomach with a dozen cuts."

"How did you get away?"

"Wal, I bout give up tha ghost from loss of blood. Then I got rescued by Alex Robinoix, who carried me half dead to Bent's Fort, then down the Arkansas trail in a wagon, finally to his plantation in Louisiana. I was nearly drained of blood when he found me, so he shot a buffalo calf and fed me the milk in it's stomach, which saved my life. He kept doing it until I could drink broth, and we traveled back east by travois and then wagon. It took me a few years to heal up thar on his plantation, get the scalp growed back and the hand whar I could use it, and then I just stayed on, blacksmithin' and trainin' LaPoint here in shooting. I didn't know about you until last night when we seen ya. I didn't know Lupita was pregnant. You say she passed away?"

"Two years ago. Killed in the square by a stray bullet from a gunfight between Comancheros and some Texans, senor."

"Goldang, I'm sorry to hear that. Did she, errr, get hitched after I disappeared?"

"No, she went to live with her brother's family, where I was raised, at Rancho de Taos."

"That'd be Chaco Rameriz?"

"Si, yeah, that's right. Tio Chaco, he was like my father, he raise me, with Tia Maria Juanita, Luis, Paco, and my mother Lupita. "

"He kept his boot-making and harness shop, the leather business?"

"No senor, he passed away, but his business is still there, run by his son, my cousin, Luis, probably starting work right now."

"So, Lupita, I shore regret leaving her, waugh....she done alright?,eeer.... yal done alright?,..after?... without me thar ta take care of my family, I mean? I shore regret not taking care o yal. I didn't know Lupita was with child, and I was near dead anyway. I see ya got the shop going, and you shore know how to hammer hot steel."

"Yes, we did fine, not to worry. Senor Robinoix sent us money, paid for my schooling, got us goat herds. Don Alex had the shop rented out by a another smith when I was a teenager, and invited me by letter to learn to be a smith, from the old German he had in here leasing the place. I apprenticed for three years, and this is my first year running the place."

"That's fine. That's shinin'. Alex. We's lookin' for him. When did ya last see him?"

"I never seen him but when I was young a few times, only heard from him through letters as of late, the last one when I took over the shop, Maestro McBride."

35

"Call me Gabe, if ya don't mind. You can read?"

"Si, yes, I learned from the brothers' school. Mr. Alex paid for my education, like I said, and the tools, the fan for the forge."

"That's good, cause I'da wanted any boy of mine ta larn ta read...iffen I'da been here ta do my duty, dang, I can't tell ya how much I regret not being here ta raise ya up like I should have been....it's a sorry thing for a man not ta tend ta his offspring."

"Gabe. It's okay. Everything turned out fine, and I am very glad to meet you at last, for I figured you were dead. We will have a long visit. Why don't I start work while we talk, if you could bring the stock around back, except for the packhorse with the loose shoe, which I will attend to first. Look at these shoes I made, with the crossbars for climbing rock. Is this what you had in mind?"

"That's exactly what we had in mind," said Gabe, as he examined the shoe with a father's pride. LaPoint returned with the oats and hand fed the stock at that time. They attended the horse shoeing and spent the rest of the day visiting with Rodney Rojo, who seemed to love to work and talk and laugh together. The ringing of two hammers resounded through the square, making locals curious about who had joined their big hammer swinger. Josh circled the square, doing some shopping and eating at cafes to get the feel of the place, while nourishing a notion of bumping into Alex Robinoix there. He asked around but heard no word of his missing father.

Many of the big blacksmith's local friends dropped by to visit and watch him work, or help turn the squirrel-cage bellows fan. Gabe was very impressed with his son's skills, and stayed back to watch with some satisfaction replacing the anxiety that had gripped him when he had learned of his abandoned offspring. The atmosphere of the shop reminded Josh of the nights of good fellowship pounding red hot steel in Gabe's shop on the Rio San Antonio. He had never seen Gabe so happy as working in that shop with his son. The longing to find his own father remained in his heart and mind, but he was happy that the trip had already brought good results to the man who had been the only real father and mentor he had known.

Seeing the deer-skin rolled with salt on the mule, Rodney suggested that Josh string it out and hang it for curing

36

behind the shop, which he did while father and son visited. Gabe gave Rodney another knife he was carrying, a large one like his own like the one he had given Charles Goodnight when parting. He also signed over his half of the shop deed to Rodney, and found out all he could about the activities of Alex Robinoix. After a good lunch together, Gabe asked about other old-timers to see if he had any old friends left in Taos. But they found out most of the old trappers had gone to the plains to shoot buffalo for hides, or died. Gabe was also sad to hear that his old pal Kit Carson had died a couple of years earlier, from some kind of blood vein bursting. That put him in a thankful frame of mind, that he had outlived his compatriots, and had lived to find a son that he did not know existed. And it made him long to find his old partner Alex, for Joshua's sake. After a few days around Taos, soaking in all they could, they decided to keep looking for Mr. Alex, in his old mountain haunts.

Chapter Two: The Great Pagosa

With all the clues they had gathered, McBride and LaPoint figured their best chance to find Alex Robinoix was to head up to the great Pagosa hot springs and the ranch of Albert Pfeiffer, in the mountains west of there. Since Gabe still had lead balls in him in various spots, along with various aches and pains form his rough lifetime on the frontier, the thought of soaking in the steaming mineral pools appealed to him as well as LaPoint, who was happy to travel further into the mountains, and now ached to find his own father after experiencing the happy meeting between Gabe and Rodney. Rodney had looked wistful as they left and indicated a desire to go with them, but quickly dismissed it and plowed back into his work.

The horsemen could not ford the Rio Grande River because of the deep gorge it had cut in the desert west of Taos. They peered over the rim into the dark canyon, awed by it's depth, with the whitewater river like a ribbon below.

"I've never seen such a steep black canyon," said LaPoint.

"Wal, thar's one up on the Gunnison that'll set yore teeth on edge, too. We can't cross for many a mile, till the banks get low, up north, in the San Luis Valley."

They headed north up the valley of the Rio Grande and kept that course for nearly fifty miles until they they reached the cone shaped volcanic-looking Ute mountain after the second day of dusty riding. They passed a peaceful camp there alongside the river on the high flat plain with pronghorns grazing nearby in the early morn. Gabe took down a pronghorn at twilight and skinned it out, hanging the meat from a piñon pine in a cheesecloth bag he always carried.

After breakfast they forded the river, an easy crossing at that point, and headed up into Cumbres Pass. Traveling slowly up the steep switchback trail, they crossed the snowy pass with some difficulty, their horses breasting the fresh snowfall. At the peak they met a survey crew that had broken a trail up, so the trip down was easier on the stock. They slowly came down into the green and grassy valley of the Chama River, arriving at the Fauster hotel at twilight after the long and arduous climb up over the high gap in the peaks. The warmth of the saloon hit them with a welcome blast as they stepped into the door. The crowd grew silent as they stepped in, kicking the snow off their boots.

"You fellas come through the pass?" asked the bartender.

"Yeah," answered Gabe.

"Survey crew still up there?"

"Yeah."

"How deep is tha snow in that bowl at tha summit?" asked a teamster at the bar.

"About three feet or so," said Gabe.

"What'll it be gents?" said the bartender.

"Brandy," said LaPoint.

"Fresh outa brandy."

"Best whiskey you have, then," replied LaPoint.

After drinking a few rounds and smoking a few bowls of kinnickinnick down by the river, they climbed the stairs and slept in a tiny room with two small beds strung on rope frames, feeling the need for deep breaths to get enough air. The ride though the pass had been exhausting, and they both slept deeply, their bodies still adjusting to the climb into the high mountain town. Both awoke early for a good breakfast at the hotel cafe, then a walk around town. Later they rode out and inspected the herds grazing along the Chama River, in the wide grassy valley, from a distance, with field glasses. LaPoint recorded brands in his book while Gabe kept a sharp lookout for Comanchero outriders.

From Chama they headed west and crossed the continental divide in a wide treeless park-like a plain, then camped on the Navajo River, south of a huge mountain peak. From there the mountains grew taller and greener as the trail ascended longer and steeper slopes and switchbacks. The pack horses labored and lathered and even the stallions were laboring on the steep hills, so they rested often, enjoying the magnificent views, and the scents of the mixed conifer woods.

The forest was mostly tall pines that Gabe called Ponderosa, mixed with several kinds of fir and light blue spruce in the shadier areas, and dense fir trees on the higher slopes. The dominant pines had a distinctive rough bark of orange and black, and were alive with gray squirrels and mule deer. The riding trails were so steep and full of switchbacks that they took three days to get to the great Pagosa hot springs, but by that time had grown more accustomed to the high altitude and were feeling more crisp and clear headed.

A few miles south of their destination they came down a mountain pass into a beautiful clear valley where LaPoint visualized a horse ranch, with a huge line of peaks in the background. He was smitten with the beautiful mountains surrounding the wide flat short-grass meadows, and thought of settling there with Kathy and raising a family on a horse ranch in the open grassy parkland. He also began to understand why his father Alex had preferred living here to plantation life or running the trading business in New Orleans.

"What about Indian troubles, Gabe," he asked. "How are things here?"

"Not bad in the old days. Like I said earlier, the Utes ain't too hard to get along with, and they signed a treaty not long ago. One of my best friends was a Ute. He taught me how ta track and live in tha mountains. Nothing like the Comanches. Hell, the word Comanches is the Ute name for the Numunu, it means those who fight everyone. Talk to Colonel Pfeiffer about all this, he's been in on most of it, owns land hereabouts, knows the situation of things here. He'll tell ya the lay of the land. It's dang sure as beautiful as anywhars on this earth, I reckon."

"That it is. I guess you'd have to build big hay-barns because of the deep winter snow in those meadows there, if you were to have a horse ranch there, huh?"

"Oh yeah. I imagine ya get three ta six feet of snow over those pastures in the dead of winter, temperature below zero every night for a few months. It would call for a big time hay raking operation with big barns, that's for sure. And ya graze them in the high meadows in spring, where the mountain lions prowl, and bears. It's a whole different set of problems, but, these are the shinin' mountains, huh? Every view is a glorious undertakin'. Plenty of timber for building, and stone for masonry work. It ain't nothing we could not do, after building two ranches in Texas. The mountains is prime for livin' the grand life. Thar's inspiration in every view."

"Yeah. Now I know exactly what you mean by that, the Shining Mountains. I'm really glad we came, whether we find Alex or not."

On the late afternoon of October third they struck the San Juan river, racing icy cold out of the tall mountains around

Wolf Creek Pass, and rode the several miles down the narrow mountain valley to the hot springs, crossing the fast current twice to do so. The pack horses were nearly swept away while crossing, and the travelers needed ropes to tow them over the fast cold current.

Huge stony peaks surrounded the place, most with fresh snow on the bare rocky tops. A small logging operation worked to the north, and the town was a mix of stone, adobe, and board buildings along a fast flowing river. They led the mules west through the small town to the hot springs, glad to be on level ground for a change. They could see a tall cloud of white steam arising as they approached, catching the scent of sulfur and other mineral salts on the breeze.

The main hot spring was a hole about twenty feet across, above the river about a stone's throw. There were various pools dug around the river bend where the huge deep smoking big spring bubbled. The central spring was deathly hot and filling the air with a pungent steam full of minerals, so there were water canals leading off from it to different pools below, where the river water could be mixed in. Setting up a camp for their horses and mules a quarter mile away, upwind of the sulfur smell, they entered the pools in cut-off pants and were stunned at the pleasure to their aching muscles from the stinking water. They spent the rest of the evening soaking in the various pools, watching big trout swim in the river below, and slept soundly a couple of miles downstream on the San Juan, with the murmur of the river lulling then to deep and restful slumber. It was the most relaxed they had felt in years of driving themselves in their ranching business, and they returned for more soaking the next day.

"This is great," said Josh as they settled into a steaming pool to soak. "No hostile Indians, no gun battles with rustlers, no stinking bawling cattle. Just relaxing with a hot soak."

"Oh man, ya got no idea how this helps my old wounds and sore spots." They sat and watched a gray squirrel with long silver hair curling out of his ears scamper up and down some nearby trees.

"Are those small oak trees?" asked Josh.

"Yep, they don't get big like the live oaks in central Texas, but they provide acorns for the squirrels and bears."

41

"I'm surprised at how many people are showing up to soak, but I don't see any sign of Mr. Alex."

"Wal, he oughta be here easin' his aches, 'cordin' ta me. This shore feels good on my aching bones. Seems like going up and down steep slopes on horseback gets a whole other set of muscles sore."

"I know what you mean. Enjoy it, ole coon, you earned it after working steady for seven years. We did alright, you know, considering we left New Orleans in the black of a rainy night with the law on our heels, seven years ago. We have two ranches and a going horse business, been shot at but not hit."

"We made it so far. And I shore am enjoyin' tha break after all them cows bawlin' across that desert."

The springs were frequented by various sorts, all mixing peacefully and quietly, trappers, ranchers, Utes, Apaches, Spanish settlers, loggers, miners, and others unknown. They decided to hang around another full day and wait for a possible sighting of Alex or Colonel Pfeiffer, and started to ask around about them. One old Ute herbalist and healer said she knew them and had seen Albert there several moons ago. She had not seen Alex in a long while, though he used to come by at times. So they spent their day soaking and fishing the nearby San Juan, discussing further moves, and a venture to Pfeiffer's ranch.

While they were soaking in a warmed pool beside the river, they heard and saw a black inflated boat come floating down in the fast current with two paddlers, one on each side, and an oarsman in the back with a big tiller oar. They hailed the shore and then the boat rammed into it, right beside the bathers in the pool made of river boulders. They climbed out and went to soak, helping one guy who appeared to have an injured shoulder, so Josh examined the boat. It was made of Indian rubber over canvas type material, they decided, full of air from pumps they carried. Josh had heard of such pontoons being used in the Mexican war to cross rivers on temporary bridges, but it was the first river running inflatable they had seen.

While Josh was looking at the boat, the main oarsman came out, and spoke with them. Gabe strolled over to join them. The river-man addressed them, after appraising the musculature of LaPoint, who stood in short pants without his shirt on, his huge shoulder, chest, and arm muscles showing."

"You like her, gents?"

"Sure do," said Josh. "Damned clever construction, different compartments full of air. Stiff and tough but not rigid. Can you patch it easily?"

"Yeah, we can. It's called Mackenzie cloth, with Goodyear vulcanized rubber over it."

"Mackenzie cloth?"

"Yeah. Best thing for river running, by far. You've got some powerful looking arms and shoulders, you ever do much canoing?"

"Yeah, but mostly I paddled a one man pirogue, a small flat bottomed boat for calm water, as a kid living on the bayou. I dug a lot of post holes and cut down a lot of mesquite posts to get the arms."

"Well, they've got one man models of these boats too. All types. Are you a good swimmer?"

"Yes, I spent a lot of time in and on the water growing up."

"Well, here's our situation. We got one paddler plumb give out, finished for the day. Got his paddle wedged between two rocks and threw his shoulder out of joint. It's running faster than he was used to. We laid him out when we hit the upper valley floor and pulled it back in place, but he's hurting."

"Yes, we saw you unloading him."

"Main reason we stopped here, to get him soaking in the healing pool, and get him a place to camp for the night. Would you like to earn some money paddling with us?"

"Well, I wasn't looking for work, but it sounds interesting. I'd like to run that river. I've never done whitewater before. Where are you going?"

"We've got some gold diggings, about ten miles downstream, in a canyon down there. We can pay you in a little dust, or we got other things to barter as well."

"What makes you think this thing will make it?" asked Gabe.

"Why sir, I know it will, done it before, several times. Why listen, an inflatable boat has crossed the Atlantic ocean under sail, several years ago, carried four men, the Nonpareil it was called. You can look it up in the newspaper files. These rubber pontoons just bounce off the rocks, if we hit any."

43

"Oh, we hit some," said his companion with a rueful look. "The way it's running now we do."

"But you can guide it with hard paddling?"

"Sure. They are easy to steer and hard to tip over. If J.W. Powell had rubber boats going down the Colorado, he'd have made it with no problem. A rigid boat crashes against rocks and breaks, these don't. With two paddlers and the oarsman in back, they are highly maneuverable, and bump their way through rapids."

"Exactly what is it?" asked Gabe as he circled the craft.

"Inflatable pontoons, turned into a boat. Gentlemen, this is scout Gabe McBride, and I'm Josh LaPoint," said Josh, offering his hand.

"Bret Haroldson," said the stocky man as they shook hands all around. "And Toby McNeil there, my paddling partner."

"I saw these things in France and England, Gabe. I read Wellington used inflated rubberized pontoons to cross rivers in the Napoleonic wars. You've done this river run before?"

"Yes sir, our third trip. It's how we explored the canyon to find the gold sands in the first place. Only way to get in there easily, without scaling cliffs. We've just come down from the upper valley, about seven miles already, with dust from our diggings there. Had a great trip. It's quite an adventure, sir. You look like you could handle it just fine."

"Good sands, huh?" said Gabe. "I thought I saw some in that black sand along the river."

"Yeah, we found a bit."

"How could I get back upriver?" asked Josh.

"There's a trail along the river down to our camp, down to the church at Trujillo, where we have a riverside camp in slower water. The river is meandering by then. We just plan to pass by the diggings in the canyon, and pick up their dust, to take it down to camp with what we are carrying. Your stout looking old pard could bring your horses down-river, and you both could use our camp for the night, and eat some fresh trout with us. He crosses the river here and keeps to the east side all the way down. But don't say yes unless you can paddle nonstop for a couple of hours in the rapids. There's quite a canyon south of town, steep drop, lots of hard turns."

44

"I'm tempted. I used to paddle all day as a kid, but it was in still water."

"In still water you have to paddle hard to move fast, in fast water you have to paddle harder to steer. The canyon below requires hard paddling for a couple of hours, non-stop."

"Well, I can dig holes in hard-packed ground with a steel post hole digger for six hours straight, I guess I can swing a paddle hard for a few hours. What do you think, Gabe?"

"Go ahead on, have some fun. Learn what ya can. Spot whar the trout are. I'll ride down to the church and meet you tonight."

"Alright then, yes, hell yes. How long before you want to take off?"

"When you're ready, we are. Put on wool clothing, for you're gonna get cold water splashed on you."

"Alright. Forget about pay, you can owe me a favor later on, if our paths cross again. There's nothing I'd like to do better than run that river right now. It would wash the dusty taste of that Texas desert out of my mouth."

Into the inflated boat they piled, and LaPoint had his first whitewater adventure that day. They all donned cork life jackets and used paddles with leashes on them. The current was swift and gave Josh a startled reaction at how quickly it carried the boat away. He paddled on the right side of the duel pontoon boat, which they had just pumped up again, and was surprisingly stiff. With both paddlers under direction of the oarsman up in back, and his steering power with the big oar, the boat was quit agile in the drops, and they traveled as fast as a horse would quickly walk down the whitewater river.

They had no problem handling the hard turn with boulders just a hundred yards below the springs, nor the merging cross currents below little islands in the stream, and the first three miles were a pleasure cruise through good ranch land, with golden cottonwood trees lining the banks, and just a little drop to make it interesting. Cliff swallows nested along the small bluffs, and hurried back and forth to their mud nests, creating a swarm of quick-flapping over their heads as they paddled under the sandstone walls. Mother ducks with lines of babies paddling behind her would appear and disappear. The river made one turn after another, with cliffs about fifteen feet high along the banks, and grassy valley beyond that. Josh noticed the good laying stone in the rocky bluffs, and the good horse ranch meadows lining the water. Then the cliffs got taller and he could not see the shoreline meadows, only beige sandstone walls, layered into good size for building stone.

Then the layered rock canyon walls got higher and higher as the river dropped into the canyon, picking up speed, turning to mostly whitewater, the sunlight sparkling on all the ripples over rounded boulders and river cobbles, the mist rising from small waterfalls and crashing rapids. They had to hit the falls at the point to avoid flipping, and the turns against the sheer vertical walls of the canyon required furious paddling to cut the corner and avoid a crash into the wall.

The walls of the canyon grew taller and steeper as they dropped into the whitewater boulder gardens. The clear green snake of the main current wound around one hard bend after another, each new turn revealing another line of boulders to dodge, or another waterfall that they had to find the point of to avoid capsizing. Their skills as a paddling team increased as the river got more difficult. To LaPoint it was exhilarating, cleansing his mind, washing him of everything but the present instant, and paddling hard to keep himself above water.

Soon the ledge-stone drops were deeper and they had to work much harder to avoid rocks and to hit the rapids and short waterfalls correctly, but the several miles of easy water had gotten Josh integrated into the team, and they had one successful dip after another through the white water, getting splashed but always upright and moving to the next rapid. The basic procedure was to avoid getting sideways and hung on a rock, and to overpower currents and back-washes behind boulders with powerful paddling. The dunks in the falls chilled them, but the furious paddling warmed them back up.

Many small islands appeared, requiring a quick decision which path to take, the rougher rapids outside or the inside stream that usually had little waterfalls in series. They usually chose the faster outside course and crashed through standing wave trains below the curve, as the two currents merged again. They had to hit the merging currents with paddling force to stay upright against the side wash, and enduring the bumpy standing waves below without tipping over. It was nearly full time strenuous paddling, but they managed to stay upright and pointed downstream as the river speed increased with the steeper drop through the canyon. There were no longer easy smooth stretches to rest on, and they were all panting with the effort in thin air of seven and a half thousand feet altitude.

For an hour in the twisting and layered sandstone canyon walls they negotiated hard turn after hard turn, and boulder gardens with stones so high they could not see around them. A series of right angle turns left them bouncing off tall cliff walls at times, or caught in back-flow eddies behind boulders. It was touch and go in that area, and at times they crashed against rocks, but they pushed off and turned straight again and stayed upright in the worst of the white water. They soon learned to cut the inside of the turns to avoid crashing into the vertical beige sandstone canyon walls, and did so repeatedly.

The drop got even steeper and the river gained more momentum, all whitewater, as far as they could see, without calm patches to rest in any more. The beige sandstone canyon walls were hundreds of feet high, with taller mountain slopes above them, covered with pine and fir. Hawks and eagles swooped overhead, and lines of yellow ducks paddled the rapids in front of them. They passed groups of big geese with tan bodies and black heads, and saw lots of mule deer and some elk on the shorelines. But always the river called for their attention, as hidden waterfall after twisting rapid appeared at every bend.

With everyone panting hard, they kept making hard turns in the canyon, each revealing another maze of boulders and white water drops to run through, and mist rising from various falls. So they soon of necessity learned to feel the long trail through the rapids, falls, and boulder gardens, as soon as they rounded a bend and sighted down it. Satisfaction grew as they were able to negotiate a trail they intended to, avoiding the holes and dead ends, skirting the sides of the standing wave trains, despite the raging power of the swift whitewater that bucked the boat like a bronco and surged powerful cold waves into their faces.

Then, when their confidence level was at its highest, they rounded a horseshoe turn and found the current being swiftly pinched into a narrow gap between boulders, where it cascaded in a misty falls. With no chance to get to shore, they tried to keep straight through the gap, and shot through only to land on

47

a boulder below the falls, surrounded by the foam of the falls. The splash was beginning to fill the boat.

"Push off, push off," yelled LaPoint, shoving against the stone with his paddle. The others did the same and they slipped off into the white foam, riding deep and taking on more water, but moving along until they could bail it out before the next falls.

"We're still upright boys, stay sharp now, not much more canyon to go!" yelled the steersman from the back. It was exhilarating to all of them, but especially to LaPoint, the eager greenhorn. He was a furious paddler when they powered it through the tough spots, the speed of his reflexes perfectly matched to the changing rapids. All the struggles of the last five years of fighting to establish his ranching business faded from his mind, and he felt only the river and the path to go.

After six or seven hard turns in the deep canyons, the river slowed and flattened out to a looping pattern over gravel bars, with wide grassy pastures on the right side. To the east stood black slate bottomed cliffs with stinking springs and hard rock intrusive dikes running through them, making falls in the river bed.

While the meadows opened on the west side, the river did meanders over gravel bars and gave Josh views of potential horse ranch land to the west. Soon they were dropping over taller waterfalls created by upright dikes of harder rock that crossed the current and stood out against the surrounding terrain like ancient walls. Then the valley widened and the slope decreased, slowing the river into even wider meanders. The paddling became less furious, though several hard turns and rapids kept them busy at times. LaPoint noticed the beautiful meadows along the river and thought of a horse farm there. Then they saw the riffle boxes of the diggings, along short sandstone cliffs on the west bank, and stopped to pick up gold dust there from the miners working the black sand that had swept down from the high mountains. After a brief visit, they shoved off again into the rushing current, the boat heavier with a fat pouch of gold dust tied to the straps inside.

They navigated the slower winding loops easily and stopped above the tiny hamlet of Trujillo with the gold dust they were carrying down from their higher altitude camps. Then they went to their campfire and wagon on the west shore and waited for Gabe. Josh inquired the address of the company that made the boats, for he was very impressed with it's value, and the unadulterated pure pleasure of running the whitewater river as well.

Their wet wool clothing had kept them reasonably warm in the furious paddling, but as the evening cooled they chilled off and made a bigger fire by the shore to warm up and dry their clothes. The miners had some pans and riffle boxes at the camp, so Josh learned to pan the black sand for the heavy grains of gold washed down from the peaks of the mighty San Juans, which towered up to 12000 feet above the headwaters, according to the miners. Gabe arrived with the stock at sunset to camp the night with them, enjoying a little gold panning too, until twilight set in. Then the old mountaineer caught some trout for dinner. They slept beside the sound of the rushing San Juan river in the high valley, their horses tied nearby to alert them to roving bears or mountain lions.

The next morning they had Gabe's sourdough biscuits with coffee and mule deer back strap, then rode back upstream to the great smoking Pagosa hot spring, soaking once again, hoping to spot Alex or Pfeiffer. The soak was good for Josh after the hard paddling, stiffening unfamiliar muscle exertion areas, but no familiar face appeared at the hot springs, and they found no further word of Colonel Pfeiffer or Alex Robinoix. The long hunt for his father was frustrating him. He had spent years trying to rebuild the family fortunes after the losses in Louisiana, establishing two Texas ranches, with the notion of pleasing the man who had left him in charge.

After their long soak they headed west up the hill from there, intent on finding Colonel Pfeiffer's place and perhaps Alex Robinoix. They nearly emptied their canteens on the ride up the valley, they were so dehydrated from the hot pools. The town was surrounded with towering mountain walls with stunning lines of peaks, prompting LaPoint to remark it was as nice a setting for a town as the Taos Valley.

"Actually, prettier, far as I'm concerned," replied Gabe. "I think that's the continental divide back thar, shore nuff tall peaks, and lots of them. The upper Rio Grande Valley is on the other side of that mountain wall. That watershed heads a different direction than this one, goes to tha Gulf of Mexico, while this goes to that Pacific. It's the divide. Backbone of the stony mountains."

"Glad to be here with you, scout."

"Glad ta have ya. We got a hell of a climb now, better tighten all the riggin's."

A very steep hill led away from the San Juan River and the steaming hot springs beside it, then several miles of level valley with plenty of grass, and a few miles later they came upon a creek coming north out of a timbered tight valley, which they followed to Pfeiffer's place. They found a log cabin and a sort of shipping building and pelt emporium beside small gauge railroad tracks, but no Pfeiffer or Alex Robinoix. There were stacks of what looked like posts for mine timbers piled around the narrow gauge railroad landing, as well as stacks of ties for narrow gauge rails. The place was boarded up and abandoned, with only old tracks on the ground.

"Look's like Pfeiffer's been here, shipping pelts and timbers, but not for a few months," said Gabe.

"Maybe he's been long dead."

"Could be, but I got a hunch he's still humpin' in the hills somewhars. I don't know whar else ta look right now, though."

McBride saw the disappointment in Josh's face and proposed riding further west to the Piedra River canyons and Chimney Rock, a prominent sandstone spire with a smaller twin, a few miles west. The old mountain man had heard about the place from, Alex decades ago. Josh agreed and they headed west for the great stone wall of the Piedra River. It was a nearly vertical stone bluff rising hundreds of feet to the west of the river. They sat on a rise overlooking the shimmering silver whitewater of a creek in the valley, and rested their stock, while Josh looked at the immense stone bluff with his field glasses.

"Looks like we ran into a solid rock wall in our search for Alex," said Josh. "It's a dead end. Like that one in front of us. That is the biggest steepest stone cliff I've ever seen."

"El Rio De La Piedra Parada, the River of the Rock Wall."

"Looks like the end of the trail on the hunt for Alex Robinoix."

"I reckon. I keep searchin' my mind for whar he might be, since he wasn't at Pfeiffer's ranch," said Gabe. "We might just drift inta him on intuition as anything else."

"Yeah, or give up the futile search. I'm game for something else. I'm glad that you found your son, anyway. I've wasted enough time and energy searching for Mr. Alex. I've got to leave that behind and make my own way, Gabe. I've wasted too much time trying to please a man who is usually gone. I don't need his name or approval anymore. I guess I'll always be the bastard LaPoint, might as well make something out of it. Let's see some more country I've never seen before."

"Wal, alright then, we'll take an alternate route back."

Gabe said they could follow the Piedra River south from there, and see some new country on their way back. They rode several miles west through a beautiful valley drained by a small creek, until another creek that Gabe called the Devil's Creek came out of a canyon to the north. They rode into that tight and twisting canyon just to experience it, and were impressed by the huge fir trees and clear rushing stream that even had a few beaver in it. Gabe was very glad to see beaver in a stream he had trapped in the past. They returned down the tight canyon to the larger valley and continued west, past steep tall rocky canyon walls covered with timber growing right out of the stone, until they saw the spires called Chimney Rock.

The Piedra River came rushing out of mountain canyons just a few miles above the spires, and they rode up that tight valley a few miles just to experience the splendid beauty of the place. A nearly vertical wall of stone rose a couple of thousand feet high, on the west side of the river, and further upstream both sides were bounded by huge canyon walls while the white water tumbled down the steep valley floor, crashing over boulders from side streams. This canyon made the one on the San Juan seem not as foreboding, for it was deep and very steep, with a much rougher torrent in the bottom. They rode up until it was too difficult to follow the river, for the stone canyon walls came right down to waterline with raging whitewater rapids and falls. Then they rode back downstream and made for the stunning sandstone spires called Chimney Rock by early explorers, a few miles below the canyon.

LaPoint felt drawn to the top, and he suggested they ride up to the plateau just below the spires and camp, which they did, though it proved more difficult than first imagined, with lots of sliding in loose scree, and eating dust. The views of the grassy valley with the winding river below made Josh think of a horse ranch there, where the river left the canyons and began it's meandering. The climb to the top took hours of switchback riding, often breathing dust from loose scree and slippery slopes.

It was sunset when they arrived, so they made a cook-fire of piñon pine and scrub oak, and they slept well under the shimmering stars that seemed very close overhead. The huge mountains to the north were contrasted by the dry mesa land to the south, as the whole horizon was visible from the plateau around the spires. The spires themselves assumed fantastic shapes from every angle, rearing their chunky heads out of a slope of fallen sandstone boulders.

That night Josh dreamed of his father, Alex Robinoix, who appeared with men dressed in elaborate feather head-dresses and danced in a circle to a slow, throbbing bass played by dancers on boards over hollows in the ground of a round building. It was a pleasant dream, and he was sorry to awake and lose it when he heard Gabe puttering at the breakfast fire. He tried to hold on to the images, but they fleeted away as Gabe muttered about the smoky piñon knots in the breakfast fire. The dream gave him no clear notion on whether his father was alive or dead. He determined to put his mind on the future, and forget the search for his father's approval.

That morning after caring for the stock, Josh hiked towards the tall stone spires as Gabe made biscuits. After a short hike the younger man found old ruins of round stone buildings, lots of them. Further up the slope, past a slippery narrow steep spot, he found similar stone ruins of great square buildings, with round foundation circles and pits within them. The stonework was carefully laid and solid, with the evidence of fire in their timber roofs, all very surprising to Josh, who was used to the tepee dwellings of Plains Indians. Some of the mortar had fired pink in the burning, and Josh examined it carefully, deciding it was ashes, sand, clay, calcined mussel shells and bones, and some kind of animal blood for a binder.

"Very clever people, used what was available, stone and plaster and timber. I imagine they plastered the roofs of their huts and put a rock curb to catch water up here, since there's no spring."

"Yeah, and maybe they diverted all the rainwater into that big rock bowl thar, dammed it up and used it too."

"But why build up here instead of down by their crops?"

"Reckon it was ta be up close to the stars, or maybe defense. Heck of a steep long walk down to tend the crops, though."

"Another mystery, like Mr. Alex, I guess. Let's eat, I want to show you some old ruins I found up the hill.

After breakfast he showed the stone foundations to Gabe, who speculated that the were dwellings of the same ancient ones who lived west of there, at the Mesa Verde, in stone buildings hidden in cliff overhangs where water seams occurred. Many of the old scouts had found such dwellings of decent stonework, over their years of prowling the hills. Gabe told him of the summer of '48 when he and Alex had explored extensive cliff dwelling to the west of there about a day's ride, homes of what Alex called the ancient ones.

They explored the ruins for a couple of hours, then descended and followed the winding Piedra River as it flowed gently southwest in a valley full of sagebrush and rabbit bush, the breeze waving yellow flowers and tracing sunlight sparkles across the softly flowing river.

"This is shore 'nuff a beautiful valley," said McBride.

"It could make a great horse ranch, with irrigation from the river, hay barns, the right stock."

"So now you dreamin' of a mountain ranch, huh?"

"Yeah, I am. It'd be a good place to start a new life, here in all this beauty, away from all the gun battles."

"Wal, it'll take more money than we got now, that's for sure."

"Yeah. I intend to make some."

"So what do you want to do now?"

"Forget about searching for Alex, and go make enough money to buy a ranch up here, away from all the rustler and Comanche troubles down south."

"Got the bit in yore teeth now, do ya?"

"Yeah. The past is over. I'm done with searching for my missing father. He's been missing most of my life anyway, time I quit wasting time on it. I was just his bastard anyway. You're the only family I have. And Jesse, and the Menchacas."

"Wal alright Josh, let's head south down this valley to the San Juan valley, then head back up it to Pagosa springs."

"Will that go by the miner's camp?"

"Yep, eventually."

"Lead on, scout McBride," said LaPoint.

The golden line of cottonwoods and willows along the river was stunningly beautiful, and fifteen miles of easy riding through good grass, and they came to the junction with the San Juan River.

"The miner's camp is upstream, maybe fifteen miles, I reckon," said Gabe. "We could check by the great Pagosa Hot Springs on our way out, back up the valley, see if any sign of Mr. Alex..."

"If news of him appears, then it was meant to, I guess. I'm done with the search. On the first two ranches, I was picking up the pieces left by someone else. I'm going to make my own ranch. Let's head for the miner's camp and get some gold pans."

In the ground around the two rivers Gabe noticed rock-lined storage pits and the round stone bases of other ancient dwellings, smaller and rougher than the ones on the plateau around the rock spires. They speculated that these were the earlier, more primitive stone-works of the ancient ones who had built so well on the plateau around the Chimney Rocks.

They turned back east and followed the San Juan through dryer country with sparse trees, leaving the thick forests of ponderosa and fir for scattered piñon and cedar bushes on the hillsides. Rabbit brush covered the valley floor except for a bit of grass along the river, which was bordered by a gallery forest of cottonwood and willow turned gold and bright yellows. They noticed trout swimming in the clear river, and bears fishing for them at the small rapids and meanders. It was not running as swift as in the canyon boating run, and the valley was wide and easy traveling.

They came to the prospectors' camp at Trujillo, and stayed to catch trout and visit with the geological experts there, doing a little more panning as well. Gabe, with his strong wrists and forearms, soon became expert with the pan, and they started their dust pouch there. And unlike before, this time Josh was intent on learning how to work the pan. He worked until dark to master a fast spinning swirling technique with a riffled pan.

As a recompense for LaPoint's paddling effort, from the miners they received a good map, with information on the whereabouts of possible gold sands on the headwaters of the

San Juan, and good pans to test for it. They decided to prospect the upper creeks of that swift flowing icy river before the heavy snows fell, and traveled upstream, west of the river. The miners warned them of the effects of the high altitude there, and cautioned them to move up slowly.

The trail turned north into a valley beside the deep canyon that LaPoint had run in the rubber raft. They traveled up the narrow canyon past the hot springs, into a broad valley full of grass. At ten miles they came upon a spectacular waterfall falling hundreds of feet from a cliff on the south side of the valley, where they had lunch and watered the horses below the spray. For two days they headed northeast alongside the sparkling San Juan, with golden cottonwoods along the banks, and brilliant yellow aspen on the slopes, contrasting with the dark green pine and fir forests of tall dense trees. Herds of mule deer frequented the grassy meadows along the river, barely moving as they rode through. White clouds hung on the peaks as they plodded up to ascend the pass.

"The map says this trail climbs up around 11000 feet," said Josh on a rest stop.

"Hell, I believe it. I'm panting, we got to go slow."

LaPoint let McBride set the pace up the switchback climb, and three hours later they reached a high valley. Wide grassy meadows filled with alpine flowers covered the valley floor, with huge towering peaks on either side, their rocky shoulders thrusting high above the tree line, frosted with recent snow and hung with clouds. The air became cooler as they climbed to the end of the valley hemmed in by huge rocky walls that were forested up their steep slopes until at their sheer shoulders heads of stone rose above the tree line. They began to spot small groups of elk, and eagles and hawks circling overhead.

When the river trail hit the northeast end of the valley, they followed the south fork up into the mountains on steep switchbacks past the waterfall at the beginning of the climb. The ascent was difficult and slow, and they walked the horses and mules at least half the time, with the pack animals protesting most of the time. They camped by a stream with adjacent hot springs, high in the mountain valley of the tumbling stream of white foam. The narrow valley floor leveled out somewhat right below the treeless zone, at 8000', according the

the map given them by the miners, with peaks on either side looming three thousand feet higher, covered with dense forest of white fir to the tree line, where their bare rocky pinnacles projected into the blue sky. Most were a deep gray, but some had tints of red and yellow in the long talus slopes. They stopped to rest often, catching their breath while they admired the view. Josh was ready to find some gold and kept panning the stream, finding a few tiny grains of gold.

They followed that winding stream up into the highest valley they had traversed, the air thin enough to slow them down considerably. After climbing for about twenty miles they camped in a broad grassy park, surrounded by stunning sharp peaks all around, covered with dark green timber and golden aspen to tree line. They spent the next morning working that stream, then moved southeast, stopping to pan the dark heavy sands as they went. The gold pouch began to grow, approaching the size of a plum. Gabe panned until his hands ached and sat back by the fire, warming them, amazed at how Josh worked at the panning. Moving slowly uphill helped give their bodies and livestock time to adjust to the higher altitude, and stopping to pan made them richer as they acclimatized. Josh got better at panning the dark sands and gravel, finding enough gold to keep him at it for long hours.

"Hey, why don't ya give it up and come ta eat these trout," hollered Gabe at twilight. "Ya don't have to pay for that ranch with yore name with one trip, ya know."

"Why not?" replied LaPoint, as he swirled the sand around in the big riffled pan, staying there until it was too dark to see.

"Folks that push too hard in tha dark often fall off a cliff," said Gabe.

Above them loomed the pointed peak of a mountain colored gray along the top ridge, then reddish, gold, peach, and yellow gray scree rested in a huge cone below it. There they found lots of gold dust and minute flakes in the sand, and increased the size of their pouch to that of a small apple. They spent a week slowly moving southeast through the high mountains, panning the creeks and rivers as they went. In the highest valley they struck pay dirt in the black sand, and gleaned a lot of flakes and dust in a day of hard work that made their wrists sore and fingers ache from the cold water. They had two pouches the size of apples when they finished. By that time Gabe's hands were suffering from the rheumatism, and he was tired of gold panning.

Then they moved south along the Conejos River as the weather turned colder, with freezing nights, fishing for their meals in the clear rushing water. When they found no fish they ate the mule deer with beans and rice and biscuits. When the mule deer ran low, Gabe shot an elk, and they spent another two days smoking the meat and panning the cold water, until they both had experienced enough ice-water for a while, and headed for Chama.

Gabe was not familiar with the trails there, but was using his instincts, the stars, the lay of the land, the flow of the river and streams, and a compass to head for the Chama Valley. After a week on the river they cut off southwest and climbed a ridge, that revealed more ridges in front of them. For several miles they traversed the bare upper ridge-lines of the divide, until passing storms with bolts of lightening drove them down. The crashing and flashing were unbearable as they saw bright bolts striking the ridge-line and retreated at a trot with their hair on end from static electricity. They waited out the storm in a deep draw, and it passed by quickly, and they resumed their southward ride. The horses were as nervous as they had ever been, and everyone was glad to leave the high rocky divide.

"Damn," said LaPoint. "That's worse than getting shot at. Those close hits scare the crap out of me, Scorpio too."

"Survival feelin's set in with all that power unleashed so close. Stands the hairs on end at time, huh?"

"I hope it's over. There must have been ten lightening hits on that ridge line. You can smell the burnt rock in the air now."

"I reckon tha worst is past, for now. We'll head south after a bit, let it move away further, get the edge of that black cloud past us."

With Gabe fairly certain they were headed for Chama, they continued a slow trek through the high mountains for another several days, climbing ridge after ridge, crossing numerous alpine valleys, when they finally arrived at Chama with two pokes of gold, each about the size of a fat apple, and diminished supplies. The mountain vacation had been a partial success, though they had not located Alex Robinoix, they had gained a substantial amount of gold, and spent their first stretch of weeks without scrapes with rustlers, after years of constant ranching.

They made the necessary trip to town to resupply, and had a meal and several drinks at Fauster's Hotel and Saloon, before riding to camp in the valley below town. They spread their tarps under tall ponderosa pines alongside the river and fell asleep listening to it's peaceful gurgling.

At Chama in the morning after breakfast, they saw that the wide valley showed an increase in the number of cattle and horse herds, grazing along the river banks and flat areas adjacent. They slipped down at sunrise and studied the herds with the field glasses, recording the brands, and again recognizing many Texas brands. LaPoint marked them down in his book to give to Goodnight when they next met.

After re-provisioning at Chama, they crossed the Cumbres Pass through knee-deep snow and emerged into the wide flat valley of the Rio Grande, with good sunny weather. After a short rest from the crossing, they rode north up the Rio Grande in the high and wide alpine valley, with LaPoint occasionally panning for gold as they went, but finding none at first. The steep mountain wall of the Sangre De Christos loomed to the east, while the tangled peaks of the San Juans and La Garita mountains reared their frosted rocky heads to the west. After a couple of days travel north they began to find traces of gold dust in the black sand, but after a few more days of panning, they had done enough panning in cold water, and they headed east when they approached a huge Peak called Blanca, and crossed the La Veta Pass into smoother country.

Within two days of easy travel on the plains along the front range, they were in the growing town of Trinidad, where they re-provisioned. They crossed Dick Wooten's toll road through Raton Pass and headed for Goodnight's Apisha ranch, a long days ride southeast, across the flat grasslands with volcanic cones in the surrounding area. When they arrived, Goodnight was in a lather over trying to get a herd across the Colorado border. The pages full of the brands of stolen Texas cattle from LaPoints journal did nothing to calm him down, but he filed it for later work, after his current jam. He had too many herds grazing on too little grass, and had to push one through to

Colorado to fulfill contracts with the miners along the front range to Denver.

He had tried once and been stopped by armed men from Colorado in the Trinchera Pass, barring his passage. He had returned the herd to the ranch, but the range was crowded with other herds from Texas, and he had the legal papers to show that the herd he was trying to move north had wintered in New Mexico. He just did not have enough men with guns to force his way across the line. He wondered aloud if McBride and LaPoint could help.

"Wal Charlie," said Gabe, his knife out and being sharpened as Goodnight made his appeal, "We ain't lookin' to get in outside fights, being as how we got enough of our own with rustlers down south. And we been on the trail a long time, headin' for tha home spread."

"Why hells-bells McBride, the longest I stayed in one place for years is three nights in a Denver hotel setting all this up."

"Hold on, Gabe," said LaPoint. "We're here. He need's our help. I'm for riding the herd over the line with him."

"You are?"

"Yeah, I am. You can wait here if you want."

"Like hell, ya say."

"Then come with us."

"Hell yeah," said Charlie. "Both of ya, salt and pepper."

"I'll come, though I'm not sure what's come over you. Why you all hell bent for leather to lasso a bunch o trouble, all of a sudden, since we give up tha search for..."

"I'm intent on a ranch with my name, not something of Mr. Alex's, and Charlie is offering good money too. I want to ranch up near the mountains, like Charlie's doing, anyway. Building a grubstake."

"Wal, don't let yore poke pull ya lop-sided in tha saddle, pard. Anybody can fall off that way."

"Oh I know, you think I'm getting' like Fremont, getting' the bit in my teeth to make a name for myself any way I can. It isn't that. It's about helping out a friend, and making some outside money."

"Wal alright, but we got..."

"He's our friend and needs our help, and we showed up right when he needed two good shooters. We're a fit."

59

"This after we avoided gun scrapes for near eight hundred miles of mountain riding."

"You coming or not?"

"Come on, McBride. I need another old ranger, and we can ride together, McBride, Goodnight, and LaPoint."

"Yeah, I reckon I will, look out for you bullheaded young'uns. I ain't disputin' that Charlie's in tha right, and he's in a bind with two herds here and not enough grass left."

"Well alright then" said Goodnight. "It's settled."

"Wal listen, I recollect thars a spring that comes out near the top of that pass. Let's have the cattle thirsty when we get thar and then hit will be hard to hold 'em back from the water smell."

"Good idea, already I'm glad yal signed on," said Goodnight. "I'm gonna have enough drovers behind them to stampede them through that pass, if we have to."

"Here's the rest of it, Charlie. The list of Texas brands. It's pretty long." LaPoint pulled his sharp knife and sliced several pages from his journal with it, handing them to Charlie.

Goodnight was very satisfied to receive that information, and intended to do something about it later, he indicated, when powers of attorney could be collected from all the Texas ranchers represented by the list of brands. The time to take strong action against illegal activity had come, according to Charlie Goodnight. Either the law in those areas would help when they saw the paperwork, or it would have to be handled in other ways.

After gathering more hands with experience in holding nervous cattle during gun-battles, they drove the herd north and entered Trinchera Pass in mid November when the air was crisp at sunrise. The plan was to keep the herd bottled up in the pass with extra drag riders, so if any stampede started they could turn it north towards Colorado with bull whips, blankets, and gunfire. Meanwhile, Charlie Goodnight, Bill Wilson, LaPoint, and McBride rode at the head of the herd, with several armed shooters riding spaced out behind them. Their plan was to force the legal crossing, with determination, and gun-work if necessary. McBride reminded the younger men that a direct approach could work without a shootout, if handled correctly.

"But they have to know we will shoot, if we need to," he said as he tightened the girth strap on Buck. LaPoint checked his weapons and said little, a grim visage showing.

Goodnight carried a ten gauge double barreled shotgun across his saddle horn, with a calm balance like he was hunting quail, riding along in his thick wool coat. LaPoint and McBride both rode without coats, only sheepskin vests, with two pistols each, the thongs and flaps unhooked for fast access. They had repeating rifles balanced on their saddles, hooked with leather thongs to the horns. When they approached the line of riders carrying carbines, about twelve men with grim looks on their faces, near the middle of the pass, the Texans stopped the herd, and the front four riders walked their horses ahead, leaving the other armed riders to stop a stampede if it was attempted. In front of the herd was an old bull who never panicked at gunfire, with a very loud bell. Goodnight's top hand Bill Williams held his horse in front of the bull, to impede his movement until the time came. The ole Texas bull pawed the ground, clanking his bell gently in the frosty air as his four foot spread of horn waved in the cool air and his breath came out in white fog.

The sun was rising over the rise east of the pass when they met the armed riders forming a blockade, and Goodnight pulled out his paperwork on the herd and notified them these cattle were heading north to Denver. The four riders behind Goodnight were spread out with twenty feet between each one, all balancing a rifle on their saddle, with LaPoint and McBride riding the wings. Behind them about twenty yards back rode another group of six, spread out likewise and carrying repeating rifles. The bull leading the herd was about ten yards behind them, followed by the herd at about the same gap.

The leader of the blockade group received Goodnight's paperwork, read it and handed it back to him, then proceeded to tell Charles Goodnight that those Texas cattle would get stampeded if they were driven another foot this way. Goodnight told them if any shooting started, his men would be the ones to finish it, and the herd would be stopped by extra drovers at the foot of the pass and run back through over their bodies. LaPoint unhooked and cocked his Spencer rifle at that moment, as did McBride and Wilson. Goodnight just sat erect on his black chunky horse and stared at the man, finally saying, "I'm done monkeying with you guys. Get out of my way."

A long moment passed while the man looked at the paper again, then said something to Goodnight in a quiet voice, and rode back a hundred yards with the paper to a group of men sitting on their horses on a rise above the pass, the steam of their mounts breath shining white with the sun rising behind them. They conferred a couple of minutes while LaPoint and McBride sat astride their Andalusian stallions with cocked rifles and stared at them, nudging their mounts into a pacing in place motion, then shifting them into a sidestepping motion. The old lead bull increased the pawing ground and swaying his head, clanging his bell louder. The white frost on the sides of the pass started to melt as the slanting sunlight hit it, and they waited like that for a minute as the bright morning rays of the sun crept like a white shaft into the high valley, warming their faces.

Goodnight looked over at LaPoint and jerked his head towards the group on the rise, where the discussion over the paper was going on. LaPoint and McBride were still sidestepping their trained mounts, moving out wide.

"I'm fixing ta read the riot act to these knot-heads. If hell starts popping, shoot those sons-a-bitches on the hill, they're the ones behind this. I"ll get these guys up close with the shotgun and pistols."

"Alright, Charlie."

LaPoint nodded and looked to see if McBride heard, pointed to the riders on the rise with his rifle, and McBride nodded back. The men behind them started slowly walking their horses forward, some taking to the sides of the high valley and dismounting in good shooting spots, some filling in the gaps a few yards behind the leaders with fighting men on horseback, their brass sided rifles gleaming in the rising sun.

After several very long minutes of discussion, the blockade leader rode back with one of the men who had been vociferously talking at him. The look on the first man's face told LaPoint that he did not want to die there on another man's illegal errand. The second man was well dressed in a suit with heavy wool overcoat and fur collar. He rode up to Goodnight and handed him back the paper.

Goodnight handed it back to him saying, "That's your copy, notarized. I got a copy, and so does the governor's office."

"We can't let you through until we send a rider back to Denver and check out this paperwork."

"*No sir, that is not the case.* We shall cross this herd by noon today. This herd has wintered in New Mexico and the papers prove it. We have legal right of entry and several of the best marksmen in the southwest staring at you, and we are coming through. That man with the rifle is LaPoint, the man who out-shot Britt Jonson with a long gun, and he's pure hell with repeaters and pistols too. The other is Ranger McBride, who taught him. I don't need to be a good shot to blow a hole in you as big as a watermelon with this ten gauge. You have no legal standing to stop us, so you are just rustlers in my eyes and the eyes of the law. We are coming through, and if any shooting starts my men will finish it. We shoot to kill when we have to shoot."

"Now wait a minute, you listen here..."

"You listen," said Goodnight in a loud voice that cut the man off sharp with its intensity. "My men will kill you and your friends on the hillside there first thing, if any shooting starts. Your drovers are no match for men who battled Comanches and Comancheros to get here. Now we're done fooling around with you guys, get the hell out of our way."

The line of riders behind the man all heard the loud voice of Goodnight, but nobody moved, except for glancing nervously at each other, waiting to start firing upon command.

Goodnight turned his head and yelled at Josh. "LaPoint, let's go through. McBride, we're moving!"

LaPoint yelled, "Ride away now and live to tell about it."

Gabe gave a loud yell, "Now git!"

LaPoint started Scorpio at a brisk sideways walk, moving horizontally to the blockage, in his trained quick sidestepping gait, as did McBride with Buck, both moving laterally with their horses, angling for higher ground at the sides of the sloping valley walls, bypassing the line of riders blocking the way, then turning and drawing beads on them as Charles Goodnight turned in his saddle, swung his hat in the air, and yelled "Bring the herd, we're crossing!" One armed Bill Williams turned the bull loose and quirted him, yelling "move!" as the bell started clanging and the horns started a swaying advance.

The blockaders were facing expert riflemen on their flanks by then, at a raised elevation, with barrels raised and aimed, and the riders behind Goodnight started moving up to support him as he nudged Blackie forward with his heels. If they tried to stop the herd, the blockaders would be caught in a crossfire with deadly accurate marksmen.

"Last chance to ride out of here alive, now get going," yelled LaPoint from the flank as the sun flashed from the side plate of his rifle. "They're not paying you enough to cover the funerals."

"Make way or eat some hot lead," shouted McBride from the other flank, aiming at the riders on the hill with his Spencer.

"Make way, we are coming through with a legal herd!" yelled LaPoint, so loud it startled everyone. Goodnight glanced up at him with a smile on his face.

"These slugs make a big hole on the way out," yelled McBride.

Wilson rode up beside Goodnight as Charlie paced his horse forward, his shotgun in his hands near the saddle horn, the leather rein straps tied to loop on the horn. Charlie stared him down, then pulled out a big pocket watch and glanced at it, then put it back in his vest pocket. The herd was slowly plodding up behind the belled bull, now only twenty yards away.

When the two leaders of the blockade turned their horses, and pulled up beside Charlie, LaPoint was nervous that he would have to shoot them with Goodnight in the target zone. He drew a bead on the well-dressed gentleman just as the man looked up and saw LaPoint sitting in the sunlight with the rifle pointed at his head. Raising his arm in alarm, the frightened man spurred his horse around, followed by the other man, then the line of blockade riders all turned and followed them back up the pass.

Goodnight kept riding at a steady pace, waving his arm for the herd to follow. The blockaders rode off in a hurry, heading back down the slope into Colorado. The herd proceeded through the easy pass, into Colorado and up the face of the Rockies to Denver without a shot fired. LaPoint and McBride rode with them as far as Trinidad, and had dinner in a cafe with Goodnight before heading south again.

The steaks were tough but the beer was cool, and they had a good visit there. After hearing profuse thanks from Charlie with a agreement to meet at the Menger Hotel at San Antonio in spring, LaPoint and McBride headed south through Raton pass, paying Dick Wooton's toll, and rode across the staked plains, leaving in the first week of November, after a mild norther had blown through and made the air chilly with a north wind waving through the golden dried grass. They walked the horses side by side and conversed at first.

"Ya shore surprised me, Josh, with joining up in an outside fight so fast this time. Even if it was Charlie."

"Yeah, well. It was Charlie. And we didn't have to shoot. I haven't had to shoot anyone since that Comanchero was after you on the Goodnight trail."

"Wal, keep your powder dry. We got lots of Comanche country ta cross now."

"So this is the Llano Estacado, which everyone says you're the scouting expert on. The staked plains, eh? I'll be watching you, McBride."

"Let's lay low and hope to avoid buffalo hunting parties. If we get chased we may have to give up the pack horses and make a run for it on Buck and Scorpio. And they'd chase us a fer piece to get them. So just simmer down a bit, why don't ya? I couldn't hardly believe when ya agreed to jump inta that fight."

"No fight to it, was there?"

"Naw, lucky though."

Josh let Scorpio graze the dried grass beside the playa where they had stopped to rest. "I'm like Charlie, I want to ranch in the mountains now, make my own place up here. To hell with those that try to stop it. That herd was wintered in New Mexico, had every right to cross. I guess sometimes bastards that try to block the way need to meet up with a bastard like me."

"Waugh! Enough of that bastard talk. No matter what name ya call yore self, we got a danged good poke now, don't go jumpin' inta any other fights til we get home, huh? So yore intent on getting' yourself a ranch in the mountains now, be shed of what Alex left you down on the San Antone?"

"Yeah."

"Wal, Pancho could manage that spread for us. I reckon the thought of moving back up near Taos sounds mighty appealing ta me, right about now. The way things are heating up around San Antone with the Comanches, and the mustangs about cleaned out down south. I'm for wrapping up things down thar and reinvesting up in the mountains as well."

"Alright then. It won't happen overnight, but I think Charlie is dreaming of a ranch up on the Arkansas as well, maybe we can work together on getting set up in ranching up here. We forced open a pass where we don't have to pay Dick Wooton's toll, for a start."

"Well, what we done put us on Charlie's list of favorites, I reckon. That and moving the herd across Texas for him last summer. You didn't commit us to getting inta that war with the Comanchero rustler crews did ya? You said ya was just gonna collect brands."

"I didn't commit, didn't say no either. They need to be cleaned out, just like the rustlers we've been cleaning out around Helena and Live Oak."

"Yeah, but we can't jump inta every fight."

"Ranching can't spread up the plains with that sort around. It's like wolves after sheep. Cougars after calves."

"Wal, let the Army take care of them, I say. For now...Keep yore sharp eyes peeled for Comanches."

"Alright. Now the Staked Plains. Why do they call it that?"

"Hell if I know, and I'm supposed to be the best white tracker on it. Maybe for the Spanish dagger stalks, maybe cause some drove stakes in for markers, don't rightly know. Maybe it was for tha buffalo steaks."

"Well, I hope crossing the staked plains doesn't turn out bad."

Chapter Three: Comancheria

With apple-sized gold pokes and Goodnight's pay in silver in their packs, the scouts paced their stallions and pack horses across the vast sun parched grasslands for the Palo Duro Canyon on the upper Red River, over two hundred miles away. They made good time across the flat plain in the cool weather, since recent rains had freshened the thick turf in the draws and left small playas, tiny lakes, so the stock ate and drank well.

As time passed it seemed to LaPoint like an endless sea of grass, with nothing but flat horizon in all directions. After riding hard for eight days through the tan and golden plains, they finally made it to the great gash in the Llano Estacado called Palo Duro Canyon, named by Spanish explorers for the dense hard mesquite wood growing in the floor of the amazing cut in the red and cream earth. Somewhat resembling the multicolored eroded hills south of Chama, with gullies fanned out at the bottom like ruffled Spanish skirts of rose and gold, the cliffs shone with various color bands of red and cream and greenish gray gypsum running through the layers of the cliffs, and streaks of gypsum sparkling in the sun. The top was layered with a crumbling mass of limestone cap rock that broke off in chunks scattered down the steep cliffs, with their fans of erosion at the bottom. The canyon deepened into a yawning hole as they followed it east, and they stopped several times on the rim to admire it's surprising grandeur.

"Incredible," said LaPoint when they first spotted it. "After nothing but flat plain for eight days of riding, and now this!"

"Every man feels that way, first time ya see it. Every time, actually, for it takes lots of long days of riding the plain ta get here."

"Are there other trails here?"

"A long trail from the west, all the way ta Las Vegas. But we still got days and days of staked plains in front of us, and good chance of seeing Comanches. Keep yore eyes peeled for dust."

Moving further along the southern rim of the deepening reddish canyon, they saw what looked like smoke or dust rising from the deep gash in the level plain, and left their horses hidden in some cedars with feed bags on, then crept towards the rim overlooking the wide gap below, where the canyon had deepened into a steep drop. A tall solitary tower of stone projected up where the cap stone had kept it from washing away, like a castle tower, or a lighthouse on the coast of England, according to Josh. The canyon wall opposite them was stunning in its red color and layered textures.

They both let out a gasp and took in a deep breath when they got to the rim and looked over. Below them they saw the haze of hundreds of campfires and blackened tepee tops trailing wispy white streams, and miles of lodge circles stretching east, down the red and green canyon. It was a beautiful and stunning sight, shot through with slanting rays of sunlight gleaming on the multicolored cliffs, one that raised the hair on the back of their necks, yet evoked admiration.

The scouts laid there in silent awe for a few minutes, taking it all in. Despite his nervousness at being so close to the great encampment of horseback warriors, LaPoint also felt the pervasive peacefulness of the villages, and got a glimmer of understanding why Gabe talked with affection of his early days trading and buffalo hunting with the Comanches.

The Indians below, Comanches, Kiowas, and Cheyenne-Arapahoes, village after village stretching down the widening river valley as far as they could see in the hazy light, were processing buffalo meat up and down the valley, preparing for winter. They could see hundreds of drying racks and women slicing meat and drying it while others tended to the hides. The men seemed to be mostly lounging around the campfires, snacking and visiting, animated in their gestures telling tall tales of hunting buffalo, according to Gabe.

Hunting parties were going out steep trails up the canyon branch to the south, and others returning with pack horses and mules carrying heavy loads of buffalo meat, using the same accessible incline to ascend the steep canyon. With the field glasses LaPoint could see where big herds of horses had been driven down. Then he began to admire all the horses, sweeping the binoculars down the valley to where the creeks joined.

Various horse herds grazed along the grassy flats besides the winding little river, as far as they could see, with a larger herd a few miles away, where the valley broadened at the merging of the two big canyons . It was the biggest gathering of horses Josh had ever seen.

"People of the horse," he said.

"Ya got that right, just look at 'em all, the horse to hunt the buffalo, and raid."

They were awed but afraid of being seen by returning hunting parties, so they agreed on a quick departure. Creeping back to the horses and walking them away slowly so as not to make an unnecessary sound, they made two miles east without speaking a word. Finally they hid in a clump of cedar at the beginning of the canyon and conferred.

"Damn, Gabe, never thought I'd live to see something like that. I'll bet we saw more than a thousand Indians there, and three thousand horses. My fingers are trembling around these reins."

"The Palo Duro Canyon. Not many white men have seen it, I reckon. Goodnight wanted to come with us ta see it, but couldn't get away, as usual. I tole him I'd show it to him someday. My neck-hairs been standin' on end for an hour," replied McBride.

"Mine too. What a sight."

"I like ta peed my pants when we got to that rim. I tole ya we might see half tha Comanche nation here in this time o' year, but that seemed like Comanches and then some. Maybe Kiowas and Cheyenne too."

"I never expected to see so many horses either, they are rich with horses."

"I wouldn't of minded being a Comanche a hundred years ago, going out ta spear buffalo offa a fine mount, running with yore pards through the scrambling herd, picking out the best one ya could get, ramming that spear through its heart and thanking creation for the great gift, then lounging in camp and counting yore horses. They got their existence pretty well balanced out on tha plains, long as they got horse and buffalo. But it ain't gonna keep workin' if they keep raidin' settlers, not with the federal army moving in serious like."

"That was a sight I'll never forget. What a horse herd. If they would just live up here and quit raiding, I'd be glad to give it to them. They have the horse and buffalo existence pretty well worked out."

"Wal I'm for letting the Quohadi Comanches have the staked plains, and buffalo and the canyon. Matter of fact, let's us do that right now, 'for tha fat's in tha fire. We need to make tracks before they find out we been around....I ain't old enough to die, or get tortured...If they do catch us, we got to go down fighting or shoot each other before getting caught alive, you understand?"

"We'll just have to make it too hard for them to catch us alive. We got plenty of ammo, and then we got McBride blades. We go down fighting."

"Waugh. I'm just sayin..."

"I know what you're saying, and I won't let them torture you. Let's make a safe departure plan."

They decided on a night ride south to the Tule Canyon, to get away from this big encampment, and made that canyon and found a hiding place by dawn. They took turns sleeping in a spot well hidden by cottonwood and cedar trees until afternoon, with Josh being disturbed by dreams of a horse stampede. Before dawn they departed southeast after a cold breakfast, heading for the edge of the cap rock, trying to stay hidden from any riders they spotted. They descended from the cap rock at Quitique, and headed for some rough canyon lands and broken cliffs where Gabe knew a good hiding spot to camp, out of the rising cold wind. Making a small cooking fire in the lee of a huge red sandstone cliff with streaks of white and green gypsum running through it in long horizontal bands, they ate and then moved the sleeping camp further up into the canyon, to a defensible stony spot.

After camping a night under tall red sandstone boulders jumbled at the base of the tall canyon wall, while a norther raged above on the plains, they ventured out the next day, hoping to track some fresh game in the light snow and sleet whitening the ground. They mounted a reddish sandy high rock pinnacle first and scanned the area for signs of campfire smoke, and saw none, though the blasts of cold wind would scatter smoke quickly. They rode in a big circle through the grasslands around the streams coming from the canyons. Finding the tracks of several buffalo, they followed them into an incredible maze of red sandstone spires and cliffs and pinnacles, up twisting sandy creek beds, until they had them trapped in a box canyon. Dismounting, they took one big female down with repeater rifle fire from a hundred yards, a shot apiece at the same time. They hung the carcass from a thick mesquite branch overhanging a small curving creek-bed with a trickle of water running down it. Using the horses' power they pulled the lariat over the stout branch and lifted the buffalo up from where they had dragged it in the course sand of the creek bed. With the carcass suspended over the dry creek, Gabe began skinning while Josh took care of the horses, pulling them down into the shelter of the creek-side and feeding them grains. It took a long time to do the skinning work, with cold fingers and bits of ice flinging down in swirls into their faces. The hard curve of the nearly dry creek with the twelve foot undercut bank lined with cedar provided a good place to work out of the howling wind. The mounts were tied in trees alongside the sandy creek-bank, a few yards back.

As they were finishing with the skinning, pulling the heavy hide down the suspended body, they were surprised by a group of Comanches. The stealthy Indians had crept up on them in soft moccasins, the blustering wind hiding any small noise they might have made. The well armed Comanches had surrounded them with men on the small river bluff, and warriors blocking every escape, holding rifles or drawn bows.

"Gol-dang-it-ta-hell, we been took," said Gabe as they whirled around and saw they were surrounded in the little canyon.

"What?"

"Don't do nothin', lemme talk to 'em first, but be ready to knife fight to the death."

"Alright, make your move, I'll follow. Talk like you never talked before."

Though both of their minds flashed the old saying of 'save the last bullet for yourself' to avoid torture by the Comanches, both decided to die fighting first. For these two, knives at their belt and a lunge at the nearest brave was the last resort, not a cyanide filled cartridge, like some of the old timers carried to avoid Comanche torture. It was something they had discussed around the campfires plenty of times.

71

Gabe began to speak Comanche in a loud voice, calling for parley. "Naki, naki, "Ekaa Wasape Nahuu. Naki, naki, naki," he began signing to what seemed like the leader, who was approaching after springing off the embankment over the creek.

The tall erect brave with long braided hair, the thick braids wrapped with dark fur, was sporting eagle feathers projecting from the ends and an eagle feather fan in his left hand. On his thick and muscular neck was a fully packed bear claw necklace, turquoise beads alternating with the big grizzle claws. He paced up the dry sand of the creek bed and began sign language. All of the warriors had face paint, their war decorations, and they all deferred to this leader.

He came closer so Josh could see him confront Gabe. This imposing chieftain was a calm and dignified looking man with high cheekbones and a prominent nose with piercing steady gaze from heavy-lidded eyes. He was armed with a tooled leather weapon belt holding an army pistol scabbard and knife scabbard, with an ammo belt full of heavy 44 slugs. Another brave stood at his side, stocky and muscular with reddish sunburned skin, brawny arms holding bow and arrow with rusty metal tip. His hair was smeared with grease, but showed traces of flaxen sun bleaching.

When LaPoint got a better look, he saw that on the chieftain's belt was a big .44 Army Colt pistol worn backward on the left side in a modified army scabbard, with the flap half gone, and a antler-handled McBride knife in a buffalo-tail scabbard on the right. The bone handle resembled the knife they had recently made and traded to Britt Jonson, and the one at LaPoint's belt. This startled LaPoint, and he wondered if Britt had gone under.

The wide top half of the big warrior's face was painted with chalky white, while the bottom half was solid black, giving him an unworldly scary look. Over his buckskin shirt he wore a small breastplate of quills and bones and beads, accentuating his regal appearance. He had a buffalo skin robe draped over one shoulder, and fringed tall legging-moccasins. He wore no white man's clothing nor tattoos, as the Tonkawas were apt to do, and kept a dignified bearing as he walked close to Gabe.

He tapped the familiar looking knife at his waist and looked at Gabe, who nodded. The thought again flashed though Josh's mind that the Comanches had killed Britt, and a wrenching wave ran through his gut, stirring hot feelings of rage, but he held still as the blood pounded in his ears. He felt that the warrior beside the leader was fixing to shoot him with the rusty arrow at any second. He took deep breaths through his nose and remained still and ready to strike if need be.

Gabe made a hand sign with flat palm down, sweeping across his middle, then walked over and wiped the buffalo blood from his hands, while squatting by the tiny flow of salty water in the bottom of the creek bed of course sand, casually ignoring the nearby Comanches. With over a dozen braves drawing beads on them, the old scout slowly washed the small skinning knife and replaced it in the leather sheath, stabbing it into his belt by his other knife. Then he stood up and walked over to the chieftain, saying, "Naki, Naki."

The big warrior chieftain walked up to McBride and poked him gently on the chest, saying, "Ekaa Wasape Nahuu."

Gabe looked him eyeball to eyeball and nodded while hand signing. Then the warrior touched his own chest and said, "Kiwih-nai."

Gabe nodded again, then pointed to the knife on Kiwih-nai's belt, and at his own, making more hand signs. "Of all people to run into," muttered Gabe, and LaPoint knew they had fallen into the hands of the rising chieftain that Mackenzie and the entire 4th Cavalry had been searching for. He also felt a glimmer of hope, as this raider had a reputation for returning captives unharmed.

"Nahuu Peta Nacona." said Gabe as his hands kept signing,as he spoke, along with the Indian's. The other warriors seemed curious and somewhat amused, and gathered closer.

Kiwih-nai smiled, nodded, and replied, touching the knife, "Tuhubitu papii tasiwoo" ....then slowly took the small skinning knife from McBride's belt and pulled it from the sheath, testing it for sharpness across his palm.

"Nahuu Tuinuhpu Kiwih-nai."

Gabe nodded. "Ehkwe One."

In a low voice LaPoint spoke. "What's he saying?"

Gabe nodded and smiled as Kiwih-nai tested the sharpness of the blade, putting a small slice on the high Venus mound of his palm, drawing blood, and glancing at McBride with his hand up.

"He says he is Kiwih-nai, and he called me 'Red bear with sharp knife', and he wants this skinning knife for his boy, I think. That's the knife that Britt traded with Peta Nacona at his waist....he got it when his dad went under. He's the son of the great Peta, but he had ta form his own band."

"That's good to hear, I thought it might be Britt's, that they killed him."

"Naw, I recognize it as his old one, the one he traded to Peta Nacona."

When the big chieftain heard those words, he grunted and nodded his head. Walking up to Gabe, the calm and steady warrior reached up and pulled McBride's hat up and touched the scalping scar with his long fingers, then replacing the hat and handing the small knife back to McBride.

"Red Bear Sharp Knife," he said in halting but well-pronounced English. He gave a broad smile, apparently proud of his English pronouncement.

With a shocked look on his face, which he quickly hid, Gabe replied.

"Eagle ...Parker", to which the warrior shook his head and scowled. The smile disappeared into an intense stony stare as his chest puffed up and he spread his legs and stood very erect.

"Parker. No! Toso Taiboo Waiyauyaupu. Censee Ann Parker. My father, Peta Nacona. Like you, father LaPoint."

Gabe nodded and made hand signs. The big warrior stared at him eyeball to eyeball and continued. " Kiwih-nai, KIWIH-NAI! Numuh! Quohadi Ekakwitsubaitu Kiwih-nai!" This was accompanied with vehement hand signing, as was everything that passed. In his belt was a fan of eagle feathers, which he took out to gesture with, pointing at McBride, LaPoint, and then the Buffalo.

"What?" asked LaPoint.

"Says he ain't Parker, that his mother Censee Ann Parker was a white girl,...but a Comanche woman, says he's Comanche, the Lightening Eagle of the Quohadis."

Kiwih-nai nodded affirmatively, hand signing, looking at LaPoint, and then McBride, satisfied they understood. His body posture relaxed some as he pulled the eagle feather fan across his chest. More hand signing ensued, back and forth. Josh began to believe they would live through it.

Gabe nodded back, signing with the flat hand across the chest again. Then Gabe took the small bone-handled skinning knife and made a small slice on his palm. He reached out and locked hands with Kiwih-nai. They gripped hard for a few seconds, a surprised look crossing Kiwih-nai's face with his big hand in the increasingly powerful lock of the old black-smith, whose grip was like a vice. Then Gabe released his grip slowly, and took the scabbard back from the big warrior, sheathed the knife after wiping it on his pants leg, and stuck it in the Indian's belt.

Kiwih-nai nodded, said "Tainuhpu nahuu," then turned to look at LaPoint, who had remained motionless all this time, ready to draw and shoot to save his friend, and go down fighting if need be. Kiwih-nai smiled, then laughed and said, "Ekakwitsubaitu Pia waioo," pointing his finger at LaPoint, then signing. He rattled off a string of Comanche words mixed with Spanish, and Josh heard the words Rio Blanco, then more signing while Gabe stared and tried to comprehend.

"Tell me, dammit Gabe, what'd he say?"

"Dammit, Gabe, Red Bear," said Kiwih-nai with a smirk, then a chuckle.

"Said the knife is for his son. Called you the Lightening Cougar. Says he knows us, from seeing us at the Blanco river once, when you shot those water moccasins, the first time, remember? The first time, when we visited the ruins of the old place, and you did a fast draw on them cottonmouths and went ta zinging ricochets at me? He musta been hiding in the cliff somewhars. Says you drew with the lightening and your spirit animal stirred and revealed itself there, a dark cougar. So they named you Lightening Cougar, son of Red Bear with Sharp Knife. He says he always wanted a knife like the McBride knives of Para-coom and Peta Nacona, and that he got his when his pa went under, and it was the best knife on the plains. Or something like that."

Kiwih-nai looked at LaPoint and nodded with a satisfied and dignified look on his face, his heavy lids giving an intriguing look to his intense and steady gaze, the two tone paint job very effective in intensifying the features.

"Ekakwitsubaitu Pia waioo," he said again, gesturing at LaPoint.

McBride nodded, then pointed at the fast action .36 Remington on LaPoint's hip in the tie-down cut-away holster. Kiwih-nai nodded and pointed to Josh, then took a couple of steps towards him, followed by the surly brave at his elbow. "LaPoint," he said. He tapped the big butt of the knife at his belt, and then to him self, saying "McBride. McBride." Then he stepped over to Gabe.

Kiwih-nai reached and pulled Gabe's big knife from the scabbard, slowly, glancing at LaPoint as he did so. Josh remained motionless, staring at him, ready to draw and shoot if he started to use the knife on Gabe. Kiwih-nai laughed, pulled the knife to his fingers, and tested the sharpness of the blade.

"McBride, " he said. Pointing it at Josh he said, "LaPoint." Then he pointed it at the buffalo hanging there nearly skinned, that his young warriors had gathered around, with some sitting on the small cliff above the undercut creek bed "Tasi-woo Numunu", he said, making more hand signs.

"What?"

"Says it's the people's buffalo, and since he's chief, he decides who gets what cut."

The big warrior smiled as he saw they comprehended.

"Comprende, senors?" he said. "Carne de cibolo es por Comanche."

"I caught that, no meat for us tonight, huh? Tell him we'll give up the meat gladly, huh, and be on our way. Hell, we can eat cold biscuits."

"Hell yeah, I'm like that church-mouse caught in a trap, I don't want the cheese, I just want ta get out! With our horses would be right fine, too."

"Kiwih-nai Quohadis!" said the big chieftain, tapping his breastplate.

"Eagle of the Quohadis. I got that," said LaPoint.

"Censee Ann Parker tukuhputu."

McBride nodded, "Say's his mother is the Parker girl,"...signed and took a deep breath, then reached slowly and took the knife from the big dignified looking warrior, went back to the hung carcass, and finished pulling the skin off, while several braves approached and pulled their knives. Josh was ready to draw and fire at them if they moved to cut Gabe, who went on working like nothing was amiss.

76

Gabe cut out the liver and sprinkled it with gall. "Tasiwoo Quohadi, Numanu..." he said, setting it on a flat stone and going back to butchering the meat while the warriors edged in closer to watch his expert butchering. He started whistling *blue tail fly....*"jimmy crack corn and I don't care."..as he continued efficiently butchering the meat.

The warrior beside Kiwih-nai began to hum along with the tune in a husky voice, even mouthing some words when it came to the *"Jimmy cack corn, hadocare....."* causing Gabe to look back with an astonished look, then return to his cutting. "This was once a white boy," he said to LaPoint.

Kiwih-nai spoke loud to Gabe, pointing to the blond warrior.   "Asewaynah."

The stocky warrior strutted forward and shook his bow in the air. "Asewaynah Quohadi," he shouted.

Gabe looked over and nodded. "Gray Blanket. Quohadi warrior"

"Toso taiboo no!"

"Says he ain't no white man."

"He sure could be, with that sunburned skin and bleached hair," said Josh, trying to calmly stare at the young man, who was simmering with rage and hostility.

Gabe looked at the fiercely scowling brave and nodded, then went back to butchering the buffalo meat. Kiwih-nai directed some braves to make a small fire, which they did with flints and dry grass they carried. Gabe cut out the hump and tongue and took it back to Kiwih-nai, who had remained standing with his legs spread and motionless, looking at LaPoint, who glanced back at him while watching the braves close to Gabe with their knives out.

Touching his head first, the big chieftain pointed to the sky, and said, "Ekakwitsubaitu no, LaPoint," laughing after he spoke.

"What did he say, Gabe, they fixing to kill us or not?" asked LaPoint.

"He says your name is Lightening Cougar, but there is no lightening today. Not exactly sure what he means, but he's smilin'. Maybe he means there's no reason to draw down on him."

Kiwih-nai nodded and laughed again. Then he pointed back towards where Scorpio was tied under a small cliff edge and said.

"LaPoint puuku espanole"

"Yes," said Josh. "Puro sangre espanole."

"Si senor, seguro, Puro sangre espanole caballo macho. Muy bueno, muy bonito, muy intelligencia."

"Si, es verdad," said Josh, nodding.

Then the big chieftain made an eagle-whistle like cry, three times, and a big dark horse nickered and whinnied in the cedar bushes on the flat above. They could hear the horse snorting and tugging on the branch he was tied to.

Pointing towards the horse, barely visible as a silhouette in the brush to LaPoint and McBride, the warrior said. "Kiwih-nai puuku tuinuhpu." He signed with his hand as he spoke, then looked at Gabe to translate.

"What's he saying, Gabe?"

"I ain't shore, his horse, yore horse, his son. I think maybe he wants yore horse for his boy. That's what I give up my skinnin knife for, his son. But I ain't sure." Gabe looked at Kiwih-nai and made a bunch of signs with his hands, sticking the bloody knife in his teeth to do so. LaPoint slowly shook his head in the negative.

Kiwih-nai laughed and shook his head no, and began signing furiously again. He seemed to be enjoying himself, completely relaxed and inquisitive. He was close to Josh's age, and around the same size, though a little stockier and shorter. He pointed to his horse again, but the animal had shifted behind brush, and all they could see was a tall dark shadow. Exasperated, shaking his head with a weary smile like these foreigners are so obtuse, the big man spoke again.

"Puuku.... mo'o no good...bad ham...bad ham....puu-ku."

"...something about horse, bad ham, bad hand, something? Shit, I ain't spoke Comanche much in years..." muttered Gabe as he sliced away at the buffalo, handing out chunks to the warriors gathered around him.

"Bad ham puu-ku, puu-ku, tuhuya ebibitu tenahpu!" said the bemused Kiwih-nai, and gave the shrill whistle that sounded just like an eagle's screech. The horse nickered again, and the others tied with it joined in. The warriors laughed and made seemingly derisive comments about the situation, finding some amusement in it.

"What's he saying, Gabe, damnit?"

"Gabe, Damnit?" said Kiwih-nai, laughing.

"Not sure. Bad ham horse, horse blue man, something like that. What horse is he pointing at, all I see is the bush?"

"There's about six tied in those cedars back by that gully, but I can't hardly see them for the branches. Both white men strained their necks to see the horse that Kiwih-nai kept calling and pointing to, but all they could see was a a black mare of considerable size, like a grain feed cavalry horse, and a big gray rump with big black hand-prints on it. The chief was smiling as he shook his head in exasperation at the ignorant white men. Some of the warriors were yelling and laughing now at some unknown joke. Some of them near Gabe began pointing at his mangled left hand and shouting something.

Not being able to see or understand, LaPoint noticed the Comanches with knives getting closer to Gabe as he stepped on a boulder to try to see over the edge of the rim to the horse, and Josh started edging that way, glancing at the leader as well. The big warrior signed to the others and said something that made them back off after forcing Gabe back down to the buffalo, where he recommenced the butchering and handing out meat.

Kiwih-nai pointed to Gabe's bad hand and smiled at LaPoint.

Gabe finished detaching the choice cuts of tongue, liver, and hump, and walked over to hand them to Kiwih-nai, who glanced over at another warrior with drawn bow and gestured with his chin at him. The other warrior with long tangled sun-bleached hair and blue eyes was painted fiercely across his face with a red band across his eyes and black band with red streaks across his lower face, but his shoulder and arm skin was a shade redder than the others, from sunburn. He stepped over and took the meat, from which Kiwih-nai cut half of the tongue off, and then a piece of the liver, and handed it back to Gabe.

Gabe looked him in the eye and bit a big chunk out of the liver, then handed it back to him. Kiwih-nai stuffed the rest in his mouth and chewed it down.

"Numuh Tasiwoo tukuhputu," said the warrior, accompanied with hand signals.

McBride nodded. "He says his people's buffalo are going down, disappearing.

More hand signs, then "Pahiitu Tenahpu Puetuyai," said Kiwi-nai, pointing first to himself, then the blond warrior holding the meat with a fierce glare at the white men, then at LaPoint.

The warrior beside him began pacing his feet on the sandy bank with a deeper scowl than before.

"What?"

"Not sure, something about you three guys are brothers in spirit, orphans, or something like that."

The blond warrior with the frightening facial paint that matched his scowl seemed to dislike what Kiwih-nai had said, and walked up to Josh and tipped his broad felt hat off, pointing to his long sun bleached hair, then slapped him across the forehead.

"Ehkweone!"

Josh held back his anger and spoke to Gabe. "What's this angry one saying?"

"Butcher-knife. That one wants yore scalp," said Gabe while Josh put his hand on his knife butt and made ready to stab the man if need be.

"If he goes for ya, draw your knife and not your gun, so they'll let you fight and not shoot you full of holes."

A loud remark from Kiwih-nai called the man off, and Josh picked up his hat and replaced it, his hand on the butt of his knife. The blond warrior circled around, kicking the sand of the creek-bed.

"Told ya to consider cutting that hair afore we hit tha plains," said Gabe, suppressing chuckles.

"You just keep cutting that meat and handing it out to them, Old Coon; they seem to be satisfied with you doing the squaw's work for them."

"Waugh. That I will. You hold yore ground."

The angry warrior walked back to stand behind Kiwih-nai, scowling, with beefy arms folded across his chest and a puffed up pouting look on his face. Josh stared at the two warriors, wondering what kinship they shared, and guessed that Kiwih-nai sensed in him the youngster who had to start over in a strange culture, abandoning his old self to build another, yet never quite being the same as the people around them.

From being sure they would die, Josh had a surprising change of perceptions. A strange feeling of friendliness emanated from this powerful chieftain with the white mother who had turned Comanche and married the powerful warrior chieftain, Peta Nacona. It was very similar to the feeling Josh got when a wild stallion had run his flight distance in the round pen and was ready to return and bond to him. He stepped closed to Gabe and spoke.

"We're breeds, adopted out, but never fully belonging, is what he means, I expect. I got a strange feeling we may get out of this alive, even though this German Comanche wants to butcher me for being a white man."

"We might slip outa this net, if Kiwih-nai keeps control of the situation. He's shown them that we're under his protection, with the blood sharing. We just got to submit with more meat til he's satisfied. We'll be on our way here shortly." Gabe expertly wielded his big knife to section up the rest of the meat, and the braves seemed impressed with how sharp it was.

Whirling his big head and swaying his long braids with eagle feathers in them, Kiwi-nail pointed to their horses and nodded his head, then stepped over to LaPoint and extended his hand, still with a blood smear on the palm.

"Puu-ku Puetayai," said the big chieftain.

LaPoint shook his hand.

Kiwih-nai pointed to the knife on his belt. "McBride," he said. He pointed to his own knives, "McBride", then pulled the big one that had gone from Britt to Peta Nocona to him. He tapped the blade on the bone handle of LaPoint's knife, so Josh drew it out. They slowly crossed the blades, then slid them against each other and locked at the identical brass guards. The knives could have been twins. Kiwih-nai drew his patterned steel blade back, then touched the points together, "LaPoint!" he said, and laughed a belly laugh, then put his knife on Josh's palm and looked at him. Josh nodded and the sharp blade slid across his palm, drawing a tiny line of bright red blood against his pale palm. Kiwih-nai held his shiny blade in front of Josh's face, and said "LaPoint" again, chuckling at his own pun, then slipped the blade back in his scabbard as the warrior did the same. "Puuku Puetayai Tenahpu," said the chieftain, tapping LaPoint's solar plexus, then his own.

"LaPoint" he said, tapping Josh's chest. He gripped LaPoint's hand again, this time a sad look crossed his noble features. "Kiwih-nai," said Josh. The blood of their palms mingled in their grip. "Tuhuya pihi kuhma"

Josh LaPoint nodded his head, locked eyes with the man, and kept his strongest grip on the big warriors hand, which was equal in power to his own. The warrior applied his hand power relentlessly, as did Josh, and they stood with locked eyes for a few seconds, their forearm muscles swelled out as they gripped each others hand. As they were at their peak of squeezing each others hands, LaPoint said in a calm relaxed tone, "So what did he say?"

"Said you were horse-heart men." Kiwih-nai nodded. Then they both grinned and slowly released, and Kiwih-nai jerked his head towards Scorpio, who felt the intensity of the encounter and was nickering nervously.

"Kiwih-nai puu-ku, Bad Ham puu-ku. LaPoint puuku tuinuhpu."

Keeping his eyes locked on the big warriors, Josh asked Gabe, "What's he say?"

"He said...hell I ain't sure.... his horse, and bad ham horse, your horse, and your horse's son. Maybe he's bragging about his horse, or his son's horse, or he want's your horse for his son. I don't get what he means, but I think we're fixing to make tracks alive. You may be riding a mule, though."

"No way I'm giving up Scorpio. I'll trade my knife like Britt."

Gabe laughed at that. "You run the bellows and do all the pounding on the next one."

Kiwih-nai pointed to LaPoint, then himself.

"LaPoint puu-ku puetuyai kuhma. Kiwi-nail puu-ku peutuyai kuhma." That was accompanied and followed by a lot of vigorous hand signing.

"He says you're a horse spirit man, and he is too, and we can go free and enjoy life until we meet again, if we hold our tongues about his location. Time for you to give him a smile and nod to agree you won't lead soldiers back to the Quohadi."

Kiwi-nail pointed to their horses. "Vamoose ala caballos, McBride, LaPoint. "

"Wal, we both know what that means. Let's go," said LaPoint.

Gabe nodded, made a gesture with his hand swinging flat across his chest, and handed the skinning knife back to Kiwih-nai, then walked back to the tiny dribble of a creek and washed his hands. With another flat hand across the chest Gabe strode towards their horses, who nickered at them from the brush where they were still tied. LaPoint made the same gesture, and mounted Scorpio.

Kiwih-nai smiled again, gestured with his hands and arms to LaPoint, as if urging him to rear his horse, so he did so, holding Scorpio there. Kiwih-nai gave a shrill eagle whistle and the other braves all started chattering as LaPoint walked Scorpio on his hind legs, his own hands free of the reins, at his waist. Then he settled the stallion down and Kiwih-nai went up to it, breathed into the big nostrils, rubbed the soft muzzle and looked at LaPoint.

"Puu-ku LaPoint. Puu-ku Kiwih-nai, bad nah," he said, and did another eagle whistle, answered again by a loud neigh and nicker on the little plateau where their horses were tied in cedar bushes. The other braves were busy skinning out the carcass and cutting up the meat by then. The blond haired warrior rushed up yelling and spit towards them as Gabe mounted, yelling "tosa taiboo, tosai taiboo!", and touching LaPoint with the tip of his bow. He looked like he was ready to kill and scalp both of them single handed. He drew back the bow with the rusty tipped arrow of barrel hoop metal, and aimed it over LaPoint's head.

Kiwih-nai spoke again. "Comanche Hahni, Quohadi Hahni, Tasiwoo Hahni," signing at McBride as he spoke. MaBride nodded, and cleared his flattened palm across his chest, then touched his heart.

Undisturbed, Gabe put the meat in his saddlebag and rode out of the box canyon followed by LaPoint, both men amazed to be set free.   "What was he saying at the last?" asked Josh.

"Said this is the house of the Comanche and the Buffalo, and made me promise not to lead the soldiers back there."

About fifty yards out while riding at a steady walk they heard an arrow whistling towards them and then heard it hit the ground ahead of them, to the side a bit. It quivered there in the sand as they rode by. They kept walking their horses at a steady pace and soon had rounded enough turns through the boulders and red cliffs to breath easier.

"How's your heart, old coon?"

"Done some thumpin' in thar, for shore."

"Mine still is. My fingers are shaking now it's over, I hope."

"Keep moving and listen for arrows, but don't act scared."

"What I can't figure is why that German-looking Indian wanted to kill me so much. Like he already had a special grudge against me. I couldn't help but think of Kathy's brother, what he must be like, and if that was him."

"Naaw. I think that's the Ficher kid that sorta latched onta Kiwih-nai as he made his rise."

"Why'd he thirst for my blood so? I was ready to grab my knife at any point there."

"If they're captured when they're young, they grow up listening to these medicine men and campfire orators go on and on about how the white man is stealing the country, and they become devotees, so ta speak. They try to out- Comanche the Comanches. This one has latched on to Kiwih-nai to rise up in the tribes with him. He wants to do the same, impress the others with his fury. He is out for blood."

"But not Kiwih-nai. Call me crazy, but he seemed friendly to me. I felt the same feelings as a horse that is ready to join up."

"He was. He loves horses, and knows what a horse man you are. You have things in common, actually, with yore mixed blood. We're lucky to get outa that scrape with all our stock and scalps too. Let's hope our luck holds."

About a mile out, they rode onto a high point to look back with field glasses. On the flat ground above where the Indians now had a fire smoking, they saw the Comanche horses tied to the cedar brake. Gabe was using his telescope and Josh the binoculars, and they both saw the big gray pacer at the same time as it swung into view, with four black hand prints on its powerful rump.

"That's big gray!" exclaimed LaPoint.

"The big gray pacer. By jehosa-fat-in-tha-fire!, that's what he was saying. He's got the big gray with hand prints on his rump! Bad Hand, Bad Hand, that's what it was.....that must be what he's calling Mackenzie now, on account of those missin fingers. Bad Hand, Bad Hand's horse, Mackenzie's gray pacer! He stole Mackenzie's horse. The rascal, that's what he told us." "Hell-fire, that's it. He's riding big gray, that's what all that horse business was about, you're right, it's him sure as hell, all painted up with feathers in his mane. He's gotten lighter colored, but it's him. I recognized something familiar in the voice, and so did Scorpio, but I was too distracted by that mean German Indian that I didn't put it together." The big stallion who had fathered the gray pacer nickered and neighed, shaking his big head up and down. " Hell, yes," said Josh. "Even Scorpio knew."

"Shit-fair and save the flint,' said Gabe. "He's got the colonel's horse, and he knows it's Scorpio's colt, and he knows you trained it! That's what he was saying....wanted us to know all he knew, that he was way ahead of the white men tryin' to catch him. He was thanking you for the well trained war horse. Waugh!"

"Way ahead, I'll say, Lieutenant Boehm waited a year and a half for that horse and paid big money for it, and Kiwih-nai humiliated the Colonel by getting it somehow, maybe killed him even."

"Waugh, that guy is something," said Gabe. "Never seen a finer looking Comanche warrior."

"I'll say. If he ever gets together with that damned Maman-ti with all his talking owl religious hocus pocus, they could spark a general uprising that would be hell to stop. The prophet to make speeches with his hand puppet, and this guy to lead the warriors."

"Waugh. That's a bad thought. Probably let us go 'cause he wants us to go back home and get to work, making knives and training horses for him. Let's see now....He's got a knife of mine that his daddy gave him, another skinning knife for his son that I just gave him, and a horse you bred from your own and trained for two years. Hell, I believe ole Britt out-traded us, he just left Peta Nacona with a knife. "

"I'm sure glad to get out with our horses, and our lives."

"Those guys were eyeballing our horses pretty well. They wanted the stallions. That's what that white warrior wanted, a horse like Kiwih-nai's, the father of his chieftain's horse. And yore scalp."

"Damn-it Gabe, I never thought I'd see the big gray here, and didn't recognize his whinny with all those other horses doing it too. That's sure enough him, with black hand-prints on his rump and eagle feathers in his mane. Do you suppose the Quohadis wiped out a cavalry unit and killed the colonel?"

"I shore hope not, my friend Jack Charlton would be gone under if that's so, and Boehm and a bunch of other good fellas too, and a general war started."

"I hope not too. Sometimes I get a hunch that they want to spark an incident with a massacre so they can have a general war and clear the west for the railroads. I don't trust that Sherman and Sheridan. I hope Mackenzie hasn't been killed. I liked him."

"Me too. He's pretty cranky at times, but always on the job," said Gabe.

"Damn, I'll bet he's pissed off for losing the gray pacer to Kiwih-nai. That's what Kiwih-nai was boasting about so much, getting Bad Hand's gray stallion. Maybe he named the stallion Bad Hand."

"Could be that too, I reckon, he had black hand-prints on each side of his haunches."

"Good chance Mackenzie has gone under," said LaPoint.

"I expect we'll find out if we make it to Fort Concho without getting scalped. If thars a war on we're going into the hottest zone of it."

"Hell, my hands are still trembling from the last visit with Comanches, lets lay low and stay hidden on the way back," said Josh. "I've got enough juice going to make a herd of horses nervous after that. I never thought we'd be surrounded like that, unawares. I was ready to knife fight if need be."

"That was on me. My fault. Got too carried away with the thought of good buffalo steaks and such. Got lulled by not havin' no redskin troubles for so long, since we run that herd."

"We got out alive, thanks to your Comanche and hand palaver."

"Waugh. Kiwih-nai has been known to let captives go."

"Yeah, he seemed to be having a good time with it, feeling so good about having the horse I raised and trained and delivered to Mackenzie, and white guys butchering meat for his hunting party."

"Yeah, 'cept he thought we was stupid not ta catch on ta what he was saying about Big Gray."

"We were stupid to get caught, Scout."

"Don't I know it, and used some of that LaPoint luck to get out alive, I reckon. Hope ya got lots left."

"I guess we'll find out, but I feel pretty good right now, thankful to be alive."

"Me too, let's ride. Thar's a chill wind risin'."

After that harrowing but intriguing encounter with the rising young chieftain Kiwih-nai, Eagle of the Quohadis, they rode south through cold weather and made steady time for Fort Concho, skirting the eastern edge of the cap-rock cliffs, always staying near places to shelter, hide, or fort up in the rocky borderline of the cap rock. There was some decent water in the creeks and they reached the fort without being attacked, arriving there on a frosty evening in early December. The first thing they did was seek out Jack Charlton and ask what happened, if Colonel Mackenzie was still alive. They found the tall sergeant at a big stone corral, working with some mules. After a happy greeting, he let them in on recent events as they rubbed down their stock and put them to stable and hay.

Sergeant Jack's tale was a difficult one of frustrated effort and near success, and it tumbled out of him as he curried his mules. He began with the long search across the plains by the 4th Cavalry, the violent ambushes and running engagement with Kiwih-nai's band at Blanco Canyon, when Kiwih-nai led them through incredible loops up and down the canyons in a wild goose chase, baffling the Tonkawa scouts. The long armed Sergeant curried the mules harder and harder as he dealt out his tale. He continued with the sad and frustrating tale of the loss of the best cavalry horses on a night raid by the Quohadis, leaving the scouts and officers afoot, and later the near apprehension of the large band of Comanches being on the verge of successful conclusion, so close to the fleeing village that they were finding abandoned puppies and cooking pots, then suddenly dampened by a raging norther and freezing weather and nightfall laced with sleet and hail, and then the wounding of Colonel Mackenzie in the thigh with an arrow, and a severe injury to Captain Carter, all of which prompted the abandoning of the chase and return to Fort Concho while Sergeant Jack's favorite mules froze to death in the icy wind. At that point of the story the big Sergeant quit currying and wiped his eyes of tears with his army bandanna.

The gist of the story was that Kiwih-nai had run them in circles and stolen their horses. The big sergeant put out his mules when he was finished with his tale, finally turning to Gabe.

"We were made fools of, McBride, for lack of a good scout like you."

"You got scouts. We're drovers and ranchers."

"Our scouts can't find 'em. And they all got extra horses to switch off with, while we drag wagon loads of grain and supplies. It's futile. But Mackenzie is driving us ragged."

"Whar is he, in the hospital?'

"Hell no, he's set up with a bed in his office while his leg heals. The man's a walking collection of war wounds. Grouchy as all hell, too."

After hearing all that, LaPoint and McBride made sure not to mention their encounter with the big gray and Kiwih-nai's band in the cap rock canyons. Glad that the colonel was still alive, they did not visit him in the stone headquarters building where he was propped up in a bed beside a desk, doing paperwork and reportedly yelling at everyone, his thigh wound adding to his list of injuries.

From Mackenzie's adjutant and other sergeants they learned more. There had been low talk that Mackenzie had failed in the final thrust when so close to the fleeing village, and this had the dedicated man more irascible than ever. Pressure was building through newspaper editors for the army to fix the raiding problems on the frontier.

The fact that they had come so close galled the Colonel as much as losing the horses, but nobody dared to mention the big gray. McBride and LaPoint did not want to have to refuse him in any requests for scouting in his current mood, nor rake over the wound of losing the big gray pacer to Kiwih-nai, the emerging young war chieftain of the Quohadis, but just one of many chieftains leading raids all over the frontier. And with the visit with Kiwih-nai fresh on their minds, they did not want to even be around the Colonel, for Gabe had given his word, and would not go back on it and lead the soldiers to the Quohadis' heartland in those red canyons. And LaPoint liked Kiwih-nai, and figured he'd be doing the same thing if he was in the man's position. They both hoped the Quohadis could continue to be the buffalo Indians and live on the staked plains, for they admired the balanced way of life the tribe had developed there. They resupplied and rested at the stone house of the chief of scouts at Fort Concho, had dinner with the sergeants Charlton and Williams, and Lt. Boehm, who tried to hire them as scouts again, and to acquire another war horse for the colonel. LaPoint offered the possibility of a similar mount within a year, but they both turned down the scouting offer. Then they headed south for the Blanco Valley, about 230 miles away, after signing more contracts to deliver horses to several forts in spring. The army was accounting for half of their business at that time, as the cavalry was in constant need of reliable mounts.

Pushing their mounts, they made steady good time in the pleasant fall weather between howling northers, and arrived at the rancho on the Blanco ten days later, intent on spending the wet winter training horses. They had no problems with bandits or Indian raiders, though heard talk of lots of depredations as they traveled through the German communities on their way home. They even heard that settlers had been murdered and captives taken at the tiny hamlet of Blanco, just a dozen miles upstream of their Clear Spring Ranch. It seemed the Comanche problem was getting worse instead of better.

When LaPoint and McBride finally returned to Helena to check mail and gather the horses at the ranch to move them to San Antonio, Josh was surprised and happy to find seven letters from Kathy. They went for a meal at Muldoon's, where Josh read through all of them, then wrote a long letter back to her after the meal, sipping brandy at a table alone near the back. When he was finished with the long letter and had it sealed and dropped in the post office outgoing box, he slowly rode home, thinking of a life with Kathy Hartman.

The rest of the winter was passed in the normal busy way, long stretches of work at training horses when weather permitted, preparing for contracts with Mr. Winger, Charles Goodnight, and the army forts along the frontier. During the cold northers they gathered in the warm blacksmith shop and folded hot steel for knives under their ringing hammers. Then while they ground the blades, the vaqueros played music and sang with their cattle soothing-voices, and the ladies danced the fandango, easing the loneliness Josh was feeling with Kathy so far away.

Chapter Four: Trailing for Captives

The spring of 1873 was wet and grassy in the Blanco River Valley, after lots of northers that set off great thunderstorms had raised the river twenty feet at times. Wanting to avoid Helena and it's gun thugs, the LaPoint outfit had made use of the grassy Clear Springs ranch that year for horse training and farrier work. When the live oaks had finished shedding leaves, Josh, Gabe, and Jesse had gathered their remuda of saddle mounts and driven them to Forts Concho, Mason, and McKavett, fulfilling contracts they had made in San Antonio with General Augar the previous fall. Tom Jackson had been left running the mustang operation with Pancho as head vaquero, since he had learned enough Spanish to work with the outfit of Tejanos, and had a knack for treating everyone fairly and keeping the outfit running smoothly.

Since Indian depredations in the northern hill country had been increasing, they were glad they had delivered their mounts to the cavalry without problems, and were a shade more relaxed in their vigilance on the way home from Fort Mason, down the winding Llano river with it's pink granite shoreline protrusions through the gray limestone banks.

A couple of days into the leisurely ride back from Fort Mason, they encountered a rogue group of Indian raiders that got the jump on them, and led them eventually into the Comanche wars, which they never intended to get into. And it turned out that the raiders weren't even Comanches.

The drovers were riding along the Llano River. The shallow stream braided over flat rocky-bedded floodplains scoured from seasonal overflows. They had just watered their stock where a southern branch joined the main stream. They were heading east for a few miles, to resupply at the town of Llano, before turning south towards the ranch on the Blanco, when LaPoint riding lead spotted the dust of a band of warriors moving fast through the parched grass along the raised banks of the winding stream. He pulled his field glasses and rode to the bluff along the south shore to take a good look, and saw it was a raiding party.

Just as he pointed out the warrior band to Gabe and Jesse, who was riding too far ahead in youthful bravado, the Indians began firing with good repeating rifles. They all wheeled their mounts and broke for the river trees, but Jesse's gelding was taken down as he plunged over the cut-bank. The young vaquero took a hard tumble off the screaming horse, scattering gravel as he hit a little bank of it, then got up and began limping for a log jam as Josh returned fire with his Spencer and Gabe rode in fast to pick him up. Jesse, who was staggering as he tried to run, apparently hit in the lower thigh, made ready for a pickup as bullets zinged off the stony bank around him, blasting chips and whirling lead into the air. The whine of ricochets echoed down the bluffs as rifle fire increased around Buck, who was racing down the flat floodplain, hooves clattering on the stone. Metal tipped arrows came arching through the air and skittered on the rocky banks after striking sparks when they hit.

The injured horse was down for the finish and continued its death screams as Jesse swung up behind Gabe and they headed for cover, about twenty yards back upstream, while the raiding party fanned out in cavalry attack, all firing at once, with arrows and bullets flying in from a wide front. The screams of a horse he had trained were tearing at LaPoint's gut. McBride yelled out, "More covering fire, Josh!"

LaPoint poured fired with his rifle at the spread-out raiders, one after another, as Scorpio locked into steady shooting position. The careful and accurate fire from LaPoint knocked one from his horse, and slowed the others in their assault with well placed shots. He steadily forced the warriors back behind the protection of trees and bushes along the edge of the floodplain, carefully aiming each shot for fullest effect. The raiders quickly fanned out behind cover, aware that a marksman had sighted them, and death was near if they weren't careful.

When LaPoint had emptied the rifle he jammed it back in the saddle scabbard and nudged Scorpio, who broke for cover at the log jam along the cut-bank, where Gabe had already laid his mount down behind the wood protection of thick fallen cotton-wood trees, and found shooting positions with Jesse. Josh saw their rifles protruding from between two logs as he jumped Scorpio over the jam where Gabe had forted-up. Gabe could be counted on to sight every potential log fort along the rivers as they traveled, one of his old ranger and mountain man habits.

McBride and Jesse began a barrage of heavy fire as LaPoint cleared them with the long jump of the powerful stallion into the protection of thick cotton-wood trees and broken driftwood logs. He quickly dismounted and laid Scorpio beside Buck. Both horses disliked being laid down with bullets whizzing, but both would do it when commanded. LaPoint then hid behind a big log and reloaded his rifle, slung it over his shoulder by the leather strap, along with a belt full of bullets, and jumped up to grab the first branch of a pecan tree in a thick grove. Within a second he was moving up the tree, looking for the perfect shooting viewpoint.

The raiders were pouring fire into their position from several different angles as he climbed up, but Gabe and Jesse were returning rapid shots, and kept them distracted while LaPoint quickly moved up the big pecan tree like a cat. When he found the branch he wanted, just above the surrounding trees with a clear view, he stood behind the main trunk and began to fire at the warriors one by one. Because they were well hidden by then, he could only harass and sometimes nick them, but his accurate fire convinced them to leave after a ten minute battle. LaPoint stayed in the tree with his field glasses as they rode off upstream, catching glimpses of them as they fled through trees and open space.

"They're heading out, it looks like. What's the toll?" asked Josh.

"Wal, I think Jesse's horse is done for, but he's alright, aside from being grazed through the leg and taking a knock on his head. I got the leg wound staunched off. He's got a knot on his forehead big as a turkey egg, though, and he's shootin' dazed. He fired a lot of shots for not hitting nothin'...reminded me of his pa. I think he's about half knocked out. How many do you make of them? Sorta cloudy cross-eyed look to him, like you had when ya got kicked by that mule when you was a kid."

"I'm okay, viejo, just shook up about my horse is all," said Jesse. "No problema, soy bueno," yelled Jesse to Josh.

"Looks like about seven warriors and a couple of small boys with sun-bleached hair. I winged a couple of them, and I think I killed one. He's still down, anyway, not moving."

"Captives? Oh no, not again! Gol-dang 'em all ta hell! Wish we'da kept an extra mount each," said Gabe, as he raised both Scorpio and Buck from their prone cover positions. The stallions arose quickly, glad to be on their feet again.

"Jesse can ride with me."

"Could ya tell what tribe?"

"Not really. Maybe Lipan Apaches, wearing some white man's clothes."

"Raiding party heading back for the staked plains with captives, I surmise, gol-dang it. They'll take 'em ta sell off, up to Quitaque, the valley of tears, " said Gabe. "The more braves get killed the more they steal kids to replace 'em."

"Assassinados," said Jesse, as he limped out to shoot his horse, who was still writhing and screaming in the gravel on the rocky shore.

"Gabe, why don't you do that for him?" asked Josh from his perch.

"No, es my caballo, I put hem down," yelled Jesse. "It's a man's job, no?"

"Alright, if you're up to it with that knot on your head, Jesse. It ain't easy."

"I know," said the teenager, and walked towards his miserable job, shooting a horse he loved that had never let him down, and was now dying through no fault of his own.

Josh went to scanning with his glasses again. "Damn them, one of them is using a quirt on those boys. Hey....could you load the Whitworth and hand it up to me, quick like? I got these guys in sight now, in the open with no bushes for awhile."

"Yep," said Gabe as he hurried to the task. A loud report echoed as Jesse shot his horse, then the teenager's suppressed choking and crying, then the sound of him retching his guts out on the rocky floodplain.

Enraged by the raiders holding captives, and at the death of the horse he had given Jesse and helped him train, Josh hurriedly broke dried branches off from a higher spot and watched the raiders ride away along the wide clear floodplain of the Llano River. One of them had dismounted and was doing something while squatting in the dry grass. Soon a little smoke was started there, and then another spot. The others were binding the captives more tightly and wrapping their own wounds while waiting. The sight of the captive boys enraged

94

LaPoint even further, as the fires in the grass grew and smoke began to billow.

When LaPoint got the Whitworth rifle he sighted for a few seconds, gauging the wind by the drift of the smoke from the grass fire the Indians had started, adjusting for the conditions of the shot, then sent a five hundred yard elongated hexagonal-shaped hot lead that hit the last rider in the center and knocked him from his horse stone dead. The big boom echoed from the rocky bluffs along the river, bouncing downstream and out over the hills as the smoke filled the air around LaPoint. This sent the others bolting for the trees that lined the upper ridge along the river valley, and he lost sight of them.

Within a minute LaPoint saw the billowing smoke of a big grass-fire that the party had lit behind them to deter pursuit, which obstructed all further sight of them. Seeing no more chance for long range shooting, he climbed down and examined Jesse. The leg wound was not too serious but the bump on the head was still rising and turning colors. They laid him out on a blanket with a wet bandanna on the knot and had him rest for a spell, despite his protests that he was bueno. After fifteen minutes he felt somewhat clear and could walk without staggering, so he mounted up behind Gabe, in case LaPoint had to do some rapid rifle shooting.

Then they went to examine the two dead warriors and found a Penataka Comanche and a Lipan Apache, both wearing bits of white man's clothing, vests, fine black wool suit jackets, and nice felt hats. One carried an old battered army bugle on a rope over his shoulder.

"Plugged him dead center, I see. I gotta get you in another shooting match where I can bet some good money someday."

"The scope makes it almost easy."

"Look at this varmint, dressed like a preacher. I'd take that nice coat if you hadn't ruint it with a hole through the back and chest. Wonder if the hat fits."

"Try it on, spoils of war, I guess."

"How you feelin' about this?"

"About what, exactly?"

"Killin' Indians, your first. First shootin' scrape since the cattle drive across to the Horsehead Crossin', when ya picked off that Comanchero that was after me in the dark."

"Had to be, only thing bothering me is the image of those blond boys riding captive, covered with blood, getting whipped like slaves. That and a favorite horse they killed, the one I gave Jesse. I wish I could have got them all."

"That's right. Don't I wish that along with ya. Hits tha worst thing, stealin' kids from folks. Glad you kilt some. These here is bugs boys. Wonder if this fancy hat fits." Gabe put the new black top-hat on his grizzled head. "Naw, too small for my noggin, tha pin-headed skunk. Probably belonged to one of those brainless preachers. Think I'll take the horn, instead of a scalp."

"No more Tophat Ranger McBride, eh? Did you really used to scalp them after you killed them?"

"Yeah, in my wrathy days when I was on a vengeance tear, to put the holy terror into the rest of them varmints. If they're disfigured they can't enter their happy hunting ground, but wander forever between the worlds like ghosts, 'according to their religion." Gabe pulled the brass horn free and gave it a few blasts that amazed Josh and Jesse for their volume and length.

"Still got some wind power......for an old fart, huh?" said Josh. "Tone deaf, though."

"That sounded awful, hurt my head," said Jesse. "Don't do no more, por favor."

"Yep. Used to blow a cow's horn. Lungs musta growed up big chasing after ole long lanky Bill Williams in my trappin' days. I hope them son's of bitches heard that, by gad. They got me pretty riled up, and I didn't hit a one of them. You sure they had white kids?"

"Unless you've seen some fair-skinned and tow-headed Comanches. Hell yes, two little boys, and the bigger one was nearly naked. Both had cuts all over them, and dried blood."

"Damnation, that makes me mighty wrathy!"

"Me too. They've been jerked away from their families and ridden through brush. Wish we had more horses, to go after them."

"Let's go get 'em," said Jesse. "I'll ride double and shoot them. I've had kinfolk stolen."

"Gol-dang-it. It pains me to think of losing their trail on the high plains. Now's the only real chance to catch 'em. But with only two mounts, Jesse's leg and head wound, we need to get him in for medical care."

"I said let's go get them assassinados!" said the young vaquero.

"You could take Jesse in while I trail them," said LaPoint.

"Naw-sir I should be tha one doin' the Indian tracking."

"No way."

"Wal alright, we take him in together."

"No, I'm going with you. We're going after them," said Jesse.

"Naw yore not. Yore shot and knocked half loco. Llano village is about ten miles or so west. Thar's a doctor thar, ah recollect."

"Alright, let's do that, take him to the village, notify some help, get more ammo and provisions, then come back and pick up the trail. I'm damned sick of reading and hearing about kids being stolen after seeing their parents slaughtered. We can keep their trail until help joins us, or pick them off with long range rifles."

"Josh, I'm okay, I need to go. They shot my horse."

"No, Jesse, not this time."

"Alright, I'm fer that," said Gabe. That's how Britt and me took down that bunch before, long range with Sharps. They never even saw us as they fell one after another. Long as you ain't intendin' on takin' them head on, the two of us."

"Hell no, they were well armed. That was rifles they were firing, not just bows and arrows. But we could whittle down the odds with the long guns if we could get close enough."

"Let's go get him doctored. You want to carry Jesse with you? So I'm free to do some shooting if need be."

"Yeah."

They headed south for a couple of miles when Josh spotted the dust of another group of riders as they topped a ridge. He stopped and pulled out the glasses to get a better look, standing in his stirrups.

"More raiders?"

"No. Look like trail hands, actually, but well armed, pistols and rifles, crossed ammo belts, some of them, with hound dogs trailing. More likely somebody after these raiders, raising lots of dust, pushing the hell out of tired horses. Could be rangers maybe, nearly twenty of them, riding hard this way. Horses are lathered. They have extra mounts too."

"They're for shore after them raiders, before they get to the plains." Gabe pulled his revolver and slung the battered and bent bugle into position for blasting it. Then he fired a shot and blew the horn three times. Josh watched the riders veer towards them, and they dismounted and waited while doing more doctoring on Jesse's leg and head, which had both started bleeding again.

"Man, you make my head throb with that shooting and horn blowing," said Jesse.

"Wal, the buttons are stuck or I'd play a pretty piece for ya ta grow that purple potato on yore head. Be still. You need a buffalo steak on that knot, but I ain't got one."

"Ouch! Let Josh do it, he ain't so rough," said Jesse as Gabe tightened the bandage on his leg. Josh took over and retied the wrapping after dousing the wound with brandy. Gabe watched the riders approach with his telescope as Josh tended Jesse and then the horses. When Josh looked through his binoculars again, he saw a particular urgency in the faces of the riders that he remembered, reflecting the feelings he had after raiders burned his home plantation and killed his mother. Gabe closed his long telescope and spoke.

"Hey, that is rangers, and I know the leader, ...it's Captain John McGregor, from Camp Verde, riding ta beat the devil, on worn-down horses, trailing hound dogs. You met him when we stopped at that blacksmith shop, thar on the Cibolo Creek north of San Antone a bit. We traded him some knives that time, stayed up all night on peach brandy and coffee, listening to those musicians and watching the square dancers, remember?"

"Yes, I do, and I recognize him."

Gabe stepped forward to greet the fast moving crowd of riders as they came pounding up in a cloud of dust. Josh checked the lump on Jesse's head, which was growing and turning colors as his eye was swelling shut and turning blue.

"Howdy, Captain John. It's Gabe McBride."

"I see who it is. It's the old hammer-man, the knife maker, the ole tracker, out here on the Llano." He patted the knife on his belt as he approached. "Got one of yours myself." He extended his hand and shook with Gabe. "Good ta see you, ole scout."

"Yal been ridin' like you chasin' somethin'."

"Hell yeah we have. What'd ya signal for, Gabe?" said the captain as he uncorked the canteen in his left hand to draw a long pull. Before Gabe could answer he yelled to his men to dismount and grain their horses while they rested. The men complied at once and took to doing things they couldn't do while in hot pursuit, tightening girth straps, adjusting tied-on gear, watering the tired mounts and themselves, shaking the dust from their bandannas.

"We just got out of a scrape with a raiding party carrying at least two white kids captive, back whar the rivers join over thar. They killed a mount and wounded one of our outfit, this young man here with this purple knot on his head where he hit the rock when his horse went down. LaPoint hit at least two of them with big slugs. They headed upstream, up past that smoke thar. They set the grass on fire behind em."

"Buck up boys, we mighta found em! You got a wounded man? Take care of their injured, this is scout McBride," yelled the captain.

The men sent up a cheer, which caused their pack horses and tired mounts to make a racket, setting off the hound dogs, who had just caught up. Word spread that ranger Gabe McBride was talking with the captain. The dusty men conferred excitedly as they rested themselves and their horses, passing a water-bag among the mounts while snacking on jerky. A young man wearing glasses and carrying what looked like a medical bag walked up. "You got injured?"

"Yep," said Gabe. "That man there got shot through the thigh when they took down his mount. I got that patched up for now, and it went clean through without hitting bone or tendon, but he whacked his cabeza on the rock of the riverbed and knocked himself silly, or worse." The young ranger went to check out Jesse's wound and head injury.

"How many did you make of the raiding party?" was the captain's next question.

"LaPoint here was up a tree with field glasses, and sighted about seven or eight leaving with at least two blond white kids, likely boys, all cut up and covered with dried blood. He killed two of the raiders."

Josh stepped forward to shake hands with the ranger captain as Gabe continued. "Took the second one down from a tree branch with a long rifle at over five hundred yards as they were leaving. I'll bet that threw a shock into the sonsofbitches. That 's when they hustled off and set the grass on fire."

The ranger captain shook the hand of LaPoint and looked him eye to eye. "This fella LaPoint just killed two of them, men," said McGregor in a loud voice, drawing another round of affirmation from the men with canteens in their hands. "Two bodies left behind, eh?" he asked.

"Yep. They were in a big hurry, musta knowed yal was behind 'em."

"They damn sure been trying to throw us off the scent. You scalp 'em, like they say you used to, back in the forties?"

"Naw. I ain't religious about it no more. Let the coyotes and buzzards have 'em. Somebody's got to get the rest of them before they hit the cap-rock, or they'll disappear on the plains. They ain't dragging no lodge poles ta leave a trace."

"Well, we're on 'em and ain't gonna let up. Been riding hard since we heard. Left Camp Verde in the middle of the night. They got my cousin's boys this time, the murdering thieving bastards. Took 'em right out of the pasture below the house, down by the creek-bank in broad daylight, right in front of their mom."

"Your kin? Not the Smith boys from Cibolo Creek, Henry's boys?"

"The very same, Clinton and Jeff."

"Damnation, I knew their Pap Henry from the old ranger days. Why, that's just twenty five miles from San Antone! They keep getting more brazen."

"It's war, Gabe. Whole countryside living in terror, line of settlement being pushed back by raiders. Maybe you ain't heard, being out on your spread, but lately they've been murdering and kidnapping all around the area north of San Antonio, Fredericksburg, New Branfels, and north up into the Fort Mason area, even around Fort Concho. Settlers are packing up and leaving those areas, the Saline Valley and Castell been about burned out."

"Wal, gol-dang, can't the army do anything? Hell, we're sellin' the cavalry mounts hand over fist."

"They ride around in circles until the Comanches steal their horses, mostly. Both the Kiowas and Comanches are murdering settlers all up and down the line. This same bunch we're chasing killed a man splitting rails a few miles back, stripped him and filled him with arrows like a damned porcupine, took his clothes, mutilated him pretty bad, had my younger men throwing up. I expect my young cousins had ta watch that. Damn-it all to hell."

"This has to end," said LaPoint.

"The bastards are having their way on the frontier."

"They need a bastard like me on their trail with a long rifle," said LaPoint. "Put an end to this slaughtering parents and stealing kids."

"By God we're going to end it now. You're more than welcome to help us get them boys back. They took the wrong kids this time. This is family, my blood kin. I'm not gonna let up 'til I get them boys back, by God, if it takes me the rest of my life. And I'm gonna kill every one of those raiders if I can, with well armed rangers to back me up. My thanks to you for taking two out of our way. Let's go get the rest. What tribe were they?"

Gabe spoke up while offering a chew of tobacco to the captain. "A Lipan Apache and a Comanche, wearing settler's clothes. The Lipan was in a damned preacher's suit. And a nice hat and an old bugle."

"So you signaled us with the bugle, huh? I thought it might be the cavalry, until I heard them sour notes. I should have known it was you, like that cow horn in the old days, three blasts. Mighty poor playing, though."

"Wal, I'll get better with practice, maybe,"replied Gabe.

"Let our hound dogs get a whiff of that bugle, would ya? They been throwed off the scent several times, that oughta freshen it."

"Shore, have 'em sniff this and the bodies too. Who's your pard?" asked Gabe as another captain walked up with the bloodhounds.

"This here is Captain Shriener, from Kerrville," said John McGregor as a man with a wide brimmed straw hat walked up from where he had been tending the hound-dogs.

They shook hands and locked eyes. "Ranger McBride and LaPoint, good to meet you. We've heard of your scouting and shooting skills, on the campfire grapevine, I guess you'd say."

"Yep, LaPoint and McBride, horse traders."

101

"Best scouts and long rifle marksmen of the staked plains, is what I heard," said the ranger.

"Gabe's the scout, and I can shoot," said LaPoint.

"He can cut sign with the best," said Gabe.

Then Captain McGregor spoke up.

"How about you joining us and helping track em, Gabe, like the old days? They've done about everything from backfires to spreading skunk musk to throw us off. And we had to bury several folks in their trail. I'm amazed we're even close, actually. A tracker like you and a sure shot like LaPoint would be a great aid. Not that you ain't a fine rifleman too, old timer. But there's word of LaPoint's pistol skills south of San Antone, and talk is that he out-shot Britt Jonson at a thousand yards in a match at Helena, and you too, using a Whitworth."

"Wal, we was discussing going after 'em, seeing those captive boys with them, but we got a wounded man, barely morn'n a boy himself. I suppose I could go with ya while LaPoint takes him in for doctoring."

"I ain't no boy, biejo!" said Jesse.

"No way," said Josh. "We ride together. The only way you're going is if I'm going with you, and the only way that's happening is if the Captain here sends Jesse back with one of his riders and one of those spare mounts."

Josh LaPoint stepped right up to the second ranger Captain and shook his hand. "Josh LaPoint," he said, looking directly into the man's eyes. "We'll help on those conditions."

The ranger captain saw the blaze started by the downing of Jesse's horse still growing in LaPoint's eyes, along with relentless determination to rescue those captive children.

"We'd like to help get your blood-kin back, sir," said Josh. "I can't stand the thought of them making slaves of captive kids, jerking them away from their mothers and kin, or worse. Sign us on, if you can take care of our wounded."

"Alright, LaPoint," said Captain McGregor, after an long swig from his canteen. "Glad to meet ya and sign yal on. You can take the varmint down from long distance for us, like those long shots that beat Britt in the shooting match."

"Might have had a bit of luck on that, Captain."

"Well we need some of that LaPoint luck," said McGregor. "Your idea sounds good, we'll send a man back with your wounded friend, and you two come with us. Gabe

McBride's been known to out sniff a bloodhound on the trail of Comanches. Sharpshooters with long rifles are more than welcome. How far is it to some good water for our mounts, they're fading fast. We ain't got much left."

"The Llano River's about two miles, and running pretty clear, but you'd better graze them here, on account of that grass fire. Pretty smoky down there now, Captain, with the horses winded already. Then we can water them well up ahead of the fire on the river, upstream where those big pecans grow, and cut for sign," said LaPoint.

"One of yal bring them hounds and I'll take ya to the bodies so they can pick up the scent again," said Gabe.

They rested the horses for a while as the saddle sore riders walked around, then headed northwest to catch the riverbed above the white smoke of the grass-fire, with LaPoint urging Scorpio to the front and aiming upstream to a point in the valley where he thought they might intersect them. Jesse was taken back by two men who rode beside him as he mounted a tired and lathered mare and headed for doctoring.

It was a crisp Friday in early March as they traveled slowly up the Llano River, with its wide stony bed and braided stream-flow, searching for the scattered trail of the raiders. There were often bluffs on the bends of the river, with a gallery forest and good places for ambushers. The raiders used the trackless stone along the floodplain to hide their trail, and often Josh was down on the ground looking for overturned pebbles, their color being a slightly different shade, driftwood sticks recently broken by horses, bent weeds, squashed river plants, scuff marks from the shod horses on the algae of the rocks beside the water, or fresh horse manure. The hound-dogs seemed confused most of the time, milling through the water or along the shore with their baggy jowls to the ground and noses twitching, whimpering in frustration.

It was slow work cutting for sign, much of it on foot, LaPoint running back and forth while Gabe held the reins of his horse a ways behind. The trail was full of crossed switch-backing and confusion of backtrack and brush drags as the raiders tried to throw the trackers off. At times Josh smelled the strong musk of skunk, which threw off the hounds, and twice they crossed small patches of blackened grass where the raiders had tried to set backfires that failed to spread. The rocky ground along the scoured flood-plain was difficult to cut sign on, requiring LaPoint to get his face down next to the stony ground. The rough country left plenty of places for the raiders to wait in ambush, so much time was taken to avoid that while searching for tracks.

For long frustrating hours they moved up the valley, grazing as they went, since they were past the big grass-burn. They seemed to be falling behind the pace of the raiders, because of too much time searching the crossed small trails, with constant smell of skunk putting the dogs into a worthless frenzy. Then, feeling the frustration and desperate urgency of the rangers, who had been riding non-stop for many hours trying to cut the raiders off, LaPoint and Gabe remounted and rode in front, cutting for sign from horseback and following their hunches upriver, and they headed northwest on the trail of the murderers carrying white children for the rest of the bone-wearying day. At times they would see enough sign to confirm that they were on the trail. LaPoint had the sharpest eyes and rode along the north shore looking for sign that they left the riverbed and headed north for the high plains. The rest of the time they guessed and moved upstream, searching for signs, presuming the raiders kept going upstream.

Captain McGregor was full of furious determination that the rangers catch the raiders before they reached the staked plains, and drove his men as hard as he drove himself. They were all very eager and well mounted riders, with plenty of firearms, but LaPoint could see that the long ride had been hard on them and their mounts. Even their few extra mounts looked jaded and sagging with every step.

They found continual signs of the trail, but never seemed to gain on the marauders, and by late afternoon the rangers' horses were fading fast. Coming upon a settler's little dogtrot log cabin, they were able to buy corn for their horses and to press on with the hard chase up the twisting riverbed and pink granite protrusions in the gray limestone banks. The twilight glow faded as the moon rose and they kept on the trail, at a snail's pace. Captain McGregor was driving himself and the men relentlessly, and they rode without ceasing until they had to rest when the moon went down, and it was too dark to see anything. They found a settler with a full corn crib in the Castell Valley, about twelve miles upstream from where they met the river above the grass burn. When he heard they were chasing raiders with captives, he said all the corn and hay they needed was free, for many children had been stolen from that area and the areas further west.

The next morning they were moving by dawn, when it was light enough to cut for sign again. The river did a series of turns and loops, each after about two miles of straight stream, each providing plenty of places for ambush. The travel was slow with the granite and limestone rocks everywhere. There was skunk musk smell aplenty, which threw off the hounds, but convinced LaPoint and Gabe that they were on the trail. Still they never seemed to catch up to the fast moving marauders with their captives. After a long day of trailing, they camped where Beaver Creek entered the river, and slept a few hours until the first light in the east.

The following day they rode north another dozen slow miles to inquire at Fort Mason, with no success. The patrols were ranging north with no extra troopers to spare in the hunt upstream. They were able to replenishing supplies and rest the horses with good feed there. The next day was the same, occasional traces of a trail up the rocky river flats and along the shoreline, but nearly a cold trail by that time. For a couple of days they trailed the raiders for another thirty miles of river meanders through valleys with lots of cliffs and caves, the stone changing to red sandstone and gray limestone.

LaPoint and McBride spent a lot of time on their knees, laboriously studying the ground for signs of recent passage, almost to the headwaters of the Llano. When they came to a fork in the upper stream, they decided to take the north stream, figuring the Indians would follow it until they cut north for the Llano Estacado, where they would disappear forever. The river-gallery trees, a mixture of mesquite, juniper, and oaks, provided plenty of cover for the raiders to hide in, as did tall cliffs with overhangs and hollow in which to hide. The fear of ambush never left the weary rangers as they rode with rifles out. LaPoint kept to the lead, cutting for sign from horseback by then. They pushed on faster than before, fearful that they were falling too far behind the raiders, and would lose the trail.

Exhausted by twilight, they could go no more that Saturday night as darkness fell and hid the trail signs. They made camp in a good grassy area beside the trickling upper stream for the exhausted mounts, rolling in their bed tarps against the chill as thunder rolled throughout the lightening-storm in the west. They all passed out from exhaustion and frustration in the flashing light, but were awakened in the early morning hours by a violent thunderstorm and sleet blowing across the ground, pelting them violently, and turning into hailstones of increasing size and density. The horses huddled in a sheltered nook beside the cliff as the wind shrieked against the stone.

Everyone hunkered down in their ground tarps, pulling the edges in tight. The wind of a wet norther howled like demon ghosts along the cliff faces of the river as the hail was soon followed by a downpour. They curled under their sleeping tarps in disgust, knowing the flooding cloudburst would wash out any tracks and scents that were left. The rain held steady for hours as they waited for daylight, cussing their bad luck. The hound-dogs were mournfully baying under a clump of junipers as the downpour increased and water began running on the ground, flooding the rivulets as the river began to rise. They had lost the trail, and any chance for hot morning coffee as well. The raiders could head north and mount the cap-rock onto the treeless broad tabletop of the staked plains, disappearing in the trackless grass between the sparse waterholes.

On Sunday morning at daybreak, after a cold breakfast, they started the dejected return home, heading south through a light rain, in the darkest of moods.

"Don't yal men think yore the only ones who ever came back empty handed," said Gabe before they headed out. "Thar's plenty of time with Captain Jack Hays when we didn't catch who we was after. It's a bitter pill, but yal got ta swallow it and go on."

"By gum I'm not giving out yet," said Captain McGregor "They've got the whole frontier living in terror with this raiding, and I aim to catch these miserable kidnappers if it's the last thing I ever do. I'm just going back to re-provision for a long trek, this ain't over yet."

"Wal, ya done tha best ya could, John," said Gabe.

"I know it. Thanks to all of you for a great effort. Let's go home for now."

They headed back and soon had to swim their horses across the south branch of Llano River, which had turned from a

106

clear braided shallow stream into a raging brown torrent a hundred yards wide. Some of the rangers could not swim, and many of their horses were spooked at the idea of crossing the wide brown flood.

Scorpio and Buck had plenty of experience swimming raging rivers, so Josh and Gabe took their boots off and hooked them upside down on the saddlebags, hooked short ropes on the horses' saddles, then plunged in, soon switching to trailing their horses in the water as their stallions swam the current, tugging their masters through the swirling brown currents.

Reaching the other side a ways downstream, they yelled for the rangers to follow as they put their boots back on. Most of the rangers crossed alright until a bunch of driftwood came floating down on a rising flood crest. Josh and Gabe readied their lariats on the shore as they saw the trouble coming.

Soon one of the rangers was being washed down stream by a floating pile of tree branches. Whirling a tight loop hard as he had learned from Pancho, Josh landed a lasso on him after several attempts, hooked the rope to his saddle horn, and pulled him to shore. Gabe lassoed another, after a failed attempt, and the rest evaded the floating driftwood jam and made it to shore. The guys who weren't soaked in the overnight downpour were soaked now, in a cold wind from the north.

The remainder of the trip was spent sodden and miserable, slipping on muddy trails and dangerous creek crossings, feeling dejected about not catching the raiders and freeing the captives. LaPoint could not free the images of the young blond boys from his mind, and the failure to catch the raiders rankled him deeply as they rode back through the rain. He remember how he had felt as a child ripped away from his mother's love, and it kept his gut churning to see the image of those boys in his mind.

The only constant sound was a rumble of thunder, the pelting of rain on soggy hats and canvas oil-cloth mackinaws, and the squeak of wet saddles, layered with occasional grumbles and curses at the whining dogs. The men argued about whether taking the dogs had been worthwhile, and about other things that had slowed them down. It was another long hard chase after marauders that had ended in utter failure. It was fortunate that no peaceful Indians crossed their path, for a boiling frustration needed venting in every man.

107

Captain McGregor spent a lot of time talking to Gabe about a return scouting trip up onto the staked plains to try and rescue the boys, as well as other white captives, but Gabe could only give him information on waterholes and canyons, and not a commitment. He had horse contracts to fill, and didn't want to get LaPoint involved in killing Comanches as he had in his early days. He had already noticed how upset Josh LaPoint was.

They rode back in the steady rain and wind and collected Jesse at the doctors house in Llano for the trip back south and their horse business. Jesse healed well with the doctoring they gave his leg, but had two black eyes for a month and a knot on his head that only slowly disappeared. He was still game and grew more confident in his skills of leading the vaqueros in the subtle arts of rounding up mustangs. He also practiced shooting more, in deadly earnest. He had heard tales from his grandfather from Mexico about Comanche raids for captives, many decades before, and it was still going on. He decided it was time to stop it, and wanted to master long range shooting.

In San Antonio for horse trading business later that summer, they learned that Captain McGregor kept searching for his nephews throughout the summer, to no avail, and that the boys' father Henry had offered a thousand dollar reward for each boy, for he knew that if they were not returned soon, they would become Comanches, or be violently abused if they refused. This was a burr under both their saddles, but they had a horse ranch to build, and daily responsibilities.

Despite their continued success at capturing, breeding, and training saddle mounts for the trail drives and the army, a persistent discontent over the white captives stayed with the LaPoint outfit in those months. Kathy often asked in her letters if any news of their rescue had reached Helena, for the discussion about the stolen children had touched a sore spot inside her about her lost brother. But they kept their minds off the feeling of bitter frustration with constant hard work on the horse operation, and building up the ranch on the Blanco.

After disposing of all the horses they had for sale and making new contracts with the army for more horses and mules, the LaPoint outfit signed on to help Mr. Winger drive a herd north across the Llano Estacado to Dodge city. They joined with Mr. Winger's crew of experienced drovers just northwest of San Antonio, at Leon Springs, with McBride and LaPoint scouting

108

and pointing the herd, Pancho and Jesse alternating at point, and Tom Jackson in charge of several well armed out-riding scouts.

They had several brushes with Indians on their long trek north, but only a couple of bunches tried to steal cattle. They lost perhaps twenty head to night raiders, while they had to head off a stampede caused by the Indians crawling up to the herd and popping blankets. McBride advised them to ignore the loss and keep pushing on to Dodge, which they did. Whenever the old scout saw Indians from then on, he parlayed with them and gave them beef for safe passage. The drive succeeded in arriving at Dodge with the cattle in good shape and only a hundred or so missing out of a herd of two thousand.

When it was over the LaPoint outfit rode together back to the Blanco Valley without incident with Indians or bandits, despite the silver they carried. They spent the spring traveling far into south Texas to find good mustangs for breeding, pushing sixty miles below the Nueces River to the wild horse desert west of Corpus Christi. They had brushes there with gangs of Mexican bandits, but were able to drive most of them away with their accurate heavy shooting. But on their return they lost a herd of about forty horses near the Nueces, to rustlers from some Mexican gangs. LaPoint fretted over losing the horses, which they had worked hard to collect, and tried to figure ways to thwart the outlaws. He pushed his outfit on the return to try and make up for wasted time and effort.

Chapter Five: Captured Comanchero

The LaPoint outfit stayed busy supplying all the contracts that Josh secured with the good reputation of their saddle mounts. The gathering and saddle training had been developed to a fine art by then, with everyone taking a task and mastering it. By '72 and '73 Josh and Gabe spent most of their time training horses on the rancho instead of gathering them, leaving Tom and Pancho in charge of that. Jesse had displayed a knack for both skills, and Josh was training him to be a horse trainer while his father Pancho worked at gathering good stock with the vaqueros. Jesse's skill with a riata from horseback was unmatched by any of the drovers, and he practiced his marksmanship a lot to try to match the shooting skills of LaPoint and Jackson.

They had large horse herds in the early summers, with over half of them ready for saddle, the rest tamed to bridle and ready for marketing. Josh had made contracts with General Augur in San Antonio to deliver saddle mounts to the cavalry forts on the frontier. After delivering a herd of mounts to cattle drovers, they gathered the mounts for the cavalry for a drive north, past San Antonio to the forts on the edge of Comancheria.

LaPoint led an outfit of nine horse drovers trailing a herd of nearly two hundred horses up towards Fort Concho, when they were hit again by rustlers. Like the year before, they were surprised and beaten by superior numbers in a well planned attack. The year before they had been able to fight off the rustlers with only a few dozen raw horses stolen. This time they lost a whole herd destined for contract sale to a trail crew going across the Goodnight trail, while camping on the middle fork of the Concho River, two days out from the fort.

At least half of the horses were saddle-trained mounts for the army, and all were the best stock available on the south Texas savanna. They had used Gabe's buckskin stallion to run in the lead of the bunch while Gabe rode another dun gelding. The outfit had the bunch pretty well in hand and were camping on the pasturage around Grape Creek, about fifteen miles northwest of the fort, when a large gang of marauders struck in the predawn darkness. The three night riders were overwhelmed and forced by rapid gunfire to flee for their lives into the arroyos, with two of them taking flesh wounds. In a few seconds the ground was thundering with the running spooked herd, driven by gun blasting rustlers, popping whips and blankets. The vaqueros were running for the remuda, trying to catch their mounts, and dodging bullets.

Gabe had been up taking an early morning leak before starting his regular sourdough biscuits, and he hid in a juniper bush during the attack, hoping his white underwear did not give away his position to the wildly firing rustlers rampaging through camp, popping bull whips and flapping blankets and yelling like madmen. His horse Buck was well hobbled and double staked and did not bolt, though he did some serious kicking and snorting during the commotion.

Scorpio, who stayed beside Josh at night, did not stampede with the herd and remuda, despite the wave of rustlers riding through the camp, so LaPoint quickly grabbed his weapons, pulled on his boots and hat, then mounted, and took out trailing the herd by the sound of thunder and the dust cloud. This was the second year his outfit had been rustled, and he was furious.

Gabe yelled as he rode off, "Don't get shot!" then found a vaquero who still had a mount, and sent him off after Josh. Tom Jackson also caught a mount and soon saddled it and took off after LaPoint. But neither mount could keep up with the dappled gray stallion, and he soon left them behind.

After LaPoint had gone a couple of miles he topped a small rise in haste and saw another rider trailing him. At first he worried that it was ambushers circling behind him, but when the rider became back-lit by the moon, he could tell it was Miguel, one of the vaqueros, by the way he rode. He decided to press on to find out which way the herd was heading, rather than slow down for aid. He pushed Scorpio towards the thunder of the running herd, following the clear trail of risen dust in the moonlight.

Within twenty minutes some well placed shots from hidden rustlers with rifles drove him back, and he hustled away, quirting and toeing the stallion under him into a zig-zag retreat. Soon he joined his drover Miguel in hasty retreat as rifle shots

111

landed around them. Tom Jackson then joined them in a clump of brush, but they were peppered with rifle fire and could not see the shooters. They raced back in the dark, and after pulling the other night riders together back at camp, LaPoint went to make plans with Gabe to recover the herd.

Gabe was hunched over his breakfast fire of mesquite branches as Josh approached, kneading the sourdough ball on an oilcloth. The pungent smells and sight of Gabe in his regular morning activity was comforting after the disaster.

"Anybody shot, Gabe?"

"One dead rustler, two or more of us winged a bit."

"Damn. We lost a herd. Again. My fault. Who do you think they were, Gabe? And where are they heading with the herd?" Gabe glanced up and gave a negative shake of his head as LaPoint said, "my fault."

"No it ain't yore fault."

"If I'd had more..."

"We was outnumbered, let it go and get ready to feed."

Gabe had progressed to pinching and rolling biscuits in two big Dutch ovens while squatting by the fire, a well gnawed ginseng root in his mouth. He had a small shovel and began heaping a glowing mound of coals onto the lids as he covered the two big cast iron cookers. There was a large blackened pot with a dozen or so eggs in it and water starting to simmer. The coffee water began boiling in the big blue enamel pot, so Gabe pulled it back from the coals a bit and poured the ground coffee in it, stirring it with his knife.

"Well don't let me take your mind off breakfast now, Old Coon," said Josh, exasperated, as he squatted beside Gabe. "Who do you figure it was this time?"

"Renegades again, most likely. Whites with Indians. Probably the same bunch that hit us last year. They headed to New Mexico, I reckon, probably La Puerta del Luna or somewhar's thereabout, to sell our stock. Hell, we might as well start running these good saddle mounts to Sante Fe, since that's whar lots are ending up anyway. Maybe we could let these sonsofbitches drive them across the Llano Estacado and steal them back at Chama."

"Well you've obviously had time to cook up some great ideas. Did you get a good look at them?"

"Yep. But like I say. Hard to know who they were. Thar was Comanches, Kiowas, Mexicans, and whites, accordin' ta what I seen and heard. I mighta seen that Bison fella, and some Comancheros, but it was too dark to tell for sure. The one that got shot dead looks like a halfbreed Mexican Apache, or a captive gone native, in Indian clothes and paint."

"Who shot him?"

"Jesse, I think."

"Damn, I suppose it had to happen. Is he taking it alright?"

"Yep. He's been wanting ta shoot a rustler ever since those raiders kilt his horse."

"And that's your best guess as to who they were?"

"Wal. Waugh. My best guess would be ole Polo Ortiza and his gang. I think I mighta seen him on a gray stallion. He always liked a fine horse and fancy Spanish duds, with one of them short fancy riding jackets. I seen a lot of guys with beards, which Indians don't have. Comancheros. They'd be taking the herd up across the Llano Estacado to sell in New Mexico, I reckon."

"You know him, this Ortiza?"

"Usta, back in Taos, and Chama, whar he hid out sometimes, at the Fauster Hotel, whar I took ya for that pool game that time and ya won all my cash. He dealt in stolen stock and captives, as I recollect. No-count varmint, in my book. Stole one of my knives, he did. Cheats at cards too. A backstabber and bushwhacker, whiskey trader, gun runner. I'm sorta surprised nobody done shot him yet, like tha egg-suckin' cur he is."

"Well, why don't you tell me how you really feel about him, then?" said LaPoint. "Heading which way to New Mexico?"

"Wal he's tha type I told ya about, give the Comancheros a bad name. I expect they was going up the Mucha-Que, probably towards Blanco Canyon, whar ole Mow-Way likes to camp and trade with 'em. There's a good road, old Comanchero trail, all the way across the Llano Estacado to New Mexico up thar. Waterholes no more than thirty miles apart."

"Not according to Major Marcy's report."

"Wal, Marcy believed what they told him so he wouldn't go across the plains. Probably had the scours from gyp-water by then, and didn't want to go out thar. They'll have back-shooters out on the trail, lots of them."

"They do. I never thought they'd hit us so close to Fort Concho. Damn it, I hate getting rustled like that. That's twice in two years, probably the same bunch getting all our hard won stock. They make it damned difficult to make a living," said LaPoint.

"I heard from the scouts at Fredricksburg that they been doing it regular around here and all the way to San Antone, along with murdering settlers and capturing kids. They're a bunch of no-count sorry son's-o-bitches that ought to be put under. They plan to sell our horses and rob us of all that damned hot work gathering and training them. Thieving trash."

"I've had just about enough of developing herds of saddle mounts for them to make off with, Gabe."

"We'll track 'em and get that herd back. We can't let 'em take the mounts we worked so hard to get, huh?" asked Gabe with a squint into Josh's face."

"I'm for getting them back. But I was dodging bullets in the dark back there, and one of them nicked Tom's saddle-horn. And they got us pretty much out gunned."

"Oh yeah, I reckon they do. I'm just making a load of biscuits ta take, and some hard boiled eggs. I'll whip up an omelet next. No use rushing after 'em, that's what they expect, they'll have bush-whackers out for a long time."

"Yes sir, we found that out already," said Tom Jackson, who came up after gathering his gear and weapons, hoping for breakfast. "And us being back-lit by the moon. They planned it just right, the sons o bitches. What's for breakfast before we go after them?"

"Same as always. We heard the shooting. Glad they didn't hit ya. Breakfast in a short while, full spread."

"I see you've got some saddle mounts back together. How many?" asked LaPoint.

"Enough for you, me, Tom, Jesse, and Poncho to have two apiece, and two pack horses. They're gettin' ready now, loading gear and ammo."

"Where are Martine, Pablo, and the other vaqueros, nobody hurt too bad, huh?

"Naw, scraped and banged up some, and a flesh wound for Pablo. I already sent the vaqueros back to Fort Concho on

114

the mules to report the raid and bring back more mounts and supplies. Maybe some help from the troopers if we're lucky. They was supposed to be sending a patrol out yesterday, according to what Sergeant Charlton told me."

"Jesse? Going with us into a probable shootout? I don't know about that, Rosita will have my hide if anything else happens to him."

"Jesse's the one that shot the only rustler we took down. Your weapons' training is setting in on him. He wouldn't be denied. They got his favorite horse, and he woulda followed us anyway. We already had that argument, no use going over it agin. He's going, "cording to Pancho, him, and me. He can ride like hell and shoot too. You know it, too."

"Damn. I don't like it, but if Pancho agrees."

"It's settled."

"I'll ride with him, boss, and keep an eye out for him," said Jackson.

LaPoint nodded. "Well let's get that herd back, then. I'm feeling pretty stupid about now. I didn't figure on rustlers this so close to the fort. I should have had more night-guards out."

McBride spoke up. "Wouldn't made much difference, most likely. These guys got a lot of practice at stampeding herds at night and running 'em away. I figure it's the same bunch that hit Goodnight last year. They had more than twice as many riders. I figure it's the same gang that got ole Dick King's herd from Leon Creek. We need to get 'em, put a stop to this. "

"Alright. We're going after our stock then. Looks like I should be ready to go in about thirty minutes, judging from those mesquite coals you're loading onto that lid."

"About right, I reckon, though we'd better eat first and drink all we can. Got coffee going for now and for the trip. Gonna make an omelet too, and pork."

"No rush, huh? Hunters' breakfast."

"Hell, I'm hungry, let's eat good first, could be a long ride and end up getting killed. I don't want to die on a gnawing stomach."

"Yeah," said Jackson, "Nothing like a stampede and chase to work up an appetite."

"They're expecting us ta rush right into an ambush, ain't they, with bushwhackers lining the trail? Ya want hot lead or hot biscuits?"

LaPoint nodded his head as he squatted by the fire. "Yeah, that they were. And I surmise you plan to circle up ahead of them and hit them after they bed down, but we're short on gun-hands still."

"Yep, that's the part I'm workin' on. There's that ranger patrol we talked to yesterday already out, and maybe other stock-men looking for rustlers. And cavalry patrols ranging northwest. And you know McGregor has been out with ranger patrols ever since his nephews got stolen. We might get lucky, run inta some help."

"Yeah, or shot and killed like Tom and I almost were. They got some good shooters."

"What' daya want ta do, just go on home broke with an unfulfilled stock contract? Gather another herd and bring it up here for these guys to get again?"

"No. At the least we can take some down with long rifles. I'm with you, just wish we had more men with guns, let's go get the horses. And thanks for sending back to the fort so quickly. I suppose you've loaded both Sharps and Whitworth?"

"Yep. We might have to even out the odds with long distance shootin'."

Jesse came riding up with several more horses he had rounded up. "I got one of them, boss. And I got four more horses. Let's go get the thieving sons of bitches. I've had it with these raiders riding up and shooting at us."

"We will. You stick with Tom or me. Get everything ready, we're going after breakfast. Check your weapons. You're alright, huh?"

"For sure, I'm ready. Listo por combate."

"After breakfast," said Gabe.

"And let them get away with our horses?"

"Nope. No use rushin' off into an ambush, though. Get down and eat, and learn ta obey orders plenty quick if ya intend ta go with us."

"Alright, alright, let's eat."

When the biscuits were done they each had two with a big breakfast of salted ham, beans, scrambled eggs with peppers and onions, and black coffee, then packed the rest into

Gabe's saddlebags and the mule packs. At sunrise they were ready to go, with everyone mounting in the first bright rays.

Fully provisioned and determined, they took out after the herd, armed as much as possible. Each man was carrying at least one pistol, a Winchester or Spencer repeating rifle, and plenty of ammo, while Gabe and LaPoint both carried long range guns as well. LaPoint had his long-barreled brass plated Remington .44 revolver in a scabbard on the left side of his belt, and the modified trigger-less fast action short-barreled .36 on his right side. They carried two big canteens of coffee for later on, and all the canteens of water they could, along with provisions on the mule. This was the second year they'd had their spring remuda stolen, and they were determined to stop the rustling of their hard-earned herds.

The sun was glaring up over the horizon in the east, a red-orange ball of fire already throwing glare and heat aplenty, as they followed the obvious trail of the running herd. Josh and Tom, the best rifle shots from horseback, rode in front with weapons ready to fire back at possible bushwhackers. Tom and the vaqueros carried brass framed "Yellow Boy" 66 Winchester repeating rifles, recently purchased in San Antonio, with lever action for rapid fire. Tom carried his older Spencer repeater on the other side of his saddle, as well.

With plenty of shod hoof-prints mixed over the running wild horse herd's prints, they knew they were greatly outnumbered by the rustlers. Leaving the trail of the herd as it swung west after a couple of miles, they headed due north for a an hour, then began looping west. Gabe said he intended to surprise them when they figured they had escaped pursuit, by coming at them from the northwest when they were camped.

With Gabe's intimate knowledge of the staked plains, Josh immediately concurred with the plan. They pushed their mounts hard, changing every three hours to rest the horses, trying to loop north ahead of the herd. The countryside was rolling prairies mixed with stands of timber near the creeks, and the grazing was plentiful. Exercising as much vigilance as they could, they rode hard and steadily to get ahead of the rustlers until sunset, when Jesse, scouting ahead with his sharp vision, spotted a detachment of cavalry from Fort Concho up ahead of them. He spurred off to meet them and returned in thirty minutes with news that they too were after raiders, and wanted to unite forces.

When they joined up with the 4th cavalry near twilight, they camped together and parleyed with the commander, a Sergeant William Wilson. It turned out that the cavalry was on a long patrol for horse rustling marauders, so two Tonkawa scouts went south with Gabe and Josh to find the herd. The scout with the most English was Old Henry, a former riding partner to Gabe from his ranger scouts, who was glad to see him and rode beside him gabbing until Gabe told him to spread out. Old Henry called Gabe 'Long Rifle' and wanted to ride with him and talk Tonkawa up front, but Gabe was intent on sensing where the herd would be.

They rode in a spread out pattern, guiding by the stars, until LaPoint spotted the dim glow of campfires of the bandits' resting place. He quickly rode to the other scouts and gathered them in silence, notifying them of his find.

It was near midnight when they carefully slipped over a ridge and sighted about half the herd, settled down for night camp around a small creek with plenty of well armed night-riders circling them, and several rifleman posted on hills nearby. LaPoint observed the camp with his field glasses from beside a mesquite bush on the little brushy rise. The fat yellow moon provided enough light to study the situation, which he did while the Tonkawas talked in excited whispers to Gabe.

Leaving the stirred-up Tonkawa scouts to watch the marauders, they headed back to the night camp with the news, arriving just before dawn. They woke Sergeant Bill and gave him the information, which aroused him greatly, and got him to issuing orders and rousting the sleepy troopers. The LaPoint outfit tightened their saddle girths and prepared for battle, checking and rechecking their weapons, thinking of payback after twice being rousted from their sleep by rustlers. LaPoint took Tom Jackson aside and spoke to him.

"Tom, I need you to stay with Jesse and make sure he doesn't get reckless. Protect him and hold him back some if you can."

"Alright, Josh, but you know he can shoot nearly as well as me. You trained him."

"Yeah, but that was without bullets flying around, and he's full of piss and vinegar after shooting that bandit, so try to rein him in some when we hit that camp. Let the army take care of the bandits, and our outfit recapture that herd. What he's really good at is controlling horses with his riata."

"Consider it done, if I ain't shot in the process."

"Goes for all of us, eh? I wish I hadn't gotten us into this."

"Hell, you didn't get us into it, the rustlers did."

"Yeah, well if I'd had more guards on the horses, we wouldn't be fixing to go to war over this."

"Look here, boss. I already done spent three years in a stupid war and got whipped bad by Sherman and his black powder boys. I ain't planning on backing down to any rustlers like the varmints that killed my brother, and there's nobody I'd rather fight with. We're fighting for what we earned, and the right to carry on the ranching business here. If we don't do it, who will? We're with you, all the way."

"Thanks, Tom," said Josh as he walked his horse over to where Jesse was adjusting his girth strap. After talking with Jesse about the situation, urging him to concentrate on the horses and not the fight, LaPoint rode up to Sergeant Bill and told him they were ready. The Sergeant went to ranging up and down his line of troopers, preparing them for a real fight.

Within a half hour the 4th Calvary detachment, accompanied by the well armed LaPoint outfit, were moving south at a fast pace to recover the herd and capture the rustlers, who had even taken cattle destined for the Army commissary in the recent past. All the Army men were brimming for a fight, after long days of patrolling in vain. They had all heard of the settlers' complaints that the army was no protection from the savage raiders, along with the endless clamoring of the newspaper editors for action against the relentless marauders. The LaPoint outfit rode in front as scouts, with Pancho and Jesse together as outriders to the west, and Tom Jackson out-riding to the east. The LaPoint plan was to let the army handle the main fight, and to concentrate on getting the horses back.

LaPoint was the first to sight the outlaw camp in his field glasses, to the east of the horse herd. He saw no one stirring, just a thin trail of smoke from the campfire. Walking their mounts to within a couple of hundred yards, LaPoint found a place to hide the horses in a clump of live oaks. He then set up with Gabe in a sheltered position on a brushy rise. LaPoint

119

pulled out his Whitworth and loaded it while Gabe did the same with the Sharps. Both drove metal rods with U shaped ends for rifle rests into the dirt. With their rapid fire repeaters ready as well, they prepared for the attack, intent on taking down the night guards on the herd so that Jesse, Tom, and Poncho could sweep in and capture the horses.

The night riders on the near side of the herd were close enough to use the repeater rifles, at a couple of hundred yards. LaPoint counted four of them, and pointed them out to Gabe. The other three drovers from the LaPoint outfit were primed to bolt after the horse herd, hiding behind some mesquite bushes, with their girth straps tightened, riatas out, and weapons readied. Tom Jackson hustled back to report their readiness to the Sergeant, who was also primed and ready for a fight after a week of searching. The 4th Cavalry dismounted and tightened their girth straps, loaded their weapons and made ready extra cartridges. As Jackson rode back to join Pancho and Jesse, the cavalry lined up and prepared to charge.

It was a beautiful sunrise, the eastern sky pink and orange and birds singing over the grassy prairie. A few random distant coyotes were giving their last howls at the setting moon. The carbines of the troopers were all out and ready, and their brown and black horses lined in a row and ready, many of them snorting and pawing the ground.

The Tonkawa scouts were given yellow army bandannas to wrap around their necks or heads and to identify them from the hostiles. They changed from their scouting ponies to their war ponies, and began murmuring a war chant in painted faces. As the sun crept nearer to the low ridge to the east, the cavalry moved slowly in attack formation of eight abreast, three lines, approaching the last small brushy rise that separated them from the outlaw camp. While they topped the rise, the sun appeared with blinding rays at the edge of the horizon, and they moved forward in a square, at a fast walk. When they were within two hundred yards of the smoldering campfires of the rustlers, they accelerated into a canter, with carbines out. Instead of a saber, Sergeant Bill rode with a revolver in his hand, pointed at the outlaw camp. The horses kept the formation but accelerated at a steady pace.

"That's it," said LaPoint softly while sighting the big rifle. "Hit them at sunrise with the light in their eyes."

"They'll be hungover for celebratin' the theft of our horses last night, most likely. What a wake-up call. Look at 'em now, thar they go, holdin' tha line real good, they are."

"Let's go for the horses," blurted Jesse.

"Hold on and wait until the iron is hot 'fore ya strike," said Gabe.

"Yeah, just wait," said Tom. Josh sighted in on the outriders without a word.

"Listo," said Pancho. "I no shoot, just go for the horses."

The troopers struck the outlaw camp at a full run, with the blazing sunrise at their backs throwing brilliant light into the bandits' eyes. Panic was the first reaction from the sleeping miscreants as the charging horses struck the camp and the troopers poured deadly fire from their carbines and revolvers. After the troopers charged through the camp, they circled around and went through again, firing the whole time.

When the front line of troopers charged the camp, LaPoint and McBride began to methodically pick off the night guards on the herd, taking the near ones first as the LaPoint drovers rode out to take the herd. Jesse surged ahead of Pancho and Tom, racing for the horse herd with pistol out as LaPoint and Gabe shot the rustlers around the herd. Each shooting from a rest with well placed shots, they cleared the hostile riders from their saddles and left the horses running free. Three of the Tonkawa scouts cut their war mounts over that way as the LaPoint drovers gathered the herd, sweeping around to help gather the horses, with the knowledge that they would be paid in good mounts. The chances of regaining the herd looked good.

One last night-rider appeared at the far edge of the herd, about 400 yards away. LaPoint reloaded his repeater fast when he saw the man drawing a bead with a carbine on Jesse. But Gabe had already taken his Sharps, quickly aimed, and took the rustler down with a shot to the chest. Jesse raced on to turn the startled herd into a mill, with Pancho and Tom right behind him. The LaPoint outfit did what they were best at, controlling horse herds, and bent the packed animals into a turn to the right.

The noise of a dense carbine battle was coming from the outlaw camp, where chaos was unfolding as wave after wave of troopers stormed through the bandits. The rustlers who resisted were shot full of holes, and the Tonkawas were scalping them. Gabe watched with his telescope from the small rise as LaPoint reloaded their long range guns. The battle was over four hundred yards away, clouded with dust. With the big guns loaded, they both set up on shooting mounts and watched each side of the action, the horse gathering and the camp battle. Within a minute Gabe had to let loose with a long shot from the Sharps as another rustler rode out to fight for the herd. Gabe knocked the rider off his horse with a chest shot and reloaded the Sharps. LaPoint took down a rider fleeing from the fight near the campfire at a few hundred yards, and reloaded. Jesse, Tom, and Pancho started to get the horse herd under control. Surprise and overwhelming firepower was winning the fight for the army, and the carbine fire was intense and nearly constant.

The horse herd was slowly milled to the right and pulled from their panicked run by the LaPoint outfit, with Jesse in the lead turning the lead mare. Within ten minutes the troopers and drovers had overwhelmed the rustlers and won the brief engagement after the fierce gun-battle during which Gabe shot three armed night-riders out of their saddles from long range. LaPoint, watching the battle around the campfire with his glasses, held his fire, saving the big Whitworth for a real need. The Army was overwhelming the gang of rustlers and didn't need his help taking the camp. Realizing they were out gunned, most of the outlaws tried to run and were shot down while doing so. Finally they surrendered and were rounded up by the troopers as the LaPoint outfit went on to contain and settle the herd, which they had milling in a tight circle as the battle wound down.

During the confusing melee of the close range battle, a swift rider in vaquero dress clothing with a big gray sombrero left the dust-cloud of the camp on a big black stallion, heading west at a full run. Josh saw him and instantly felt that this was the jefe, from the flashing silver conchos on his leather pants to his fancy vaquero jacket, his big ornate sombrero, and the silver studded saddle on the big stallion. The pale full moon was still gleaming along the horizon and back-lit the fleeing rustler in a silvery blue sky as the sun rose in the east. The horse was very fast, and left a long trail of dust as he galloped towards the setting moon.

LaPoint lined up a shot for the fleeing man, hoping to wing him and knock him off his stallion using the accurate

Whitworth with its twisting octagon firing tube and long octagon bullets. The rider was moving away from him at a slight angle, and he aimed for the shoulder with the high powered scope he had acquired from Britt Jonson. By the time the rider had pulled into the rising sunlight, he was nearly seven hundred yards away and moving like a streak, laid down over the big stretched out black stallion with its long tail streaming.

Gauging the wind from his dust-trail, and the rider's rhythmic motion on the galloping horse, LaPoint triggered the big Whitworth and watched through the scope as the crack-boom of its thunder rolled over the prairies.

"You got him," said Gabe, looking through his brass telescope.

The rider flew over the head of the running stallion when the big slug hit his shoulder, twisting and falling off as the horse went down in a tumble. The black stallion cartwheeled over the man in a whirl of dust and tried to rise, then staggered back to his front knees and stalled, snorting in distress. This gave LaPoint an awful feeling in the pit of his stomach. The man had flipped in the air and slammed down, laying motionless on the ground. LaPoint immediately mounted Scorpio and surged out for the spot, while Gabe took one more shot towards rustlers near the herd, knocking another rider off his horse with the big Sharps.

"Gabe. I'm going to go check that guy and get that stallion."

"Go on, we got this here. I'll be thar directly. Don't let them get away. You think he's alive, ya just winged him?"

"Yeah, I think so," said LaPoint as he rode away in a hurry. Scorpio raced the seven hundred yards at a full gallop while the firing at the outlaw camp settled down to a few random shots.

When LaPoint reached the downed bandit, the black stallion had regained his footing, and was shaking his big head, while the rider lay barely moving, still sprawled in the dust. Josh dismounted, checked the stallion for broken limbs, calmed it some, secured it to a mesquite branch, then got his canteen and poured water on the man's face, letting him revive as Gabe came charging up on Buck, skidding to a stop in a cloud of dust.

"That's it, cover me with dust again, ya ole coot. Can't you ever ride up without skidding that horse?" said Josh, glad to

123

see Gabe was not injured in the battle, and full of piss and vinegar from hitting several bandits with perfect shots.

"He likes ta stop like that,...Hey...Lookee thar, a Spanish stallion, that's a fine horse. Is it alright?"

"He'll live, no broken bones, but he's shook up from the tumble. How's the fight going?" There was scattered firing and the sound of running horses in the distance.

"Most of 'em are shot down, dead and dying, and the rest captured. Sergeant Bill is tryin ta rein in the Tonks from scalpin' and butcherin'. That red headed guy I seen before wasn't among 'em, far as I could tell."

"Any of our outfit hit?"

"Naw, they're out settling the herd now while the soldiers mop up. Jesse's gone after the few horses that got away. The Sergeant wants a captive to question, though. Is that who I think it is?" asked Gabe as he dismounted into the settling swirl of dust.

"You tell me, he's just reviving. He looks like old Pedro Serna from the Cavalier ranch on the Nueces, to me. Nice leather trimmed riding jacket he's got. That was quite a tumble he took, must have flew twenty feet and flipped before he hit hard on this big ant mound here. Might have broke his back. So I left him there with ants crawling up his legs."

"Wal, long as that horse is alright. Be nice if he could talk though. He knows a lot."

"Where is Jesse, is he alright?" asked Josh.

"Yep. He's after the horses with Pancho. Tom kept him out of the camp fight, and is over there with 'em, riding guard while they circle the herd. There's Tonkawa scouts helpin 'em too, hopin' for horses."

"Good. So you think you know who this is, eh?"

Gabe took his boot and rolled the sprawled out man over by the shoulder as Josh stepped back over to soothe the stallion. The Whitworth slug had made a small hole in the top of his shoulder and a big one going out the other side. It seemed to have missed the bone and gone through, for he could move the arm, and it wasn't pouring much blood.

Dressed like a Spanish gentleman in elegant breeches and fancy gray short riding jacket was this middle aged man with a well trimmed goatee that was graying at the edges, moaning from his clean wound through his shoulder. There was dust and bits of dried grass all over his face, and both nostrils ran blood into his mouth. His big ornate gray felt sombrero was crushed and hanging back on his neck, the cord tight around his neck. He was starting to groan and move by then, his eyes rolling around, trying to take in his situation.

"Well howdy Polo, remember me?"

"Chinga su madre, viejo bastardo, was et you shot me. And my horse?"

"He's alright,and you just been winged some, with the bullet clean through. You been shot by LaPoint thar, who's claimin' yore horse. You stole a horse herd from the wrong fellas this time. LaPoint don't miss."

"I felt it hit before I heard it. It was a damn Sharps, eh?

"No, Whitworth."

"Hey senor. I know you maybe, viejo hombre?" asked the downed Latino as his hand crept down towards his knife scabbard. Gabe's powerful grip was instantly on his wrist.

"Sure ya do, tried to cheat me at cards back in Chama plenty of times, at tha Fauster Hotel. And you're wearing a knife you stole from my shop in Taos."

"McBride? Gabriel? Rojo Cabeza? No?"

"That's right," said Gabe, as he drew the knife from the belt of his old acquaintance.

"Rojo Cabeza? Cabron. You still alive, you old mula. I heard you went under. Your hair went from rojo to blanco, eh, Gabriel? I went by your shop in Taos to pay for the knife, and they said the Comanches got you. Why you guys shoot at me, cabron?"

"You stole my horses, mine and the fella that's tending yore mount thar, LaPoint. We don't allow such. Anybody shoots at us gets shot back at. So whar are the rest of 'em? This is about half of the herd, I reckon."

"Hey Gabe, let's parley, we can cut a deal here, good for both of us. We got these horses from Bise McCairn and his outfit. We didn't know it was your herd. The Kiowas and Comanches got the rest of them, a half day ahead, with Bise and his riders. You could pardner up with us too, Gabriel. Good money in it. Bise is an ole redheaded Scotchman like you was before ya went all gray. He's smart too, they never catch him. He knows how the army operates."

125

"Yeah, crap on that, ya done gone a bit gray yourself, ain't ya?" Gabe slapped the dust out of the long black hair of the fallen man. "Or maybe it's just the dust of Texas. I'm surprised somebody ain't put ya under by now."

"Some have tried, cabron. But we cut a deal instead. I make good deals."

Gabe slapped the man across the face, twice. "Thar'll be no deal from me, ya scurvy dog, ya done gave Comancheros a bad name. Don't rank me with no murderin' marauders."

"There's a whole country full of stock gathering, Gabriel. Did you buy those horses?"

"Waugh. You raise the wolf hairs on me, ya gaddam marauder. We gathered and trained those horses and yal stole our hard work. You guys ain't nothin' but renegade horse thieves using the road I helped lay out for trading to run stolen herds back ta New Mexico. I know about that rustler's nest at Chama, ya ole thief."

"Jus tryin to make a livin, Gabe, buying and selling, you sabe, no? Taking horse herds from those who stole 'em, es jus business, no?"

"Attack the livin', ya mean. Business my ass. You just keep raisin' my wrath, don't ya, Polo? My guess is yal been attacking lonely cabins for the loot and captives you can sell too. I'd just as soon gut ya now if that nice Sergeant Bill warn't around. Maybe I will before he shows up, say you fell on your knife. Or here," said Gabe as he scraped up a bunch of big red ants from the mound nearby, "take some of these ants here and see if ya like 'em."

"Hey, cut that out, you ole bastard," yelled Polo as the ants fell on his neck and started crawling and stinging.

"That's just a start, ya cur."

"Chingasumadre, bastardo cabrone!"

"Hey, don't talk rough to him, I'm the bastard that shot you," said LaPoint as he stepped over to the bandit. "Are you going to bleed him out, Gabe?"

"Come on Gabe, we gotta make a livin too, eh? These Texans just steal the stock from the Mexicans, and we New Mexicans take them back. Come on, old frien', mi biejo amigo, no? We could cut a good deal, make you more than you woulda made with that herd. We'll collect lots of herds. You getting old, you need something to fall back on, eh? Let's the

126

three of us ride out of here and parley, I'll make you rico hombres. For old time's sake?"

LaPoint stood shaking his head with a slight smile as the Comanchero was trying to weasel Gabe. He walked back to sooth the horse some more. The stallion was settling down as he stroked it's muzzle. "Well have at him, Gabe, I'll keep the horse settled down if he starts screaming."

"No, no, no, Gabriel. I make you the best deal."

"I oughta slice you with my knife you stole for ole times sake. You was a snake in the old times and a snake now. Josh, how's that stallion of 'ourn?"

"He's fine. He'll sire some fine colts."

"Wal, this fella here won't when I'm done with him." Gabe ran his thumb across the long lost blade, testing the sharpness, then held it to the outlaw's throat. "Ya let it get dull, ya lazy thief. Ya got that horse taken care of now, LaPoint?"

"Senor LaPoint, don't leave me alone with this old loco hombre."

Josh was soothing the stallion and rubbing it all over, breathing gently into its nostrils. "He's alright, just shook up. Nice horse, a breeder for sure. I'd better get back and help round up our horses before they scatter, Gabe. You got this guy under control, eh?"

"No senor, don't leave me with him," cried the rustler.

"Yeah, go on, I got this varmint. I'll bring him in directly, after he tells me what I want to know, or I make a gelding of him."

Josh gave a searching look into Gabe's face. "Sergeant Bill's gonna want in him one piece, old coon. Don't stick him too deep and bleed him out all the way, like that other guy, last month."

"Aaaiiieee chingacabron. Don't leave me with him."

"I got him now," said Gabe.

A grim and foreboding expression clouded the bandit's features, and his face began to twitch in fear as he whimpered in protest. Gabe gave a look like he was deliberating whether to stick the guy or not.

"Leave enough to put in jail later, Gabe."

"Oh, I'll leave him in one piece if he talks," said Gabe as he slowly slid the blade along the man's throat and drew a little blood, drawing a squeal from the downed rustler.

LaPoint urged Scorpio across the prairies towards the sound of the running herd. Putting the knife away, Gabe pulled rawhide hobbles out of his pocket and tightly secured the rustler's hands behind him, then booted him back over and questioned him with the repossessed knife at his throat for a few minutes until Sergeant William came riding up with an escort of four men.

"Sergeant William Wilson, let me introduce ya, this here is yore captive, Polonio Ortiza, and he done told me some things yore gonna be glad to know. He's a renegade marauder, a horse and cattle thief, and murderer, and he can tell you where these son's o bitches hide, including that Mow-way band you'ra seekin', which is the only reason I didn't slice his juggler vein, right here in his neck. He's yorn now, and I'm hopin' we got some of our horses back."

"Senor. Officer. Get thes loco viejo away from me. He slice my neck," said the bandit as Gabe hauled him to his feet. There was a small trickle of blood running into the ruffles of his white shirt and his collar-less gray jacket.

"Aw, ain't nothin' for a guy like him. The horses?"

"Probably near a hundred horses, McBride. LaPoint is riding back to see to it, and your vaqueros are trying to keep them contained. That was incredible shooting you two did with those long rifles, especially that last one by LaPoint. I was watching the miscreant fleeing when I saw LaPoint take him down from that little rise you both were firing from. Amazing shot."

Two of the black troopers dismounted and moved to the man and his horse. "You men take the prisoner off Mr. McBride's hands before he faints and falls on a blade. Take him back to the camp."

"On his horse, suh? The animal be bleedin', and de scout gots a hold on him."

"Hell no, that horse is mine now," said Gabe.

"Ours," said Josh.

"McBride and LaPoint get the horse. Put a rope on the bandit's neck and walk him back, then bind him completely onto a mule for delivery back to the fort. And keep the rope on his neck."

"That's the proper procedure for him. He's a slippery one. Don't let him get away or I'll regret not killin' him."

"We'll keep him wrapped up tight for the Colonel, sir."

"Wal, alright then, that worked out well, all in all. Nice scouting with ya, Sergeant Bill. Thanks for the help with getting our herd back."

"Likewise, I'm sure. I've heard of you for years from the rangers and out scouts, Mr. McBride, and was honored to work with you. I'm riding one of the saddle mounts you guys sold us last year, you know, and I sure do like him."

"Good to hear that, since we just lost half of an army herd."

"You sure you don't want to join in with us in finding this village of Mow-way's band, where they're gathering these stolen herds? These renegade marauders like Bise McCairn have been thieving all the stock around here and San Antonio, moving it north with the aid of some of the Kotsotekas, we believe. He uses hit and run tactics and is so far impossible to catch. He even steals from around Fort Concho and Fort Mason. We could sure use a scout like you, who knows the Comanche ways and the watering holes. Colonel Mackenzie will wring me out for letting you get away," said the Sergeant. "Lt. Peter Boehm has already been wrung out for not hiring you guys last year. The Colonel means business, and wants the best scout for the staked plains he can get."

"That bulldog Col. Mac could find 'em and whip 'em, I reckon, with Sergeant Lawton for supplies, Charlton for the front line, and this fellow Polo for a guide. I don't care to scout for him, though."

"Why not, sir, if you don't mind my asking?..."

"Cause I'm in the horse business, not scoutin', and he seems heavy on the fussing and light on the recognition."

"He's demanding, that's for sure, but he gets the job done. He's whipping the 4th Cavalry into a real Indian fighting unit."

"Waugh. According to what I heard at the bars in San Angela, the colonel seems to spend all his daylight hours wringing folks out and all night studying maps. He's had Lieutenant Pete badgering us to be scouts for over a year now. Every time we meet up about horses."

"So why don't you help clean out these miscreants?"

"'Cause the Colonel don't need us to do his job. He can find that village, with ole Polo here."

"Well that may be correct, sir. But with a scout who knows all the watering spots, we could be more effective. The colonel is determined to stop this raiding and captive taking, and to rescue the captive's that the hostiles are holding now. Even the reserve Indians are getting out of hand, driving the Quakers to despair. Another family, named Lee, was massacred near Fort Sill, and captive children taken. The head Quaker agent has called in the Army to attack Mow-way's village and get the captives back, for he defies them."

"Wal hell's fire, so much for the Quaker peace policy, huh? I know'd they're takin' kids for ransom and otherwise, partly 'cause certain fools made it profitable by buying back captives. And it damn sure puts a burr under my saddle, and LaPoint's too, but we got a job to do, contracts to fill."

"Wouldn't that job be a lot easier if we cleared out these raiders and rustlers?"

"Wal, shore, go on ahead, Sergeant, ….hell, if ya want to settle them yal just head on up the Mucha-que Valley to Mucha-que Hill, hit them by surprise from two sides, when the time is right. But ya better take plenty of limes, citric acid, and New Orleans Sazarak Brandy for the gyp-water, and always test for quicksand at water crossings, and keep a knife on the throat of ole Polo thar. He knows whar to take ya."

"I need a man I can trust, Mr. McBride. This scallywag is liable to take us on a wild goose chase."

"Not if you keep a rope on his neck and a sharp blade handy to persuade him. Make him cross first if you suspect quicksand at the crossing. He's a coward, under all his macho posturing with the fine Spanish gentleman outfit. Sumbitch cheats at cards too. He hangs with a crowd of cutthroats up in Chama, thieves and rustlers to a man, who all deal in stolen stock and captives from Texas."

"We've caught a couple of these guys before, but they escaped before we got any information."

"Wal, I always use a sharp knife to persuade his type. Usually don't even have to draw blood, just let him feel it on his neck. He knows they will kill him if possible, for leading you in, later on. So he has to know you will kill him slowly on the spot, which has more incentive than a future possibility, especially if you shave some hairs off his chin with the blade."

"Ranger McBride sir, listen, there's reported to be a whole bunch of captives in Mow-way's camp, over a dozen. There's ranger outfits out now searching for them, and probably going to get massacred if they rush the camp. There's reportedly two young boys from Boerne and reportedly a five year old girl, and several other children. The Smith and Lee families are going through hell wondering about those kids. If we could go out with a small force we might rescue them like you've done before, sir."

"Not likely, too late."

"But your reputation as a guide of the staked plains is unmatched, Mr. McBride. Lieutenant Boehm has already spoken of you highly. And scouts Strong, Old Henry, and Johnson. Ole Henry says you know the waterholes and Comanche hideouts heap better than anyone. "

"Henry can track better than me, Bill. And LaPoint's better with the long gun."

"Sure, we've got good trackers in the ranks of the Tonkawas and Seminoles, but the tracks are gone in a day on that buffalo grass country, and the water is scarce. They don't know the staked plains like you do, and we end up with nothing but gyp-water to drink, lost."

"Wal then, listen to me. You ain't gonna sneak up on them when they're running with well armed marauders and gathering stock, for they'll have outriders everywhere on the lookout, and be ready for a fight. Them sons-o-bitches all had good repeating rifles and two pistols each. So while their back-riders hold you off, the rest will scatter with the herd and meet up later. The most of the Comanche hunters are out after buffalo now, which is getting scarce, so you ain't gonna find a full village."

"So what would you suggest?"

"Bide your time, then use this Polo fella for a guide. Best thing to do is wait til summer's over and catch 'em settling down in a canyon with good water and processing their winter food. They always set up to dry their buffalo meat in a canyon at the headwaters of the rivers."

"What about Mow-way's bunch? According to our sources at Fort Sill, there are still a large number of captives in his camp. He says they were purchased from Lipan Apaches, and refused to give them up."

"Mow-way. I usta know him, as a young buck, before he rose up ta be a chieftain. Stronger than most men. We hunted buffalo together, with lances. He's got one of my knives, I reckon, if he ain't lost it. Traded two buff robes and a horse for it. Later I heard he killed a grizzle with it, single-handed, and wears a necklace of the claws now. He'll put up a hell of a fight, I reckon."

"If we could ever find him. Where do you think his band will winter?"

"My guess is they'll be on the North Fork of the Red, along with some Quohadis, maybe Para-coom's band, maybe Kiwih-nai's. They are all fierce fighters, with as many rifles as bows now. They even say Kiwih-nai's bunch fights with revolvers and carbines now. And they don't close their eyes like Mexicans when they pull the trigger, I've heard. These renegades got long range guns too, probably Sharps with the new long scopes. You'll have to outnumber them with well mounted troops using carbines and lots of ammo, overwhelm them in a surprise charge, like yal done with these rustlers. Surround the village and capture everyone, hold 'em hostage til the raiders come in to the reservation, and they give up their captives. Take the horse herd and don't let them steal it back at night. Hold their folks until they bring the white captives in. Turn their tactics on them."

"Sounds simple, but...a guide like you...."

"I just gave ya the varmint to lead ya in. Polo's an old Comanchero, of the bottom dweller type. He knows the trails and waterholes as well as I do in that area. He knows the way they run stock back to New Mexico too."

"Yes sir, he's known to be in league with a renegade named Thomas McCairn, among other names, who was thrown out of West Point back in '48, and has been a rustler and raider since then, running with a rogue band of Comanche, Kiowa, and Apaches."

"That's the one ole Polo called Bise?"

"Yes sir, Bison, Bise McCairn, formerly cadet Thomas McCairn of West Point, til he was thrown out in 48."

"West Point! If that don't beat all. What'd they throw him out for?"

"General bad behavior, whoring at Benny's Haven, fighting, lying, cheating, then stabbing another cadet, according to what Major Hatch told us. I figure maybe he got syphilis from the whores there and went crazy from it. He's fully bent on fighting the army, looking for his old classmates to show them up. He was near the top of his class, they say, clever with strategy and languages."

"Why'd they call him Bise?"

"On account of he's got dark red bison looking hair and beard and thick body hair."

"I mighta known this guy, from a long time ago, when I scouted groups to California. Met a red bearded guy who was living with the Gila Apaches once, during the 49er rush, who was intent on attacking soldiers. How else would you describe him?"

"Six foot tall, stocky, powerful build, gray eyes, ruddy complexion, awkward gait, excellent horseman, several scars on his face, and his right ear missing the bottom half now, according to a recent sighting by Major Hatch in Fredricksburg. He's very clever, speaks several Indian languages, good at manipulating folks, but has an ungovernable temper and religious delusions."

"Waugh. Could be the same guy. Missing part of his ear, how'd that happen?"

"Reportedly in the war, maybe in Kansas when he was marauding. I don't know exactly. Could have been in Louisiana near the end of the war, where he nearly bled out from wounds. I'm just piecing this together from officers' scuttlebutt over the years. It's discussed among the West Pointers a lot."

"What else do ya know about him?"

"That he rode in the Kansas border wars and won a federal captain's commission there, with a different name, from his mother's side of the family. Last official word is that he was wounded at the end of the war, maybe in Louisiana, and was mustered out as a captain. Then we heard he went west, got in a brawl in Galveston and killed a man with a knife, then he killed again in north Texas and again in New Mexico, and California, and he then joined the Indians to fight against his old West Point classmates. The law in three states has wanted posters out for him, dead or live reward. The officers all hate him and want him killed and forgotten. They talk about him in whispers, and dark

133

grumbles. Whoever leads troops and kills him will get a sizable betting pool."

"Wasn't he already riding with Apaches raiders before the war?"

"Yes sir. He already rode with the Apaches against the army in the fifties, then apparently went to Kansas to loot and pillage before and during the war. They say he rode with Quantrill and the Redlegs both, looking for loot. He somehow wrangled a federal commission out of that and went down to southern Louisiana to loot plantations, then came back west after the war and formed a renegade band of Comanche, Kiowa, and Apaches. He works with those Mexican bandit gangs as far down as the Nueces, and raids the Pecos trail, and around here."

"I think I seen him that night they rustled us, big shock of red hair and red beard. I think that's who took our herd, and probably took Goodnight's herd last year."

"Might well be so. Since the war he's stolen thousands of head of livestock, led raids on settlers' cabins, raped, tortured, mutilated, murdered and taken captives to be ransomed for gold."

"And the Army can't catch him?"

"Not yet, though the officers have a betting pool that puts a big reward on it. Hell, he's been stealing Army horses as well. He was recently spotted walking the streets of Fredericksburg."

"Wal why can't yal grab his sorry ass?"

"They've always got a number of spare mounts to escape on. Apparently he was leading a gang of horse thieves up around Fort Sill, rustling the reserve Indians' and the army's horses, and led an attack on Lawry Tatum and some peaceful reserve Indians. After the troops at Fort Sill began to scour the countryside for him, he came down here, and has been spotted in San Antonio and Fredricksburg. He's high on our list of wanted men, dead or alive rewards out for him from several states. But he's the very devil to find, he raids and disappears. The Comanche and Kiowa he rides with know the plains, and they always have extra horses for each man."

"Yeah, probably our trained saddle mounts from last year's herd."

"Maybe so. They can live off the grasslands while we have to drag supply trains with grain for a lot of our big northern

134

horses. We can't catch him nor his band of raiders, and sure could use your help."

"From what ya just told me, I more than wish I could, if I wasn't committed to this horse herd business at hand. Losing half that herd means we got contracts still to fill, and LaPoint is a bit like yore Colonel, he don't let up on an idea onct it's fixed in his head. I ain't ruling out helping ya later on, but right now I got a job to finish. You can rest assured that I will shoot Bise McCairn if he comes into my sights while I'm hunting for the rest of our horses, which I reckon he's got."

"Well sir, I wish you well on that, and hope our paths cross again. We'll be heading back with these captives to Concho and inform General Augur in San Antonio. We may be still looking for that village when you're done with your job. Col. McKenzie is a very determined man, and will not give up."

"Oh I know, we sold him that gray pacer he was riding a while back, and made other horse deliveries to him, so I've dealt with him some. He don't bend much on horsetrading. He badgers me ta come scout for him every time we cross trails."

"Well, he's determined to find the hostile encampments. The raiders think they can strike the settlers at will and then hide on the staked plains. He means to disabuse them of that notion. And now General Augur has given him the go ahead, after some recent massacres."

"You keep ole Polo locked up tight and use him to help find that village. He knows the roads across the plains that these renegades use, the old Comanchero cart trails. Thar's waterholes every twenty to thirty miles all the way to the New Mexico settlements. In the old free trading days we had cart trails all along the Canadian as well. If he balks on ya just stretch him or put a blade to his skin, or drop some ants in his pants. He'll talk. But I'm tellin' ya now, the Comanches go to the canyons in fall to make ready for winter, and that's the time to find em. Otherwise you might just be hunting the wind. They're out for Buffalo."

"I'm listening, Mr. McBride."

"Usually, come the fall, that damned Maman-ti who butchered those fellas on the Warren wagon train and set Sheridan off ta Indian killing, will be in the upper Palo Duro, or the upper Red to the east of thar, hunkering down for winter. Use that damned Polonio Ortiza to tell ya where ta water on the

135

way, and use plenty of outrider scouts. And don't drink gyp-water without doctoring it with citric acid or limes and brandy. That's about all the help I can give ya now. Except to tell ya that drinking horses' blood is better than bad gyp-water."

"No gyp-water for me if I can help it, sir."

"Polo can lead ya to good water, but don't let him lead ya inta quicksand.

"Having him will help, I'm sure."

"From what I heard and seen of your Col Mackenzie, that should be enough. Contrary to what Major Marcy was told, there is and has been a trading road across the staked plains, several of them, in fact. The early Comancheros traded in peace with the Comanche for buffalo robes and meat for the New Mexico settlements, and left cart trails all over. Now these rustlers come down out of the mountains from Chama and Las Vegas area, using the roads we laid out for peaceful trading."

"My last appeal, sir. For the captives? Some of these children, the Smith brothers, were taken right from the Guadalupe Valley, near your ranch on the Blanco."

"Naw sir, not til I clear my mind of these intentions, but thanks for the offer. We aim to get all our horses back and delivered. I'm signed on to finish a job. Ain't my war anyways, not no more. But squat with me on this dusty ground and I'll show you the watercourses."

Gabe hunkered down in the dust, grunted, spat, and began drawing in it with his knife-blade. LaPoint came walking up to listen to the long parley. Gabe used the point of his knife to show the sergeant. "Lookee here, this line be Blanco Canyon, this here is Rescate Canyon, sometimes in fall you'll find Mow-way's band there processing their winter meat. This here point is Mucha-Que hill, where they meet with these here rustling renegades. This here is the Mucha-que Valley heading up thar. Now up here is the Palo Duro, on the Red....and this area around McClellan Creek on the North Fork of the Red is sometimes where old Mow-way has his winter camp." The sergeant took out a notebook and copied the sketch and recorded the information as Gabe talked and drew his map in the dust. LaPoint memorized the map.

After a long parley with Sergeant Wilson, Gabe and Josh gathered their horses, about half of what they had before the rustlers' attack, and headed for Fort Mason. The 4th

Cavalry detachment took the prisoner Polonio Ortiza back to Fort Concho, where the information was relayed to Col. Mackenzie, and preparations were made for an expedition onto the staked plains, using the Comanchero as a guide. When Gabe rode with Josh and the other drovers to move the herd, he did not tell LaPoint of the new details he had learned about Bise McCairn, the missing earlobe and cheek scar, or the army history. He didn't want to stir up old hatreds and deter Josh from the job at hand, and he wasn't sure that this was the captain who burned the plantation. But he took to pondering it and seeking more information on it.

"What took so long with Sergeant Bill," asked LaPoint.

"Wal, he wanted to know how ta find and catch Comanches, and being as how he's the first army fella that come out and axed me, I went on ahead and tole 'im. He listens."

"Oh hell, he listens. Lucky we weren't waiting all night then. Did you show him your scalping scar and relate the tale?"

"Naw, I drawed him a map and showed him whar the Comanche's would be in fall, and how ta cross tha staked plains."

"Well, let's move what's left of this remuda."

The LaPoint outfit ran their horse herd, diminished by half, to it's destination at Fort Mason, fulfilling part of their contract, then returned and made a fruitless search for the rest of the stolen horses, wasting over a week on the trackless grassy flat tabletop of the staked plains. The dense grass that sprung right back in place within a few hours of being trampled, made tracking next to impossible. Mostly they found a few buffalo tracks and chips, but no horse herd.

After abandoning that frustrating scout on the dry wiry trackless grass, they returned home with cracked lips and sunburnt faces to hire on with Mr. Winger and run his last herd of the season to Dodge City. The bitter taste left by the fruitless search was not as galling as the useless search for the captives had been, but it was aggravating enough. They were glad to start another drive and try to make up for it with wages and part of the profits from Mr. Winger.

That drive went through without major incidents with rustlers nor many Indian attacks, though many Comanches were begging for wohaw, beef to replace the once plentiful

137

buffalo. Gabe, riding scout for waterholes, was saddened to see the northern Comanches, the Quohadis who had always disdained contact with the white man and remained proud and free, reduced to begging for stringy longhorn beef. Since he disliked the stringy beef himself, and preferred buffalo, he had been hoping to get meat from the Comanches, not the other way around. He always gave them the beef they asked for, having the drovers cut out some slow footed steers, therefore making the drive proceed without much Comanche trouble. The remuda was always kept in tight between the herd and chuck-wagon, knowing the Comanche's lust for horses.

It was like the other cattle drives, dust and monotony and the constant bawling of cows on the move, trying to find enough grass to keep from burning off weight, always searching for the best waterholes, avoiding gyp-water and quicksand crossing, always nervous of stampede from rustlers or lightening or a dropped cook-pot, always eating the same food, smelling the same cattle, breathing the same dust. At least on this drive they had constant grass and rivers to water the stock, unlike the Goodnight trail west.

The Llano Estacado, called the Staked Plains by most whites, had fierce storms from the cold air masses rolling down the Rockies and hitting the warm moist southern breeze from the Gulf of Mexico. Since this drive for Mr. Winger was late in the year, they had their problems with lightening storms and howling wind with sleet and rain that turned dry gulleys to brown torrents. One such line of thunderstorms passed north of them, full of spikes of lighting and rolling thunder, but they felt fortunate to miss it by a few miles. But soon LaPoint saw a black cloud of smoke, then the flames of a prairie fire sweeping towards them. Whipping out his binoculars, he spotted Gabe hustling back towards him, nearly a mile out. He spun Scorpio and fired off a shot to signal Tom to come quick with help.

By the time Gabe had arrived Tom and Poncho came riding up. They all spotted the roiling smoke and licking flames of a grass fire raging towards them. Gabe yelled out, "Lightening set the grass afire. Backfires. Stop the herd. We got ta light some backfires."

LaPoint had dismounted by then, and was digging in his saddlebags.

"I'm on it." He found a can of beeswax saddle dressing, and smeared it all over an extra cotton shirt.

"You guys set backfires over that way, I'll drag this burning shirt this way," yelled LaPoint as he remounted. Everyone spread out to start fires in the golden dry grass on the left while LaPoint took off to the right with the burning rag trailing in the red tops of the golden grass. Soon they had a line of fire started in the middle, and kept spreading out with the flames as the big prairie fire approached with a roaring windy sound. Whirlwinds of burning grass were spiraling up from the intense front line of the racing flames.

As the big fire approached the tiny line of flames they had started, it drew a big wind and started the small line blazing. Soon it flared and raced to the big fire, blackening the ground in front of it. With no fuel, the big fire stopped, and LaPoint had the drovers stall the herd until the other flames moved away. Aside from breathing a lot of smoke and entertaining the idea of burning alive, not much damage was done, though the cattle went hungry through blackened plains for a few hours. The black dust of the charred dry grass had everyone covered in feathery soot and coughing for the rest of the day.

They later had a stampede just north of the Red River, due to a lightening storm and fierce wind-driven hail, but they were able to hold the herd together enough that rounding them up was not too difficult the next day. At one point LaPoint was riding alongside Pancho and Jesse near the front of the herd when lightening struck the wet horns of the cattle. The horns were all sparking flames of foxfire for a few seconds, and gave off an immense heat and the nasty smell of burning bone. The ground lightening could even be seen on their horses ears, but they felt no burn and kept riding to control the herd. The amazing sight was discussed later, after the nightmare of catching up to and turning the frightened herd to the right was accomplished, and the herd was milled in on itself until it slowed to a walk on the muddy ground.

The storm had dampened everyone's bedroll and spirits though, and the rest of the drive was a rush to finish, which burned a little weight off the cattle. There was none of the usual buffalo herds to push through around Dodge, but most of the grazing was gone, eaten by earlier herds of Texas cattle. The herd still arrived in good shape and brought a good price at the rail-head. Everyone was glad when it was over, and spread out to celebrate in their own ways.

Dodge City and the surrounding area was full of drovers and buffalo hunters, the stink of hides, stockyards, coal smoke from the trains, and boozy revelers, a rowdy mess. The novelty had long worn off for LaPoint, for the town reminded him of Helena, and he contented himself with attending to business, catching up on the news, and planning for the return trip. He wanted no gun-play with drunken rowdies, for he knew his reputation would spread if he outdrew anyone in Dodge.

While in the Longhorn saloon drinking and gabbing with Billy Dixon and Bat Masterson, Gabe had learned how Britt Jonson had been slaughtered along with six other freighters, with all the corn and all the mules stolen and the wagons burned with the mutilated bodies in them. When McBride heard this his ruddy face went ashen white and he staggered outside and threw up, then went to the hotel and to bed. LaPoint was also deeply affected when Gabe told him in a choking voice, for he had grown to like the big black man in the short time they had visited, and had carried the illusion that the experienced frontiersman could never be put under by Indians. The news put a damper in any more enjoyment, and they pushed through the necessary work of delivering the herd at the rail-head stockyards, then paying off the outfit.

Finishing their business and saloon visiting quickly, by September fifteenth Josh and Gabe were heading south from Dodge, while the rest of the outfit tarried in Dodge city, intending to head back to the San Antonio spread together, after a few days of celebrating. The two scouts had been discussing heading west to the Cimarron Canyon and into the mountains for a while, but had come to no decision, for Gabe was taciturn and grim lipped, plodding along on Buck with glancing back for mile after mile. Josh rode behind, knowing it would do no good to push the stubborn old man on anything.

The grass was good and the horses did well as they headed south at a canter. For relentless hours LaPoint and McBride pushed their stallions across the open plains around the Canadian River, hoping to come across buffalo and get some good meat for their camp. They were relieved to be shed of their cow-herding responsibilities, and had a pouch of silver and gold coins for their season's work. But there were grim signs in those times.

That was the second year they noticed an appreciable drop in the number of buffalo on the southern plains. All the giant herds around Dodge and north of there were gone, reduced to hides and bone, and they rode for five days through areas where the buffalo herds had been endless, without seeing any. What they saw was spirals of black birds above bone yards of the buffalo, with the tracks of heavy laden wagons heading north.

Disturbed by this, the slaughter of Britt Jonson, and other things, Gabe remained preoccupied and grim on the ride south, putting the pieces of a puzzle together in his mind, and Josh rode ahead, keeping a sharp lookout for Comanche sign. They did see some small groups of buffalo being chased by what Gabe called 'immigrant Indians' who had gathered in the Indian Territories nearby. But they never encountered hostile Kiowa nor Comanches, so their progress was unimpeded.

Near midday they were leaving the Canadian River watershed when Josh spotted a fairly fresh trail because of the lines from the dragging lodge-poles. When the Comanches traveled they had the horses pull the long lodge-poles with basket-like platforms suspended between them, leaving definite marks, drag lines that stayed for a day or so, depending on moisture content. The sharp eyes of LaPoint picked out this pattern, faint as it was.

Heading south as they were, the trail revealed itself to be marks from at least twenty horses dragging lots of lodge-poles. They followed it for about ten miles to see where the big encampment was, then made camp when they reached good water on the Canadian River. LaPoint kept remembering his last view of the Smith boys, torn away from their mother as he had been as a child, tied on horseback and receiving a beating with a horse quirt. He remembered the pain in Kathy's voice when she spoke of her captive brother. Gabe had told him of all the captives being held in Mow-way's camp, and he felt the urge to find them.

They were settled in under cottonwood trees just a few miles downstream of the old ruins of a Bent Brothers trading post on the small river for an early camp. Gabe was telling Josh about a battle his old friend Kit Carson had engaged in nearby, when a party of eight Rangers and two Tonkawa scouts came riding up on well worn and lathered mounts. The rangers and their horses were soaked with sweat and pretty tired, bleary eyed and staggering as they dismounted.

Their captain was John McGregor, who had been looking for his young cousins, the Smith boys, for months on end, one scouting expedition after another. He was much worn since they had seen him last, his cheek bones standing out high in his wasted visage, the raging fire of quest in his bright blue eyes burned down to hot coals of dogged determination. He was surprised and glad to see LaPoint and McBride again, and immediately started a parley over information.

The rangers said they were looking for Mow-way's village, for the Smith boys and other captive children, lots of them. They had word from the Quakers at Fort Sill that the Smith boys were at that village, along with recent young captives from the Lee family, the rest of whom were savagely murdered. They said that the Quaker Indian agent Lawrie Tatum had called for an attack on Mow-way's band for refusal to bring hostages in, including the Smith boys and more recent captives from the slaughtered Lee family.

Josh offered buffalo jerky, day old biscuits, and good water to all the rangers while they talked. Grateful for the break, the famished thirsty rangers parleyed with Gabe and Josh for awhile about their search for captives, fed, watered, and rested their mounts, and then moved off south, following the trail left by a moving village where the captives were being held. McGregor wanted to get the last bit of daylight moving south, and all Gabe could do was force some jerky and water for them to carry, and send them in the right direction. Josh scanned the horizon with the field glasses as they rode away, standing on Scorpio's back to do so.

"See any dust or smoke?"

"No."

"Waugh."

"They've had those captured kids from Cibolo Creek a long time, Gabe. It's been bothering me since we saw them riding off, then lost their trail up the Llano...and now these other kids. They've got everybody living in constant fear, even close to San Antonio and Austin. I'm worried for the ranch on the Blanco now."

"Yep. It's a general war of terror on settlers now, pushing people out."

"We'll be pushed out of the Blanco Valley if it keeps up. I can't raise a family there with the Indians raiding and stealing women and kids. Kathy is just getting over her fear."

"Wal, it's been bothering me too, ever since we failed to track the raiding party. Henry has offered a thousand dollar reward for each kid, trying to get em back before it's too late, and they was tryin' to get me to go scout for 'em, but we been pretty busy minding our own business, and I told 'em I wouldn't know where to look until fall." Gabe lit up his pipe and took a snort of brandy. "I shore hate ta see John go off like that, too tuckered to think sharp. He's gonna push til it kills him for those boys."

"He's determined, alright. He's been on the trail since we saw him, last spring."

"Yep. He's a McGregor, and they never give up. Comes from a long line of blood-feudin' Scottish borderland reivers. They're a match for any Comanche."

"He's been on the hunt this whole time, but he's liable to catch more than he can bite off."

"Blood kin. You know what it's like. You took out after those marauders that kilt yore ma as soon as ya could, didn't let up 'til ya got all ya could."

"Yeah, but he's been many months on the trail for those boys, all the while that image of them has been stalking my dreams, being quirted and tied on horseback."

They didn't speak for a while, tending to camp chores and rubbing down the horses. The evening campfire was very small and smokeless, and they weren't very hungry, but both had another cup of brandy after the small meal. Josh finally broke the silence as Gabe puffed on his pipe and ran a whetstone along his big blade.

"You reckon that little worn out ranger patrol will find those captives, Gabe?" asked Josh while stirring the fire of old buffalo chips.

"Maybe. From what we told 'em about that trail we been followin', and what they already sighted. They may catch 'em in camp on the Red with the renegades, waiting for some wet northers to fill the playas and creeks so they can move their herds ta New Mexico."

143

"How far is it to the Red River?"

"About forty miles to the north fork, couldn't get there til tomorrow."

"But then what?"

"Hell if I know. It's likely to be a big village, the winter gatherin' spot, where they'll be processing buffalo meat. The warriors will be mostly in camp then."

"That little party of tuckered-out volunteer rangers will just get wiped out if they try a rescue."

"Yep. I told 'em so."

"Well, exactly how did you rescue captives before?'

"By moving fast as soon as they were taken, trailing them night and day on two horses and hitting the raiders before they got back to a big village. Then me and Britt took 'em down one by one, from long distance. But hell, dozens of times we went out and found nothin'. You need the army for a big village. Ya ain't gonna sneak up on all those outriders and dogs yapping."

"Well, we know the army is out here somewhere too, according to what we learned at Fort Concho on the way up."

"Yeah, but whar? Could be lost and eating their mules or dying of the scours from gyp-water."

"Well, it's fall and we're done with our work for a while. Why don't we go help them find these captives before those worn out rangers blunder into something they can't handle. They were all near too tuckered out to think straight anyway. Maybe Colonel Mackenzie is coming up after them, like we heard at Fort Concho. That's what the big fella, your pal Charlton said, wasn't it?"

"Wishful thinking. He was just agreeing with me that hitting the head-water canyons in fall made the most sense. Mackenzie was champing at the bit to go in summer, after General Augur gave him the go-ahead. That's why we didn't see him at Fort Concho."

"Well, summer's over. This is late September, you know."

"I know what durned month it is, just been in Dodge and read the newspapers. The paper said Mackenzie is lost and presumed dead with all his troopers."

"Well. Newspapers are wrong half the time. Maybe we ought to pitch in with the rangers."

"Thar ya go, fixin' ta jump into another fight that ain't ourn. For all we know Mackenzie's lost on the Llano Estacado with all his men dying of gyp-water scours and raiding Comanches, like that St Louie paper said. We're just two more guys against a big village of Quohadi warriors."

"Well, we're both better scouts of the plains than those guys, and could at least locate the camp and relay the information. This stealing kids has got to stop. I can't get that image of those raiders riding off with those Smith boys out of my mind. Damn all the slave raiders of this earth, as far as I'm concerned. They're asking for a swift killing."

"Waugh. I know, stealing kids is warfare of the worst sort. It shore calls for killing those that do it, from the blood kin of those that were taken. These Comanches didn't know who they were takin' on when they hooked inta these Scots. Why they got rieving blood-feuds that go back ten generations. McGregor ain't never gonna stop lookin'. And neither is Mackenzie, if he's still alive."

"Damn right. Neither would I if they stole Jesse or Kathy. If they won't stop raiding, they're asking for a warrior's death in battle, which I'm willing to oblige them on. I might want to have some kids of my own some day, and I don't want to live in fear that they'll be stolen by Comanches and turned into slaves, or bucks or squaws. These raiders have all of Texas living in terror. It's got to stop."

Gabe gave a surprised look at Josh, and studied his face for a moment. "Kids of yore own, huh?"

"Well what else, being a bastard son all my life?"

" Alright, then, Joshua. You sound like a Robinoix I know. We could join 'em tomorrow, if you want. Headin' that way anyway. They ain't gonna make it far on them worn out horses tonight. We'll leave early, catch up with 'em. That suit ya?"

"Floats my stick, Gabe."

"Wal, alright then, Young Coon, and don't be thinkin' ya ain't got family, 'cause we been together too long for that, here, have a draw on this pipe to simmer ya down. You been the one who wanted to avoid this Indian war, as much as me. I'm thinking yore hopin' ta find Kathy's brother too, just ta add to tha unlikely."

145

"I know. But this damned raiding for captives won't stop, and everyone is living in terror of losing their kids. Let's help end it."

"Well, alright then. War it is. The trouble is, whar the hell are they?"

"Out thar, yonder, I guess. You're the one that can guess that."

"Wal alright then, maybe I will."

"Damn, I didn't think you'd agree so fast. Those Smith boys and that young girl been preying on yore mind too, huh?"

"Wal, yeah, that, the raiding settlers, murdering, raping, kidnapping, and some other. If they'd just live on buffalo up on the plains and leave settlers alone below the cap-rock, but...the young bucks won't listen to wiser heads."

"What other...what have you been ruminating for the last few days? You've been as silent as a possum since Dodge."

"Wal...From what I been piecing together, this Bise McCairn rustler varmint, the guy with the shock of red hair and beard, the one that likely got our herd one year and half our herd the next, could likely be the fella that burned down your home-place and kilt your ma."

"What?....... the hell are you talking about? Did you break a blood vessel in your head with that arm wrestling in the saloon?"

"Alright now, Listen. I run up on this strange fella, way back on the Gila River in my mountain guide times, around '49 or '50, when I was guiding miners out to California. A big stout fellow, ginger hair like a buffalo beard on his head, he was, with dark rusty red fur that just about covered his whole body, said he hated tha army and was whipping up the Apache to fight em. He was a big medicine man with the Apaches, but said he used ta be in the army. Called himself the Bison. That's why I remembered him, a really strange character that had a more attractive bushy red scalp than mine in those days, living with the Apaches, with two fine squaws and a band of renegade followers. And he could outdo two Kiowas on speechifying about fightin' the whites. Ya know tha type, like a hellfire preacher. I figured back then he was mainly intent on looting the travelers to California. "

"Hard to believe. You think it's the same guy?"

146

"Wal, back when we got our horses back from old Polo, that Sergeant Bill tole me that this fella Thomas McCairn was thrown out of West Point in 48, and rode with the Apache, then with marauders in Kansas whar he somehow got a federal captain's commission. I figure he used it mainly for lootin. Then he went down to the Bayou Teche area til the end of the war, whar he was wounded and mustered out, then killed folks in Texas and New Mexico, and left towns entirely to go live with these renegades, leading these marauders stealing livestock and terrorizing settlers. They lived off rustling the herds around Ft. Sill for a while, taking the Comanche's only wealth, then came out here to rustle the last few years."

"Yeah, well, may be. I knew some of that from when you figured he got our horses near Fort Concho. Except I thought he was a renegade, so I don't see how he got a federal captain's commission."

"I reckon the war in Kansas was a mass of confusion, just right for a clever marauder looking for opportunity and free looting. We both seen how some folks use war to turn into mad wolf-packs, ain't we? This blowhard is sharp, and he had the Apaches believing he was a powerful medicine man and giving him their best squaws, so I don't disbelieve he could convince the Federal Army in Kansas that he was raiding for them, and get a commission. He had an uncle who was a northern senator, I heard in Dodge, name of McSheeran, same as that captain."

"So that what's been roiling through your mind these last few days?"

"Yep. I been pondering it a long time, then the other pieces of the puzzle fell into place when I talked to those fellas in the saloon last night. They seen this Bise McCairn lately, in Dodge, shaved up for a change, and swore to me that he's missin' half his right ear and has a bullet scar along that cheek, from a sniper wound he got in Louisiana. His thick hair and beard had the scar hidden before now. I think it's our Federal captain that kilt your ma and burnt out the plantation. And he's leading the worst band of renegades ever forked a horse, doing 'bout the same on the frontier, marauding, murdering, raping, and stealing captives, along with stealing horse and cattle herds."

147

"Well, damnation, Gabe, that puts another twist to it. Let's get him now."

"It's killing time on the plains, 'cording ta my mind. If we have to, we can pick the sonofabitch off from long distance and outrun the danged Comanches. I'd be glad ta do it, to avenge yore ma, I owe her that, at least. Shoot him with long rifles, turn the pack animals into extra mounts, and skedaddle after we plug the sonofabitch. We'll shoot at the same time, and one of us is bound ta plug 'im."

"It's strange, Gabe. I had a dream about that son of a bitch the other night in Dodge, the first one in years, but he had a smooth face then, no beard. Why haven't you told me this before?"

"Wal, you ain't mentioned him in several years, and we was occupied with filling contracts for horses, and building on what Alex left us thar on the river. I didn't want to fire up a forge with no outlet, get ya to stewing over him with no way to find him. Stewin' for vengeance ain't no way ta live, and ya done forgot about it, far as I could tell."

"I never forgot, I just held my mind to other things."

"And I wasn't sure 'til I got some more information from those buff shooters in Dodge. Now I'm pert well sure. It's mor'n likely him, and he's likely close by. He needs rubbin' out. Time ta strike the hot iron."

"Alright. Let's go help them find the damned marauders in the morning, find the captives, and finish off this killer. I didn't want to get involved in this war, but if these Comanche are raiding and holding captives in their camp, then they're at war with us and the people we live with. And these renegades are just asking for a killing. I'm ready to help end this mess."

Gabe nodded and stared at Josh. "That's ...."

"How your stick floats, I know, Old Coon. Give me a pull off that pipe, then let's get a good rest. Here's some new Sazarak brandy I got in Dodge. My mind is going to whirling all night about tomorrow unless I get a few drinks in me. I'm worked up with that news."

They pulled on the red-stone pipe and brandy flask for another hour, discussing the possibilities they could encounter the next day. That night Josh dreamed again of the federal captain he had grazed those long years back, and still felt the need for blood revenge when he awoke. But more than that he felt he had been put in a position to rid the world of a man who did nothing but perpetuate evil. And at the same time he might help end a war that had been dragging on for decades. He began cleaning all his weapons and sharpening his knife while Gabe made biscuits by a small buffalo chip fire.

Chapter Six: Red River Battle

The next day arrived cool for late September, and they tried to follow the trail of the lodge-poles again, but it dispersed into many smaller trails that were hard to trace in the dense turf. Wasting too much time on the ground squinting at the resilient turf for signs, they decided to head for the nearest good watering spot, so they pushed their well-rested horses, changing mounts every two hours and pulling the lead ropes as fast as they could manage it.

After riding south a few hours towards the upper branches of the Red River, Josh stood in his stirrups and spotted a cavalry detachment with his field glasses, in the far distance. The patrol was headed to cross in front of them, sweeping in from the southeast, with Indian scouts fanned out in front. Josh thought he saw a similar dust cloud in the heat haze to the southwest. They rode towards the closer detachment, and Gabe signaled the scouts with his bugle, which brought them riding in. The lead scouts turned out to be John'son, Old Henry, and a Seminole scout named Sam, whose dark skin was covered with pale dust so that he looked nearly white until he wiped his cocoa-colored face with a wet bandanna. They were all glad to see McBride and LaPoint, and asked for their help in finding the Comanches.

Following a parley with the Tonkawa scout John'son, the most fluent and able to absorb and relay information, they found out that Mackenzie was coming up from the southwest, on the trail of a good sized horse herd with lodge-pole drag marks and abandoned cooking gear and puppies left behind, indicating rapid movement of a large band, fleeing from the troops. He had been harassed along the way by night raiders and attacks on his scouts and wings, but he had kept coming. He led a strong force of seasoned cavalry, with which he had just crossed the Staked Plains twice, to New Mexico and back, using Polonio Ortiza as a guide. And Ortiza was with the cavalry now, leading them in, with the full force of scouts fanned out wide and picking up trails of various horse herds.

"Waugh! Skookum! Ole Polo is leading them in. Now that's a fella that shore better hope Colonel Mackenzie wins this battle, or these Comancheros will catch him and torture him for a month," said Gabe.

"Maybe we did some good turning him over, instead of you bleeding him out like I thought you might."

"He had to believe I would before he would spill the beans. That Sergeant Bill listened and told it all to Colonel Mac, I surmise. Now the Comanche got a Scottish bulldog on their trail, with Irish and black troopers, and McGregor and the rangers ta boot. There's gonna be a hell-of-a fight."

"Heap big fight soon, McBride," said John'son. "Get many horses, many Comanche scalp. You find village."

After sharing more information about the sign they had been cutting, along with Gabe's educated guess as to where the Comanches were settled down, they sent John'son's fellow scout Old Henry back with the information to inform the 4th cavalry.

Gabe, Josh, and John'son then moved south until they spotted some grapevine thickets along a creek emptying into the north fork of the Red River. Gabe was extra tense and feeling the presence of Comanche's nearby, the hairs on his neck bristling. This had John'son sort of spooked as well, always peering around with squinted eyes while muttering low in Tonkawa tongue. John'son kept badgering 'Long Shot' LaPoint to keep scanning with his 'heap good glasses' for riders. Gabe kept signaling the usually stoic John'son to keep quiet so he could find a hunch as to where the Comanches were camped.

They felt the big village was close, and scented the fairly sweet aroma of buffalo chip fires vaguely on passing breezes. With all the columns of soldiers out pushing the bands from the east, the scouts figured the bands had moved west and settled on the headwaters of the Red River, with the deep water holes and cottonwood shade. But exactly where was an open question to ponder.

They rested their horses in some tall grass for grazing while they surveyed the situation with field glasses. There was no sign of Indian riders or smoke on the horizons, except for the dust raised by the several columns of soldiers in the distance. The scouts were just a few miles from the north fork of the Red

River, where there was grass and good water for Comanche fall encampments.

Finally, after a long silence, LaPoint questioned Gabe, who had a sixth sense about Comanches that often revealed more than what Josh could understand.

"So what does it feel like, Gabe," he quietly asked. "You seem pretty stirred up. What's your hunch?"

"I think they're on this river, nearby, but can't figure whether it's upstream or down. Thar's another good-sized branch heading northwest, with a good grassy valley up thar, and deep waterholes, down out of the wind. Could be thar, or down that other fork which old Marcy called McClellan Creek, after his son in law, who didn't want ta invade the Confederacy and ran against Lincoln for president. We usta call it Grape Creek, on accounta thar usta be loads of grapevines and wild plums thar. Waugh. Always a good stoppin' place."

Gabe dismounted and conferred with John'son by drawing maps on the ground with his knife. Low Tonkawa muttering and sign language mixed with Spanish and bits of English as they conferred. LaPoint tended to the horses and scanned with the field glasses, unable to understand most of the conversation, but getting the gist of it from the blade scratchings. He had vague mental flashes of hand to hand combat from his dreams of the night before, and put his hand on his knife to make sure it was tied down. He thought about how Gabe had taught him to knife fight as a teenager, and how he thought then he would never use the skill back then. But his dreams had been full of it. Gabe got up from his squat and rubbed his green sandstone along his knife blade.

"Well, what's it going to be, scout McBride," said Josh LaPoint.

"Shuddup, I'm feeling my hunches." Josh turned away and scanned the horizon with his glasses, knowing better than to rush intuitive genius. The only sound for a moment was the wind and the sound of Gabe's knife blade grinding the sandstone.

"Alright, let's go," said Gabe, putting the knife and stone away.

"Where?"

"Yonder. McClellan creek."

"Because?"

"It's six of one and a half dozen of the other, so we might as well get some grapes and plums if we can. And that's whar my hunch leads."

"Make's some sense, let's go."

They rode the several miles over buffalo cropped grassland, crossed the upper Red, then topped a small rise above it to study the little creek valley near the junction with the Red River. With the binoculars LaPoint thought he saw several riders chasing buffalo to the west, in the far distance. The creek below had running water, shining in the sunlight, and was bordered by thick vines over plum bushes and small oaks.

Josh studied the grapevine thickets with his field glasses, hoping to see Comanches in there gathering food. He saw that the vines were heavy with wild grapes, and with plum bushes as well in the damp bottom alongside the creek. He also saw the dust of many riders moving fast in the south, and after watching for a while, determined that it was the cavalry column rapidly approaching with several scouts in front.

"Gabe, I see a cavalry patrol coming this way. I also see those grapevine thickets have some grapes. If the Comanches are camping nearby, maybe they have been gathering some?"

"Right you are, good chance. I know I want some. Keep a sharp lookout and we'll mosey on down and cut for sign while we get some grapes. They might even be sweet by now."

"That'll be a first. Usually they're about as sour as your socks smell."

"That's what I said, sweet as my feet! Come on, keep a sharp lookout with them young eyes of yorn. We might flush some Comanches out of that thicket."

"Okay, Old Coon, never mind the murdering marauders, lets go have a picnic on wild grapes."

"Why the hell not? I got some honey in Dodge, ya know, if they're too sour for yer refined Creole tastes. Here, want some jerky to gnaw on while we search, get yore juices goin?"

"Why sure, let's eat, best way to finish a war I can think of, Ole Coon, want to stop and make biscuits too?"

"Oh, I still got several, and buff jerky too, here, chew on that...til ya sight that Bison fella."

"Well, thanks for offering me some, but no thanks..."

"I's savin' it case we didn't find any buff."

"Yeah right. Hoarding it, more likely."

153

"Wal, let's get on down thar. Keep a sharp eye out. This here is yore day ta take down tha Bise McCairn."

"I hope so. I'd like to drive that mess from my mind."

Moving slowly while observing for Indian sign in all directions, they descended into the little valley that fed the creek into the Red River. Josh thought he saw the smoke of campfires in the far distance before they left the high ground, when he made his last scan with the field glasses, but wasn't sure if it was smoke or dust from buffalo chasing hunters. They finally decided to dismount when they saw grapes in the vines and on the ground.

When they stopped to gather grapes in the thickets by the little creek, they came across very fresh sign in the damp ground that Indians, probably squaws and kids, had been there, packing grapes onto a couple of shod mules. Filling themselves with grapes, which weren't too sour, while scanning for returning Comanches, they decided to send John'son back to inform his captain, Wirt Davis, with his column of mounted troopers nearby, about the trail of the loaded mules. LaPoint and McBride ate grapes and plums slathered with honey while scanning the ground along the creek, waiting for the troopers. They had it figured out from the prints on the ground and condition of the grape-vines, by the time the troopers approached. A small group of Comanches had been harvesting grapes and had departed with loaded mules, leaving a little line of fallen grapes for a trail.

"Hell, they left an easy trail," said LaPoint.

"Probably some visionary tole 'em they'd be forever safe up here on the Red," said Gabe.

"Well, we've not won anything yet, so they're still undefeated, you recall."

"Yeah, been safe so far, for centuries."

"I want to pick off that McCairn with the Whitworth, even if we can't get close."

Gabe put a ginseng root in his mouth and said, "Waugh. Me too."

"You know, I've heard you say that seven hundred damn times and I still don't know what it means," said LaPoint.

"It's what a bear says when he's surprised by a fool greenhorn scout..."

"Look, here comes the captain."

"Waugh! That's Davis, my sergeant pals have given me good reports on him."

"Hell, I hope he's no greenhorn."

"He ain't. Let's sign on with him as scouts, right now."

"Alright. Let's do this."

Captain Davis rode down the hill with John'son, and saw the mule trail leading from the grapevine thicket after the two scouts pointed it out to him.

"Excellent work, McBride. And you surmise this will lead to a main encampment?"

"Yes-sir, further up the Red River."

"Finally, Colonel Mac finds his Comanches, after a long summer of searching."

Josh and Gabe offered to scout the trail after John'son told Davis they were "heap good scouts and trackers". Davis had already heard of their skills and immediately accepted their offer, though with a question.

"Why would you want to take the risk, after turning down the colonel for years?"

"Because we were in the original ranger tracking party after the Smith boys, and we know their family, and had one of our outfit wounded by the same raiders," was the quiet answer given by Josh LaPoint.

"Vengeance? You rode with McGregor's rangers?"

"Naw, it ain't vengeance, it's tha captives," said Gabe.

Josh spoke up. "Mainly a desire to end this thing, Captain, like you, I imagine. We spotted the captives and helped track the raiders, but we lost them in a rainstorm. Sure, I know folks who have family missing, captives. There's not time enough to tally all the vengeance strokes some folks are due, and it goes back to the beginning of time. What it boils down to is they're making war on us and our people, so we're aiming to end it. If this damned Mow-way won't give up his captives, and the Quakers are calling the attack in, I'm willing to help all I can."

"That goes for me too," said McBride.

"Mucho good scouts, long rifles," said John'son. Ojo de Aguilar, 'Long Shot LaPoint' him. Shoot Ortiza one thousand yards! McBride best scout."

"Yes, we've all heard of the shot that brought down Ortiza. You are both engaged as scouts by the United States Cavalry. Now listen, scouts. We already ran into McGregor's ranger party looking for the captives, and sent them south to join Mackenzie and help with scouting and collecting the hostages when the attack begins. Ride ahead and cut the trail so we don't spook them with the sound of the column."

"Alright. And we'll signal back with our mirrors so ya can see which way we're heading, Captain, just to keep you right on our trail. When we see the village or outriders we'll flutter the mirror continually for a while."

The captain agreed with their plan and readied his men for silent pursuit. The troopers were excited and ready for battle, with the sergeant barking orders down the line, getting them prepared for a battle after long summer months of a scorching search.

Then the three scouts, Gabe, Josh, and John'son, followed the mule trail for a while, staying a mile or so ahead of the troopers, just within binocular sight of their dust, signaling back with mirrors, even eating the fallen grapes that littered the easy trail, heading a few miles northwest. Finding a small grassy rise by a wet playa lake, LaPoint stood in his stirrups and scanned for riders. Looking to the north, he spotted an Indian whipping his horse away from them, in a big hurry, about five hundred yards away, traveling west.

"Uhh-oh. I think we've been spotted. I see a scout high-tailing away from us, and lots of smoke in the far distance ahead of him."

"We need ta take him down. Can you do it with the Whitworth?"

"Long Shot LaPoint shoot 'im now," said John'son.

"Yeah, probably." Josh got down and slid the big gun from it's sheath, and knelt on the ground, jamming his forked metal rod in for a rest. Loading quickly, he then laid on the ground and rested the heavy rifle. The rider had moved a couple of hundred yards further away, leaving a dust trail behind him, leaning low and racing his mount. LaPoint sighted in with the long telescope and quickly fired, and the telescope hit his eye socket, bruising it.

"Ouch, that smarts. Everything takes a toll. Damn, that will swell up. Rushing the shot, it'll get you with that telescope right by your eye."

"Yeah, and he's still up and ridin', but slumpin'," said Gabe, peering through his own telescope.

"Shoot 'im again, Long Shot LaPoint," said John'son. They looked through binoculars and telescope. The Comanche scout, about 800 hundred yards away, was slumping as he rode, then fell from his horse and did not get up.

"Ya got him down. Now that's some LaPoint luck."

"Good, I paid for it with a black eye. Told myself I wouldn't do any more sniper shooting."

"Wal this is war."

"I don't need to hear that damned speech again. He's down, let's go."

"That was a fine shot. Too bad we ain't got some fresh buff meat for that eye. I guess ya hurried it a bit ta catch him, huh?" asked Gabe as he mounted Buck.

"Yeah, a bit. I can see alright, anyway," said Josh as he calmed his mount.

"If he'da made it back to tha village, it'd been hell poppin' afore we's ready for it."

"Right. I didn't like killing him, but..."

"It's war."

"Yeah. Let's get it done and over with."

"If we can. Gonna need some more of that LaPoint luck. Comanches never been struck hard by the cavalry on their home grounds before like this."

"Well, times are changing," said LaPoint as he nudged Scorpio into a slow walk.

They moved ahead another mile until they spotted dust from a big horse herd, and many small smoke streams from a big village. They left their horses grazing in a depression around a small playa lake, then went to scout the village on foot with binoculars. They ended up crawling to a slight hilltop and laying down with field glasses in shock. They saw lots of smoke rising from the river valley, and lots of crows and buzzards in the air, but no scouts in the immediate area, so they decided to walk their horses even closer for a better view, but be ready to mount and flee if necessary.

LaPoint spoke after drawing water from his canteen while the horses drank from a tiny playa. "That's pretty strange. The easiest trail to follow that you could imagine, full of grapes and blackbirds eating them. Never thought the trail in would be so easy."

"Waugh," replied Gabe with a smile. "But we had to know whar to find the start of it, didn't we?"

"Wal waugh back at ya. Human nature to go for grapes on a hot dry plain, eh?"

"Ya got that right, and thar's whar we found tha trail. Waugh."

"I'd pay ya ten bucks silver not to say that again."

"Oh yeah?"

"Yeah."

"Silver?"

"Yeah. Your favorite color, right? I'll pay you later, because if you get rubbed out today the Comanches will get it."

"Speakin' of color, that eye of yorn is really turnin' colors now. Got some purple and yaller round the edge now."

"I told you, I rushed the shot, and the telescope bruised it. It's throbbing a bit."

"Wal, you got a black eye comin', but that Comanche is down and we still got surprise on our side."

"Well let's canter up there in case that scout gets back up."

They rode until they found the scout's body, with his horse grazing nearby. Gabe saw the shot had hit him in the middle of his back, but he was still barely breathing. Josh did not want to look at the body, but did not want to leave the warrior to a certain slow death in the sun. Gabe dismounted quickly, and slit the Comanche's throat to finish him off.

"I guess I should have done that," said LaPoint with a shudder.

"You done yore part, pard. Take a deep breath or three," said Gabe as he wiped his blade on the warriors buckskin.

"We're in it now," said LaPoint.

"Let's get it done," said McBride, and walked on, as did LaPoint, who quickly scanned with field glasses towards the village, looking for riders. The horses followed along nervously, their ears pricked and scanning forward. After a hundred yards in the dry grass, they stopped when LaPoint caught a strong whiff of smoke from buffalo chip fires. A vague column of haze appeared to the north, and LaPoint remounted to stand in his stirrups with field glasses.

"Yes, it is something, a smoke column, or lots of little ones. A whole lot, all the way up the valley."

Then they slowly walked their horses towards the smoke of the village. Creeping into a hidden spot beside another wet playa with tall dry grass to scout it out with field glasses, they realized they had come upon a huge village of over two hundred lodges, large and small, and thousands of horses, probably Mow-way's band, on the south bank of the North Fork of the Red River, in a grassy valley. The large encampment stretched out upstream as far as they could see beyond a bend in the river, with smoke trails being visible beyond that. The camp was surrounded by several large horse herds, grazing on the flat banks above the stream-bed, and plenty of outriders, so getting closer was too risky for them. Slipping away quietly, they walked their horses a half mile, then mounted and raced back to inform the cavalry detachments approaching behind them, and those approaching from the south.

Captain Wirt Davis received the information and had it relayed to Col. Mackenzie while he positioned and prepared his company for attack. The dust from Mackenzie's columns was clearly visible to the naked eye by that time.

Having given what information they had, Josh and Gabe continued riding south until they encountered the 4th Calvary columns led by a Captain Beaumont and Col. Mackenzie. In the front of Beaumont's column was Sergeant John Charlton, Gabe's drinking buddy from Fort Concho and San Angela. The big man with handlebar mustaches and a ruddy face dripping sweat smiled and nodded his head when he saw Gabe.

"There's a scout for you, Captain," he said. "That's Ranger Captain McBride, following his partner LaPoint on that charging pearl gray stallion there."

"I recognize the man and horse...it's the horse trainer you got your gray pacer from, sir."

"I know that, Captain," replied Mackenzie curtly, seated on a bay gelding. "That stallion is the sire of my horse, Big Gray, the one the Quohadis stole from us."

"Yes-sir. Partially my fault, sir."

"We may remedy it today, Sergeant."

Gabe and Josh rode right up to the two officers and skidded their stallions to a dust churning halt, with LaPoint being the first to arrive and speak.

"I'm Josh LaPoint, horse trader and drover, sold you that gray pacer, Colonel,... we met last year at Ft. Concho."

"Yes, I recognize you, Mr. LaPoint. And I still miss that fine horse, which was stolen by Kiwih-nai's Quohadis one miserable night. The same bunch that put an arrow in my thigh."

"He's done the same to lots of folks, sir. Good to see you. And good to see you using old Polo there for a tour guide."

"Yeah," said Gabe. "Good ta see ya, Polo."

Ortiza just glared at Gabe, a worried look on his face, his hands trembling. "Cabron," he muttered.

"McBride and LaPoint," said Mackenzie.

"LaPoint, you shot me and took my stallion. My curse is on you," said Ortiza, who then spit towards Josh.

"A pleasant surprise," continued Mackenzie. And Ortiza has been invaluable as a guide, all summer long. He's a couple of inches taller, too. Lets move away from him a bit." They walked their horses to a spot where they could converse in private.

"By God that's a fine horse you ride, LaPoint. I guess I've told you that before. Any chance you'd part with him?"

"No sir, but I have a colt out of the long legged mare that produced your mount, same color, another big gray pacer."

Colonel Mackenzie nodded with a slight smile. "Sounds good. You have solid information for me, LaPoint?

"Yes-sir. We found the Comanche village you're seeking."

"You found the village, you say?" queried an astounded Mackenzie as Gabe chimed in.

"That we did, sir."

"Finally you scout for us, Ranger McBride, eh?"

"That's right sir. We found a big Comanche village, Col. Mackenzie, sir, about two hundred lodges, at least, and we request further engagement as scouts until this affair is concluded."

"Actually Captain Davis already hired us on when we showed him the trail to the village, though we didn't sign scout papers yet," said LaPoint.

"That's outstanding, excellent. I remember trying to hire you quite a few times, Scout McBride, you and LaPoint here, as guides for the Staked Plains. It turned out that Polonio Ortiza was almost enough, though."

Sergeant Charlton came riding up and joined them. "These are the guys who captured Ortiza, sir," he said to the Colonel.

"We'll sign on right now as scouts to lead you in,.... to try to rescue the captives when you attack, if that's agreeable to you, sir."

"Agreeable?! Gabe McBride! Why goodness yes it's agreeable, man. I've been searching the whole staked plains for hostiles, to Alamogordo and back to the Palo Duro, and you say you sighted the village. Where are these confounded Comanches?"

"About six miles north, sir, on the south bank of the north fork Red. They're spread out along the river sir. Lots of horses. Over a thousand, I'd guess," replied McBride.

Sergeant Charlton could not suppress an expression of joy when he heard that. Beaumont was staring at Gabe and Josh in disbelief. "Finally," he said. Mackenzie was showing a rare smile and shaking his head from side to side. Looking at Gabe, he spoke.

"Can you believe it, Beaumont, like sweet prune pie in camp. How many times did I say we need to hire these guys for guides? Then Gabe McBride and LaPoint ride in and tell us where the village is, right out of the blue. Were you scouting for those rangers out seeking captives, McBride?"

"No-sir, we was comin' back from Dodge when LaPoint cut sign of Indian ponies and lodge-poles. We told McGregor and his rangers about it when we saw them yesterday, but this village is way too big for them to take on. This village is full of raiders and renegades with herds of stolen stock, some of it likely belonging to tha LaPoint outfit. It's likely several bands, maybe including Para-coom or Kiwih-nai's band. They'll fight like hell, sir."

"Gentlemen, you arrived just in the nick of time, it seems. I've been searching for this village for months. This is where the biggest nest of captives are held." The Colonel turned to his troopers, black and white weary soldiers wearing blue wool uniforms covered with dust.

"Captain Beaumont. Make ready for silent approach and attack in columns of four, upon command, at a canter, Captain. Tighten girth straps and prepare for battle, carbines out, extra ammo. Pass the word."

161

"Glad to ride for ya, Colonel," said Gabe.

"Glad to have you both. With your help we can end this war."

"Let's do it."

"Where did you get that bugle sticking out of your saddlebag there, McBride?"

"Took it off one of the renegades that took the Smith boys, sir."

"We aim to get those lads back, as well as at least a dozen other captives. Do you play?"

"Waugh. Wal, some..."

"He doesn't play, sir. He wails on it like an old hound dog," said LaPoint. "Or a broken bagpipe, out of tune."

"I'd like to hear you do so....but not at the moment."

"I'm with you sir, I can blow this thing when we get the scouts in position, if you want."

"Good idea, when you're as close as you can be to make a dash for the captives and you see us ready to charge. Don't blow any fancy calls, just wail on it three times, like a sour bagpipe if you can, eh?...while LaPoint watches the main circle of lodges nearest you with his field glasses and long range rifle. You are both famous for the long shot. Try to hit the first warrior that comes out to lead the defense, when they respond to the bugles. Take out the leaders first."

"Alright sir, will do."

"Right now.... I need you to report to Lt. Boehm for duty on guiding us in and rescuing the captives, Mr. McBride. Have him spread the Tonkawas out front with word to stay hidden and not spook the village until we attack. Mr. LaPoint, would you ride with us for now sir, and fill us in more on the lay of the land?"

"Gladly, Colonel."

Mackenzie turned back to Gabe. "Are you ready for this fight, Scout Chief McBride? The scouts aren't required to fight, you know, and I'd rather keep the Tonkawas out of it, if possible. They get too carried away. We're not here for scalping or unnecessary slaughter, but to kill every warrior who fights, and destroy the whole village and capture the horses, women, and children."

"I know what you mean, sir, about the Tonks. They'll be butchering and feasting on sliced Comanches if you let them.

162

We'll try our best ta curtail that. We're sort of amazed to see you, Colonel. Heard you was lost on the Llano Estacado. Read it in the newspaper at Dodge City."

"You and McBride are the last scouts I expected to see as well. I thought the best I would get out of you guys was the capture of Ortiza."

"Did his information prove valuable, sir?"

"Hell yes, man. Polonio Ortiza showed us the smugglers road to New Mexico and another northern route back, that met the Palo Duro Canyon. Took most of the summer, and I don't carry a newspaper reporter with me like some bucking for a General's star. But we haven't done what we set out to do, find a village of hostiles with captives, nor stop the damned raiding. The Quakers can't get any co-operation out of this Mow-way over the captives, and we need to find his village and rescue them."

"You've got that village now, sir. Give 'em hell, Colonel Mackenzie,Sir!" said McBride.

"We intend to. This is the only way to end this war and captive taking, strike them in their homeland. We've ridden hundreds of hot thirsty miles for this engagement. Are you men ready?"

"We're ready sir. I'll ride with LaPoint when hell gets ta poppin', sir. LaPoint is the one that actually spotted the village, sir. He has good field glasses and good eyesight, so we'll guide you in and then try to sight the captives while you get your charge ready. After you make your move and we fire off our long range guns at the first line of defense, we'll go for the captives. And we think there are renegades there, with better weapons than bows or old muskets. And it wouldn't surprise me if there are more villages nearby, upstream or down, maybe Quohadis, the hardest to whip."

"Alright, scouts McBride and LaPoint, hired on just in the nick of time. Report received. Glad to have you. See the only officer with a non-regulation white hat out there with the Tonkawas? That's Lt. Peter Boehm, conferring with a ranger party that has just joined us and reported about the trails you guys had found."

"We both know him, Sir."

"Sign his roster book as scouts. Report to him with your plan, tell him I approved it, while Mr. LaPoint rides with us for a while and gives us more details."

"Yes-sir. And Col. Mackenzie, you got to get that horse herd, no matter what, sir. Even stampede 'em if ya have to. The warriors can't hold you off if they can't get to their horses. Without their horses they are plumb whipped."

"We're thinking alike, McBride. We intend to capture their horses, free the captives, capture the Comanche families for hostages, and burn the village and provisions. Then we're going to use the hostages to force the remaining hostiles to bring in all the captives."

"Turn their tactics ag'in' 'em, huh? Probably only way that will work, actually. Beats the hell out of buying captives back one by one."

"Right. That's part of what has encouraged this child stealing. We'll rest here and prepare for the attack while you go give Lt. Boehm a map of the area, right? Inform Mr Henry Strong over there as well, with those rangers, the civilian scout leader. Then you and LaPoint will lead us in, silently. When all the rangers and scouts are in position with your long range rifles for the defense leaders, and you see us in position, blow that horn. You men can pour fire into them there from set positions as we charge, then follow us in."

"Yessir. Sorta sneak up on 'em like Comanches, huh? Glad to hear ya ain't gonna fire a cannon off upon departure like old Cannonball Miles, sir."

That remark elicited a loud guffaw out of Sergeant Charlton and a grunt out of Mackenzie. LaPoint thought he detected a half smile on the colonel's face, the first he had seen since he had delivered the big gray pacer.

"What do you mean, McBride?" asked the Colonel.

"What I heard is that Miles announced his position every morning with a cannon, so all the Comanche for thirty miles around knew exactly where he was every morning. Save's 'em having to worry about that, and helps 'em lead him on a wild goose chase..."

Mackenzie gave Gabe a hard look, trying not to smile, shook his head at Beaumont who was about to speak up, then nodded at Gabe.

"Well, with any luck he's driven them to us, McBride," he said, "Instead of letting them run back to the reservation like Kicking Bird's bunch did."

"Wal, we got 'em cornered now, sir."

"That's what this long search has been about. Now we deal with them like they dealt with everyone else."

With that Mackenzie turned and went about readying his men, heading down the line of troopers intent on making sure of every detail. Turning his head as he rode off, he paused and called back to Gabe. "Try to avoid the main fight, find the captives and protect them with the scouts and rangers, and help keep the Tonkawas from going wild, will you Mr. McBride?"

"Yassir. But they're hot to kill Comanches."

"Killing warriors is alright, no butchery, no scalping. Nor killing of women or children."

"Yassir. We're with you on all that, Colonel."

"We'll find the captives, sir," said LaPoint.

Gabe rode over and joined up with the scouts under Lt. Peter Boehm, the only officer wearing a big straw hat for sun protection. The scouts squatted on the ground while Gabe starting signing to them and drew out his big knife to draw a map. Gabe looked up to Boehm and said. "Hell Pete, the Comanches are gonna think you're the big chief 'cause you got that big white sombrero. Ya maybe oughta put on one of these buffalo soldiers caps."

The lieutenant laughed out loud, obviously glad to see the old scout and horse trader. "McBride, it's the same kind of hat you wear, to keep the sun off. You finally decided to join us? What information you have for me?"

"A map of the village," said Gabe as he squatted like a Comanche on the ground and began to trace lines with his knife.

"Hot damn, here we go!" Peter Boehm and the scouts gathered around the sketch on the ground. There was a low murmuring in Tonkawa as Gabe parleyed with them in the dust.

Busy issuing orders, Colonel Mackenzie rode back up to the front of the column where LaPoint waited.

"Mr. LaPoint, is that gray-haired half-scalped old man up to a fight like this? He looks pretty stout, but he was a legend before I even got to Texas, and must be pretty long in the tooth now. Is he up to a big battle? How old is he? He looks fifty. I don't want to get him killed, or have his heart give out like Kit Carson."

"Oh, he's up to it, sir. Nobody I'd rather be with in a scrape, and we've had a few with rustlers. I would guess he's about sixty or so, but could whip a couple of thirty year old guys in a knife fight. You won't be able to keep him out of it. He knows the Smith family, actually he's friends with the boy's pa."

"Yes, that's the word on him from Sergeant Charlton, and I heard from Sergeant Williams and Lt. Boehm that I have you two to thank for helping capture that rascal Ortiza, who has proved very useful."

"Yes-sir, we helped on that, and got half our horses back in the bargain. Sergeant Bill was a good fella to ride with, listens well too. Gabe gave him an earful on Comanche hunting on the plains."

"Yes, advice well taken, as it turned out. We found that road to New Mexico that McBride told the sergeant about, and traveled it. So tell me exactly the lay of the land around this camp, LaPoint, as we ride. Damn, I admire your stallion. What a fine arched neck and head on him, looks like pictures of Napoleon's horse, sir."

"I imagine you might admire him, Colonel. He was the sire of the big gray pacer I sold you. Bred him to a Kentucky mare for that horse."

"Yes, I know. I remember well our first meeting with that big gray. Reminds me of that wonderful mount, best I ever had. Not as long-legged, but the same head and smooth gait. He's lighter in color. Seems like he was darker the first time I saw you, the first time you sold us saddle mounts."

"Yessir, turning to white, he is. I still have the Kentucky mare, sir, maybe I can bring you another one when this is over."

"I'd like that, though I'd also like to get that first one back from Kiwih-nai...now what about the camp...?."

"Well, it's stretched out along the river where there are cut-banks and deep waterholes. Also quite a few ravines. Best we could tell they're mostly involved in processing their hides and meat for the winter. I might have seen some kids that were captives, but it's awfully hard to tell. There's camps on both sides of the river, and the valley is hidden below the plains. There's some ridges to the south we can use for cover in order to sneak up on them. They had one horse herd on the this side of the river, watched by young braves, and another big one across the stream. I counted around two hundred lodges up to the bend in the river, but there was smoke coming from beyond that. It's a big village, stretched out along the stream-bed."

"Excellent, man. You've done an invaluable service, LaPoint, capturing Ortiza and providing this information. They gave Billy Dixon the medal of honor for the Adobe Walls fight, and I'll put you and McBride up for it as well, for your valuable scouting here and now."

"Thanks, Colonel. Glad to be of help."

"Are you going to take that valuable horse into battle?"

"Yes-sir, he's trained for it, you've seen him kick out in both directions, back at Fort Concho. If I get killed you can have him, Colonel, rather than some Kiowa medicine man."

"I wish we could get that damned Kiowa medicine man Maman-ti, he's the one stirring up all this religious killing fever. Save your sharpshooting for that type. Don't get killed, LaPoint, I may have further need of you. Anyway, I like your stallion's colts just fine, and need another one. Now tell me every detail you remember about this camp. I wish I had paper for a map to pass to the Captains."

Pulling out a page of paper from his pocket journal, LaPoint drew a small map. After making sure that Col. Mackenzie had the camp size and location, the lay of the land, the depth and bends of the river, and location of the horse herds, Josh rode out to catch up with Gabe and the leading scouts. They then rode in the lead with John'son until they spotted the village and found shooting spots nearby. John'son rode directly back to Mackenzie to report while LaPoint scanned the village with his high powered glasses, trying to identify the captives. He could not see them. Everyone looked busy processing meat and hides, while some were swimming in the river.

With the scouts under Lt. Boehm and Mr. Thompson, as well as ranger McGregor's men, Gabe determined to try to rescue the captives when the attack began. The entire exhausted patrol of rangers had joined forces with the scouts and were ready to help with that job. They had crept up as close as they could without being spotted, and waited with rifles aimed from set positions, ready to pour fire into the leading edge, then attack and race through in search of the captives.

167

Both the old ranger and LaPoint tightened their girth straps and put on spurs to control their war horses, then readied their pistols and repeating rifles as Col Ranald Mackenzie and the 4th Cavalry prepared to strike the village. Then they took out their long range single-shot guns and set them up with shooting rests, viewing the peaceful village through the telescopes.

"I can't see any captives, but Mackenzie looks ready. The officers have their swords out, I can see them flashing," said LaPoint as he swung the field glasses back and forth between the village and cavalry.

"And my bugle is just a flashin' in my hand, ready ta toot."

"If your mouth is as dry as mine, you're not going to blow that bugle much," said LaPoint.

McBride took a pinch of Black Mule tobacco into his mouth to make some saliva, and got the horn ready, while Josh alternated between scanning the village and watching John'son approach the column in his field glasses. They were as ready as they could be.

"We take down the leaders when they come out," said LaPoint.

"Right. Stay steady 'cause hell's gonna be poppin' soon."

Josh spoke down the line to the rangers, in a louder voice. "It's about the captives, men."

McGregor went up and down the line, exhorting his rangers to hold steady and make ready to give them hell.

LaPoint spotted the 4th cavalry commander in the field glasses, wanting to make sure he got the word from John'son. The Colonel was issuing orders and paying close attention to every detail while firing up his officers with strong encouragement to do their best at their first chance to win an engagement in the enemy's home grounds.

The mounted troopers, men who had traversed the staked plains to New Mexico and back seeking Comanches, were eager for a fight. LaPoint could see buffalo soldiers, as the Tonk scouts called the black troopers, and lots of sunburned Irishmen in the ranks. Until that time they had been mainly chasing after raiders in vain, and they were ready for a real engagement. Mackenzie rode back up the line of cavalry in columns of four as John'son reached the head of the column.

Josh watched them confer, and knew the troops were informed and ready. He flashed his mirror once more, and Mackenzie acknowledged with a wave of his hat, then pulled his saber.

"Those troopers looked really tired and famished," said LaPoint.

"They are," said Gabe. "Charlton says they ain't et nor slept in so long he can't remember when it was. There's plenty of buffalo meat in that Comanche camp, prepared by the best. All we got to do is win."

"Oh, is that all? Ain't ya gonna say waugh?"

"Waugh. Can ya spit?"

"Barely. I'm pretty scared but I have it under control. Usually we don't have time to sit and wait for the action, now seconds seem like hours. I've got my mind reined in as best I can. Breathing deep and planning my moves."

"All we can do. Yore used ta having folks attack ya without time ta think. This waiting to attack is worse. Don't think about what can go wrong, think about what yer gonna do."

"Keep us alive, if I can."

"That'd be the first thang."

"Don't get shot, ya old bear."

"You neither, young cougar."

"Let the soldiers sweep through and then let's get those captives."

"Right," said Gabe as he sighted with his long brass telescope.

"I think they are fixing to charge," said LaPoint.

"Remember, no matter how hot it gets, we gotta help McGregor find his kin," said Gabe.

"Right. I'm in this because of the captives. Here they go."

The column began moving forward at a rapid walk towards the edge of the sloping sides of the river valley, to where they would soon be charging down onto the valley floor and be sure to be spotted by the outriders. LaPoint signaled back with a mirror in a long flutter, waited until the columns reached the valley floor and were spotted by outriders, and the bugle calls began. Then LaPoint nodded to Gabe, who gave three long blasts on the battered bugle, which set off a barrage of rapid fire from the rangers and scouts. LaPoint sighted in with the long Whitworth and took down the first warrior coming out of the nearest big lodge. Gabe, firing both Sharps and Spencer, took down warriors emerging from lodges near the edge of the encampment. LaPoint switched to his repeater rifle and began to drop warriors with accurate shots to their bodies. The rangers were laying down a barrage of rifle fire as well.

The scouts watched the column break into a canter, then a gallop as they crashed into the camp, then another blast from Gabe's trumpet got everyone remounted. Another blast sent all the fanned-out scouts and rangers towards the side and back of the village while the cavalry bugle-man sounded the charge and the column struck the first big lodges and the horse herd at the same time.

It was around 4 in the afternoon when the 4th cavalry engaged the village, with Capt. Davis leading company F while Beaumont and Mackenzie led company A, Captains Wint and McLaughlin led companies B and C in a direct charge through the village, and company D under Capt. Lee went after the horse herd. Meanwhile the scouts and rangers began the nearly impossible task of finding the captives in the pell-mell dust-storm of the village. The noise and confusion was terrific in the afternoon sun, with scattered action everywhere. The Tonkawas were in full battle paint and fervor, killing indiscriminately and scalping whomever they could. LaPoint and Gabe had their trained stallions quick-stepping through the edge of the village, backing quickly, then racing forward out of hand-fighting melees, trying to spot captives.

The troopers under Capt. Davis, led by Sergeant Charlton, encountered fierce resistance by the stream and sustained several casualties while the other companies swept through the camp in surprise, milling horses and people in the dust cloud, with scattered and confused fighting among fleeing woman and children mixed with warriors scrambling for their horses and firing off their bows with arrows from up close. Warriors were scrambling and fighting back with spears, bows, and firearms. Some women fought back with lances and were killed, while others began to gather their children and surrender, some holding babies up high in front of them to stop the soldiers from shooting. The officers began to take charge of these as prisoners, and gather them away from the fiercest fighting, under guard. Other officers broke away from the fighting to try to restrain the Tonkawas, who were flailing at fallen warriors

170

with their tomahawks, and slicing heads for scalps. LaPoint and McBride were quick-stepping their mounts through the confusion, looking for captives as the din increased to a solid roar.

The troopers had carbines and plenty of cartridges which supplied steady firepower that overwhelmed the surprised Comanche men in camp, causing panic and confusion as people ran in all directions through a stinking haze cut through by the sharp rays of the afternoon sun. Two cavalry horses that had been taken down with spears in the initial charge were screaming in agony on the ground, and LaPoint put bullets in their head from a distance, then went on looking for the Smith boys. As if drawing the gun attracted them, two warriors assaulted LaPoint with spears, and he shot them both in the chest and moved on, searching.

The scouts and rangers could not find the captives in all the hellish mayhem of the battle. Gun-smoke and dust, screams of wounded horses, women firing arrows and being shot, angry yells of warriors calling for their horses and hurling spears, the constant shrill keening and shrieking of the Indian women, death cries, moans from the dying and wounded, scalping chants and screams from the Tonkawas, and rapid firing filled the scene with confusion and horror as LaPoint and Gabe led seven scouts and several rangers into the village of over two hundred lodges, which had just been overrun by two columns of charging cavalry. People were scattering everywhere, with random shots and arrows flying this way and that in the panicked confusion of killing action.

The horse herders had been trying to run the herd down to the warriors for combat when the columns under the command of Captain Lee broke their efforts and turned the herd. The warriors were scattered and ineffective in their defense of the village, lacking the mobility of fighting horseback, until they began to rally at the cut-bank of the stream. Then the sky filled with arrows coming from there, which drew concentrated return carbine fire from the troopers. The sound of horse and yelling from upstream soon joined the sounds of battle at the creek-side cut-banks. Larger volleys of arrows began to arch in together, hitting trooper and Indian alike. Battle lines formed at the gallery forest along the stream, and the rapid carbine fire filled the air with noise and smoke.

171

Unable to find any of the captives in the whirling dust and confusion of the battle, Josh and Gabe stayed on their mounts and rode through the camp, sidestepping their light-footed steeds, shooting warriors when they had too, rapidly backing their stallions when they had to, then surging them forward, searching for captive children and women. At times LaPoint used his warhorse to batter resistance, walking the furious stallion on his hind legs while he kicked warriors with his front hooves. At times the agile stallion quickly turned and kicked warriors with his back legs. Groups of people would scatter from the lodges as the scouts and rangers battled their way in. Some young girls speaking Spanish ran up, and were included with the Indian women under guard, for they wore the same buckskin clothing and looked about the same as the squaws.

While LaPoint was engaged in pistol-shooting a warrior in a bush who had been arching arrows at the ranger group, Gabe led the way to the large painted lodges of the head men, hoping to find captives there at the inner circle. The fighting was not intense in this area, and it looked almost deserted, as many of the warriors had moved to the creek-bank where they had cover to make a stand. Tall poles hung with scalps stood in front of several lodges, several holding painted buffalo sculls on top them. McBride and the rangers began searching the lodges and finding young captives.

After killing the warrior in the cedar bush, LaPoint spotted an old man and two younger fellas who might have been white captives on a mule, and went after them. The old man carried a shield that had a four inch hole blasted in it from some ranger's shotgun, and was leaking torn and printed pages of a bible in a trail across the village. The paper flew out of the shield each time the old man waved it, nearly knocking a boy off the back with his unbalanced gesture at one point. LaPoint and the sidestepping agile Scorpio followed the paper trail through the melee for fifty yards upstream, trying to keep sight of the boys on the back of the mule, which was staggering from the load. Sometimes he had to fight for his life and knock down whoever was opposing his advance, using pistol or rearing horse's hooves. The bible pages kept fluttering out of the ragged shield and into the breeze as they fled on the wobbly mule, leaving a trail of Hebrew scripture through the chaotic battleground. By following the paper trail, LaPoint kept the mule in sight through the smoke and confusion of the whirling battle.

The mule staggered under the weight of the three riders, overloaded and off balance, soon went down from exhaustion as Josh was stopped by a warrior running at him with a lance, screaming at the top of his voice. Swinging in the saddle he dodged the lance and shot the man in the chest as Scorpio reared and kicked, but the man keep swinging the lance and poking at him, so he shot him three times more before the man collapsed. Then another warrior came rushing at him with a lance over a dozen feet long, the revolver clicked in his hand, empty, and Scorpio jumped up on a quick command and struck the man in the chest with both front hooves, knocking him backwards and onto the ground, then stamping him once in the chest and setting him still.

When Josh looked up the blond boys were running with the old man towards the creek, while the mule flailed its legs on the ground, it's energy spent. The old man was tiring and the boys were helping him along, lifting him when he went to his knees. The old man used the shield to try to protect the boys, waving it around as he thought necessary, fluttering paper out of it. LaPoint thought it was the Smith boys, and did not want to lose them in the chaos, since they had been on his mind since they were stolen. But the ferocious battle was centered on the bluff by the river where the warriors with rifles had dug in and poured deadly fire at Charlton and his men in front. And the old man was foolishly leading the boys right past that area, hoping to cross the river to where the Comanches were gathering on the other side.

LaPoint nudged Scorpio forward and was gaining on them when a mounted group of warriors came charging into the battle from upstream, rushing up the creek-side, firing revolvers and carbines from the opposite shore. Emerging groups of warriors on foot began to send volleys of at least twenty arrows at once from the other shore line, where they hid behind a little bluff with capstone rocks on top of it. Slugs were zinging off the rocks, buzzing like dragonflies past his ears, one after another sending multiple bursts of stone chips into the air. Dodging the fuselage became more important than catching the boys at that time, and LaPoint pushed Scorpio into trees at top speed to survive. He heard a rush of horses from upstream as he hid behind pecan tree trunks, scanning the confused scene for those blond boys.

The mounted warriors were shouting 'Kiwih-nai Quohadi', following a charging Comanche chieftain with his lower face painted black and long braids, wrapped with dark fur in them, streaming back behind him as he rode forward with pistol and rifle in each hand. This enraged leader was a big man on a fine gray pacer that LaPoint recognized as the stallion he had sold to the army to be ridden by Colonel Mackenzie. He thought the warrior flashing by was Kiwih-nai, and guessed that the big chieftain following him at a short distance with more mounted warriors was Para-coom. He could see Para-coom had a big antler handled knife that looked like a McBride in a sheath at his belt made of a buffalo tail. He could not help but marvel at the horsemanship of these Indian leaders as they rallied their warriors along the cut-bank. He saw a danger that the battle could turn against the soldiers, with more warriors joining the fight from upstream. The yelling from the riverbed was intense, and mounted warriors were bringing extra horses with them.

The loud and powerful Para-coom behind Kiwih-nai was a striking figure of a horseback fighter, a master rider who controlled the stallion with his legs and feet while carrying weapons in each hand. He was very brave but not foolish, often leaning behind the big neck of the black stallion in defense, always moving, spinning his great stallion one way and another, a fearless Comanche chieftain leading a group of hard charging fighters. Whenever warriors faltered and started to fall back along the defensive line at the river, Kiwih-nai and this other big chieftain would charge over that way and yell at them while firing their guns, inspiring renewed effort. More warriors from upstream kept arriving and joining the fight. The troopers had decreased their carbine fire as they exhausted their ammo. Sergeant Charlton sent runners for more firepower, and two were hit with arrows.

The activity along the shoreline had dislodged rabbits, coons, a badger, and several diamond backed water snakes and moccasins with big viper heads, which were swimming away from the warriors' tramping towards the shore where Kiwih-nai and the other chief rode back and forth. Comanche warriors were being hit with carbine fire and falling back into the water, turning it towards red. Continued volleys of arrows flew

174

across from the other side, some striking into trees near LaPoint. Confused and panicked horses were running around and through the pink water, unsure which way to flee. A thundering sound came from where the big Comanche horse herd was kept, and scattered firing punctuated with bugle calls. Smoke from the constant shoreline firing was thick, obscuring some of the view among the gallery forest. The Comanche resistance was growing more intense as volleys of arrows kept flying in towards the line of troopers, and gunfire erupted from approaching warriors on horseback. Then two army runners returned with ammunition and ran along distributing it to Sergeant Charlton and his men, as Colonel Mackenzie sent another group to the supply train for more.

Kiwih-nai rode away from LaPoint downstream along the shore at high speed, emptying his rifle, and then his pistol, at Ranald McKenzie, who dodged the fusillade behind some oak trees. Troopers near Mackenzie started returning volleys of fire at Kiwih-nai. Enraged, Kiwih-nai yelled at the top of his lungs, gave his shrill eagle-whistle scream, then whirled the big gray, spraying gravel as he charged back upstream along the shoreline, slamming his rifle into a fine-fringed scabbard on the great stallion and bending low behind the stallions neck.

Sighting a big headed snake at least five feet long just swimming to shore about fifteen yards in front of him, he urged the big gray down the shoreline at sprinting speed, leaning down lower and lower until his long fingers trailed along the top of the water, and quickly snatched the cottonmouth viper by the tail as it recoiled with the splash of the stallion's front hoofs.

With a yell of triumph he snapped the snake in the air and whirled it over his head like a sling as he rode towards LaPoint, his horse going chest deep into the pink water. LaPoint watched him in amazement from across the river, thinking he looked like David with his sling in the Bible story. Skidding his perfectly controlled mount to a stop in the water with a foamy splash, the Comanche flung the snake towards LaPoint, yelling "Ekakwitsubaitu Pia waioo," and then giving his shrill eagle whistle cry, as it dawned on LaPoint that he was actually throwing the snake at him.

LaPoint had to move quickly to dodge the snake as it flew twirling at him, the tail flicking his face as it passed. He saw the open white mouth go by with fangs out, then bolted into some trees and reloaded his seven-shot rifle to try to flank the Indians while Kiwih-nai rushed off, reloading his rifle as he rode up the river-bank to meet arriving warriors and exhort them to attack. Soon a solid mass of warriors were fighting from around a deep part of the river where horses could not charge through the water at them, while others arched volleys of arrows from a gully coming down the small rise. The battle grew more fierce than before as the Comanches dug in along the cut-bank with rifles, with the outcome in question. Runners were kept busy carrying resupplies of ammo to the solders who were firing their carbines to blistering hot to try to overwhelm the stubborn warriors. Mackenzie rushed from place to place, trying to control the battle and capture the women and children unharmed. The battle lines of the troopers held firm, and Mackenzie kept them supplied with ammunition.

These enraged Comanches of various bands were regrouped and firing revolvers, bows and arrows, and carbines at the soldiers, while their chieftains exhorted them. Some youngsters were even hurling rounded river stones across the water at the troopers, along with the volleys of arrow. Unless Josh could break free of the copse of trees where they had him pinned with heavy fire, he would loose the chance to catch up with the boys with sun-bleached flaxen hair. The boys were hiding behind a dead horse, trying to help the old man to hide, and looking for a chance to run across to the river and flee.

Deciding to take a chance just after another volley of arched arrows stuck quivering into the trees he hid behind, LaPoint spurred his mount to catch up with the tow-headed boys, who were approaching the cut bank of the river. Kiwih-nai did the same, taking aim with his brass-sided Colt revolver as he came, controlling the powerful horse with his legs and feet. Scorpio jumped a fallen shrieking horse and sidestepped grappling fighters to make his way where LaPoint directed him, as bullets whistled by his head. The boys bolted when they saw him riding towards them again, scampering fast, but not as fast as the accelerating stallion under LaPoint.

As Josh nearly caught up with the bigger boy, the youngster stumbled over a tree-root by the river's bank, and turned over to stare at the approaching stallion, then started singing, *"Old Dan Tucker, too late for his supper, Old Dan Tucker, too late for his supper..."* at the top of his voice, over and over, holding his hands up as if to ward off a blow. The other lad scrambling as fast as his short legs would carry him for trees along the shore at that time, and disappeared. LaPoint was then sure they were white captives, and felt he was seeing the captive Smith boy he had seen years ago, now grown into a Comanche but still remembering childhood ditties learned on a dirt cabin floor.

Stunned, Josh holstered his empty pistol and reached down to try and grab the boy and lift him onto the saddle. As he did so, Kiwih-nai charged directly at him into the shallows of the river, screaming at the top of his lungs and firing a revolver from twenty yards away that sent slugs whizzing by his hat, clipping one edge. LaPoint spurred Scorpio to the left to dodge the fusillade and miss running down the boy, who had jumped up and was scooting into the river swimming hole where he leaped in feet first and began paddling furiously for the other side through the reddened water.

LaPoint then nudged Scorpio into a grove of pecan and cotton-wood trees to avoid heavy rifle fire and reload his revolvers and rifle again, shocked and disappointed that the boy would run from him. Kiwih-nai skidded to a halt at the river's edge and the man had a good bead on LaPoint with his pistol, but did not fire, instead just stared at him through the tree-trunks for an instant, locking eyes. He gave a blood curdling and very long yell, which ended like the scream of an eagle, holstered the revolver, grabbed a short spear he had been carrying attached to his riding rig, and hurled it like a javelin at LaPoint. The feathers near the tip fluttered in the air as it approached.

Without time to think, LaPoint instantly dodged by jerking back as the spear with a white buffalo bone point narrowly missed his shoulder. In dodging the sharp point he fell backwards over the rump of his mount, turning over in the air and landing on his feet in a crouch. Instantly he grabbed a rounded river stone and flung it at Kiwih-nai as he had thrown pieces of brick at alligators in the bayous of Louisiana. The stone was round enough to spin, and sailed true, striking the stout Comanche in the chest and knocking him back onto the rump of his horse. He recovered, leaned forward again, and rode towards LaPoint and the river, approaching the boy while nodding at LaPoint and rubbing the sore spot in his chest. LaPoint leaped back on Scorpio's rump and worked up into the saddle, ready to bolt into cover, only to see Kiwih-nai staring at him.

LaPoint was again amazed at the actions of the rampaging warrior who kept throwing things at him across the river. He knew he had nailed the warrior with the rock at full force from fifteen yards, yet the big man shook it off. After rampaging around trying to kill him several times the chieftain was approaching him at a walk on his horse without weapons drawn. Kiwih-nai simply raised his chin and nodded in recognition of LaPoint, pointing at the boy, who was struggling in the deep pool colored red with bleeding warriors.

LaPoint saw the boy flailing pink foam in the swimming hole, struggling in the deep end of the pool, with bodies floating nearby, looked back at the big warrior, and nodded to him. Kiwih-nai then rode into the deep water, right below LaPoint, yelled Comanche words at him in a very loud voice, "Pi wa-oo Ekakwitsubaitu!", then bent down and pulled the boy onto his horse, gave his eagle shriek, whirled in the pink froth of the stream, and rode away and over the opposite bluff, carrying the boy with one arm.

Josh took a deep breath and felt a strange upwelling surge of appreciation for not being killed, thankful to draw breath, mixed with admiration and wonder at the incredibly cool and agile Kiwih-nai, who rode as well as anyone LaPoint had seen, and who had spared his life in battle. Looking down at his revolvers, he saw only two slugs left, and reached for his ammo bag, reflecting on the encounter. Kiwih-nai could have shot LaPoint but had chosen not to after seeing him dodge the lance. LaPoint could have draw his long barreled Remington .44 pistol, which had been reloaded by then, and easily shot the warrior while he rescued the boy, but had chosen not to.

Glad to be without a wound, Josh took the opportunity to reload all his weapons again, hiding behind the timber on the riverbank, then joined in repulsing a charge by the warriors at the river's edge. He took deep breaths to calm his hands so he could reload proficiently, meanwhile glancing up to scan the battle.

There was a surge on the Comanche side as the steady firing from the troopers waned. Kiwih-nai had returned into the intense fray and began whipping up the hunkered-down Comanches. They began to make assaults and were driven back by renewed heavy carbine fire, since Mackenzie had the troopers well supplied with ammo runners by then. The disciplined line of troopers could not be moved by the recurring attacks by Kiwih-nai and Para-coom, who dodged bullets on horseback in their fury.

Seeing the battle in doubt, Josh began using his rifle to knock down warriors by the swimming hole, where they fired from cover of trees. He picked them off one by one with careful shooting from the rest of a branch on a tree trunk. The fighting grew intensely heated as more joined in from both sides. Volleys of arrows were soon directed at LaPoint to still his effective shooting, but he hunkered down and shot from a rest. The firing was nearly continuous, by then mixed with war screams and yells from both sides. Tonkawas were screaming and officers shouting at them, the women keening a shrill irritating noise, and smoke from scattered campfires and gunshots rising into the breeze along the beautiful grassy valley.

Within minutes, with the daring leadership of Kiwih-nai and the big warrior, and another unrelenting chieftain, there were nearly a hundred warriors making repeated charges at Captain Beaumont's men, but each time they were driven back with heavy fire, with the troopers using trees and driftwood for cover. Repeated volleys of continuous fire came from the disciplined line of soldiers led by Sergeant Charlton.

Colonel Mackenzie, fully engaged in fearlessly overseeing and directing the battle, sent McLaughlin's company to reinforce Beaumont, and they began to overwhelm the warriors and renegades who were gathered near a long waterhole on the river banks. Without horseback mobility, many warriors were trapped in the US Army's style of warfare, with discipline and superior firepower turning the battle against the Comanche in their heartland.

The few horses the Indians had and many warriors were cut down by volley after volley of carbine fire, thanks to all the ammo supplied by Sergeant's Lawton's men, who braved heavy fire to run it in. The river water was turning bright red with blood, which began to flow downstream and tint the whole river with delicate trailers of pink. LaPoint could see Kiwih-nai and Para-coom as they continually rallied the men for another charge against the overwhelming firepower of the troopers with repeating carbines. With an urge to end the battle, he decided to try to take down Para-coom with his repeating rifle, and trotted into a cluster of trees along the river to brace against a tree branch and take a steady shot.

As LaPoint aimed his rifle, Kiwih-nai came cantering along the opposite shoreline and firing his big Colt revolver, the third shot striking LaPoint in the right side of his chest, where he carried his journal, and knocking him off his horse for the second time in the battle. Landing like a cat on his feet after a flip, LaPoint grabbed Scorpio's long tale and pulled himself up, gasping for air, thinking he was shot dead through the lungs, and desperately wanting to die with his horse. Scorpio circled around and LaPoint quickly remounted and ran the stallion into trees while trying to catch his breath. He felt for blood and there was none, but the throbbing pain was like somebody had hit him with a club in the front of his ribs. He reached down and felt the hot lead slug flattened out and stuck into his journal. He sighted the head of Para-coom moving along the river's edge, bobbing along on top of the cut-bank as he raced along the shoreline. LaPoint fired, but missed him, his aim and accuracy shaken by the wrenching pain in his chest. A volley of arrows came in and one stuck in his hat brim, pulling it over his eyes, so he retreated to cover and reloaded. Shaken and still unable to catch his breath, he rested in the trees as the battle raged on and the tide swung to the side of the troopers. He felt a throbbing pain with every breath, and could barely straighten up, so he hunkered down and watched the battle.

Many of the woman and children were giving themselves up in the village, coming out of their hiding places in the trees and bushes along the stream, and being taken prisoner by the troops there. Mackenzie was riding back and forth yelling, issuing orders to not harm those who surrendered, shouting at the Tonkawas to quit the killing of women and scalping of men. Some warriors began breaking off the assaults in the village when they saw the women being captured, and heard the Tonkawas shouting their bloodthirsty cries among them.

Though some women had been killed in the initial charge as they fought back with spears, the killing of the first assault in the long village had diminished greatly as the fight had shifted to the creek-bank. The soldiers in the village were starting to secure prisoners and burn lodge-poles to make hot fires. Several Tonkawas were dismounted and finishing off wounded

Comanches, starting to scalp again when out of sight of the officers. A wagon with some civilians and an army escort was approaching the village, and the captives were being gathered back at a point beyond.

The Red River at this point looked like a blood-vein of the earth, leaking the vital fluids out of the Comanche heartland, downstream in trailers of maroon water turning to pink. The shrieking and shrill keening of many squaws across the river grew very loud and piercing as they dumped dead warriors into the deep pool to keep the Tonkawas from scalping them like they were doing across the river. The sound was driving LaPoint to distraction, and he tore his bandanna and put little wads in his ears. He tried to resume normal breathing as the throbbing eased in his chest and he replaced the journal, scanning the battle for Gabe. Not seeing him, Josh rested beside Scorpio in the underbrush, hoping to avoid further battle, since he still wasn't moving as well with the bruised ribs.

Within a few minutes the sounds of the chaos dimmed as LaPoint hid behind trees to survey the scene and recover. Gabe was nowhere to be see, nor were the rangers, as the smoke thickened on the ground. It was a sickening scene, which was only fully absorbed when stopping to reload and surveying the stream. The battle was continuing unabated, as there was determined fire coming from both sides, with many more warriors than they had figured on, still arriving from upstream to join the fray.

Seeing things stalemated along the river bluffs, LaPoint took one last deep breath, and broke from the trees and went back into the yellow smoke cloud to find and join Gabe and the others looking for captives. As he did he saw reinforcements being brought into position to flank the Comanches, by Colonel Mackenzie. Signaling Scorpio into a quick back-step, then a quick sidestep, he avoided the line of troopers and went off looking for Gabe.

He soon spotted Gabe near the back of the first village, peering into tepees as the rangers and scouts rode pell-mell throughout the stretched-out village looking for the captives, circling through lodge groups large and small, moving upstream past the nearly dead and dead bodies of horses and people. Scorpio bolted towards Gabe on La Point's command. There were arrows flying out of cedar-brakes at the troopers still, some

181

shot by women or youngsters. The cloud of dust was now joined with smoke from lodge pole bonfires burning buffalo skin.

"Hey Gabe, any luck finding captives?"

"They got a few, not many. Mostly Mexican. One lil white gal from that Lee family. Whar'd ya go? Had me worried."

"I think I saw the Smith boys and I went to grab them, but I ran into the warriors coming from upstream."

"You're riding sorta strange, crooked like, you get hit?"

"Yeah, took a slug in the journal, from Kiwih-nai's revolver, bruised the hell out of me."

"Waugh. Stay close, dang-it, we're here ta get captives, not get in the battle."

"Alright, but that's what I started out doing, going for those boys. Let's keep moving, find where the captives are while they're fighting by the river."

The two Spanish stallions were very good at quick-stepping around the lodges and campfires, which put McBride and LaPoint a ways in front of the other rangers, whose horses were shying and spooking at the situation, slowing them down. Gabe was right in front of Josh, both riding with .44 caliber Remington pistols drawn, calling out in English and Spanish, searching for the captives among the lodges.

When McBride approached a wildly decorated lodge with a tall well-festooned scalp pole out front, a Mexican in vaquero clothing, firing a carbine, burst out of the low flapped opening, followed by large and burly red headed man with a short copper beard. The red bearded man came rushing out shooting a long revolver, bent over and firing wildly as he looked up at the mounted rangers led by Gabe. He was ducking behind the Mexican for cover, trying to hit Gabe with pistol shots. Seeing LaPoint approach while firing the long barreled Remington, the renegade aimed a shot at him and grazed LaPoint's left forearm in its bulging muscle. Josh nearly dropped the weapon but kept coming, trying to draw a bead on the man who ducked behind a firewood pile.

Gabe began firing his pistol at the same time, putting two slugs into the Mexican in front, but the other renegade crouched and fired well-aimed shots right back at him. Gabe took aim over his forearm and nicked the man in the left shoulder, but the man just hunkered down and kept blasting away with his long-barreled revolver, using both hands in a

182

deliberate manner. His fourth shot winged Gabe in his clawed hand, blasting out a red mist in the air, and as the renegade took aim again Joshua spurred Scorpio forward and threw him into a skid, throwing a cloud of dust while LaPoint shot at the red-headed man as the renegade dropped down and rolled, causing LaPoint to miss him.

The renegade came up swinging a big knife as Josh rode up, knocking the pistol out of LaPoint's hand while slicing his fingers. Instantly LaPoint kicked the man in the chest and flung blood into his eyes while trying a punch with his wounded hand, but the big fellow reflexively grabbed LaPoint's leg and tugged, causing him to tumble from Scorpio, his sore ribs screaming in pain. As Josh tumbled he grabbed the man's hand on his leg and twisted it loose, making him yell out as he kept twisting the thumb with all his might. The man fell back as LaPoint landed on his chest, and got his own left arm loose to do some damage.

One good punch to the head knocked the redhead back and down, so LaPoint could snake his powerful right arm around the man's neck. They tumbled on the ground, rolling over as each sought advantage, with LaPoint never relinquishing his headlock while suffering repeated blows and gouging. The right arm had a flesh wound and was throbbing in pain and dripping blood, but LaPoint held on. The pain from the bruise under his journal was intense as he wrestled the man, who was wildly slashing at the double thick buckskin on his shoulder as LaPoint's powerful arm crushed his neck, cutting off his air and the blood supply to his brain, slowing his slashing to wild flops of the arm as they tumbled in the dust.

Grappling with the powerful man into the campfire and out, the renegade slugged LaPoint in the crotch, knocking him loose, then came at him with the blade again. In deep pain but still scrambling, LaPoint grabbed a heavy mesquite branch with glowing coals on one end, and swung it at the man's face, which cause him to jump back. LaPoint lunged and stabbed the red coal to his head, but the man dodged again and swung his big knife, knocking the firewood from LaPoint's hand with another slice that nicked his thumb.

The injured hand pulled in to his chest, LaPoint winced in pain for an instant as he took a backward step, looking for a weapon on the ground.

183

"Got you now, bastard," uttered the renegade.

"No." Instantly LaPoint's left hand jammed with lightening speed into the man's throat at the Adam's apple, staggering him back while Josh drove a bloody fist into his solar plexus, stunning him into gasping for air, sending him to his knees. The powerful hand that had dug scores of post-holes in tough caliche and limestone gripped the throat and would not release as LaPoint cut off his air while his knife arm flailed about.

At that point Josh was finally able to get a hold of his knife hand to stop the slashing with his powerful grip, then kneed the man in the solar plexus again, and was able to draw his own knife. The man rolled over hard and carried LaPoint with him, ending up on top and breaking his knife hand free just as LaPoint's blade entered his heart and stopped the movement. LaPoint jabbed again, deeper, feeling the tip hit the spinal column, stabbed again and twisted the big sharp blade into the heart, rolling the man over into the dirt with a hard lunge.

"No, not this time," said LaPoint as he rolled on top of the man's chest, ready to stab again. The resistance had ended.

"You're done."

The red-headed renegade stared up at LaPoint, motionless, suspended in time, took a gurgling gasp and then settled into a dead heap with his small closely-set gray eyes glittering at nothing, and his jaw dropped open in surprise. LaPoint withdrew the knife and saw the heart was not pumping blood from the wound any more.

Gabe yelled, "Hey, you alright. Did he get ya?"

"I'm okay. I got him. He's gone under."

"And 'bout time for tha varmint."

"How about you?"

"Minor wound, but bleeding like a stuck hog. Need some time to wrap it, stop the blood. Got me a bit light in the head."

"Me too, I liked to got whipped by this cur," said Josh, trying to catch his breath. "Let's reload and bind our wounds while the rangers round up the rest of the captives."

"Look out now," yelled Gabe. "More varmints in that lodge."

Several men went tearing out the back end of the lodge by slicing a hole in the skins with their long knives, but they were shot dead by rangers who had come around that side by then. Captain McGregor was around the back of the tepee ring, calling out for his captive kin. Several more children came from the lodges towards the rangers.

"Could be more rascals in thar," said Gabe, down on one knee and swaying.

"I'm reloading as fast as I can, just hit the ground for a minute there."

"Alright," said Gabe as he slumped to the earth. LaPoint and McBride reloaded and faced the other lodges. Both were bleeding onto the ground from hand injuries, and LaPoint was gasping in pain from his bruised ribs. But the red headed man was not moving a bit.

Then several white children came running out from under the flap of the lodge doorway, and LaPoint holstered weapon, then knelt down to embrace them. They ran to his open arms, which he enfolded upon them. McGregor came running up and searched their faces one by one, looking for his kin. Soon several Mexican woman and a teenage boy named Francisco, along with several other captives, joined the group. Rangers crowded around to protect the gathering group of frightened youngsters.

Gabe, whose hand was squirting blood about like LaPoint's, still felt woozy and sat down on the ground by the small fire, while LaPoint called for the rest of the scouts and rangers, who formed a protective ring around the group of captives who sat on the ground, while the battle raged all around the edge of the village and into a deep draw beside it. They paused from fighting and put quick wraps on their wounds. Gabe did some deep breathing and began to recover his equilibrium.

The fighting was still fierce along the riverbank as the warriors made their last stand and final sustained effort to save the horse herd, and fight off the heavily armed troopers at the same time. The shrill wailing of squaws was so intense as to be unnerving to many of the rangers. Several of the Tonkawa scouts broke off and went to join the main battle at the creek, eager to kill and butcher Comanches, chanting their high-pitched war songs. Horses flopped around in agony on the

185

ground, screaming their death agonies. LaPoint felt the urge to go and shoot them, but didn't want to leave Gabe again.

Much of the fighting had moved a little ways upstream to a deep swimming hole to keep them out of the hands of the rampaging Tonkawas with their ancient blood feud. Some of the Tonkawas were getting into a scalping frenzy with dead warriors felled by Beaumont's men along the near edge of the water, downstream of the main fight, until Mackenzie charged up and ordered it stopped.

Henry the Tonkawa scout, who had just wrestled a scrapping Comanche down to have him shot, protested loudly, "I need scalpm heem...He no good Comanche. Why no let me scalpem heem?" Mackenzie spurred his horse right at the scalp hungry scout, scaring him back off the body. "There will be no scalping. NO!"

Henry jumped back and released the dying Comanche, beat the body with his bow, then turned and ran towards the battle, several of the other scouts following him. Mackenzie rode over to direct officers in taking captives, his voice heard above the chaotic din of of the fight. Gabe and Josh guarded the captives as the rangers located more and brought them to the central location

During the heat of the battle the determined Colonel from West Point was ranging all over the village trying to control the action, oblivious of danger. On the ground with the captives, LaPoint saw what looked like a well tanned Caucasian-looking young warrior, with a bow and arrow, slipping in a bush to hide with his weapon. Thinking it might be Kathy's brother, he felt the urge to go and fetch the young brave before he was killed, and he turned the care of the captives over to the scouts and rangers while remounting Scorpio and heading that way. About the time Scorpio was able to wend his way out of the tight mass of lodges and campfires littered with fallen bodies of people and horses, the youngster in the bushes notched an arrow in his bow and aimed at Colonel Mackenzie, who was yelling orders to take the women and children left in camp prisoner, trying to rein in the sullen Tonkawas, who wanted to go their own way in an orgy of butchery.

LaPoint spurred his mount but the brave was twenty yards away in a cedar-brake and took careful aim at the Colonel as Josh approached from the other side. LaPoint drew his revolver and tried to aim, but by then the over-excited Scorpio had broken into a bouncing trot over bodies on the ground, making focus difficult. The young warrior drew back the bow, hidden in the bush about twenty yards from the Colonel, who was approaching at a fast walk on his bay gelding, yelling orders right and left.

Seeing the Colonel about to be shot by the young buck from ambush, LaPoint skidded Scorpio to a halt and took aim to wing the warrior with the long-barreled revolver. Fearful of a mortal wound to a white captive, he erred on the side of safety and missed him entirely, hitting a branch right near his drawn back bow-string, causing an instant release of the arrow from the startled warrior.

The arrow deflected on a branch yet still hit Mackenzie in the front of his stiff jacket, but without enough force to penetrate it deeply. Still, the shock of seeing their leader with an arrow stuck into his chest sent several troopers into a panic. The Colonel jerked the arrow out and continued about his business as if nothing had happened. The young buck who shot it took off running for the bank of the river, flinging himself off the edge into the deep water and disappearing below.

As the frenzied fighting shifted away from the central village, LaPoint went back and bandaged Gabe's hand with his bandanna soaked in brandy from a flask in his saddlebag, then took a close look at the red-headed man he had killed. Though the dead man had a thick mane of red hair, his face had only a short but thick rusty stubble, as if he had shaved recently. He saw that Gabe had fired a slug into his forehead to make sure he was dead. The .44 caliber slug that punched the small hole in the front of his head had blown out the back, and the long red hair was matted and caked with drying blood, bits of bone, and brain matter. The knife wound in his heart was not even very bloody, since the heart was stilled as soon as the big layered steel blade entered it.

"Hey Gabe, what'd you shoot him for after I stabbed him in the heart."

"He needed something from me, anyway, how do I know, you coulda stuck him with a Bowie knife."

"Don't get me started. You know I hate slavers."

Gabe nodded. "You just kilt one of the worst sort."

LaPoint felt strangely indifferent to the gore dripping from the hole in the man's head. He had to know if this was the object of his blood feud. He squatted down and pulled the woolly soft reddish brown hair from the right side, showing a long crease leading to half an ear. Staring at the face, Josh realized he had killed the murderer who had killed his mother. A great wave of relief rolled through him. He shifted his balance, dizzy in waves of emotion, to keep from falling over, his eyes tearing in relief from the weight of vengeance that had left him.

He took deep breaths to steady himself. An image of his mother's face drifted through his mind's eye. He pulled his bloody knife from the scabbard and wiped the blade on the man's sleeve, several times, cleaning both sides as Gabe walked over.

"Wal what da ya think? Is it him? Is he the villain from the Teche killin's?" asked Gabe.

"Yeah, it's him. It's done. I don't have to carry that anymore. I feel really free for the first time since we came to Texas."

"Lemmi get a good look at that varmint," said Gabe as he bent over to the body, dripping his own blood into the dust amidst the smoke of the scattered smoldering firewood

"You'd better sit down, you bled out some...and it's still dripping."

"Aww-hush, yore the one that's swaying in the breeze...I gotta get a look at that varmint."

"Okay. So look," said LaPoint as he sat back and reloaded both revolvers, the blood from his hands and forearm having covered his pants. Then he got up and went to soothe his stallion, who was still fired up from the battle.

"By gad, that's Bise McCairn, alright. I recognize him from my days on the Gila. No mistaking that shock o red hair, even more outstanding than mine was. His face is a lot more weathered and wrinkled, but it's him. Same face I saw rustling our herds too, though his beard was a lot longer. Damn he's a hairy sum-bitch, ain't he? Ya could make a warm pelt out of him. And he's sure enough got the cheek scar and missing earlobe. So that's the guy you saw through them field glasses back at the plantation, huh?"

"Yes, it's him, I'm sure, and I'm damned glad to be shed of that. And I'm glad it was hand to hand, and I had a McBride knife."

"Yeah, I know what ya mean. If you had not jumped him he might have put me under."

"I didn't actually jump him, he grabbed my leg and pulled me down. Strong guy. Took a while to get control of him. He smashed my nuts once, still hurts. I had to choke the miscreant before he'd quit slashing at me. Seemed like it took forever. But it's done."

"Yeah, done for good, the crazy turncoat varmint. Most everyone in this world will be glad to be shed of this damned murdering renegade. And it should free up all of yore mind for better things than killing a skunk. Kathy will look on ya different, now that it's done. That vengeance smell will be gone from your soul. Ya mark my words on that."

"Yeah, maybe so. Hellfire and brimstone, smell that. They're starting to burn the lodges, and I don't want to be here for that. Let's get these captives out of here."

"Wait just a second," said Gabe, and pulled his big pistol. Aiming carefully at the hand of the dead man, he blew a finger off, then crawled over on his hands and knees to find it and put it in his pouch. "That's just in case there's anything to that Comanche superstition about the maimed being lost ghosts."

"Why hell, why not get his ear for a souvenir?"

"Alright," said Gabe, whipped out his big knife and sliced the man's half ear off, putting it in a small piece of buckskin cut from a hide and into a pocket.

"Oh crap, Gabe. I was kidding."

"Wal, ah warn't. Damn his hide. Waugh! And that's the last time I'm sayin it."

"That will be the day," said LaPoint, with a chuckle, glad they were still alive.

Gabe smiled and said, "Yore a free trapper now, time ta get that gal, LaPoint!" then pounded Josh on the shoulder, dripping blood on his buckskins.

"Hey, don't get blood on my buckskin, you know how hard that is to get out," said LaPoint.

"Wal hell, 'scuse me, but you're a bloody mess anyway. Still, yore a sight for sore eyes, thought I lost ya thar for a second or two."

189

"I'm glad we're both alive, let's stay that way and let the Army do the rest of this."

"Hell yeah, I'm for that."

Josh felt light enough to smile to himself, even in the heat of battle. They carried the captive women and children back to safety a quarter mile or so from the fighting, where the mules waited with supplies, behind where some civilians had parked a wagon and were busy with something on a table in front. It looked like they were getting tables set up to cook something.

There they waited and talked to the captives while the battle continued around the creek-bed and horse herds. Pouring more brandy on their wounds, they wrapped them with cotton bandages from the army supplies. LaPoint pulled out his journal, which held the .44 slug that had penetrated it near the binding. His ribs had a huge red and purple bruise where the impact was felt.

"Damnation, that's what yore walkin' so funny for. Got shot in the chest, in yore book."

"Yeah, looks like that journal saved my life. It was Kiwih-nai, shot me with his pistol."

"Dang, if that ain't LaPoint luck, it ain't never been seen."

"My chest doesn't feel too lucky right now, though."

"My stomach is growlin', wish we could find some buffalo meat."

"Not much going on in the village now, maybe we can. I'm weak from lack of food and sleep too."

The firing was less intense as fewer Comanche returned fire. The two chieftains could still be heard yelling like buffalo bulls, but the roar of troopers' carbines predominated. Clouds of blue gun-smoke drifted on the breeze and mixed with the fumes of burning buffalo skins.

In the village, the hungry and worn out soldiers had found the cache of dried buffalo meat and were passing it out to hungry troopers, who had not eaten or slept in a long while. Gabe saw Sergeant Jack Charlton near where the civilians in long white coats were boiling some big copper pots on one of the campfires. They rode over to talk with him.

"Did ya get hit, Jack?"

"No, but I had some men wounded. It was coming in hot and heavy. We got right into the thick of it. But we whipped their asses."

"Yeah you did, Jack," said LaPoint. "Made a fine job of it. We got a bunch of captives back."

"Do you know what we done, boys?" said Gabe. "This is the first time in a century and a half that the Comanches have been struck hard in their heartland. Mow-way is done with strutin' and talkin' big to Lawrie Tatum about how them puny soldiers got ta come out to whip him before he gives up captives. He done been whipped on tha Comanche plains, first time ever."

"It was the only way to end this war, the way I see it," said LaPoint. "That Mackenzie was their nemesis. McGregor too."

"These Comanches didn't know what they bit off when they decided to challenge these Scotch-Irish," said McBride. "The Celts is a tribe that knows about fightin'."

"Sergeant Jack, I saw you leading your men in the thick of it, and I'm truly impressed. You're one heck of a fighting man. If you ever get tired of the army, come ride with us."

"Likewise, LaPoint. I saw you hit that brave hidden in the bush right before he shot that arrow at Mackenzie, probably saved the Colonel's life. And I saw you use that stallion to put a lot of braves down."

"Why hell, why should he get tired of the army?" said Gabe. "He was just a private when I first met him, and he's liable to be a lieutenant next week, and with the medal of honor, by rights."

The colonel at that moment came riding up on a stocky black gelding, his second horse of the battle, the other being shot out from under him. "Sergeant, are your wounded being tended too?"

"Yes-sir."

"My compliments to the scouts, McBride, LaPoint."

"And ours to you, sir," replied LaPoint.

"Are you alright, LaPoint? You're standing a little crooked."

"Well, I took a slug in the journal, got my nuts smashed, and gave myself a black eye. I'll be alright in a few days."

191

"That's good. And our legendary scout, McBride, did you fare well, sir?"

"Yep, shore did, and mighty impressed with the way you tended yore business today, sir."

"Excellent. Thanks for your invaluable help."

Then the colonel rode off without another word towards a clump of Tonkawas down by the river and yelled at them, one word, "NO!", and they scattered leaving a Comanche body on the ground with scalp missing. He charged the black horse in their direction and pointed to the battle, and they ran that way. Riding back, he stopped momentarily and yelled to Sergeant Charlton, "Watch for the damn Tonkawas butchering and stop it if you can. Send them up to the line, I'd rather have them butchering live Comanches than dead ones."

"Yes-sir!" The big sergeant stood to full attention, his frame towering over Gabe, who stood beside him eating jerky. Watching the colonel spur his horse off towards the front line of battle, Gabe remarked. "Didn't he start out on a different horse?" asked Josh.

"Yeah, had it shot out from under him," said Jack.

"Wal, I reckon thar's no doubt who's the big chief on the staked plains now. That man just done something that no army's been able ta do, turn the Comanche's tactics on them in their homeland. This is a turnin' point in tha war that's been goin' on a century and a half. Mark my words, with all them villagers held hostage, these renegades will start bringing the captives in."

"Then it was worth it," said LaPoint. "I sure hope so, because I take no pleasure in something like this, with all the villagers in the way."

"You two scouts had a big part in it, first giving us Ortiza, then leadin' us in to the village. You'll probably never get the recognition you deserve."

"Hell," said LaPoint. "We were just passing by at the right time. McBride is right, you should get the medal of honor for the fight you led Jack. I'm glad and amazed you're alive. All we want is to do our business of horse ranching in peace, and now maybe we can."

"You two sure kept moving on those Spanish chargers. Hell, I saw LaPoint use his to kick over a brave with a spear when he ran out of ammo. His horse must have taken down four warriors with perfect kicks. I'd sure like a horse like that."

"Ya reckon they'll make Mackenzie a general and you a captain now, Jack?" asked McBride.

"Well, we haven't got newspaper reporters, only those scientists over there, here to study Comanche bodies to see what makes them so mean, or some such craziness. How are your wounds, any lead still in there? What about those hand wounds? Lots of blood on both of you. And your arm, is the bullet still in there?"

"Went through," said LaPoint. "My ribs in front here are really sore. Kiwih-nai hit me in the journal with a long shot from his pistol. Knocked me off Scorpio and bruised the hell out of me. Then I had a hell of a wrestling match with Bise McCairn, and got my nuts smashed and fingers sliced a bit."

"Bise McCairn? Did you kill him?"

"Hell yes he did," said Gabe.

"Yeah, I put him under."

"Jehoshaphat! Wait until the officers hear about this. And what about that damned Kiwih-nai, you were tangled with him as well, right?"

"I thought I saw you throw a rock at him from the ground when you went off your horse once, after a lance came flying at you. I thought you were a goner when I saw you fall and flip off the back, so it was inspiring when you popped back up and flung that stone."

"I did, nailed him in the chest. He's got a bruise too. Look at this journal, saved my life, quite a punctuation for today's entry."

"Damnit all, look at that, slug still there. Army .44 caliber too. That's the LaPoint luck they talk about, eh? But I see you've got a hell of a shiner happening on your right eye. Did McCairn give you that as well?"

"No, I got that earlier, when I shot a scout that was riding to warn the village. I rushed the shot and the telescope hit me."

"Not a bad toll, considering what we done. How 'bout you, Gabe?"

"Naw, we're okay," said Gabe as he held up his bandaged hand. "Warn't all that good a hand anyway, lucky he didn't hit me in the good arm."

193

"A warrior with a pistol shooting at you, besides Kiwih-nai?"

"Naw, when we ran inta Bise McCairn in the lodges with the captives. LaPoint jumped him and stabbed him in the heart after we emptied our guns at each other."

"Bise McCairn? You sure? The officers will be drinking cheers to that if its true."

"When have I told ya anything that wasn't? We got the son of a bitch, and he's laying thar dead by that ring of big lodges. I got his half ear and finger in my pouch here."

"Well, that was a job sure needed doing," said Jack as he drank from a canteen, the water washing through his dusty mustache and down his chin. LaPoint was rubbing his horse and watching Mackenzie direct the battle, wondering if he should go and help. He felt that he had accomplished what he was there to do. He did not want to have to shoot Kiwih-nai, and he knew the mopping up operations would involve sharpshooters, of which he was known as the best. He pulled out his repeater and reloaded it, just in case.

"Gonna take your rifle over there, LaPoint?" asked Jack Charlton.

"No, I think they can do without it."

"That's right. You guys done your part, leading us in, and getting the captives. How many did you find?

"Around a dozen or so, Jack. And I want to thank you for fighting so hard to free them, and all your men. You guys on the front line by the river were a solid wall of fire. Never let it be said again that you guys don't put it all on the line to protect the frontier."

"Damn, it's good to be in an engagement that worked for a change," said Jack.

The Tonkawa scout John'son came riding up on his painted war pony, more animated than his usual stoic self. "Sergeant Jack, Scout McBride, Long Shot LaPoint! Big victory? We get medal now, lots of horses, yes?"

"Horses maybe," said LaPoint.

"Wal, this is what ya wanted, to kill Comanches, huh? Since we first met back on the Colorado."

"Yes, McBride," said the animated Tonkawa.

"What about the horse herd?" asked Josh.

194

"Horse herd captured, plenty horses. Plenty Comanche scalp. Need meat now. Much hunger, long time no eat." John'son dismounted, went into a nearby lodge, and returned out the door with parfleches of dried meat. He opened one parfleche and it had two compartments with two colors of meat, which they began to eat. Charlton saw him eating and reached for some, so John'son handed his sergeant the parfleche. The big sergeant was famished after not eating for many hours and fighting furiously, so he dug his big hands in and began stuffing his mouth with both dark and light meat. Some buffalo soldiers gathered round to eat as well, everyone being famished. Charlton commented on how good the lighter meat was, and asked John'son what it was.

The Tonkawa scout turned and gave Gabe a half smirk, "Mabeso white man, I reckon, sergeant Jack."

The big sergeant Jack spit it out in furious sputtering rage, and swung at the Tonkawa, who leaped back like a deer, while Gabe and LaPoint burst out laughing. The several sweaty buffalo soldiers burst out laughing, though one of them spit out some jerky and began retching.

Jack Charlton didn't think it was funny and chased John'son away while shaking his fist. The wily Tonkawa with the painted face was too light on his feet for the big lumbering soldier in tall riding boots to catch, and Jack soon gave up, panting and starting to laugh in relief. On his way back he stopped to see if the copper pots boiling steam over a hot fire were being used for stew or what. Several men in civilian garb and white smocks where setting up a small table with boxes and some kind of calipers and notebooks fluttering in the light breeze.

Inside the boiling brass caldrons on tripods were the heads of three Comanches that some scientists were collecting for study. Jack spotted them, turned, and staggered a few steps before throwing up. When he was done, he straighten up, wiped his mouth with his yellow bandanna, and said "What a day, lads. I'll stick to hardtack."

"Here Jack." said Gabe, laughing. "Here's buffalo jerky, I guarantee."

"I've lost me appetite, men. Might as well go back and join the fighting if this is what the commissary is like. See you lads later. I'm gonna tell the officers about you finishing McCairn."

The fighting continued for another half hour along the river, with the superior firepower of the troopers winning the day. There was a constant din of rapid firing and squaws' grieving chants. The constant high pitched grieving sound was very unnerving to LaPoint and the stallions. Both scouts stuffed their ears again and moved away from the heat of the battle. From their different viewpoint they could see some Comanches were firing while others rode off.

Within another half hour some Comanches began to surrender, while many rode away to the northeast. Mackenzie went down there immediately to restrain the Tonkawas and take charge of the captives. When he had officers handling that, he spurred off to check on the horse herd, with only one mounted guard riding behind him.

"Well I see why that busy Scotsman gets wounded so much, he charges around like he's tryin' ta catch every bullet in tha air," said McBride.

"He's done a damn good job of directing this battle," said LaPoint. "He never lets up."

A soldier came and got Gabe to translate for the Captain interviewing the captives, whose number had grown as others crept in. Ranger captain McGregor had not, however, found his kin the Smith boys, and was still looking desperately. Mow-way was nowhere to be found, and the other chief captures said he was in Washington talking to Big Chief Grant.

LaPoint stayed to sooth and rub their stallions, and tend to nicks and scratches on them. He did not want to think about captives, knowing that both Smith boys had fled from him, and a young white warrior in a bush had shot and nearly killed Mackenzie with a bow and arrow. It had dawned on him that the captives wanted to be Comanches, and that thought was reeling in his mind. While he had been stewing about the Smith boys being kidnapped, they had been learning to ride bareback on the endless plains, instead of the drudgery of farm boys. They wanted to remain as Comanches. Though it grieved him, LaPoint understood the attraction of a horseback life on the grassy plains.

When the battle was over, LaPoint and McBride figured at least fifty Comanche warriors had been killed, while the

Fourth Calvary had captured about 130 prisoners and over two thousand horses. There was no telling how many bodies were thrown into the deep river hole, but the water was deep maroon red. Only a few soldiers, mostly Charlton's men from the front line, had been hit with serious wounds. The lodges and winter food supply were all burning on stacks of dry lodge poles, trailing giant columns of nasty yellow smoke into the fair afternoon sky.

There was plenty of evidence of stolen stock connected with depredations by marauders across Texas in the camp, including branded mules from a recent freight train massacre. Many of the horses were branded with Texas ranch brands. Mow-way was not found in the village, but over a dozen captives were rescued, though not including the Smith brothers from Cibolo Creek.

The failure to find those boys was a major disappointment to Gabe and Josh, and they were greatly chagrined by it, despite the success for the war effort. Captain McGregor was beside himself with frustration, and vowed to continue looking. The red stain from the battle was spreading downstream like a leaking wound, gory testament to the first victorious engagement against the Comanches by any army. McBride and LaPoint were exhausted but satisfied they had accomplished what they set out to do, horrible as it was to see the village burn. They knew the army, with the captured villagers, had the ultimate bargaining chip with the renegades holding captives, finally. Gabe was certain that holding the Comanche women captive would end the captive problem.

Colonel Mackenzie and the 4th cavalry had lost several men and about ten horses, and had destroyed a village hidden in the Comancheria for the first time. The fourth cavalry had traveled over a thousand miles across the staked plains during the broiling summer, searching for Comanches, and finally had accomplished their goal.

The Colonel rode up and informed Josh and Gabe that the big warrior on the gray stallion was indeed Kiwih-nai, who had stolen the horse awhile earlier on a midnight attack of the horse herd.

"I was pretty certain of that, Colonel," said LaPoint. "They came down from the upper village in droves, with him and another big warrior leading them. I think the other was Para-coom. Have either been shot, sir?"

"No. They moved too fast from cover to cover, and ride like whirlwinds. Kiwih-nai led the remaining horseback fighters over the hill in back of the river, with my horse performing admirably for him. And we're also pretty sure that Para-coom was the other big fellow leading them. He escaped also, but we got another chief or two. And the captives."

"You made history here today, Colonel. I admire your work, doing what had to be done. I'll get you another horse like that big gray."

"Get me one that fights like yours in battle. All the men are talking about your horse. And they tell me you startled that warrior that got me with an arrow in my jacket, causing him to flub his shot. I thank you for that. You likely saved my life."

"You're welcome, Colonel. You didn't seem to be too concerned with your own safety at the time."

"It's my job to run the battle properly. I started doing this right out of West Point, in the war. It's what I do best."

"Wal," said McBride. "I ain't seen anybody do it better, and I think this will go a long way to winnin' tha war, if ya hang onto that herd and those hostages."

"Maybe it will, my thanks to you and McBride for the help you provided, capturing Ortiza, and now this, finding the village. And maybe I'll get that big gray back from Kiwih-nai yet."

"Glad to ride for you, Colonel. You did a fine job of controlling the battle," said LaPoint.

"Not as fine as I would have liked, with those vengeful Tonkawas, but good enough. We have the horse herd and all those villagers as hostages now. Kiwih-nai and Para-coom have a lot of thinking to do now, anyway. That Kiwih-nai was a hell of a fighter today, on my gray pacer, wasn't he? One of the finest horseman in battle that I've ever seen, though your horse impressed everyone as well, and that buckskin of McBride's. Amazing riders, these Comanches chieftains, especially Kiwih-nai, eh?"

"Yes-sir, he was." Josh remembered the instant when Kiwih-nai had locked eyes with him when he was out of ammo and Kiwih-nai had a bead on him, then let him live. He wondered why. He had the feeling that they could have been good friends in another lifetime, away from this bloody war. He was glad that neither Kiwih-nai nor the gray stallion had been killed. He could not help but admire the way Kiwih-nai and Para-coom rallied their warriors time after time, always in the thick of the battle. He realized that he would be doing the same if he was in their place.

After the battle cleanup, the Colonel tried to enlist Gabe and Josh as full-time lead scouts, but they refused, saying they were glad to help this time, and would again if the opportunity and occasion arose. The bonfires of the burning village roared behind them as they spoke.

"Maybe this victory will do it, Colonel," said LaPoint. The rest may come in, for this striking them in their homeland has never been done before."

"Maybe, but I doubt it. We'll see. You sure you won't scout for us some more right now?"

"No thanks colonel. Neither of us want to see that kind of smoke and dust again for a while. Going back to the horse business. Can we select some horses from the herd now?"

"All you can handle, but be careful heading south with them. There's Comanches out there yet, and will be until you men decide to come back and help me finish this thing."

"You can do it without us, Colonel," said Gabe.

"We've hit a good lick today," said LaPoint.

"That we have," said the Colonel as he saluted the two scouts and cantered off.

Selecting the best horses they could find in the big herd, they headed south for their ranch on the Blanco. They warned Mackenzie to watch for night raiders on the huge horse herd, out of which the colonel had allowed Gabe and Josh each six top picks, for their aid in finding the camp. They took a group of well-formed mares and young stallions to help build the next herd at their ranches.

As Josh and Gabe herded their dozen new horses south, Col. Mackenzie and his cavalrymen tried to contain and hold the huge horse herd, but the Comanches later regrouped and stole them back at night, which Josh learned later in San Antonio, while dealing with Mr. Winger at the Menger Hotel. The big cattleman gave them lots of news before letting Josh know that he was courting Delores, his former steady gal who now ran the kitchen. Josh was happy for both of them, and happy to hear the rest that Mr. Winger told him.

The cattleman told them over dinner that Mow-way had been in Washington bargaining for reserve Indian status when the raid occurred, and was now bringing in captives. He further mentioned that Quohadi chief Para-coom had brought his band, camped upstream during the Mow-way battle, in to Fort Sill, within a week after the battle, saying the Comanches had their battle with the blue-coats and were whipped. Another interesting bit of news circulating the hotel lobby was that a Comanche chief named Horseback was going from band to band, persuading them to give up the white and Mexican captives.

It seemed the Comanches were shocked and convinced by Bad Hand and the 4th Calvary, and were actually bringing back the captive children. Having their own women and children held hostage in a stone stockade at Fort Concho had helped convince them to relent. Then finally Josh and Gabe learned from an army adjutant that the Smith boys had been brought in to Fort Sill, and they drank a misty-eyed toast of good brandy to that event. Although he was satisfied that they had played a vital part in bringing the Comanche war to a close, Josh still wondered about Kathy's brother, and if he would ever be found.

Gabe kept repeating that the Red River battle marked the beginning of the end for the Comanche, and viewed this, and their participation in guiding the troopers to the village, with mixed feelings, as did Josh LaPoint. Although they regretted that the situation had come to war, they did not regret their part in it. Josh pondered his encounters with Kiwih-nai and marveled at the halfbreed warrior's skill on the great gray stallion, remembering the spear and snake throw with equal ease and audacity, but with the feeling from Kiwih-nai that there was some sport involved between them. He felt no hostility towards the man, but also knew they might meet in battle again and try to kill each other, for the war was general now, with no quarter.

While riding for remudas south of San Antonio they pondered and discussed the issue of the continued Comanche and Kiowa raiding into the settlement areas, the renegade rustling and raiding, and the rescued captives speaking of others still held, which finally convinced the two scouts they had done the right thing. They knew that the medicine man Maman-ti, a vicious and uncanny war leader with total hatred of whites and a lust for power over Indians, had instigated the Lone Wolf band to many of recent depredations, and that they were still at large. They hoped Mackenzie would finish the job and catch them. They thought about their friend Britt and the butchered freighters who had owned all those mules in Mow-way's camp, and the more than a dozen captives rescued, and they were satisfied with their part in the battle.

When they rode into Helena to attend to horse business after a month on the prairies, Josh learned that Kathy had returned and was teaching school in Panna Maria again. He heated up a bath, shaved and washed, dressed in his best clothes, and rode hard and fast to her little house. He intended just to chat with her but he kissed her, and she responded. Holding the kiss for a while, when it was over, he told her he thought of her every day and night while she was gone, and asked her to marry him, the words tumbling out without planning it. She said yes and asked him to stay the night, which he did, to the prolonged delight of both of them.

After that they were a couple, and Josh avoided Muldoon's saloon, instead playing chess with Kathy in the evenings, or reading his books together, and sharing walks in the flowered meadows, long horseback rides down the river valley, or romps on her bed. They planned to wed in spring, when her brothers and dad could attend the wedding, which was to be held at the big springs on the Blanco, where they would live in the stone house Josh had built, and raise and train horses. It would mark Kathy's return to live in the hill country, the beautiful land of clear springs and rolling hills that she had left after seeing her mother slaughtered by Comanches. But this time she would be surrounded by the best marksmen in the land. Events would intervene to postpone the marriage.

Chapter Seven: Forked Tongue at Medicine Lodge

With the Clear Spring Ranch on the Blanco River built like a fireproof fort surrounded by high stone walls with rifle ports, they felt secure enough to continue horse training under the watchful eyes of sentries in their high perches, despite the increasing Indian troubles. The training went well and large remudas were sold, then most of the outfit signed on to drive another herd for Mr. Winger to the rail-head up north through the staked plains. With the seasoned crew of drovers, the drive was run smoothly and the herd delivered to the stockyards beside the steaming locomotive with good weight on them. The crew was paid off with bonuses, and the extra money helped LaPoint build a grubstake for another ranch, further north, in a mountain valley.

It was in Dodge City, in late August of 1873 after that year's cattle drive for Mr. Winger and the trip to Cimarron Fort to deliver saddle mounts, when Gabe started pondering the idea of going to see Buffalo Hump down at the Comanche reserve near Fort Sill. When he finally revealed the notion to Josh, it was something unexpected and caught the younger man by surprise, sort of like when Gabe revealed the situation with Bise McCairn at Mow-way's village. After LaPoint had dealt with his vengeance vow, Gabe took another angle on his own.

Finishing up the last of their business arrangements at the rail head stockyards, collecting money, dealing horses, paying off bills, and such as that, they were anxious to leave the brawling town. The drive, using the farthest western trail possible, had been a solid success, thanks to Gabe supplying beef to any Indians who asked for it, and the lack of severe thunderstorms causing stampedes. Lack of water had been the only bad problem, for it had been a rainless summer. But with the best high plains scout, they managed to keep the stock in shape, sleek enough to bring a good price. While Josh signed the contracts and got the money, Gabe was talking to lots of folks in Dodge, learning the latest, including the fact that Lone

Wolf and Maman-ti were still loose and raiding with mixed bands of Kiowa and now even the Cheyenne-Arapahos. Dodge had quickly become the gathering place for every white man who used the plains, for it was the furthest terminal west of the great railroad. Live cattle and buffalo hides filled the trains headed back east. It was still a raw lumber town full of cattlemen, cowboys, and buffalo hunting crews on the prod. The stink of hides, cow-manure, coal smoke, piss, and cheap beer and tobacco mixed with gun-smoke, fouled the air. The rancorous mood of the staggering drunks was soon as tiresome as the smells. There was a constant bawling of cattle from the stockyards, as if weeks on the trail listening to them wasn't enough. It reminded Josh of the gun thug haven of Helena, Texas, and he was always glad to leave it.

The LaPoint outfit received their money for the drive and spent the rest of the afternoon and evening in town, at bath and barber, restaurant and saloon, talking to folks, with Gabe and Tom Jackson examining the new Sharps rifles the buffalo hunters had. Josh had it in mind to take off quickly for Taos for some fall hunting and searching for signs of Mr. Alexandre, but he could see Gabe wasn't ready, so he sipped brandy and made plans for the future while Gabe was jawboning with the saloon crowds. The inevitable arm wrestling matches began to occur, with Gabe winning one after another. None of the younger men could down the old blacksmith with forearms as big as their calves, even though Gabe was at least a couple of decades older than most of them.

Gabe was interested in acquiring the latest Sharps from one of the hunters, to try to out-shoot Josh with his Whitworth. Josh told him to forget it, for he wanted no more truck with the hunters. On the trip back from Cimarron, where they delivered a remuda, they had spotted a few buffalo, and Josh had taken one down at around nine hundred yards, for dried jerky and fresh tongue meat. It was another impressive shot for a windy day with the big Whitworth.

So naturally, in the saloons of Dodge with some of the best shooters in the world sitting around, Gabe got to bragging about LaPoint's aim with the British Whitworth precision engineered gun, and several suggested a shooting match at a thousand yards the next day, putting up the best of Europe rifles against the best in the States. Gabe was trying to arrange a

203

match with the prize being a new Sharps. He was willing to wager up a part of his share of the herd profits, and was putting on his best barter talk to set the deal. The good shooters in Dodge had heard of LaPoint out-shooting Britt Jonson and taking down Polo Ortiza in dim light. They wanted to see him shoot the big Whitworth against Billy Dixon and Bat Masterson.

Josh put a damper on that idea as soon as he could, saying he had some business meetings to attend to, and was more than happy with his Whitworth. He had already learned that fame with weapons led to unnecessary shooting scrapes, and he aimed to avoid more. He was pondering the notion of talking Gabe into a trip back to the Piedra River valley, with intent to buy some grassy acreage there. He avoided the buffalo hunters and sat by the piano listening to the rollicking tunes and drinking brandy, with his eye on Gabe, then retired early. He admired the pretty saloon gals, but the images of Kathleen's smiling angelic face filled his mind, and he turned down offers of bar-girl company. As usual, he and Gabe both awoke early, an hour before first light. With a kerosene lantern in the livery stable they readied their gear and discussed the trip south, deciding to take two extra mounts and a mule for supplies.

They were having an early breakfast at the Dodge Cafe & Grill when Gabe mentioned his idea. "I want to go down through the territories and visit with Buffalo Hump down there at the Comanche reservation near Fort Sill."

Josh looked him square in the eyes and said, "Uuuuh-oooh. Damn. Here it comes. I thought you said you gave up the idea of stabbing him, since he gave up the warpath."

"I did. He done took the peace road, and his tribe went through hell after that, I heard. Disease and starvation forced 'em back off the reservation into the Wichita hills, and the army attacked 'em there. They been through hell, according to what the Fort Sill interpreter, Jim Shaw, told me. I ain't carrying no grudge for him now. The peace road was hard enough on him."

"Except maybe you'd like to go put him under like I did that Bise McCairn."

"Naw. That's past, far as I can tell. I ain't felt that in a while. A life without regrets is worth a lot more than vengeance over wartime killings. He was fighting for his country, and once ya start up a war, ain't no controllin' it, especially after whippin' up them young braves over the council house fight. You know, this all started back then, when they brought that pore Matilda Lockhart in covered with scars and bruises and her nose cut off, for that's what set those men off in killing rage down thar. Buffalo Hump was responding to the massacre at San Antone, at the old Bexar jail they called the council house."

"Then why would you want to go down and see Buffalo Hump? Why not let that sleeping dog lie? I was already making plans for a trip to Taos. I figured you'd like to see your son again, hammer a bit of red hot steel, show him some more about knife making, then go up to the Great Pagosa. Why the hell would you want to go down and find Buffalo Hump, after all we've been through with the Comanches?"

"'Cause I want to talk to him, by God. Taos will be there when we're done, with all them elk waiting to be shot. There's stuff between me and him ought to be talked over 'fore we both go under."

"Like what?"

"I want him to convince the other bands to stop raiding, like what Wild Horse tried. Because from what I seen, thar's only one way the Comanche are gonna survive, and I want to talk to him about it. The only buffalo that's left in any numbers is the southern herd, on the staked plains. That herd's got to be saved for them to survive."

"Yeah, that was a disgusting trip to Cimarron, all those bones everywhere. Buzzards and bones. Amazing change in three years. The northern herd is about gone, it seems."

"This Moaar fella finding an outlet for tanned buffalo leather set a wheel in motion that won't stop 'til all the herds are gone. I seen it happen with the beaver, and lived long enough to regret it. The end of the buffalo will doom the plains tribes, and we'll be stuck eating cows."

"I think you're right."

"And if the Kiowa and Comanche don't quit raiding and interfering with the railroads, Sherman will wipe them out, I guarantee. That Warren wagon train massacre showed him how close he come to laying dead with his brains scooped out, his privates cut off and stuffed in his mouth, and a fire on his gut, like them fellas. He musta had some bad dreams after that one, for he shore gave the go ahead. He's hot to wipe 'em out now; that massacre gave him all the excuse he needs to do the railroad's dirty work, and this is their last chance to survive."

"How?"

"Stop the raids on settlers, turn in all the rest of the captives."

"Yeah right, after a century and a half of raiding, just stop?"

"A lot of them done it already on account of Mackenzie holding them hostages we got him at Mow-way's village. If they cut a deal now, after this year of not much Comanche raiding, they may be able to hold onto the Texas buffalo grounds, market meat and hides like they did in the old days with the New Mexican folks, and survive as a people. Hell they could ship buffalo meat and robes right out of Dodge, for it's a dang site better than this old stringy longhorn. At least the Quohadi and Yampicari got that last chance, maybe."

"I see. Your old Comanchero dream. Peace with the Comanche through trade, like the old shining times in Taos."

"It happened then, and around the German settlements in Texas for a few years too. My departed wife said they used to trade old cheese kegs to the Comanche women for drums, get baskets of pecans in return. It could happen again. White folks can't handle livin' on the staked plains anyhow."

"Well, I wish it could have continued, but... I think you're too late with that. There's too many renegade bands that won't come in to the sorry reservation life. The government isn't keeping it's side of the deal, and the Indians are wise to it and won't go along. Besides which, they all get sick when they're penned up there."

"Maybe, but since I'm one of the few that might be able to parlay it, I reckon I ought to try. A lot of the captives have been returned, since our raid on Mow-way."

"And you think it's worth the risk to go talk to Buffalo Hump, your old sworn enemy, about it? It's bound to rake over old scars."

"Yep, I do. I'm already raked over like a spring garden anyway. Them scars is crusted over and plowed under several times by now. I think it's our last chance to prevent a general war, with the Kiowas raiding again now, and their last chance to survive as a people, and I want to see that happen. It's a way of life that should not be wiped out like we done to tha beaver.

And we don't need no more massacres to stain this land. I've been hoping that battle on the Red River last year was enough to end the damned war, and I can't get the sight of the river full of blood outa my mind."

"Me either. And the smell of those burning lodges. But I doubt you can convince the hostile bands to do much. Lots of the tribe got wiped out by cholera recently, and they can't be too happy about reservation life."

"Yore probably right, but I need ta try. Don't ya see, if he and I can shake hands, maybe there' hope to end this war."

"Isn't this best left to the government, Gabe?"

"Listen, the cold fact is that Sherman developed total war in Georgia and intends to use it on the Plains tribes, with his pal Sheridan."

"How do you know that?"

"I conferred with John'son about it when we stopped at Fort Concho in spring. He pretends to not understand English and listens to the Sergeant's talk. The 4th cavalry has gone after the Kickapoos and Apaches raiding across the border from Mexico, but they'll be back after the Comanches when that's done, I reckon."

"They send Mackenzie on all the tough jobs."

"Yep. That man means business, he's relentless, he learns from his mistakes, he uses the right scouts and lots of them, and he's figured out how to whip the Comanche, I reckon. He's probably found those Kickapoo and Apache raiders by now, and is coming back to finish this job with the remaining hostiles. And he takes orders from Sherman and Sheridan, who want to wipe them out with total war. They will find the winter villages and wipe out the horses, lodges, and food, if the tribes don't submit to reservations. The Quaker peace policy is over. They want to come at them from all sides in winter, and want us to scout for them."

"Scout for Sherman and Sheridan, them that made total war on the south?"

"Naw, scout for Mackenzie to end this damned raiding and get the captives back."

"And you know all this from your parley with John'son?"

"Yep. I learned about Mackenzie from him and that scout chief Strong. Mackenzie wanted Strong to persuade us to scout for the Fourth Cavalry after the drive. The colonel finally talked to me about it again, you know."

"You never mentioned that to me."

"You had enough on yore mind then."

"So you think Colonel Mackenzie is coming back up on the plains to whip the Comanches.

"Yep, and the Kiowas, this fall. They want us to come scout for them again, find Maman-ti's bunch. He's the one that led that Warren wagon-train massacre, and they're raiding the frontier settlers again. The colonel even sent ole Jim Shaw to recruit us. And they got ole Chisholm out looking for captives."

"Scout for the cavalry again? We already done our part in this war, finding Mow-way's bunch, and it worked. It was mostly about the captives with me, and that experience shed a whole new light on that situation in my mind. Those kids didn't want to be rescued, even though their blood kin searched for them a whole year."

"Wal, they can either go Comanche or get walloped with sticks every day. We was too late."

"Still, it threw a hitch in my loop when I tried to grab that kid, and he dodged me like I was going to hurt him. And I have a notion that it was Kathy's brother who shot that arrow into Mackenzie's chest, too."

"Wal, lots of captives have been brought in since that battle."

"Yeah, right. Most of the Comanche bands moved near Fort Sill and brought in the captives, so why can't they hold the buffalo hunters off the southern herd and let it rest? The Quohadis can have the buffalo plains, as far as I'm concerned. I'm not leading them to Kiwih-nai's village."

"Me neither, we gave our word to him."

"Let them get that damned Maman-ti and Lone Wolf's Kiowas, they're the ones stirring up raids now, from what I heard."

"That's why I didn't mention it, knew exactly what you'd say. But they're gonna do one last big sweep in fall, and want us for scouts again, to finish the job. You'd be miffed if I didn't tell ya."

"Damn, the raiding has decreased, why can't they let it simmer down, leave the staked plains to the Comanches.?"

"'Cause Sherman and Sheridan are mainly for protecting the railroad routes and putting all the central plains Indians on reservations under the care of the Quakers, so the plains can be filled up with immigrant farmers to keep the railroads in cash. I heard this all from the sergeants as well, ya know."

"What about this peace policy with the Quakers?" asked Josh.

"It's like thinkin' that singing hymns to a hog on ice will teach him to walk straight! Raiders is always gonna be raiders, and they all get blamed for what the young bucks do. Anyway, it's just the public spiel from the Grant Administration in response to all the pressure from the churches after them massacres on the Washita and Sand Creek, from what I gathered out of the newspapers in Dodge, and talkin' ta folks. Anyway the Quakers 'bout done throwed up their hands and called for attacks on the remaining hostiles."

"Well, it doesn't work well with the Indian ring in Washington stealing all the money for the Indian's food, then starving the tribes while they die off from diseases, all packed in the reserves."

"Exactly," said Gabe. "But that's the kind of big gov'ment we got now, thanks ta Lincoln's war and his railroad gang. Grant's gang of crooks are robbin' the public till as we speak."

"I know it. But maybe the Quakers..."

"I talked to that fella Shaw, the head interpreter at Sill, over at Fort Dodge. He says that cholera, smallpox, and starvation are putting the reserve Indians under. The tribes are between a rock and a hard place. The hard place is a reserve trying to farm where crops won't grow, and waiting in line for food that don't come. The rock is what we been seeing around here, piles of buffalo bones and no herds. The only good time the warriors have is the paltry fun of chasing a few skinny cows around on feeding day, dreaming of the old buffalo hunts."

"They've sure been reduced to a sad state, after living on the buffalo so long. They drove everyone out and claimed the buffalo ground because they were stronger, and now it's happening to them."

"Right. Ever since the Mooar brothers found a way to tan and market the leather, it's been a general slaughter to get hides to market before the other guys do. It was bad enough with all the immigrant tribes and the droughts thinning the herds, but now they're being wiped out as a species."

"I'm afraid you're right, Gabe. They used to be lots more around here. Good God, remember that time in '70 on the Red River?..pushed that herd of longhorns through them for miles, all day and into the night. Like a brown hairy sea of buffalo. One of the most incredible sights I've ever seen. And even down around the Concho back on the Goodnight drive west, when we had to drive the cattle through that big herd. The one your friend the crow told you about."

"I know I'm right. We're witnessing the end of the buffalo. It'll be just like the beaver, which I've lived long enough to regret being a part of. I remember what it was like three years ago out northwest of here, herds so thick it took all day to pass through. Now nothing but bleaching bones out there, all that meat gone to waste. Word among the shooters in Dodge is that the central herd is gone and they also done cleaned out all the buffalo around here on the Arkansas and are heading to the Llano Estacado in spring to wipe out the last of the southern herd. Already got a supply base started."

"What about the Medicine Lodge Treaty? It set the Arkansas River as the boundary for white hunters. It's been in effect since '67. That should keep the peace."

"In effect my ass. Another damned fraud. The army is looking the other way, according to the hunters I talked to last night. They're all headed to set up a new post down near Adobe Walls, where Carson had his scrape, on the Canadian upstream a few miles of whar we camped before the scrape at the Red River with Mow-way and Kiwih-nai and Para-coom."

"Below the Arkansas? No."

"Yep. They intend ta use that as a central post to range out over the Llano Estacado, gather and press the hides there, get supplies, and ship the hides back to Dodge by wagon. Even setting up a store, a saloon, and a cafe. Same location the Bent Brothers picked, years ago, in the trading days."

"But I thought that was off limits to buffalo hunters, the law of the land since the treaty, no white hunters south of the Arkansas. That's gonna set every buffalo hunting tribe on the warpath. Hell, it's right near the Alibates quarries, their sacred source of flint, the last place they want to see white men. Isn't the army obliged under orders to enforce the treaty, keep the hunters out of there?"

"Yeah, you'd think so, and so did the chiefs who signed the treaty. They believed the Arkansas was the line and everything south was theirs forever. They thought it reserved the staked plains of Texas for them."

"So did I. I read the damned thing, and that's what it said."

"Trouble with that is the Federals don't own that land to give away, the state of Texas does, since Texas reserved all public lands when it entered the union. If the buff hunters wipe out that herd, it will force the Comanches to raid south into the settlements to survive, or more likely spark a general war, which we'll be drug into, whether we want to or not," said Josh.

"Well the first thing they'll do is wipe out that adobe walls post, huh?"

"Well yeah, sure they will, or die trying. Probably do that this spring, after gathering all the medicine and warriors they can. And then kill all the hunters they can find, to protect the southern herd."

"You know Kiwih-nai and the Quohadi never signed the treaty anyway, nor did Para-coom, and others of the northern bands."

"Wal shore, they'll attack that mess at Adobe Walls, if they can prevail against forted-up rifle experts, and that will give Sherman the excuse he needs to come wipe 'em out with winter campaigns. But I heard they was shipping lots of repeating rifles down there as well as Sharps fifties and forty fours, turnin' that adobe walls into a fortress bristling with weapons. Long guns and repeaters."

"Is that the old washed down adobes we saw, where Carson had his fight? Why those ruins wouldn't ..."

"Naw, they're building a new bunch, some adobe, some jacales with thick timber from the riverside thar, filled in, chinked with adobe. Got a store, saloon, big hide pressing lever setup, corrals, everything they need to collect and ship hides and keep the hunters supplied."

"This is going to...hell Gabriel, it will mean general war all along the frontier, more raids on Texans. Kathy and all the other settlers in central Texas will be in danger."

211

"Right. Now you see what I been pondering while you been thinking of marrying that lovely gal of yorn. I want to prevent the war, if I can. It don't have to come to all-out war. If a warrior like Buffalo Hump can take the peace road, so can the other Comanche chieftains."

"So what's your notion of finding him, and then what?"

"Shaw told me the last he heard that Buffalo Hump was trying to be a farmer and raise corn now. That really got me to thinking. I considered on it plenty, and I figure he's the man to convince them to stop the raiding, if anybody can. We could go around to the bands together, show how old enemies could make peace, convince 'em to come in with all the captives, and stop the raids."

"Maybe so, maybe not. You said it didn't work out so well for him."

"Wal, he survived, and if it comes to Sheridan and Sherman against the Comanches, they ain't gonna survive another campaign, especially if Sherman lets the hunters destroy the last herd. We already seen what kinda total war those two can wage in the south, huh?"

"Sounds like it's already come to that."

"Maybe. But I'm thinking that Texas might allow the Comancheria and let the tribe survive on the Llano Estacado, if they quit raiding and return all the captives. It ain't farmland anyway, so white folks can barely use it for cattle-drives, as we've learned, and the Comanches are the only ones that can survive there. They could continue to live on the buffalo and start serious marketing of the meat and hides, on a sustained basis. White folks can't do it, and the meat is a sight better than this old tough longhorn we been trailing. Texas could let the Comanches have the Llano Estacado. They could ship buffalo meat back east on the railroad."

"Good lord, you have been pondering, Gabe. I don't think they will. The new wells and windmill pumps will spread ranching all up here, eventually."

"Naw, not for many decades. White men will never tame this place for their own use, not for a hundred years. Too much gyp-water, drought, grass-fires, storms, downpours, floods, twisters, blizzards, and such. Hell, we are some of the few whites that can even cross it. We could have a line at the existing counties to separate us, let the Comanche's keep the staked plains and the whites live in peace in central Texas."

"Houston already tried all that, didn't he? The Texas legislature would never agree to a line of demarcation to stop the spread of settlements. And now that well drilling and windmills are changing the chances for ranching success out here, I'm skeptical."

"Wal all right, maybe its a slim chance, but I'm saying the line should be the cap-rock, anyway. The Quohadi could survive up there, like they have for over a hundred years, in perfect balance with that last buffalo herd. Thar was a slim chance we'd turn from refugees into prosperous ranchers one time."

"Maybe that might have worked earlier. But now, too many settlers have been killed, too many captives taken, too many villages have been raided, and blood vengeance is running high on both sides. Even after the Mow-way raid and hostages, the really pissed off Indians are still out raiding. I can see it going to general war pretty easily if the southern herd starts getting slaughtered, so somebody's got to hold the line at the Arkansas. It should be the army stopping the hunters, to prevent this war."

"But nobody aims to. That's what I learned last night with all those rounds I bought 'em. It's already happening. There's some hunters down there around Adobe Walls already, according to the low talk, sending wagon-loads of hides back and setting up more buildings down thar on the Canadian for a big hunt in Spring to finish off the southern herd. "

"Damn stinking scallywags, Sherman and his bummers again. That's what he does, destroy the whole country the people live on. Damnit, Gabe, it's a sorry situation, but what the hell, we're just two guys trying to make a living."

"I know. So's everybody in Dodge, one way or another. But we all gonna be thrown together in this general war, ya know."

"Damn. Lot's of these buffalo hunters look and smell like the dregs of humanity, in my opinion. I heard you jawing with them last night, thought you were going to get me into a long distance rifle shooting match with them. I don't want to have anything to do with them."

"Aww. That's the skinners look and smell so bad."

213

"Now you say awww instead of waugh all the time."

"Yeah, and whar's my ten bucks silver for it?"

"Waugh," said LaPoint. "Scout me past this Comanche war, and I'll double it."

"Gonna be hard to get around."

"Yeah, with you buddying up to the buffalo hunters in the bars. I saw you trying to get a match with Masterson and Dixon for a good hour."

"Yeah, wal ya shore damped the powder on that idea. But anyway, the shooters are a better class than tha skinners, guys like Dixon and Masterson, just fellas trying to make a living on the plains and rise up in the world, like me trapping beaver as a young fella, or hunting buff for meat up at Bent's Fort, and Taos. They been driving freight and riding dispatch and scouting for pennies, and want a chance to make something of themselves, get a place and a family, like you want to."

"Aw, come on. You didn't take down a hundred beaver a day like these modern buffalo shooters."

"Listen, they see it as a chance to make a stake. Nobody's gonna buy a ranch on freighter or scout wages, that's for sure. It's their one chance to make some money, and they're going to keep at it as long as they do. They're tired of working for peanuts, being guides and messengers and freighters, and they're gone after the elephant."

"Well it's gone from a few to a stinking swarm of them up here in the three years we've been trailing herds. You seemed to already know some of them."

"Yeah, a couple, and they introduced me around. Some are old trappers that went to buffalo hides when the beaver ran out, and silk hats came in. A pelt's a pelt to them. Them bleary-eyed old farts ain't the ones making stands of a hundred buffalo like them youngsters with keen eyes and the latest Sharps rifles mounted with scopes, though."

"One way or another the buffalo is disappearing."

"Yeah, ain't it so. Instead of me and Alex buying a few hundred choice robes from the Comanches, it's gone to slaughter by the tens of thousands. Anyway, this whole operation of removing the herds is all approved up at the head offices of the gov'ment, I reckon."

"I think you're likely right on that. Or the head offices of the railroad."

"Yep. It's all of a piece. The buff hunters are just pawns being used by the government and railroad powers to destroy the Indians commissary, simple as that. Guys like Sherman and Sheridan and that secretary Delano fella make the policy, the hunters are just trying to make a buck to buy that ranch, like you and me. That the hide market developed at this time is just bad luck for the Indians, like not being immune to the new diseases of the white men."

"Bad luck for sure. They were screwed by new diseases as soon as the first Spanish got here, and didn't know it. I guess this is the final screwing."

"Yep, that they were. Speaking of which, I notice you didn't get a gal last night, which I interpreted to mean that Miss Kathy is still in yore heart."

"That ain't up for discussion right now while we're talking about diseases and wiping out Indians. Anyway, I doubt one could mess with one of these gals without catching something from one of these scurvy skinners. No more whores for me, sheath or no. I was more interested in getting out of town and heading for that Cimarron Canyon and Taos, actually. "

"Wal, we're fixing to see a general war right soon unless somebody stops it. It'll turn the frontier into hell on earth, and probably mean the end of the Comanches, if I gauge that Mackenzie rightly, and his boss Sherman."

"Probably so, but I doubt we could affect things one way or another. Best thing at this point would be for all of them to come in and to get the Quakers back to feeding and educating them. If only the government would fulfill the annuities side of the deal, and hold the Arkansas line against the hunters, but I guess the Indian ring stole all the money instead. I'm for staying out of it."

"Fine for you to say, you ain't been a part of exterminating a species like I have. Maybe I'm the only one who can effect things much, 'fore it goes to the warpath. I lived to regret rubbin' out the beaver, I don't want to regret not tryin' ta stop this."

"How do you know the army won't enforce the line? It's held so far, hasn't it?"

" 'Cause Dixon and Harrahan told me that Mooar talked to Major Dodge over at the fort. They came right out and asked what would the army do if they was to hunt buffalo down below

215

the Arkansas. Dodge said if he was a buffalo hunter he'd go to where the buffalo are."

"That can't be right. The army is letting them go down without protection? They'll be slaughtered."

"And that will trigger an army campaign to wipe them out. Don't ya see, it'll be like the council house fight all over again, it will give the tribes a cause to unite around and create general war, like with Buffalo Hump in the forties. Thar's already talk of a new prophet rising with the Quohadi. A young fella called Isatai, predicted the comet we had, and other tall tales, magic paint ta turn bullets, spitting up wagon-load's of cartridges, and such further religious palaver as that. They gonna rise up. Once that happens, the pressure will mount to wipe them out with all these troopers leftover from the war."

"Probably. When folks are desperate they listen to crazy folks in religious garb more," said Josh to Gabe's nodding agreement. He continued on.

"So who's gonna stop the hunters from going after the southern herd, if the army won't? And who's gonna stop the Comanches and Kiowas from raiding?"

"I don't fuggin' know who's gonna stop the hunters, Josh, for the man who coulda done it is dead, ole Sam Houston. He's the one got Buffalo Hump to come in. If he coulda just drawed a line at the caprock to divide Indian land from the whites before he died. Damn. Gotta be somebody in Texas we could talk some sense too, to avoid a general war. Maybe Charlie Goodnight, or Lawrie Tatum, maybe some of those religious folk in San Antonio, maybe go to the governor, even."

"We? We? I just got done with a near impossible job of driving a herd late in the season, that I didn't really want, trying to make up for rustler losses. I was ready to head to Taos and hunt elk and scout out a new ranch site. How in the hell are we gonna get an agreement to stop raiding from the Comanches?"

"We ain't. I'm gonna convince Buffalo Hump to, iffen he wants to save what's left of the Comanches. If that warrior could take the peace trail, then he's the one to convince others to. If I can make a personal peace pact with him after we talk out the raid of 1840, then anything is possible, ain't it? And you can help me convince the Texans."

"Me? Why me?"

"Well you're a lot better at talking to high muckety-mucks and writing letters and all, with yore 'lightenment education and suchlike. You got the schoolin', the lettering, and ya don't say 'waugh' nor whaar nor thar so much."

LaPoint laughed. "Hell, I never could understand whar thar was, and waugh happened to my floating stick, and what the hell the difference between whar and war is."

"Thar ya go agin. I need you 'cause ya cut your teeth on dealing with officials back in New Orleans, representing the company. I'd need yore help talkin' with the Texans. But it ain't gonna happen unless the tribes give up raiding the settlements."

"What the hell you been drinking, anyway? Did you come upon some absinthe or something? Let me see if I got this straight. You want to talk to Buffalo Hump about saving what's left of the Comanche nation? After his raid burned you out, and you chased after him for years trying to kill him?"

"Yep, I reckon that's how it boiled down. I respect him a lot more than some of these white trash mealy mouths around here that's for wiping out all the Plains Indians, or some of them marauders who call themselves rangers and wipe out villages full of women and children just for the pain and plunder."

"You sure you aren't going to stab him first, then talk?"

"Ain't sure about nuthin', but I don't aim to stab him," said Gabe, his serious expression touched by a slight smile.

"You might have a change of heart when you see him."

"I knew you'd say that. I ain't aiming to kill him. I ain't denying I want to talk to him about my homestead and the Plum Creek battle."

"That could set off some of that old blood revenge feeling, don't you think?"

"Wal, I won't rightly know how I feel about that until I talk to him, I reckon. But I ain't hankering to stick nor slice him anymore."

"You sure?" asked LaPoint as Gabe pulled out his knife and began to rub his small sandstone along the blade. "Naw. Our war is over. He was a great war chief, a great warrior fighting for his own country and people, and now they say he's tried his best to be a peace chief. I'm a right fair hunter and tracker, and he avoided me for years, so I'd have to admit he's a good warrior. I just gotta talk to him, that's all. I'll go by myself if you got other plans."

217

"Like hell you will, you stubborn old fart. If you're going to attempt the impossible again, I'm going with you."

"Alright then, let's go see how a man can change."

"You mean Buffalo Hump, or yourself?"

"Both."

"Alright Gabe. We'll head down to Fort Sill and see if we can contact him. I doubt those Quakers will let you see him, with the legend of Top-Hat Comanche Hunter still alive."

"Maybe so. Maybe not. We'll just deal with it as it comes."

" Alright, let's go see this old buffalo hump man."

"Poo cha na quar hip, war chief of the Penetaka Comanches. Chief Hard On. We'll pay him a call."

"I don't see how you remember those Comanche words."

"My ma made me memorize every night when I was growin' up."

"Must have been nice, to have a ma, growing up," said Josh. "Let's get this over with, then. You ready, I paid for the meal, with a tip."

"Shore, let's get the hell out of here."

They left Dodge city, traveled light and fast on down to Fort Sill, and found out that Buffalo Hump had died a couple of years before, from slow starvation and disease, while trying to be a farmer, like many of his band.

Sorely disappointed, they met with some agency interpreters before they headed west for the cap-rock bluffs and the staked plains beyond. From the Comanche interpreter they also found out that constant raids were being conducted by the Kiowa chieftain Lone Wolf, who was avenging a lost son, while many of the Comanches were avoiding raiding and returning captives in order to get their own women and children released from the rock stockade at Fort Concho where they had been held since the Red River victory. Mackenzie's strategy had worked to some degree, but trouble was brewing over the buffalo slaughter.

The most disturbing news they heard at Fort Sill was that the prophet named Isatai had gained prominence among the fierce Quohadi, and allied himself with Kiwih-nai, now striving to fill the place of his father Peta Nokona as a great war chieftain, advocating general war. They were reportedly going to kill all the Tonkawa scouts to start with, and cripple the army's ability to navigate the staked plains. Then they would wipe out the buffalo hunters and settlers pushing into their hunting grounds. The Tonkawa scouts related this with fear in their eyes, knowing they would be the first victims of the Comanche's rage.

They heard other disturbing news from the military officials at the fort. Buffalo hunters were being killed when they were caught by Indians on the plains, and freight wagons ambushed. The army was involved in a multi-pronged expedition to sweep the remaining free-roaming Indians from the plains, with Nelson Miles already in the field a month, driving hostiles west, and Mackenzie coming up from the south. Mackenzie had been in the field for months, chasing hostiles. The Comanche war was far from over.

Saddened and discouraged by all this war news after the months on the trail, they departed south from Fort Sill without extra mounts. The Indians were close to starving and wracked with diseases. McBride and LaPoint had felt badly about that and given their extra mounts and mule to the agent at Fort Sill, who was waiting for supply wagons stuck in the mud of sudden rainstorms, and had hungry Indians to feed. Horse and mule meat were better than starving, so LaPoint and McBride departed on two horses without a pack mule, thankful that they had left Leon and Josie at home for this trip and used strange mules. They headed back towards the Blanco Valley, traveling fast without the pack mule tagging along braying in constant complaint.

It took a day to reach the Red River crossing, so they camped on the north side and swam the horses across in the morning. On the afternoon of the crossing day they heard the rolling boom of big guns on the high plains, and rode over to take a look. From a distance they watched three buffalo hunters take down over a three dozen buffalo from a small herd, in the space of fifteen minutes. While they peered through their field glasses and telescope, the hunters decimated the herd and four skinners went to taking the hides and leaving the meat to rot. A swarm of black turkey vultures cruised on the hot air in constant circles above the carnage, waiting for their turn. Coyotes waited a mile away, resting by a playa. It was a disgusting sight to both of them, but they decided just to move on and be extra vigilant for Comanches who might be drawn to the noise.

219

They headed southwest until they sighted the cap rock bluffs, then skirted them as they headed for Fort Concho. The edge of the cap-rock always provided them with hiding places as they moved with caution. Around noon of the third day, they heard gunfire ahead of them, as if a small battle was raging. They hurried the horses towards the sound, and within ten minutes they topped a little hill and saw a group of Comanches attacking a buffalo hunter camp. They both wheeled their mounts around when they saw the situation held far too many braves to engage.

"Shit fire and save the flint, thar's too many of 'em to take on, let's get back behind them bushes and look with the field glasses."

They did as the older scout wanted and soon Josh was peering at the scene with binoculars from a cedar bush along a wash, while Gabe fumbled in his saddlebags for ammo and his telescope. He pulled out his Sharps rifle and crept with it and the telescope to hide with Josh in the bushes and survey the scene.

"Looks like over twenty warriors, closing in on several buffalo hunters," said Josh. "Put your long gun away. We are not getting into this one."

"Holy fire. They're done for," said Gabe as he adjusted his telescope.

"They are," said Josh LaPoint. "Three skinners are already down and scalped, and it looks like just the two shooters are holed up under that wagon half full of hides. They haven't got a chance. Hell, I see more warriors on horseback beside that clump of mesquite to the west. Another six or so. They're making a rush for the wagon now."

"Yeah, I see 'em comin'. We could pick off a couple with long rifles, but that'd just bring the whole nest of hornets down on us."

"I'm not going to go under for some damned buffalo hunters killing down below the Arkansas."

"Me neither," said Gabe. "They made their bed, let 'em lie in it. Poor sonsobitches."

The group of Comanches on horseback started their charge. The rolling booms of two big Sharps fifties reached the scouts' ears after two warriors fell from their horses, but the others kept charging the hunters. The air was filled with arrows

220

and the sound of rifles firing, with dust stirred up by riders around the wagon.

"Hell's a poppin' now," said Gabe.

"I don't want to watch, but I can't stop."

"Thar it goes, got lassos on the wagon, gonna pull it over, thar it goes, got one hunter with a lance, the other with arrows, son of a bitch!"

"Well that was a lopsided battle," said LaPoint.

"Got what they was axin' for, ya ax me."

On horseback and on foot the Comanches had attacked the two hunters from all directions at once, eventually dragging them out from under the wagon as it flipped, and chopping them to pieces while LaPoint and McBride watched with field glasses and telescope from five hundred yards away, feeling waves of revulsion and fear roll through their guts. Two braves ran about waving the bloody scalps, while others dismembered the hunters in a frenzy, tossing out body parts as blood spurted.

"Damn, that is gruesome. I've seen enough. Nothing we can do. Let's circle back and get the hell away while they're doing their butchering," said LaPoint.

"Alright, I'm for that. Them fellas took a mighty big chance comin' down here way past the Arkansas to slaughter buffalo, and they done got slaughtered themselves."

"But damn, what a butchery. Now I understand why you old timers carried a shell filled with cyanide."

With a morbid sense of revulsion they backtracked, then headed east and southeast, traveling as fast as they could for as long as they could see, to get away from the rampaging Comanches. They finally made a cold camp when the moon set, and slept in shifts, in a gully with rifles out. The next morning they ate jerky and left before dawn, after both had nightmares of the torture scenes they had seen.

On the way the next day they discussed what they saw, and each vowed to not let the other be captured by the Comanche. They each determined to save the last bullets for themselves, if it came to that. Gabe's advice was if that failed they should each attack a warrior with a knife, forcing the others to shoot them. That discussion was followed by hasty travel to get off the staked plains while avoiding vengeful Comanche parties looking for buffalo hunters.

The next afternoon LaPoint spotted smoke, and they rode to it cautiously and found a smoldering wagon with pile of hides inside it, and massacred hunters and skinners laying around the area, cut to pieces and scalped. The corpses looked like porcupines, with dozens of arrows sticking in the trunks. The coyotes were already gnawing on the scattered limbs, and buzzards were landing nearby, so the scouts quickly left the scene and continued south with great fear of discovery by the rampaging Comanche bands.

When they finally made it to Fort Concho after several more days of stealthy travel, they learned that warfare was erupting all over the staked plains as the Comanche made a last desperate effort to kill all the buffalo hunters. Mackenzie and his troopers were off chasing the Quohadis and other bands, and the frontier was in turmoil.

They traveled south and came across settlers with loaded wagons, leaving the valleys around Fort Mason, having been raided and burned out. They rushed home towards the Blanco ranch mulling over the turn of events, fearful that the war would spread to the frontier settlers' cabins, and to their ranch. When they reached San Antonio, they heard news of scattered raiding all along the frontier north of San Antonio and Austin, and read newspapers full of atrocities and editorials screaming for protection from the Army. By the time they reached the Blanco River, they also reached the grim awareness that their hopes of ending the war with the raid on Mow-way's village had been premature at best. And they settled in with the realization that they had to prepare for war at home, for it threatened to spread to the whole frontier.

The fall and cold weather time was spent fixing up the stone cabin on the Blanco where Josh and Kathy would make their home. With long cypress boards he built bookshelves and spread out his boxed collection of books he had brought from the Eagle Ford Ranch. After reading comments by Napoleon about building a secure defense before launching an audacious offense, LaPoint spent lots of time fashioning clever rifle ports in the stone wall at various points, to defend against raiders. The ports were centered in niches so that the rifleman could aim in a wide arch and remain protected by stone walls. He also build a tall stone wall around the house, with rifle ports, and benches to stand on and fire over the wall. A windmill tower held a perch below the mill for a rifleman to guard the ranch. A small cabin was built for Gabe near the new blacksmith shop there, with metal roof like the main buildings, so they could not be lit with raiders' torches. The interior walls were plastered with smooth creamy lime mortar, and the floors done in flagstone. Two Rumford fireplaces and chimneys were built to keep the lodge warm. It was as fireproof and defensible as they could make it. Lookout nests were built in high cypress trees, cliffs, and a perch on the chimney.

The next late winter and early spring, they spent rounding up mustangs deep in south Texas, below the Nueces where the herds were still thick. They had one running gun battle with Mexican rustlers, and lost two dozen horses, but nobody was hit, and the rest of the season proved uneventful in terms of rustler scrapes. The horses were trained at both the Eagle Ford Ranch on the south San Antonio River, and Blanco River ranch they called Clear Springs.

While in San Antonio for a horse sale in early July, they heard of the Adobe Walls battle, where a huge group of warriors had besieged the compound there in a protracted gun battle, which ended when Billy Dixon sent a slug over a thousand yards into a warrior. That was one of many battles centered on buffalo hunters on the staked plains, and many more were happening further south as enraged Indians raided the settlements. Everything that McBride had predicted was coming to pass.

Despite the war raging to the north, the LaPoint outfit was able to capture and train large remudas of good horses for all the drives heading north and west. The breeding of mustangs to stronger blood and larger horses was also yielding good results. Business continued unabated by the war, with even more horses being sold to the cavalry.

After the sale of the last of their horses at San Antonio in late July, they drove another herd of mixed cattle up through the staked plains for Mr. Winger, with the normal thunderstorms, stampedes, and paying for passage with beef to hungry tribes. The drive ended in September at the rail head in Dodge, which was crowded with herds from all over Texas.

When they got to Dodge that year, they swore it would be the last time they entered that stinking rowdy town. To LaPoint it was like the dreaded Helena across the river from the southern spread, but worse, the only improvement being that

LaPoint wasn't known there as a fast gun, inviting foolish bravados to draw on him like in Helena. The boom-town conditions there had only worsened with the increased hide gathering and buffalo slaughter combined with many more herds from Texas. Huge piles of hides waited beside bawling cattle for the train to take them away back east. The buzz around the hotels and saloons was of the Indian wars, with news of many buffalo hunters killed down south, including the big raid on the Adobe Walls post. There were constant gunfights and arrests in the town, and after getting paid and paying off the crew, Gabe and Josh left after only one day at the barber, bath, and saloon.

Chapter Eight: Palo Duro Battle

Heading due south at a rapid pace without pack animals, they took to discussing the Indian wars after riding in silence for several hours across the endless vista of grassland.

"Seems like all hell has broken loose, despite our trying to end this mess with the Red River battle. Do you think we should go help Mackenzie finish this thing off?" asked Gabe.

"If it means helping capture that butcher Maman-ti, yes. They're slaughtering freighters all the time now. To hell with him and his talking owl... these medicine men that are stirring up the remaining hostiles. I can understand them attacking the buffalo hunters, but they're making general war on everybody."

"I think we ought to finish what we started, end this damned war. Lead Mackenzie to the sons a bitches," said Gabe.

"Alright then, I feel the same, no use building a homestead to get burned out by raiders, let's swing by Adobe Walls and see what's going on, maybe pick up trails from there, after these rains."

"Might be as good a place as any ta start, ah reckon."

So they traveled fast and light on Scorpio and Buck, without being slowed down by pack animals. On the second day some dark clouds from the west brought rains to break the dry spell. They covered the distance in five days to the old fort at Adobe Walls, enjoying the freedom of the big sky country without bawling cattle to attend to. The grass was still thick near the playa lakes spread about, and water courses flowing from recent rains, so they often stopped to let the animals graze while they shared a pipe and sip of brandy and water. LaPoint scanned the plains with binoculars and noticed a lot of buffalo bones.

Finally the old adobe ruins, where Kit Carson had his battle a few years before, came in sight around a bend in the small stream. Finding little sign of activity there other than old tracks of unshod ponies, they moved upstream until they saw the gristly gnawed-on fly-specked heads of Indians stuck on posts around a crowd of ragged buildings, the more recent

Adobe Walls buffalo hunters' village. It was a sickening sight, the ramshackle jacales with broken mud chinking, full of bullet-holes, surrounded by the grisly trophies and black circles of vultures, which squabbled over landing on the heads.

"Damned buffalo hunters. Look what those savages have done. Hell, Comanches got nothing on them for gory," said Josh.

"Savage is right. They caused this as much as anybody, in my view. This was a war that didn't have to happen," said Gabe, disgusted and spitting on the ground.

"Aren't they all? Damn it all. Look at those rotting heads stuck up like the days of the Roman empire. They just got to show how damned savage they can be."

"More like on a Scottish castle. It's a sign to the Comanche. Indian can't go to happy hunting ground with his scalp or his head cut off."

"Yeah, so you told me before, but that's disgusting. They could dismember them without sticking the heads on poles to look at every day, not to mention the damned smell."

"It's war on savages with savage ways."

"Well I hate being on the same side as these curs."

"We're on the side of the settlers and the captives."

"Well, lets get it over with, then, by damn. I don't want to go any closer. Lets see if we can cut sign further south, maybe run into cavalry patrols and find out who is where and what for. Nothing but stinking hides and skinners here anyway. I really despise them, Gabe. This thing could have ended with the Red River battle if they hadn't moved down here for the buffalo slaughter. I don't blame the Comanche for trying to protect their only food source. Damn the government for not enforcing the Arkansas line!"

"I'm with ya thar, pard. But we got ta end this thing 'afore it erupts all along the frontier."

Disgusted by the sight of the rotting heads on posts, with red-headed ugly buzzards landing on them to pick the remaining rotten flesh, they veered south and cut for sign of war parties in the thick turf, moving steadily on without stopping, heading for the north fork of the Red River, where the engagement with Mow-way's band had occurred. Covering that distance in another long day, they found no sign of major encampments nor fresh trails, so they headed south the next sunrise, pushing their sturdy mounts without breaking down their stamina with lack of rest, water, and grazing. They cut sign for small bands of unshod horsemen several times, but continued south, into the wind. More rains blew by in the night, freshening the grass further as the long scorching summer drought ended with fall showers.

In two more days of hard riding they had reached the stunning sandstone canyons of the cap-rock near Quitaque, where they camped next to a sheer cliff of brilliant red as the sun set over a few grazing buffalo in the sheltered canyons. The wind from the south had increased, whipping and wailing around the red sandstone bluffs and boulders. If it weren't for the sense of danger from ambush, they would have enjoyed camping and relaxing there among the spectacular red cliffs and sheltered narrow canyons.

It was after the middle of September and a violent norther bearing sleet, hail, and driving rain blew in near morning, making them glad they had found a camp sheltered by the cliffs, as Indians had done for ages past. The hail came in on the horizontal for hours, keeping them awake with the shrieking wind and pelting ice pellets the size of cherries. After weathering the all night pounding of the norther under their robes and tarps, they made for Quitaque Canyon to gather some of the sweet water there, and in the grassy valley they encountered Col. Mackenzie and the 4th cavalry. Their camp was a quagmire of horse trodden mud, and loudmouthed mules.

The scout chief Henry Strong was glad to see them and asked them what they knew about trails of Indians, and possible campgrounds. He filled them in on the recent activities of the cavalry skirmishing with Comanches. They met with Mackenzie and agreed to scout for him and the 4th cavalry, to help end the war. They told him what they knew of the situation, what sign they had cut, and where they figured the major Indian encampments were.   He told them to get ready to lead the troops to the Comanche encampments again.

After they left the discussion with him they conferred in private while preparing their horses and gear.

"Listen Josh, like Mackenzie says, we're lead scouts now, and we could either lead him down to Kiwih-nai's band southwest of here on the headwaters of the Pease, which I don't know well, or we could take a chance and lead him up to the

Tule and the Palo Duro, whar I got a good hunch ole Maman-ti is hiding with Lone Wolf's Kiowa band and the last of those Cheyenne Arapahos and some renegades, maybe Comanches too."

"Yeah, that's what I figured you were thinking when I heard you agree and mention Palo Duro in the same breath. I'm for finding the Kiowas under Maman-ti and Lone Wolf, they're the ones doing all the raiding and slaughtering freighters. I got no quarrel with Kiwih-nai trying to drive the buffalo hunters back by attacking Adobe Walls anyway. The Quohadis are being driven out of the plains by a people more powerful than them, just like they drove the Apache out. I'd expect them to fight back. And those breaks on the upper Pease are full of hiding places."

"In those canyons they'll be ready to ambush and rub us out. I'd rather head north and find Lone Wolf and Maman-ti than break my word to Kiwih-nai and get scalped in the process. That's why I told the colonel about Palo Duro," said Gabe.

"If you think they're in that canyon, let's go there. And you've been there plenty of times, and can find it in the dark. I don't want to fight Kiwih-nai again. I could even find the Palo Duro now."

"Nor do I want to fight the Quohadis again. I knew several of those freighters on the Warren train, and I know that damned Maman-ti started this war with that raid and butchery. I want Mackenzie to find him. That damned Lone Wolf was with the bunch that tortured me, the way I recollect. They're my quarry now. This war can end if they quit raiding and bring in their captives."

"Exactly where do you think they'll be? Lots of long canyons nearby."

"With this cold winter coming in, my best guess is they'll be in the upper Palo Duro, up near the head, where the Blanco Canyon joins the Red River. They'll be thar processin' meat, like we saw them before. We'll lead Mackenzie and tha boys thar."

"Alrignt. I agree," said Josh. "Maman-ti is the main villain left, the way I see it. Him and Lone Wolf. Let's take them to Palo Duro, if you think that's where those two are."

"I do. It's always these danged medicine men, craving to make a name for themselves, that causes this mischief. They got no more chance of beating the whites than a hog dancin' on ice," said Gabe.

"Seems that way. Zealots cause wars. Pragmatic men have to win them."

"Pneumatic?"

"Pragmatic. Guys who figure out the particular situation with common sense and use tactics that work."

"That'd be Mackenzie, I expect, 'cording to your notion?" queried Gabe.

"Yeah. And us, leading him to them. I hope you know the way from here, I'm not sure with all these canyons, which way to the Tule...though I know Palo Duro is north of there about twenty five miles."

"Oh yeah, I know the way, from the old days of peaceful trading. Got a lot of fine buffalo robes round here, old days. They called this the valley of tears, I guess for all the captives that was traded here. Dang, I regret it's come to this danged all out war again," said Gabe as he sharpened his knife.

"Well, I thought the Red River battle would be enough to end this, but lets get it over with. It will never stop until the raiders know we can find them and destroy their villages. Maybe one more army attack will convince them. If they don't stop raiding, Sherman and Sheridan will wipe out their whole race, all the plains people. The best thing that can come out of this is that we destroy the raiders' stronghold, and that the Quohadis get to live free on the buffalo."

"The raiding ain't gonna stop until Maman-ti and Lone Wolf are dead. We got to put them under while the Quohadis makes their own way."

"Alright then, we lead them to first to Tule Canyon, then Palo Duro, near the head where we saw that huge encampment before. We'll use John'son to relay messages," said Gabe.

"Better eat up and grain the horses while we can, eh?"

"Yep. I'll get us some grub and meet you at the picket line," replied Gabe. After taking care of provisions for the morning and rubbing down the horses in a sheltered niche in the rocks, they strung up a tarp and slept under it with a shared buffalo robe, sleeping the sound sleep of the extremely weary. As usual Gabe was up at dawn making biscuits, which they ate early. There was something very comforting about those sourdough biscuits before heading out for battle.

At six the next morning, September 19, 1874, in brisk cool air, they ascended the Quitaque Canyon up onto the staked plains, with the blue-clad troopers behind in a long double line. The grasslands past the rocky ascent were yellow against a blue sky with clouds scudding across it at high speed. The pennants of the 4th Cavalry fluttered in the stiff breeze as the soldiers walked their mounts up the incline. Many of the mounts were geldings delivered by the LaPoint outfit, personally turned into saddle mounts by Josh. The ground was soaked and slowed the progress of the wagons, the mules protesting with their brays and snorts, some resorting to kicking in the traces. Sergeant Lawton's voice could be heard yelling at them over the popping of whips as his wagons sunk into deep ruts. The men were singing some tune about "Come back John, come back to your chickadee," while the wind increased from the south.

"What tha hell them soldier boys singin' 'bout, Chickadee?" asked Gabe as he pulled on his pipe and watched the troopers trudge in a long column up the hill.

LaPoint chuckled. "Chickadee something or other. Not too sure what it has to do with fighting Comanches.

"Wal that's every rider's dream, huh? A little chickadee waiting at the ranch house door."

"Maybe so, I know it's mine. Let's mount up and move on ahead of all this quagmire. They are churning it to a soup on that incline."

"Alright, one last time, going out for Comanches," said Gabe McBride, as he put his pipe away and mounted his warhorse.

"Yeah, that's what we said last time, if I recall correctly." LaPoint led off up the hill on his quick-footed stallion, and McBride stayed right behind him on Buck, as they passed the column and went ahead to scout.

The two scouts rode together, often up to several miles out in front of the columns, but within sight with field glasses. The army traveled in a northwesterly direction, stopping for a noontime lunch break, then heading for the Tule Canyon, where Gabe and Josh were leading them, signaling back all day with mirrors and small smoky short-lived fires. The Tonkawa and Seminole scouts ranged out wide and reported back to Gabe and Josh every hour. The slow moving blue columns followed flashes of mirrored light and tiny pillars of smoke across the

230

trackless grassy plain. Some of the outlying scouts ran into roving parties of warriors, probably Comanches, and engaged with them. The well mounted Indians led them on wild chases and disappeared, only to attack them as they rode back. A pattern of constant harassment developed and continued throughout the afternoon, twilight, and night, with arrows and bullets coming in out of the darkness. The hours dragged on, full of constant danger and harassment as the breeze from the south grew into a light gale.

The unpredictable weather turned against them, and on the 24th of September, after more running skirmishes on all sides but no real engagements, another fierce norther struck them, bogging them down in a muddy encampment. The supply mules and wagons had a hellish time, slogging in the mud. Sergeant Lawton displayed great drive and ingenuity in keeping them moving, at times using lots of horses and ropes to assist traversing gullies and muddy bottoms. Comanche skirmishers made attacks on the wings while the troopers were distracted with hauling the wagons out of bogs. Finally the column moved ahead of the provisions train, which was moving at a snail's pace in the deep mud. Gabe worried that separating could lead to an attack on the supply train, but wasn't about to tell Mackenzie how to do his job. The colonel was suffering from recent wounds suffered in Mexico, and the gyp-water scours, and was not in a good mood, so after a brief conference with him, McBride and LaPoint returned to the field, looking for the best route to Tule Canyon.

After another dreary day of muddy slogging the column made it to Tule Canyon, and camped at the head of it, down out of the wind. Captain McLaughlen had been ranging about the columns with patrols and scouts, engaging Comanches but then losing them as they scattered. Sergeant Lawton and the wagons were many hours behind, slogging forward slowly. Gabe and Josh worried about the supply train getting attacked without much protection, but didn't dare to tell Mackenzie his business. The traveling up and down muddy slopes had everyone and their horses exhausted, but unable to rest for fear of attack. Mackenzie kept plenty of scouts all around his command.

Early on the 25th Josh and Gabe went out to look for the main body of Indians while the troop improved the encampment at the Tule Canyon and rested, drying out their gear in the cool north breeze. That night while the scouts were out searching, the Comanches struck the camp at the Tule Canyon, trying to steal the horses. This time Mackenzie had them so well staked to the ground with double ropes to deep pins, that they did not bolt into the darkness as before. Running and standing fights went on all night as the Indians tried to obtain the army horses, with no success. The colonel had learned adjusted.

Mackenzie had learned his lessons well, and maintained his horse herd. The firing went on all night, but no horses were lost to stampeding Comanches. Arrows came flying in out of the dark sky. Rations were reduced to hardtack biscuits as the supply train was still south, bogged in the mud and crawling along. Nobody could catch any real sleep with the constant sniping from the darkness. In the middle of the fight the provisions train came in, undisturbed by the Indians, to the amazement of all. Lawton's luck, they called it as more dry biscuits and ammo were passed out.

Still the sniping continued, and nobody was able to sleep that night, nor to recover the lost sleep when the norther had caught them the night before. Weariness piled up on the sleepy men in blue, and gave them the red-eyed staggers. Gabe was one of the few that could sleep through the random fuselage. LaPoint kept the horses pulled against a canyon wall to protect them from the arrows arching in through the dark night.

The Tule Canyon encampment was soon full of droopy eyed slow moving troopers, black and white, and Mackenzie drove them on to continue engaging and pursuing the remaining Indians, and to return fire at any flash in the predawn darkness, when he suspected a big attack. The Indian attackers came at them from one side, and then another, and all the soldiers could do was pour fire at their positions, while the Tonkawas led riders in circles after the mobile raiders. It was the nearly silent arrows arching into the soldiers camp that were the worst, burying their rusty barrel hoop steel points into things or people with a last second hiss and thud. Occasionally one would land in horseflesh and set off a round of screaming until somebody tended to it. It was an unnerving situation all night long, and the hours drug until daylight, when the attacks ceased.

In the morning the scouting parties sent out to reconnoiter counted fifteen dead warriors, and only three army

232

horses were lost to wounds. There were a variety of minor injuries to troopers, but none serious enough to incapacitate. That encouraged the exhausted men somewhat, with Sergeants Charlton and Williams pumping them up. Only a few troopers had been wounded by the firing through the night, and the other side had paid dearly. After another meeting with Mackenzie, LaPoint and McBride galloped out to investigate the tracks of the various groups of riders, and see where they led to. The Tonkawa scout John'son lit out after them when he learned they had gone.

Then under Mackenzie's command the other scouts fanned out to guard the camp so the men could rest, for the weary troopers in it were passing out. The scouts made a protective perimeter guard around the entire body of troopers, with mounted outriders. The soldiers and horses were rested until 3pm, when Gabe and Josh came rushing into camp, followed at a one mile distance by John'son, whose gelding could not keep up with their stallions. They were thirsty, hungry, and stiff from constant riding, but had important news to deliver after drinking, taking a few bites of army grub, and having their horses tended to.

They asked for and were given an immediate parlay with Thompson, civilian scout leader, and then with Col. Mackenzie. They reported the details of their scouting, that they had crossed trails too numerous to count, both horse herds and lodge-poles trails, all leading to the western end of the Palo Duro Canyon, so they had crept to the southern edge and seen a long series of camps stretching along the bottom of the canyon.

Mackenzie was impressed and satisfied with the information, and made his plan. They had informed him the main concentration of Indians was nearly due north of the Tule Canyon encampment, only twenty five miles away, and that the night attackers and raider feints to the east were meant to draw him away from the big village at the Palo Duro.

Mackenzie asked them if they were too tired to lead him back right away. They said they were ready, after some more food and feed for their horses. They went to the mess wagons and stuffed themselves with hardtack and coffee, after making sure their horses were taken care of. LaPoint acquired a pan of hot water and scissors from the mess corporal, and proceeded to cut his beard and shave his face. Then he changed his wool shirt to buckskin, put on moccasins and a headband over his long hair with a braid in back, and he looked Indian. Then he borrowed an army kerchief to wear around his neck, but stuffed it into his buckskin pocket.

After eating they went to examine the horses, and they debated whether to ride other mounts rather than possibly damage their worn out stallions. But because of the battle-fighting abilities of their stallions and the uncertainties associated with leaving them behind, they chose to stick with them for the battle, but to take extra mounts to rest them. Both of them had pretty well decided that if the Comanches were to steal their stallions, it would be over their dead bodies, not some sleeping Tonkawa guard.

An hour later Gabe, Josh, Johnson, and Sergeant Charlton were walking towards their mounts when big Jack Charlton asked Gabe if he still had his battered bugle.

"Yep, shore do Jack, got it in my saddle bags thar."

"Well, why don't you blow it after you hear our bugler sound charge, like ya done at Mow-way's. The bugler is old Henry Hard, and he's real fussy about the right notes, so it oughta get his goat if you blast a couple after he's done. He got pretty miffed about that bawling you did at Mow-ways with it. You remember him, we was drinking with him at San Angelena."

"I thought it was San Angela?"

"I've heard it called both by the troopers I met drinkin' thar. What does it mean, anyway?"

"Holy angels, I guess," said LaPoint.

"Some band of angels," said Gabe. "More like Celtic warriors. You gonna bugle the start of this march?"

"Yes. Mackenzie's orders. He wants to make sure the Comanches see us riding southwest up the canyon, to fool them that we're retreating, then turn north later. That's why he pulled the guard back in."

"Damn, he acts more like a Comanche every day."

"Yeah, him and your pal LaPoint both. Good thing he's wearing that army bandanna, thought he was a Comanche for a second or two."

"What about the grumpy Colonel now? You sure he ain't gonna wring my ass out for it?"

"Hell no. He said to tell you to do it for good luck, like Mow-way's village. Beaumont too, they both said to tell old

Gabriel to blow his horn. The Colonel was almost smiling about it. It'll give you a chance to show how you've improved with your playing, and piss ole Henry off, which I love to do."

"Wal, I've improved the volume, I could say....but the buttons don't work right, so it ain't much better than a cow horn."

"Oh no, here come some notes as sour as wet buckskins," said Josh as he tightened the girth on Scorpio. "About the only thing he can play on it is..."waugh".

"Yeah, I always wondered what that means," said Charlton.

"It means the bear has indigestion, I think," replied Josh.

"Bear farts through a trumpet, huh? Just what these varmints need," said Charlton. "Gabriel blowing his horn."

Gabe began digging through his saddlebags for the old bugle, found it, and hung it on his saddle horn by the leather thong.

"Might be the end of their time out here," said Josh. "Maybe us too, if we don't watch out."

"When in doubt, fight harder, eh Jack?" asked Gabe.

"That's it," said Jack. "Let's get it done, boys."

They mounted and moved a mile or so ahead as the column rode slowly with much fanfare and yelling and bugling southwest up the Tule Canyon. They all started singing "Come back John, Come back to your chick a bi dee...."

"Gol-dang I'm already tired of that song, and I've been with these guys just a few days."

"Well, just don't think you're going to keep playing that damned bugle when this is over. I'm going to shoot it."

"Might improve it. Tell ya what, I'll not play it again if you sing that Chick-a-biddy song, come home Josh, come on home..."

"Hush up and ride, ya ole coot, and don't get shot."

"I intend ta avoid it, and ya better hope no trooper shoots ya for an Indian in that getup."

After a few hours they paused briefly at the head of the canyon, waiting for twilight, then rose out of it and slowly made a sweep to the north as the sunset light faltered and a cool dusk set in.

Then they made a long march through the starlit darkness towards the much larger Palo Duro Canyon, led by Gabe, Josh, and John'son the stone-faced Tonkawa, by that

235

time all painted and primed for battle. He even offered LaPoint some war paint when he saw him dressed in buckskins without his customary wide straw hat. So Josh made a few marks with his fingers dipped in red and black, around his eyes, with a dot in between them. Then he opened his saddlebags and fetched three soft deerskin headbands with diamondback rattler skins sewed on them, tying one around his head, and giving the others to Gabe and John'son, who did the same. They left their wide-brimmed hats with the supply wagons.

John'son couldn't have been happier with the rattlesnake sash, which he tied across his shoulder and chest. He strutted proudly around in his completed war regalia, then ran to leap on his war horse from the rear, circling the horse around urging the two scouts to hurry. Ever since they first met John'son years before, he had been obsessed with killing some Comanches. His first request to them at that time had been to help him get a job scouting for the rangers to go kill Comanches. He had moved up to scouting for the Army, all with the goal of killing Comanches in mind. He wore a weapons belt with Colt .44 pistol, knife, and tomahawk, with carbine in his army saddle holster. With his face painted with red and black stripes, the top hat festooned with eagle feathers, and his clothing a mixture of Indian and cavalry castoffs, John'son presented quite a sight.

They still had the bow and arrow set he had traded to Gabe for the top-hat, which the Tonkawa scout was wearing with a leather chin strap. LaPoint looped the bow on his shoulder and mounted, with Scorpio showing some excitement and pawing the dirt in place.

Gabe looked at John'son, then turned to Josh and said, "Hell, don't he make ya feel under-dressed for the party?"

"No, I feel about right, being it's my first war paint, didn't want to overdo it and look like a greenhorn. You look great in that snake headband, covers your scar nicely, you should model it in town sometime."

"Yeah, so do you. I told Rosita these little skins would never sell as headbands, but you know what, they work pretty good. These and the buckskins and moccasins got us looking like Indians in dim light. Beats clomping down that deer-trail in boots and spurs with a big hat to let everyone know it's a white man."

"I dreamed we'd have to do this, and slip down a tiny trail and silence the sentries."

"Wal, let's go before John'son wears a hole under that horse circling around."

The stars gave these scouts all the guideposts they needed on the vast trackless plain. The ground was table flat and covered with wiry mesquite grass, the only danger being prairie dog holes and the chance of Comanche scouts. They skirted and flushed a bunch of coyotes near the side canyons. By the time the first dim light of dawn was skirting the eastern sky, they had come to the edge of the great canyon and smelled the abundant smoke of many lodges burning mesquite, juniper, and other driftwood in their lodge-fires. They could see the water of the Red River glistening in the middle of the valley below where the Blanca creek joined it, and the dark cones of lodges stretching endlessly along the flat floor of the canyon.

Gabe lay on the rim with his telescope and memorized the entire layout of the camp while John'son lay beside him in a fevered excitement. LaPoint searched the rim until he found tracks leading to a switchback trail down into the valley, and he crept down with the Tonkawa weapons of stealth for ten minutes to see if the horses could get down it. Returning out of breath, he told Gabe that the cavalry could make it down, but would have to lead and walk the horses in a single line. When he mounted Scorpio, he noticed his stallion was favoring one side, and he switched to his extra mount to rest his loyal warhorse. They walked the horses back from the rim a hundred yards and sensed direction by the stars, then took off at a canter.

They rode back several miles and found the main column camped and resting their horses in a bare and grass-less spot, the men weary from lack of sleep and constant riding through the darkness. John'son rode alongside, over-excited, escorting them in.

Riding up to Colonel Mackenzie and Captain Beaumont, they dismounted and went to give the news. Mackenzie paced forward and looked expectantly at them.

"LaPoint. I thought you were a Tonkawa scout, and I could not figure which one. Never saw you without your hat before. You look like an Indian. Rattlesnake headbands to boot."

"Sorry sir, but I had a hunch it might come in handy when we go for the sentries."

"Good idea, I mistook both you and McBride for Indian scouts...what's your news?"

"Colonel Mackenzie, sir," said LaPoint. "The main concentration of lodges and horses is about three miles north of here, in the Palo Duro where the Blanco Canyon joins it. That's the place to strike the horse herd, in the delta between the two streams."

"Time to give 'em hell, Colonel, and get that horse herd," said Gabe.

John'son spoke up from the side. "Palo Duro, correcto General Big Chief. Plenty Comanche. Plenty horses."

"Shut-up Johnson," barked the Colonel. "LaPoint. where is the main entrance where they take herds down?"

"At the east end, a slope coming up south," replied LaPoint. "But it's well guarded with plenty of riders. We found a trail down at this other spot, due north of here...and I made it nearly all the way down on foot without spotting sentries. We could best sneak down there and surprise them."

"Can we get the columns down there, with horses, LaPoint?"

"I think so," replied LaPoint, "but it will be leading horses single file for most of the way. All of the way, actually. It'd be best not to use mares, to keep down the noise of nickering, for there's stallions in the Indian herds...., put geldings first, sir."

"Are you ready to lead us down?"

"John'son lead," said the scout.

"Shut up, John'son," barked the Colonel.

"Yes-sir. Sooner the better, since it is almost light enough to see the ground now. I want Gabe with me, though. He knows their ways better than anyone, and we may have to knife some sentries near the bottom. Or shoot them with a bow and arrow for silence. Keep John'son here with the horses, out of our way. He's been bird-dogging us too close. He's anxious to get credit so he can get a bunch of horses and get married, is what Gabe thinks. And he's anxious to butcher and scalp."

"Alright, get some water for yourselves and your mounts, then lead us to the rim as quiet as possible."

Gabe spoke up then. "Alright sir. How about letting Sergeant Charlton lead Captain Beaumont's men down first, sir?

He's got the long legs to navigate it, and thar's no backin' up when he leads the fightin'. We might need to string some rope at some places, and he's big and strong to help with all that. Have him pick the first group to come down."

"And keep John'son back out of the way."

"Yeah," said Gabe. "We don't want John'son, we want Charlton."

"Alright, my choice as well, with as many of the scouts as we can round up, with Thompson leading them down after the first troopers and horses, Charlton's squad. You men have to silence the sentries, and take Charlton to overpower them if you need to."

"Alright then, let's finish this," said Josh.

Mackenzie moved to the side, alone with LaPoint, for a short parley.

"You have no idea how many nights I have bad dreams of the soldiers I have lost in battle, LaPoint. They wonder why I stay up all night, looking at maps. It's better than dreaming of men I led to their death. Please help me keep from getting my men wiped out in this risky venture. Secrecy is of the utmost necessity until we get ready to charge. You have to silence the sentries, or we could get wiped out."

"I realize that Colonel, and I think I've seen how to do it. We'll get the job done, Sir."

Both Josh and Gabe grabbed extra knives and sheathes for the trip down, as well as riatas. Josh strung the Tonkawa bow and got the arrow quiver ready. When they got to the rim they crept up to it with Sergeant Jack Charlton just as the sunrise was turning the eastern sky orange and pink, revealing the cream and red and yellow of the canyon walls. It was a surprising and awesome sight, this deep canyon through the flat tabletop grasslands of the staked plains, a great red ditch full of cedars, mesquite, cottonwoods, and willows. A perfect home in the deep cleft of the high plains to winter the howling northers and hide from the cavalry, sheltered by tall eroded cliff walls.

As the daylight dawned they saw that it was a larger village in the canyon than they had realized earlier in the dark, the lodges stretching as far as they could see in both directions, with hundreds of horses grazing the grassy bottom-land. The sunrise had revealed the bright multiple colors of the canyon, the crumbling cap-rock of white and gray, underlain with loose rock of rusty red color, then yellow and gray, then dark orange with strips of white and green gypsum running through it at various levels, revealing the rock that tainted the water on the plains. The bottom was full of scattered small mesquites, cedars, cottonwood, and willows by the stream deltas and the running water from the braided steam. There were lots of scattered lodges of all sizes and decorations, and a massive horse herd. LaPoint studied the trail down from a bluff opposite the switchback, looking for sentries. He spied two sleeping near the bottom, and felt a strong memory flash from his dream of the night before.

He told Gabe the exact locations of the sentries, waited for him to change from boots to moccasins, and then together they crept down the trail, keeping low to avoid detection and falling on the slippery weathered rock. Half the time they were on their hands and knees, or sliding down on their butts, to stay out of sight. Josh carried the bow he had practiced with years ago as well as his usual weapons. The arrows were all dipped in deadly coral snake poison.

It took about thirty minutes for them to creep down the several hundred feet to where the sentries slept, leaning against boulders, about halfway down. When they got there they both took a sentry and crept up behind them on the ground. When LaPoint saw Gabe in position he tackled the sentry from behind and got his powerful forearm around the man's neck, jerking his chin up to stifle his grunt, then slicing the side of his throat and across to the other side.

Gabe caught the other sentry with his forearm around the head and cracked his neck, laying him flat in the dirt, finished. Then both lunged with the limp Comanches into a clump of cedar bushes, and laid low under their branches to see if anyone heard the slight commotion.

Gabe was panting hard after the exertion, and LaPoint stood up to get a good look around, viewing a scene that seemed familiar. He felt a strange detachment, as if watching himself from above. He closed his eyes while Gabe was catching his breath and saw the lean face of an Indian medicine man with bulging eyes, looking at him. He remembered feeling the same in his dream, and his mind moved ahead to his next job. They rested for a while to calm their breathing and settle their nerves, while both felt as if they were being watched. They saw nobody stirring in the villages.

Then LaPoint hustled back up the trail to bring the scouts and first troopers down, while Gabe hid the bodies further back under mesquite trees and cedar bushes. When LaPoint approached the top of the long steep trail, he was panting, and paused gasping for air before swinging up onto the cap-rock. A bright green lizard about ten inches long, glistening iridescent in the morning sunlight as the great orange ball topped the eastern rim of the canyon and lit the colored walls, paused on the trail in front of him and stared at him. The calm unmoving reptile looked so beautiful there in the rising sunlight that Josh paused and stared at it for a moment, catching his wind. He felt a knot rising on his forehead where he had bumped heads with the sentry in the collision. It was throbbing, and the quick climb had him a bit dizzy, so he closed his eyes and again saw the fierce face of an Indian medicine man in full regalia looking at him. He felt the bump to see if he was bleeding, but it was under the rattlesnake headband.

Then he took a deep breath, jumped up and climbed the cap-rock on his knees, seeing the scouts a ways back when he did. He reached down and helped Gabe, who had come up behind him, to climb the thick and crumbling capstone. The soldiers up top were startled by his sudden appearance, and almost fired, for Josh looked more like an Indian than a soldier, with buckskins, moccasins, his hat replaced with headband, and the army bandanna in his pocket. The bow and arrow quiver were strung over his shoulder, and John'son pointed to them and began talking, which LaPoint ignored to go and talk to Scout chief Thompson and Sergeant Charlton.

Thompson and the scouts were ready, and he led them down the trail, each leading his horse behind him, a quiet line of soldiers shushing their mounts as they found their way over the crumbling colored dirt. Jack Charlton led the troopers down behind the scouts. Each trooper gave a startled and stifled exclamations of awe at the depth of the canyon and the size of the Indian village when he reached the rim. The next gasp was when they saw the tiny trail they were supposed to descend on. For horses and men used to the flat tabletop, it was a frightening sight, and the trail was very narrow as if made by deer or buffalo. The horses went only unwillingly, with constant urging

241

forward on the slippery multi-hued scree. The soldiers were wary but willing, and the long line moved slowly down the canyon wall.

It took about forty five minutes for each to reach the bottom, where they began to form up in attack lines, most holding the noses of their horses to quiet them. When the last of Captain Beaumont's company mounted up, an old Indian coming out of his lodge to piss spotted the soldiers, ran back to his lodge, and fired a shot out the entryway, then disappeared back inside.

Fearing more rifle shots would alert the sleeping villages, Gabe and LaPoint ran to his lodge to finish him off with knives or the silent bow and arrow. Dismounting in a hurry and cutting through the back of the lodge, they found him squatting down putting on war paint with both hands, so Josh shot him with the poisoned arrow from eight feet away, driving it into his chest near the heart. Gabe crawled inside and clamped a big hand on his mouth while he slit the juggler and held him as the old warrior quivered and died while his blood squirted from the neck slice. Although they accomplished this without much noise, they fully expected to be stormed by warriors who had heard his carbine shot at any second. Peering out from under the edge of the tepee, they looked for the best escape routes while the Indian's body did some spasms from the coral snake poison. Surprisingly, no general alarm was raised in the village, though they saw some woman scurrying about near the closest lodge circle.

LaPoint took the Tonkawa bow and arrows and they moved up the valley to where two braves were guarding about a dozen horses. The braves were on either side of the herd, so Josh crept up close in the cedar brush near the stream-bed until he was twenty yards away from the nearest one. With the bow he shot the man in the chest, knocking him backward from his horse, then scurried over to knife him to death across the throat and then into the heart, giving him a quick warrior's death.

Creeping around to the other side, LaPoint did the same to the other night-guard with the bow, sending an arrow into his chest. When he got to the downed warrior by crawling through the grass, he saw it was a young man about Jesse's age, probably part Mexican from his looks, and that the poison had killed him already.

242

LaPoint drew a sigh of relief, for he still heard no general alarm as he slipped back from bush to bush towards Gabe. Removing these sentries silently had cleared the way for the columns to form up into battle formation unseen on the reddish dust of the valley floor. By that time there were enough troopers to form a good first line and their confidence began to grow. The two scouts watched from the bushes, alert for the next problem to develop. Some scattered horses came by and they used their lariats to rope two and secure them under mesquite trees. They both put bright army bandannas back around their necks and heads, as the Tonkawa scouts did, to keep from getting shot in their buckskins.

"We ain't in the best of situations, with strange horses ta ride if we got to," said Gabe from under the cedar bush.

"I know. I wish we had our stallions. Let's just lay low unless we're needed."

The soldiers on the narrow trail down began hustling to reach the bottom while the men with Charlton's squad below mounted up to charge. The sunlight hitting the tall wall of the canyon revealed a long line of blue troopers and their dark mounts carefully stepping and sometimes sliding down the narrow trail, then forming up quickly at the bottom. A cloud of pink dust rose from the horses hooves as they clamored and slid down the steep narrow trail. Seeing a blue line of troopers forming up amidst the huge Indian village was an ironic and amazing sight to the scouts. Not too many Indians seemed to be stirring yet, despite the carbine shot from the old man. Charlton kept busy, getting his troopers lined up in a charging formation, as Mackenzie showed up and began hissing orders.

Gabe and Josh were flabbergasted that the alarm had not been spread after that rifle shot. They hid under the bush and watched the soldiers form up under Charlton's direction. Soon there were two lines of troopers mounted and ready to charge, and some yelling was heard upstream after the army mounts began making noise in their excitement.

Mackenzie saw it was time to charge and gave the order to Beaumont, who passed it on. Henry Hard the bugler sounded a charge and the line of blue troopers rushed forward, shocking the villagers into panic, with people running in every direction. Charlton was soon on the leading edge of the fighting, firing his carbine at every warrior who showed his face.

243

Mackenzie led the charge upstream with curved saber drawn and voice yelling along with the bugle, while the men yelled in return, scattering people in front of them. Gabe and LaPoint hid in the bushes and watched the battle unfold, not anxious to join in the killing. But they both watched for chiefs, hoping to see Maman-ti or Lone Wolf to take them down. The troopers were selective in firing their carbines, trying to cut down all the warriors as the women and children dove into hiding and the braves stepped up to defend the village. Soon the warriors were returning fire from the cover of boulders and cedar bushes.

On Colonel Mackenzie's command they made a long charge through the villages, with one column going after the horse herd. The scouts went after the herders and the sentinels on the stream, who began rifle fire as the columns charged upstream. Puffs of smoke began to sprout from behind boulder piles near the canyon walls as Indian snipers used their carbines on the charging line of troopers and the others forming up behind them. LaPoint directed army sharpshooters to their locations and points where the snipers could be fired upon. Men and horses were rushing down the tiny trail and raising a cloud of pink dust in the sunrise.

Each column charged as soon as they formed up, attacking different parts of the villages. The rest came hustling down the trail, the red dust flying from the sliding dirt as they hurried down the layered red canyon walls, surprise being no longer a factor. Clouds of dust and gun smoke were erupting everywhere as the noise increased, with yells, gunshots, and the women keening and shrieking.

Warriors found red sandstone boulders along the canyon walls to hide behind and shoot. The horses coming down the trail were neighing and whinnying in fear as the soldiers tugged their reins to hurry them through the rising cloud of pink-orange dust. If Indian shooters had gotten close, they could have easily picked off all the men snaking down that narrow trail. Mackenzie ordered men to guard both the bottom and the top of the trail with carbines. Mules with extra ammo had made it down the trail by then, and runners were distributing it to the rings of riflemen so they could pour a heavy fire at the scattered Indians. Volleys of arrows began arching in towards the bottom of the trail, and Gabe led some sharpshooters to where they could draw beads on the bowmen.

More troopers on the bottom meant another charge upstream to reinforce the front lines bogged in heavy fighting. Panic struck the buffalo-skinned tepees and people were bursting in terror and anger from every lodge circle as the additional troops charged upstream, the warriors firing their weapons while the woman ran to climb the opposite wall of the canyon and hide in boulder fields or amidst the mesquite and juniper bushes. Shrieks, angry war whoops, and the shrill keening of the women mixed with the shouts of officers and soldiers and the constant carbine fire. The battle raged on as riflemen from both sides fired from cover and the charging columns pushed upstream.

A large group of warriors were making a determined stand up the bend in the cliffs of Blanca canyon, regrouping there and charging back on mustang war ponies while their fellows unleashed barrages of arrows arching towards the mounted soldiers. Mackenzie rushed to take charge of those assaults, followed by about twenty troopers on dark geldings. Henry Hard the bugler sat tall to blow another charge and was hit by a rifle slug in the stomach, knocking him off his horse. Some green troopers began to panic then, yelling, "How are we gonna get out of here?"

Colonel Mackenzie paused firing his weapon long enough to yell, "I brought you in, and by God, I'll lead you out, sir. Keep fighting! And stay behind cover until we charge, Charlton, pull those men back, damn-it. Surgeon, attend to that bugler!"

Sergeant Charlton was so engaged in exchanging rapid carbine fire with an Indian sniper that he raced forward from boulder to boulder until he got close enough to kill the sniper, then he raced back on his long legs, only to get yelled at by the Colonel. He reloaded and kept firing from cover, while Mackenzie moved on to guide the battle.

There was enough cover in the valley to avoid the loss of many men, but the same cover helped the Indians escape while taking continual potshots at the troopers. By the time the third column charged the village, it was practically abandoned by fleeing occupants, many of them running upstream while warriors skirmished with the troopers behind them. The ground was littered with their possessions and tons of meat and hides that were being processed.

When Mackenzie came riding back after leading that charge, he saw troopers trying to scale the valley walls in pursuit of the snipers hidden in the rocks there. The men were exposed to sniper fire, with their carbines slung on their backs, and bullets were pinging from the rocks nearby.

Mackenzie shouted above the din. "Who sent those men up there? They'll all be killed in no time, order them back here to fire from cover! You men pour fire at those snipers so they can make it back. Look sir, see those puffs of smoke, pour fire into there, volley after volley, and get those men back alive." Then he rode on to direct another charge at the heavy resistance upstream and help direct the capture of the horse herd.

That had been his primary objective in this raid, to put the remaining hostiles on foot and burn the village. To that end he kept sending available mounted troopers in whichever direction necessary. Mackenzie wanted no repeat of the Mow-way village battle, where the Fourth Cavalry had won the day, but lost the horses at night. The two scouts took that opportunity to go and help round up the herd on Indian ponies, with their yellow bandannas showing around their necks.

About forty minutes into the battle LaPoint spotted a mounted group of warriors moving south along the rim to the spot where the troopers had come down. Realizing that Scorpio and Buck were kept there by a small group of troopers, Josh rode to notify a scout, who reported to Mackenzie with the news. Quickly the colonel sent a detachment to defend their only route of escape if the battle turned sour on them. That action sent the mounted warriors scurrying back south along the rim, and fighting began to diminish as warriors ascended the north canyon wall and fled. Within two hours the fighting had died down and most of the Indians had retreated. It was impossible to chase them with the cavalry horses down in the canyon floor, so attention was then given to destroying the villages.

Inside the lodges the troopers and scouts found large supplies of government flour, sugar, and coffee, and ammunition for carbines from Fort Sill. Different bands were represented by the artwork in and on the lodges, Comanche, Kiowa, and Cheyenne/Arapaho. Many Texas brands were scattered throughout the huge horse herd, as well as native mustangs without shoes or brands. There were Indians still fleeing

246

through the brush and boulders, climbing up the walls of the canyon, and fleeing upstream to escape, while warriors made desperate stands to protect their escape, firing pistols and rifles as well as arrows. Pops of sniper fire came from the wall of the canyon opposite where the troopers came down, for huge broken pieces of the cap-rock had tumbled down there and provided cover. Many of the bushes and clumps of mesquite hid Indians waiting for the chance to flee.

Despite the constant sniper fire, the horse herd was finally surrounded and captured by A. company, with the assistance of several scouts riding with Gabe and LaPoint, who were both bareback, riding Indian horses. The two scouts rode southwest up the side canyon of the Blanca creek, looking for the route where the horse herd could be driven up out of the canyon before the Comanches regrouped. It was easy to find the well beaten track that followed a mild slope to the southeast.

After surrounding and controlling the horses with the aid of the valley walls, the troopers and scouts began to drive them back to the wide spot in the valley where they had been grazing, and the fighting was then least intense. With Indians now firing from behind the boulders at higher elevations than the troopers, many men were still pinned down by fire from many directions, but very few were being hit.

There was one group of Indians upstream, hiding behind a turn in the cliff, then charging out and attacking on horseback. LaPoint borrowed a Spencer rifle from a trooper and set up on a flat boulder with a rest, as did Gabe. Together they began to pick off the warriors every time they came out from behind the cliff. After taking down five warriors, the scouts saw no more forays from the others. They stayed in place while troopers charged the position on horseback and found it empty, except for two bodies on the ground, and marks where the warriors had picked up the other bodies and carried them away.

The Comanches and Kiowa lacked the discipline that Mackenzie had instilled in his 4th Cavalry soldiers, and with his fierce and determined leadership, the soldiers held their own without many casualties, out-shooting the Indians with more ammo and better accuracy. The fact that the horse-herd was kept from the warriors, for the most part, meant the Indians could not mount deadly counter-attacks in their usual style. In both of his village raids, Colonel Mackenzie made certain to take the horse herd away from the warriors.

The fighting continued in scattered bursts with bullets flying everywhere as Indians fled in all directions, firing as they went. Many made a strategic covered retreat to the northwestern entrance of the canyons, with warriors hiding behind boulders and firing at the troops as others mounted horses and escaped. Several attempts were made to recapture the horse herd by desperate mounted groups of warriors, but LaPoint and Gabe, along with the other scouts and troopers, poured a withering rifle fire into the Indians and held them off. The warriors carried off their wounded and dead, so it was impossible to see the death toll of the battle.

The battle raged all morning and into the afternoon, with flareups in different places at the Indians regrouped and tried to strike back at the soldiers and regain the herd. LaPoint and Gabe were pinned into protecting the herd during the whole battle and did not know how the main battle was faring until afternoon, when they rejoined the main body under Mackenzie, after finally getting enough help to drive the herd back. They informed Mackenzie about the cleared way to the southeast to drive the horse herd out of the canyon. Then they joined soldiers in feasting on the dried buffalo meat.

By that time the snipers near the villages had been driven back enough to start fires of the dry lodge-poles and buffalo grease, layered with firewood and brush and then skins and winter meat. Billowing clouds of yellow smoke were rising from these fires as Mackenzie directed operations, riding up and down the valley, well on his way to his objectives of capturing the horses and destroying the village and food stocks for winter.

With fires going near every lodge circle, the soldiers started burning everything while LaPoint and Gabe began to organize drovers to get the horse herd up the steep trail out of the canyon. The columns of smoke from lodge-pole and mesquite fires turned dark with the roasting hides and meat and clothing piled on, and the stench was overpowering at times. Riding fast up various gulleys in the Blanco Canyon, they led the horse drovers with the herd towards the southwest slope out of the canyon. The sound made by the massive horse herd was a low rumble like thunder from an approaching storm. The acrid stinking smoke from the stinking fires assaulted their nostrils on their way up the slope.

With the aid of Sergeant Charlton and a detachment of troopers with wrangling experience, the scouts and soldiers followed LaPoint and Gabe up the sloping exit to the southwest and drove the herd up onto the plains on the south side of the canyon rim, with a view of the smoking bonfires below, drifting with the dust and gun smoke. Reaching the top rim, McBride and LaPoint watched the herd come up, exultant. They had captured another major horse herd after another major victory, but they knew they had to keep it away from the Indians, something the army had always failed to do before.

With a great fear of the Indians regrouping to steal the huge horse herd back, the 4th Cavalry formed a large moving corral of mounted troopers, and fighting exhaustion, the troopers began driving them thus contained back down towards the Tule Canyon. The giant herd, well over a thousand horses, was moved in a huge rectangle of troopers acting as drovers, in the largest horse drive that anyone had seen. The noise and heat from the fast moving herd was incredible as they moved south towards the base camp at Tule.

LaPoint and McBride watched the amazing sight as the dust cloud enveloped them, then went back to fetch their own stallions, left at the top of the canyon when they went down on foot. Buck and Scorpio were rested and ready, and they moved fast back down south to pass the horse herd, with Scorpio only showing a slight hitch in his gait. The knot on LaPoint's head was swollen and throbbing, and his eye was turning black and blue. He stopped by a playa to water Scorpio and take some swigs from his canteen to sooth his aching gut.

"Dang, you need a buffalo steak for that eye, shore gonna be a black one. Ya ain't so dizzy that you might fall off yore horse, are ya?" asked McBride as he walked Buck alongside Scorpio and let him drink in the shallow water.

"Not now, but it's throbbing. I'm wondering what's going to happen to all those horses. Even if we divide it up, it's a hell of a lot to handle. We'd be strained to handle a couple of dozen, the shape we're in. I'm getting mighty sleepy."

"Wal ya know Mackenzie's got some plan in his head. He already said all the scouts get all the horses they can handle."

"Maybe we could drive them back up to Dodge and sell them to herds going up into the mountains, or to Goodnight over on the Apisha. We could use the Tonkawas and some of the troopers," said LaPoint.

"Wal, dunno 'bout that. But we got ta stay awake and keep these troopers moving the herd like drovers. If they scatter, the Comanches will get 'em back."

"I've got some coffee and brandy in this flask, here, take the last of it. I just had a few swigs," said LaPoint as he handed the drink to his mentor.

Josh and Gabe were both feeling the fatigue of riding for nearly twenty hours, then fighting a battle down a steep cliff. Most of the troopers had been up too long to stay awake, and many nearly tumbled from their mounts in the long drive, and some eventually did. LaPoint and McBride rode around and tried to keep them awake and in position, since they had spent the last eight years working horses and were expert at moving herds, though the biggest was one fifth the size of that one. The dust cloud was enormous and choking, so they alternated the drag riders to swing, to let them breath.

As he was circling to the left point of the huge thundering herd of beautiful horses, LaPoint had a feeling of dread as he remembered the rest of his recent dream, the part that had jerked him awake in a hot sweat. He saw an image of the horses running over cliffs into a deep canyon and screaming in death. This broke him into a hot flush, but he pressed on in keeping the herd contained and moving south. He pushed Scorpio to move to the front of the herd, to keep it from stampeding over the rim. Several big stallions were running near the front, and Scorpio ran close and screamed a challenge towards them. LaPoint just tried to hang on for dear life, groggy from lack of sleep and the blow to his head. He eventually moved to the front of the herd and observed the stars, navigating due south for the rim of the Tule. He had to keep slapping his face and pulling his hair to stay awake as the miles passed. Soon the cottonwoods around Tule Canyon were in sight, and the swing riders moved up to the point of the herd as it approached the smaller gash in the plains. Together, under the leadership of LaPoint and McBride, they bent the herd to the right and milled it about a mile before the rim.

With the huge herd contained and being slowly fed into the Canyon, LaPoint and Gabe arrived first at the supply camp on the northern, and changed back to boots and hat while LaPoint washed the smeared warpaint from his face. They were pouring coffee down their throats trying to jog their minds into wakefulness as the tail end of the herd arrived and were shunted down into the canyon. By a rough count they figured over twelve hundred horses, and LaPoint had a horrible premonition of dread gripping his solar plexus. The coffee did not affect their sleepiness, and they both laid down to rest with their horses standing above them. The toll of deep weariness laid them into a long sleep, though LaPoint awoke with fitful dreams occasionally, and twice found Gabe awake chugging on his canteen. Fatigue held them on the ground and they alternated between sleeping and drinking water, occasionally rising to eat.

Within twenty hours the rest of the troopers arrived with Mackenzie and Beaumont in the lead. Charlton gave a shout and wave to the two scouts as they rode by to help with the stragglers from the horse herd, which was corralled in the north end of the canyon.

"Hey laddies, I'm a bloody horse drover now, eh?" said the big Sergeant, happy with another victory that so far secured the horse herd. "That village is burning, all the food and all the lodges and all the robes. They'll have to come in now."

"Damn I hope so," said LaPoint, still groggy from his long sleep.

"I know that's right. I'm too dang old for this, stiff as a dead possum. How many day's did we sleep?"

"I don't know, too sleepy to remember, but look at all those horses!" said Josh as he staggered stiff-legged to the rim of the canyon. "I dreamed they plunged over the rim. We've got to devise a plan to move them."

"Colonel Mackenzie's already got a plan. Better get ready to pick all you want. There's some real beauties in there.""

"Alright, we're on it. Where's the Colonel?"

"Over in his tent by the wagons, waiting to hear from you guys."

Gabe and Josh went to give a final report to Mackenzie and take their leave. When they heard Colonel Mackenzie say he had to shoot the horses, and they should take all they could handle, they were thrown into panic, and went down with the rest of the scouts and picked out the best of the lot, in a hurry. The huge herd was milling around at the end of the canyon, with horses and mules of all kinds and colors. It was difficult to pick through them, but they did so, pushing their strong mounts through the herd to rope the best, then dragging each to a rope corral above the rim. It took two hours, while all the scouts were doing the same, a continual line of horses being pulled from the herd and gathered into small bunches above the rim. With a burning desire to avoid the slaughter, they led their strings southwest as the Tonkawa scouts picked all the horses they could handle. They pushed their small herd of two dozen to the south wall of the canyon on a steep switchback trail, and looked down at the largest herd of horses they had ever seen, pinned into the head of the canyon. Still feeling dehydrated, they drank from their canteens and watched the impending slaughter being prepared.

"I've seen enough of this, Gabe. A horse slaughter I can't take. It's the innocent paying for the guilty again. And I led them to it."

"We led them in to end this war, Josh. When ya sign on with the army, the commander calls the shots."

"Yeah, I know. But I think I begin to know what you felt about the beaver now. I'm going to regret this until I die."

"Why hell, it ain't killin' off a species, just a big herd of stolen horses."

"We could have driven them to Dodge, maybe, with some luck," Josh's eyes were running tears as he spoke, with the right eye swollen and going black from a thump he had received while killing the sentry. His face was twisted in pain like it was when Gabe saw him learn his mother had been murdered. But LaPoint soon controlled it into a grim look, and urged Scorpio into a fast walk beside McBride.

"We could have done it. Trapping them in that canyon to be shot was pure hell. I'll regret that forever."

"It's god awful, alright, Josh, but what else can he do? Every time the cavalry has gotten a herd so far, the Comanche get it back the next night."

"I know the colonel decided he had to do it to end this, but I wish I had been awake to argue my idea to him. We've driven herds with over two hundred horses before."

"We'd been attacked by every Indian on the plains if we tried it, and you know it. How could we make expert drovers of delirious Tonkawas and worn out troopers in one night?"

"Damn-it-all, Gabe. The horses are going to die for our mistakes. Without the horse we'd never been able to even come out here, all they do is serve us, and now through no fault of their own they are being slaughtered. This is the worst thing I could imagine, and I was a part of it." Josh broke into sobs as he spoke, the long strain of this warfare pouring out in his rage and disgust at the necessary slaughter, the pain of the impending horse massacre reaching deep inside him to the little boy who fell in love with horses after he was torn away from his mother. He could find no logical argument against it, but it was tearing his heart and wrenching his gut. All he had ever really wanted was a horse ranch to raise and train horses, and now a whole herd was to be destroyed, with his help.

"It can't be helped, Josh."

"I know," said Josh as he reeled, dizzy and nauseated, and took another drink from his canteen.

"So let's move past it."

Josh walked over to the edge of the cliff and squatted down, then threw up, retching over the edge of the cap rock into Tule Canyon. Standing up and spitting, he felt able to move again, and walked back to where Gabe was drinking coffee. Gabe handed him the enameled metal cup, and he took a swig to rinse his mouth.

"This is the bitter part, I know," said Gabe.

"Alright, thanks," said Josh as he rinsed and spit. "Let's get our horses and go. We've done our part. I don't want to be around when the firing starts."

Gabe and Josh mounted and drove two dozen select horses south towards Blanco Canyon as they heard the carbine firing begin on the rim of the canyon, the mass killing of over a thousand innocent and willing horses. The second Red River battle was over, with another hidden Indian encampment destroyed, and this time the horse herd with it. Most of the last free roaming southern plains tribes had been dealt a killing blow, and the affected tribes included Lone Wolf's Kiowas, along with

Maman-ti, and several Comanche and Cheyenne Arapaho renegade bands. The last bands out were the Quohadi, led by Kiwih-nai, hiding down in the head-water canyons of the Pease River, according to Gabe's hunches. But they wanted no more part in the Comanche wars, and were bothered by the sound of the mass carbine firing for hours.

They raced their mounts and the herds south until Scorpio began favoring his right leg some more, and Josh switched mounts and slowed everything down, with the sound of the slaughter dim in the distance. After riding until mid afternoon without talking much, they stopped and rested at a full playa of an acre's size, letting the horses fill themselves and grazed on the nearby tall grass.

"Well, I hope that ends it," said Josh, his face grim and rigid. "I'm done in. I've had more than enough. That horse herd will run through my dreams for the rest of my life, I'm afraid. I can't get the image of them trapped in that canyon out of my mind. It's almost like they knew as we rode through them, selecting these best ones we're taking back, and each one was saying, 'pick me, pick me', to save them from the killing. No more Comanche war for me."

"I've had enough too. Though I imagine they will go after Kiwih-nai and the Quohadis next, unless he brings them in. I ain't gonna help with that battle, though. No more for me. We done our part."

"Me neither. I've smelt all the burning village I care to, for the rest of my life. But I don't regret either battle, but I damn sure regret the horse killing. The raiding hostiles had it coming, and if us leading the army in helped to end this war and raiding for captives, then I'm satisfied with what we did. I hope Maman-ti got killed in that battle, along with Lone Wolf and Isatai, if he was there."

"Me too. To hell with 'em. It's these medicine men who keep stirring up these slaughters. Visionaries with their fantasies do nothing but create misery for everyone else. They won't face the plain truth, which is they are whipped. The Comanche fighting the army is suicide for them now," said Gabe. "Hell, the huge military establishment from the civil war will just smother them, wipe them out with more total war. If they had stopped the raiding and focused on maintaining their hold on the staked plains, they wouldn't be in this fix."

"That is, if the army had enforced the treaty and stopped the buffalo hunters at the Arkansas. A better outcome was possible, but it seemed to just slip through our fingers, and concluding the war became the only move left for us." said Josh.

"Hell, Sam Houston had the best chance of establishing a line of separation at the cap-rock, but it slipped through his fingers too."

"It is strange, though, us leading them in both times. Much as we tried to mind our own horse business and avoid this war, we ended up right in the thick of it. As if fighting rustlers and Comancheros wasn't enough. I hope Kiwih-nai realizes the futility of it, and goes in to Fort Sill before they destroy his band too. The hunters won't stop until the buffalo are gone. Their way of life out here is finished, turned to dust."

"Wal I reckon you shouldn't have learned the staked plains so well. I guess that made us likely scouts. We done kept our word to Kiwih-nai, though, way I figures it....no regrets."

"The only thing I regret is having to lead that horse herd to the massacre in Tule Canyon. There were probably some from our own herds in there, horses I gentled and trained. Damn, that was horrible. A slaughter of horses as bad as the slaughter of buffaloes."

"Warn't no way around being a part of it, not for us. Couldn't be done with any other way. Like that ole gal in the swamp said, ole Cypress Sally, cain't be helped, about the horse herd. With the Comanches either, really. It was either gonna end up with a few left alive because they came in, or all dead with the buffalo, their bones turning to dust. Their time is over out here."

"I know, but it still makes me sad. I never would have gotten into this if I'd known that would be the final result, all those horses slaughtered. All this makes me want to leave, make a fresh start in the mountains, maybe. Too much of a killing zone around here."

"Wal, can't be helped now, let it float downstream, like all the rest of this killing, and go get hitched up to that fine little lady who loves you. And leave that hell hole down in south Texas where every gunslinger in Live Oak and Helena is itching to outdraw ya, move up to the Blanco Valley. With the Comanches whipped, it's gonna be safe for women and kids now. Kiwih-nai ain't gonna raid settlements, I expect. He's that smart, anyway.

255

The hill country should be safe for you two to make a home there."

"I intend to. And I want you to come live on the Blanco again, up on the Clear Spring Ranch."

"Alright then. Pancho can run the Eagle Ford Ranch just fine. He can use it to gather cattle herds, too, like he was wantin' to. Ah reckon ah kin take livin' with yal, if you can, long as I'm far enough from the sound of those bed springs."

"Alright then, let's put this chapter behind us. No more agreeing to scout for the Army, no matter what, eh? We have done our part."

"Skocum," said Gabe. "Floats my stick. Let's go."

They traversed the golden tan grass of the staked plains again, hoping that their involvement in the Comanche war was over at last. LaPoint spent fitful nights dreaming of the horses, but did not want to speak of it in the day, and pushed the trip towards home. A day south of Blanco Canyon they came upon a butte that the Comanches call Whistling Mountain, and there they spotted a village of Quohadi Comanches, stretched along the creek at the base of the cliff. They watched for a while, then circled around to the southeast and continued their trek to the home ranch. Gabe said his best guess was that the band was the Quohadi led by Kiwih-nai and Isatai, and they had been smart to hide down there while the 4th Cavalry cleaned out Palo Duro Canyon.

"Maybe they will survive," said LaPoint as he put his binoculars back in their case. "Survive on what's left of the southern herd, and the army will enforce the Arkansas line to stop all the hunters from being killed."

"Yeah, and maybe the priests will pray the war to an end," said Gabe. "We ain't seen much of the southern herd, have we?"

"No, but I'm hoping the Quohadi are better at finding them. Let's get home and see what's happened since we left"

They traveled in haste to the south, crossing the Concho, the Llano, the Pedernales, and finally reaching the upper Blanco and riding downstream along its rocky banks.

Meanwhile, back at the ranch on the Blanco River, Jesse and Pancho had just finished building the second round pen for horse training, and began to work on the mixed breed horses for next year's remudas. Intending to join them there, Josh and

256

Gabe herded their small but select group of horses south for another week until they reached the ranch, where they rested from the war and trained the horses. Jesse stayed on to help while his father went south to work at mustanging. Josh soon left for a visit with Kathy at Panna Maria, and stayed there with her working the southern mustang herds. He avoided the town of Helena with its gunmen, letting them think that LaPoint was gone for good.

As soon as the school term ended in early summer, Josh LaPoint married Kathy Hartman, and they settled on the Blanco River horse ranch, with Gabe and Jesse living in a small bunkhouse about fifty yards away from the house, far enough to avoid being kept awake by bed springs dancing across the stone floor every night. Only rarely did he have a nightmare of the slaughtered horse herd, turned to ghosts, running wild on the Llano Estacado, plunging over cliffs screaming to their deaths.

Chapter Nine: Buffalo Bones

The double-walled limestone ranch home on the Blanco River, across from the big springs that rushed out through a hole in the gray limestone cliff, proved to be secure for newlyweds Kathy and Josh LaPoint. Gabe McBride took to living in the outbuilding and adding a lean-too shed to blacksmith in. They began a new life on the Clear Springs Ranch, under the shade of huge pecans and cypress trees.

When Josh had proposed marriage to Kathy at Panna Maria, he had revealed his entire hidden past, beginning with the fact that he was the illegitimate son of Alex Robinoix and an octoroon house-mistress who was a healer and spiritual leader of the black community there on the plantation on the Bayou Teche. He had asked her if she wanted to marry a bastard, and ex-slave, and a man who had killed in the past and would again. Then he told her about the cavalry striking the Comanche villages, and the slaughter of the horse herd after the Palo Duro battle. She put her arms around him and her head under his chin, and told him to tell her everything while she felt his heart pound in his chest.

After revealing the retribution killings at the plantation on the Teche, he also told her how he had killed Bise McCairn, the last of his mother's murderers at the Red River Battle, and how he had scouted for the army in the Comanche war, and taken down lots of rustlers with his rifles, as well as outdrawing Ike Covington and two other fast draw gunmen. Kathy had heard many of the stories already, and was unfazed in her desire to be with him. She understood that he had paid for his involvement with the slaughter of the horse herd, and how it bothered him still.

For the first time in Josh's life, someone besides Gabe knew all about him and was allowed close to him. After being torn from his mother's care and sent to an orphan boarding school at age four, his main emotional attachment had been with horses and his salty buck-skinned old mentor. He had never been able to have a happy family life before, to the full degree he wanted with Kathy, who was very much in love with him, as he was with her.

Having lost her mother to murdering marauders in her childhood, Kathleen Hartman needed a man who could protect her and still her fears, and she understood Josh's feelings of vengeance towards Bise McCairn, but was relieved they were gone so they could concentrate on building a new life there. She knew that only by working with horses could he ease the deep pain he carried over the horse slaughter. Her longtime fear of marauding Comanches was subdued by the presence of the several expert riflemen, and the reduction of Comanche raiding after the battles they had led the 4th Cavalry into.

The wedding had been filled with Poncho's family and Hartman relatives, along with Gabe and Tom. Kathy's stout blond German brothers were farmers and ranchers along the Pedernales Valley, and hated Indians with a deep passion, wishing every one was dead. They had ridden with ranger expeditions after captives, but had been unsuccessful, like most. They were stocky men with wide faces, sunburned skin, light hair, and blue eyes. They were known as industrious and stubborn pioneers in their community, men willing to live out on the edge of the settlements and trust in their rifles to protect their land from raiders while forted-up in limestone buildings. The older generation spoke highly accented English and German, while the younger ones spoke more like Texans, and they pumped Gabe for stories of his ranger scouting days. They were under the misapprehension that Gabe always found the Comanches when trailing after captives, and scout McBride soon disabused them of that notion, mentioning that about one time in ten did he catch the raiders. Gabe eventually led the story into how he had hunted and traded with the Comanches in his youth, slowly enrapturing them with the excitement of hunting buffalo from a well-trained mount with a lance.

These men were glad the troublesome war was finished and brimming with resentment at the strictures of the reconstruction. They had all avoided serving in the Confederacy, being pro-Union and anti-slavery like most of the Germans where they lived. With their European heritage and good educational backgrounds, they had figured Texas would be easy pickings for Mexico if it were not protected by the United States. They had begun raising horses and selling them

259

in the growing settlements of central Texas. They spent hours admiring the LaPoint spread and the horses, and invited the newlyweds to come visit their places on the Pedernales.

Since they sometimes drove buggies out to Enchanted Rock for picnics since the Comanche presence there had diminished greatly, they badgered Gabe to come up and show them where Captain Jack Hays had stood off the Comanches in the old days. Captain Jack of the early Texas Rangers was a legend in the hill country, and Gabe's former association with him made the old scout and marksman the subject of much questioning.   So Gabe told them about the tiny depression on top with a small live oak growing in it, where Captain Jack made his stand.

Gabe spun his yarns at the rate of about a tale a stein of dark beer. The Germans and the Tejanos loved beer and dancing the polka and waltz with their wives, and partied until late in the night, moving their beer keg down by the river after Josh and Kathy made moves for the bedroom, and carrying on with their party in the moonlight.

 LaPoint had collected the best of the hybrid horses to train that winter, including several nice two year-olds ready for saddle training that he acquired from the Hartman brothers, and worked between northers on that, to fulfill the contracts with trail-boss Winger and the Army for spring.

With new construction work of adding two round-pens for training, adjoined with sheds and corrals, they stayed very busy in the green Blanco Valley with its winding spring fed river. Warm sunny weather alternated with blue northers and grass freshening rains that year, and the winter was a peaceful interlude from the Comanche wars. LaPoint was able to purchase an adjoining spread, which brought the ranch to nearly four hundred acres, with plenty of grassland in the valley to graze the remudas. He also acquired cattle for teaching the mounts to herd, and for steady meat supply, as buffalo were becoming difficult to find.

After leaving Helena and its gun thugs who were always looking to outdraw LaPoint because of his lightening speed when shooting Ike Covington and other gunmen, Josh was glad to set aside his fast draw pistol and just carry his Remington .44, worn backwards on his left side in an army holster with a flap on it. The industrious German settlements in the hill country were not so full of gunmen, like the area around Helena and Live Oak, nor Comanche raiders, since the successful attacks on their villages, and it was a pleasure for Josh to be able to relax and take his wife to town without concern for running into needless scrapes with would-be fast draw artists or raiding Comanches. Kathy still could not bear to be left alone for long, and there was always a rifleman at the ranch, either the scouts or vaqueros who helped with the stock.

The German towns of Fredericksburg and New Braunfels were well organized, solid stone buildings, double walled with squared off limestone blocks, laid out with common sense and good planning, with churches, libraries, and community halls. LaPoint much preferred living around them and gathering mounts to finish in that green Blanco River Valley. With Tom Jackson and Pancho Menchaca running the ranch on the lower San Antonio River, LaPoint was assured of a continuing flow of good mustang stock to breed in with the horses he was purchasing around San Antonio, Fredericksburg, and New Braunfels. The cross-breeding of mustangs to larger eastern mounts remained a central part of the work.

Jesse Menchaca, who just turned 18 the day after their wedding, came up to visit and train horses with Josh, for he also was tired of Helena and the daily concern over racist attacks there. He and Josh worked well on training the horses together, with Jesse using a small herd of beeves to teach them cutting skills when they had adjusted to saddle. The winter was an excellent time for exploring the river canyons, since the vipers were asleep in their holes, and the woods were still green with live oak and cedar. They hiked for hours upstream and found a spot where the river narrowed into a tight chute of solid stone, then hit a wall, did a dog-leg turn, and tumbled over a cliff into a deep hole in a dark canyon. They named it the Narrows of the Blanco, and spent many hours exploring the slim stone canyon below the falls, with vertical gray sculpted cliffs on both sides, and deep blue-green circular holes in the floor, that went directly into the aquifer. The place was verdant with ferns growing from the wall and mossy shorelines below the pounding of the falls and boil of white water below it, rushing through the narrow canyon.

While hiking along the clear river they found a large dead cypress that had dried perfectly. Together they used a long

261

crosscut saw to fall the thick tree along a dry ox-bend of the twisting river. They cut the long seasoned log in two, and hollowed out each twelve foot section with ax, adz, and hot coals. Gabe fashioned rasps and curved wood chisels to do the finish work. They hollowed out the front end while leaving a deck above, and put ledges for their feet to push on. A greased parfleche padded with raw wool was turned into a seat, and the bottom was rounded into a modified v hull to track straight in a lake while still being able to run rapids. They worked unceasingly as they smoothed the final form and sealed it with several coats of shellac, anxious to try it in the rapids. With waxed canvass they made pockets to hang inside the cockpit and spray covers with a hole for the paddler. They fashioned both double and single paddles out of the long lower boughs of cedars with smoothly shaped cypress planks on the ends. Gabe fashioned deck hardware to hold nets for gear bags and fishing poles, with a stout ring on the front deck for towing.

When they were finished they had two streamlined small pointed canoes with covered front decks rising to a high wave breaker, and Mackenzie cloth covers that fit around their trunks and the rim to keep the foaming water out. Then they ran the clear Blanco for seven miles at a time, through white water drops and twisting turns around rocks, then clear green pools, followed by more rapids, having Gabe and Kathy bring the horses down the merger of the Blanco waters with a creek they called the Clear Cypress, which flowed direct from a deep blue well in the aquifer. They would troll the deep pools with lines baited with minnows they had caught with a throw-net, and catch bass on the way down the river to the camp Gabe would prepare. There they would fry fish to eat with sourdough biscuits, beans, and rice, then ride back in the sunset, invigorated by the beauty of the fast moving stream lined with giant Cypress, Live Oak, Spanish Oak, Hickory, Cottonwood, Sycamore, and Pecan trees.

Josh also ordered a rubber pontoon boat for running the steeper mountain rivers, and found it could be used as an excellent ground cloth or small waterproof tent when not inflated. Soon Kathy learned to handle the rubber boat in the Blanco, and she paddled the exciting stretch of the twisting river through the gray limestone canyons with Josh and Jesse in their cypress dugouts. With her lighter weight the wider boat moved

262

almost as fast as the streamlined cypress dugouts, giving Josh and Jesse time to fish the pools. Gabe would bring the horses, and they would sight his cook-fire when they came around the last bend. All through the winter they practiced their river running skills on the small drops and jade green pools of the clear running Blanco, paddling beneath gray sculptured limestone cliffs and grassy meadows.

For Kathy the mild winter in the north again, among the evergreen cedar and live oaks in full foliage until spring, was a new awakening to the beauty of the hill country, with its rolling hills of limestone and its many bubbling springs and clear river. The river yielded bass, crappie, catfish, and perch, and the sun was out often between northers. The thick woods in the canyons were full of birds from up in the snow-covered north, and in later winter thousands of robins showed up and filled the woods with their sounds, hopping through the dry Spanish Oak leaves. Mexican eagles, great blue Herons, snow white egrets, and several kinds of hawks circled overhead, reinforced by swirling black buzzards that cleaned up any carcass. They never saw or heard of Comanche raiders, nor did they lose any stock to rustlers that winter. It was the first winter in years where they had not been forced into gun battles, and they enjoyed the peaceful interlude.

It was easy for all of them to fall in love with the tumbling and clear Blanco River, with it's winding course through the tall canyons of the limestone hills, eroded and carved for centuries into overhangs and ledges of hard gray stone. Clear springs bubbled out with water warmer than the winter air, and they made a sweat lodge along the shore near a plunging pool, using bent saplings and buffalo skins. There they would heat rocks and have a dry heat sweat followed by steam and a plunge into the clear pool.

With buffalo meat becoming scarce, they began to eat from the river more often. They would bait lines on one river run, then collect the fish on another the next day. Kathy's brothers came to visit several times for all night fishing trips yielding huge catfish and stringers of bass, and in spring they returned again to tell her of a teaching job offer in Fredricksburg. Although Kathy loved the homestead on the Blanco, she was still afraid to be alone there because of her early bad experience with Comanche raiders, and knew Josh and Gabe would be

263

gone a lot as soon as the weather warmed. After much discussion with Josh, she decided to take the job while Josh fulfilled his several spring contracts previously agreed to. Living with sharpshooters at the ranch was different than being alone with memories of the Comanches slaughtering her kin, and she wanted to build her teaching career as well.

They all took a trip to Fredericksburg so that she could interview for the teaching job, and decided to swing by Enchanted Rock. It took them three days of easy riding northwest in a warm stretch in early March to reach the huge granite dome. They spotted it in the afternoon of the third day, the afternoon sun glimmering on the round pink bowl. The huge dome had a smaller dome to the immediate south, and a sharper peak to the north, making small canyons between them.

Making a camp along a creek with course granite sand littered with gleaming stones, they enjoyed the view of the up-swelling of algae encrusted granite in the sunset. Kathy spent an hour walking the creek to pick out the polished quartz and other gems. She remembered doing the same with her little brother, before he was stolen by Comanches, and broke into tears. Quickly hiding them with her kerchief, he called Josh for a walk up the gentle incline. The walked up to some cliffs and sat enjoying the view and being in love with each other.

After listening to the granite dome creak in the fast cooling evening they slept well and awoke to explore the top after breakfast. They spent several hours climbing through the broken boulders at the bottom and walking the gentle rise to the top, where Gabe showed them the depression that Captain Jack had laid in to repel the attacking Comanches for hours. After sharing a toast of brandy there, Gabe went back down to the camp while Josh and Kathy climbed the small but sharp peak to the north, and made love on the top.

They camped beneath the peak and slept well, with no fear of Comanche attack. Then they went to finish their business in Fredericksburg, a well laid out and prosperous German community of white squared-off stone buildings with wide streets and a clean appearance. Every Hartman relative showed up, and they all spent hours in the beer garden on main street listening to accordion and tuba music while toasting Kathy's new job. They found a small stone cottage, called a Sunday House by the Germans, adjoining her cousin's house in

264

town for her to live in. Josh persuaded her to test out the bed while the others were away to prepare another German feast. On the ride back they went through Blanco to pick up supplies and made it back in two days of hard riding across the sixty miles of hill country.

After a winter of training horses without being forced into shootouts with rustlers nor Indian raiders, Josh, Jesse, and Gabe McBride delivered their trained officers' mounts to San Antonio in early spring of 1875 after Gabe finished fitting them with horseshoes, bringing Kathy along to drop off later at her brother's home in Fredricksburg. Jesse rode to the corrals at the old mission ranch south of town to meet Tom Jackson and the remuda he had brought up from the mustang ranch down south. With this horse herd they aimed to supply saddle mounts for the Army and for trail drives.

The rest of the party checked into a downtown hotel and had long hot baths and a good dinner. Josh and Kathy enjoyed a night of fine dining and dancing to a German polka waltz band at the elegant Hotel Menger, near the boarded up Alamo building the night before the meeting. Kathy was the most beautiful woman at the dance, with a maroon dress of flowing silk, and caught the eye of every man in the room, repeatedly. The army officers lined up to cut in as soon as one of them got a dance with her. Josh felt proud of her and friendly to the officers, many of whom he knew, but was glad when he got his arms around her and refused any more cutting in. Gabe spent the evening in the lobby, watching the dancers and spinning yarns for curious listeners who found out who he was and asked him of his ranger days. Josh and Gabe left for meetings with the military early the next morning, while Kathy shopped for school supplies.

General Augar, whom they knew from previous meetings, had been replaced by a General O.C. Ord in a military reorganization that had sent Colonel Mackenzie to Fort Sill. Edward Ord was a stout and striking looking man with a shock of gray hair and bushy gray walrus mustache, and he stood close to LaPoint and stared at him with an intense and piercing gaze under bushy gray eyebrows. At the meeting they learned that Mackenzie had stayed in the field after they had led him to the Palo Duro battle, looking for Kiwih-nai and the Quohadis until the brutal winter drove the 4th Cavalry off the plains in late

265

December, without their finding any trace of the Quohadis. They also learned that Kiowa and Comanche leaders Maman-ti and Mow-way had been captured, and that most bands had given up the old life of the Numunu, as the Comanches called themselves, and had come in to Fort Sill. The important news was that on Mackenzie's recommendation, the army was requesting that Josh and Gabe scout for and accompany a party of negotiators headed by Dr. J. J. Strum, agency interpreter at Fort Sill, in a last attempt to bring in the Quohadis peacefully, before Mackenzie launched more expeditions from Fort Sill, where the 4th cavalry was now headquartered.

The general asked to speak to Josh LaPoint alone for a few moments, so Gabe stepped out and smoked his pipe out in the sunshine.

"LaPoint, I want you to hear me out and think hard before responding. I've already discussed this with scout McBride, early this morning when all you young men are still asleep. As it happens, we met in California at Sutter's mill back in 1850, so we had a lot to chat about."

"Is that right? He sure got around, and seems to know everyone from the old days out west."

"That's a fact, hell of a memory on that man. I remembered him, though he had red hair then, and he remembered me. Now listen. You both have proven invaluable to the Army with your horses and scouting work. Now some warrants have come to light, issued from New Orleans in 1865 and '66, with the name John Bobindough on them, over an incident with a dappled gray Andalusian warhorse stomping a soldier to death during the occupation. Your dappled warhorse is as well known as you are, Mr. LaPoint. It's closer to white and dappled pearl gray now, but we both know these Andalusian horses get lighter in color as they mature."

"Yes-sir, some do."

"There are also reports of sharpshooter killings with a Whitworth rifle in retaliation for the burning of LaPoint plantation on the bayou Teche. Again scout LaPoint, your reputation as a long range shooter with a scoped Whitworth is well known. When you took down Polonio Ortiza in that dim light at near a thousand yards, you became famous."

"It wasn't that far, sir"

" And your reputation as a long shot was cemented when you took down that Comanche scout heading to warn Mowway's village at around the same distance, which that Tonkawa scout John'son told everyone about for months after the Red River battle, which made your horse famous as well. Your warhorse was seen kicking men in battle, with front and back kicks, like it was reported in New Orleans, at the battle of Mowway's village."

"Sir, I can explain..."

"Hear me out now. There is also a report filed by several officers in New Orleans describing extenuating circumstances in New Orleans, that the soldiers injured and killed were engaged in an assault of a local woman. And it has come to light that the marauders who burned the LaPoint plantation and killed the inhabitants were raiders from Kansas led by Thomas Bison McCairn, using an alias at the time. Bise McCairn had a stack of warrants from five states for murder and rustling, and he was killed in the Red River Battle, by you it is reported."

"I killed him in battle, sir."

"Well and good, by God. But let me speak, sir, then respond. You will have a chance to get your points in. The Army considers the capture of Polonio Ortiza and the elimination of Bise McCairn a service, which is as great as scouting the way into Mow-way's village and Palo Duro Canyon. We intend to return a service to you, sir."

"How long have yal known about this, sir?"

"These papers all came into the hands of Randald Mackenzie in his new position, in a pile of circulars delivered to Fort Sill regarding renegades. Mac saw the names while pouring through paperwork on one of his insomnia bouts and knew well of your sharpshooting with the rare Whitworth rifle. So he made inquiries to New Orleans and Camp Pratt near the Bayou Teche, after which he appealed to high command to quash the warrants. He argued your case for you and won a likely quid pro quo agreement. You know what that means?"

"Yes sir. Discretion on both sides, to start with. Then mutual consideration, so to speak. Gabe would say something like, 'ya scratch my back and I'll scratch yorn."

"Let's be clear now, we don't want to be quashing the wrong warrants. Joshua Alexandre Robinoix LaPoint is your real name, correct? From New Orleans and LaPoint plantation on the Bayou Teche?"

"I think Alex Robinoix is my father by blood, sir, but he has never given me his name, since I was born illegitimate, and a slave."

"Remarkable what you made of yourself, sir. But to clearly lay this out... you are the man who trampled the would be rapist in New Orleans with that warhorse, and shot two marauder soldiers on the Bayou Teche, as well as capturing Polonio Ortiza and killing Bise McCairn with a knife, correct sir?"

"Yes-sir. Correct. A knife, a horse, a pistol, a piece of firewood, and I strangled the sonofabitch a bit..."

"LaPoint, what happens here between us is never to be mentioned, and I will deny saying this if ever questioned, but our mutual friend can get the warrants disappeared forever if you help with this mission. Your past record will be completely cleared. There will be no warrants with the curious misspelling by a young Lieutenant who happened to be a friend. There will be no warrants at all, you will clear the past with this mission."

"You've got a deal, General. I trust the Colonel to keep his word. He should be a general too, in my book, for what he's done."

"I agree, LaPoint. But Miles is in the race for limited stars in a smaller Army. I think Mac will receive his star soon. Anyway, I'm glad we see eye to eye on this. Your work, as well as Gabe McBride's scouting, in finishing this Comanche war, is strongly appreciated by Ranald Mackenzie, and he's a very loyal friend to have. Your well-trained mounts that can live on grass have made the 4th Cavalry more mobile on the plains, another reason we are winning this Comanche war. Mac is solid on this. His word is firm as his honor is deep. He has already argued your case, and says he can get the warrants quashed. He's already gotten pardons for several of the Comancheros who guided him. Even that Ortiza fellow you guys captured."

"Not sure I approve of that one, sir."

"Be that as it may, Ortiza guided the 4th cavalry across the staked plains to Fort Sumner and back, then up to find Mow-way's village, which you and McBride helped on."

"The son of a bitch has been rustling and killing in the process for years, sir."

"Maybe, but his services were essential in the Forth Cavalry learning to traverse the staked plains. There's lots of things one has to do to win a war."

"I guess I learned that the hard way, sir, when those horses were slaughtered."

"Yes. Unfortunate but necessary, that. LaPoint, here it is in a nutshell. Mackenzie states that your services have been invaluable in finding the Comanches, and that you risked your life in battle in efforts to save his. He feels he owes you and cannot reward you other than this."

"This is all I want, personally, sir. It'd be good if he could use his influence to stop the buffalo hunters at the Arkansas River, like the Medicine Lodge Treaty stated."

"I'm afraid it's too late for that, and Mac isn't running things at Dodge, that letting the hunters take down the southern herd, that came down from the top. Nothing we could do about that."

"Well, it was a sorry deal, and I think Major Dodge should be held accountable for it."

"If wishes were horses, eh? We may agree on all that, but it's time for you to make a decision."

"This is for sure, from Mac, the past will be cleaned off?"

"You will be taken care of by the officer corps, every man of which is very grateful to have Bise McCairn gone, sir. Your record will be cleared so you can continue your horse ranching and supplying the army with mounts. Now, make your points, sir."

"That's the last load on my mind, General. Every one of them federal marauders had it coming. I shot those curs after they killed my mother and burned the plantation. The New Orleans incident was with a rapist and his gang. They all deserved it and left me no choice. And you know about McCairn being a renegade West Pointer, don't you?"

"Hell yes I knew. If another officer had asked me who needed killing more than anyone out here, his name would have burst forth, followed by Maman-ti. Don't get me started on McCairn. That son of a bitch was raiding the parties going to California in '49, dressed as an Apache with his own band. He's been a thorn in the side of every one who went to West Point. I'm damned glad I don't have to think about him any more,

269

thanks to you. And I approve of the other killings as well. Rapists and marauders have no place in my army."

"Thanks again to you, and Colonel Mackenzie, sir, for this. I've just gotten married and want to raise a family, and this helps a lot."

"That's what McBride conveyed to me when I conferred with him on this, early this morning. He made some sourdough biscuits that were better than my mother's. Quite a lively guy, and we had a great talk about the old California gold rush days, when he was guiding parties out to Sutter's mill. Remarkable memory he's got, to the degree of what I was wearing, which wasn't army clothing. He's in full agreement with this plan. Of course, his scouting abilities and linguistic skills are highly regarded, and he doesn't seem to age either."

"So you cleared it with him first? My old raw-hided mentor?"

"Yes. Ranald's suggestion there, and he knows how to plan an assault, doesn't he? Fact is, Mackenzie indicated that McBride was the only one to know of this, for he is well-trusted. He said if McBride agreed, you'd go along for sure. Spry old rooster, isn't he? Fought at both significant battles of the Comanche war. Is he ever going to get stoved-up and dream of retiring, like some of us?"

"No sir, he keeps active. He can scout non-stop for days. When he isn't scouting he's pounding hot steel. We have a lot of farrier work for him. And he makes knives. He can ride until hell freezes over, and then some, as long as Charlie Goodnight."

"Yes, I know. I've wanted one of those knives he makes for years, and got him to promise me one."

"He'll deliver. He always does. So will I, with his help. We might have a notion of where to find the Quohadis. I really appreciate this deal, sir."

"Very well, a deal it is," said the General as he shook LaPoint's hand. "Your past will be clear when you leave out with the negotiating party on this mission, LaPoint, even if you don't succeed. Just going out and trying it is enough to sweep the past away as part of the war. Mac seems to have a lot of faith in your abilities, thinks you can find Kiwih-nai and persuade him to come in. You and your old partner, he seems to think that you both have known where they hide for a long time."

"We've got some hunches on it."

"Yes. Well. Maybe an educated guess, I figure. Give it your best shot and don't get killed. We need to end this thing without more killing if we can."

"Alright, we will do it, sir. Is it true what I heard, that you were at the surrender of General Lee?"

"Yes, another brilliant warrior who saw the hopelessness of his position and surrendered to save his men. Hopefully you can accomplish the same with this Kiwih-nai, or we may end up chasing him forever. He's even been hiding in the Guadalupe mountains, and from there he can slip away to Mexico."

"I think we can parley with Kiwih-nai, and I think Gabe can probably find him, and he speaks their language well."

"Oh, is McBride the best scout then, like they say?" asked the General, a slight smile touching his lips and a twinkle in his eye, which were framed by huge bushy eyebrows.

"Well, yes. He's the old master, especially up on the cap-rock, the staked plains. I only know a few words of Comanche and a bit of signing, while he is fluent in several Indian tongues and signing. He's got a perfect memory for every trail he's been on, a nose for water, and strange hunches that usually pan out. It was his hunch that found Mow-way's village. He followed the trails to Palo Duro. He got Polonio Ortiza to talk and turned him over to Sergeant Willams."

"After you took Ortiza down with that rare Whitworth rifle by expertly wounding him at a great distance as he fled, I'm told."

"Scratch shot, and it wasn't any thousand yards, sir. Those stories grow in the retelling. And there's always luck involved on a shot like that."

"There's luck involved with everything. What about the scout going back to warn Mow-way's village on the Red River?"

"That one was a little further, but in daylight. Maybe eight hundred yards, hard to say, and some luck was involved, to be sure."

"Yeah, the LaPoint luck, is what they talk about. The luck of Long-Shot LaPoint. And you first spotted the tracks to Mow-way's village coming from the north, I'm told. This morning McBride informed me you were the best scout, because of your eyesight, and your being the best long range shooter on the plains. He also said you were better with horses than any man alive."

"Well, like I said, he's the best for dealing with Comanches on the staked plains, but I've been riding with him a long time, and we've crossed the plains together some. Actually we found the final trail to Mow-way's village because Gabe leaned towards going where he thought he might eat some grapes and plums, believe it or not. With this mission his knowledge of the favorite camping grounds of the Quohadi will be the key to success. And we have met Kiwih-nai in battle and in parley, so we have a chance. But they could be anywhere, for they keep moving."

The officer put his strong grip on LaPoint's shoulder as he spoke, "Get the job done, sir," he said, then leaned in near his ear and said, "Thanks for killing that renegade son of a bitch Tomas McCairn."

"I guess it was meant to be, sir. He was trying to stab me when I stuck him with my McBride knife."

"I'd pay you dearly for that knife, sir, to pass around amongst the officer corps. We've been wanting him dead for a long time, a damned disgrace to all West Pointers, he was. If ever a scout deserved a medal..."

"I might give it up after this mission sir, and make myself another with ole Gabe. Right now it's my lucky piece."

"That Tonkawa scout John'son spread the tale that you stabbed McCairn in the heart and cut his ears off."

"The first is true, with a lucky stroke. Later Gabe cut the mangled ear off and blew a finger off his hand, for some Irish Comanche superstition, I imagine, or maybe to mark the end of a bad era."

"Dismember an Indian and keep him from the happy hunting grounds. And the reign of terror that McCairn spread lasted many a year."

"So they say. I was just relieved to stick him before he stuck me."

"That renegade is the worst thing that ever happened to West Point, and one of the worst killers in the west. Good riddance sir, a valuable service rendered. And good luck on this mission." General Ord offered his hand, and they shook on the deal, and it was settled.

LaPoint walked from the meeting with a wave of relief, then quickly let scout McBride know of his agreement to their participation, and the quid pro quo of removing the warrants which had hung over his head for years. Gabe already knew the situation and the interpreter Dr. Sturm, who was married to a Caddo woman and well-liked and respected by the Indians. His plans were already set for finding the Quohadi, and he was listing their haunts in his mind.

They met Tom Jackson and Jesse Menchaca south of town at the corrals of the old mission ranch, where they held a remuda of trained saddle-mounts brought up for a Winger cattle drive up the staked plains to the rail head at Dodge city. Trail-boss Bud Winger had men there to collect the horse herd, and LaPoint made the exchange for silver, with more contracts for delivery later in the season. As the large remuda was being driven out of the corrals, the LaPoint outfit gathered by the watering troughs for a parley.

LaPoint paid off the hands and gave them new orders for more horse work. They left to blow off some steam in a nearby cantina before heading back to the ranch. Then Gabe and Josh told Tom and Jesse of their commitment to re-enter the Comanche war, after surviving the two battles. Tom Jackson was incredulous and Jesse upset when they heard the news of more involvement in the troubles up north. They had just been discussing how glad they were that Comanche raids had been lessening along the settlement line, according to the San Antonio paper they had just read.

"You gonna what?" exclaimed Jesse, when he heard the news.

"Lemme get this straight, boss. After nearly getting killed several times in two Comanche battles, and both of you getting wounded, you guys are going back up there? I thought ya both swore off that stuff to stick to stock business?" asked Tom.

"Yeah, how come you gotta go back since most of the Comanches and Kiowa have surrendered at Fort Sill, and you said the General told you that the captives are being returned?" asked Jesse.

"Because we committed to finishing the damned Comanche war, that's why, and it ain't quite done," said Josh. "We want to bring Kiwih-nai in and let the army wipe out the rest of these renegade rustler bands hitting the trail herds and remudas. There's not as many horse herds to work this season anyway, with Goodnight living up north on the Arkansas now. He wants us to come up there and run herds to the miners in the mountains, according to a letter his wife Molly wrote which I just got."

"Boss," said Tom Jackson, "Might as well tell you now, Mr. Winger is contracting this herd to Goodnight at Dodge if he can't get the price he wants. What with the grass greening up early this year, there are already lots of herds ahead of us. It's turned into a grand rush for the rail-heads. If he can't get the price he wants, then Winger wants us to run them up to the Apisha ranch in New Mexico to replace a herd that wintered there, and drive that herd into the mountains for Goodnight. Goodnight has already made an offer. Also, Mr. Winger done married Delores."

"Oh yeah?... first I heard it. Glad to hear it, actually. The driving west to the Apisha Ranch sounds alright, as well. We'd be getting paid to go to the mountains. I guess we'll make all the final arrangements by telegraph at Dodge. And good for Delores, Bud Winger's a really good man."

"Mr. Winger's pretty happy about it, that's for sure. He just got a more recent letter from Charlie's wife, since I reckon ole Charlie can't write. One of the smartest guys I know, can't write."

"What did it say?" asked LaPoint.

"That son of a gun can count a whole herd of two thousand cattle passing by, steers, cows, and calves, better than any man, too," said Gabe. "I seen him do it at Fort Sumner," said Gabe.

"Yeah, I know. Shows how rough it was where he came up in northeast Texas, no schooling on that frontier," said Jackson.

"The letter," said LaPoint.

"We gonna need you two for driving this herd," said Jesse.

"What about the letter?" asked LaPoint, louder this time.

"Charlie is begging for herds to take to the miners in Colorado, and ranches up the face of the Rockies, and he wants us to do it," said Jackson.

"He wants us to take this herd to the mountains?" asked Josh.

"We can't take Texas cattle direct to Colorado," said Gabe.

"Charlie's got herds wintering over at the Apisha every year, and we'd just drive this one there to replace the one we take to Colorado, but we need your scouting," said Tom Jackson.

"I think I should go with you, boss," said Jesse. "I never seen this Kiwih-nai."

"Wal, we'll be done with all the Comanche parley by then," said Gabe.

"No Jesse, you're needed to point the herd, and anyway, if we take the herd to the mountains or not, doesn't change things with the herd getting to Dodge," said LaPoint.

"That's right," said Gabe. "Listen to the boss now."

"You can get on the remuda contracts by hiring another vaquero or two. All you have to do is train one remuda for Mr. Winger and six more officer mounts for the army to be delivered here, then meet him in San Antonio with it, then join up to drive his herd up north, where we will meet you. Jesse rides point, Pancho stays home to train another remuda for the army."

"If you don't get killed by the Comanches or renegades," said Jesse.

"We won't. They've already had plenty of chances, like all the thugs around Helena."

"That don't mean they won't kill you this time. You were stove up for a month after the Red River battle, had all black eyes and sick like after the Palo Duro. They might kill you this time."

"I don't think so," said LaPoint.

"If they do, then that'll be that, and ya make a fresh start," said Gabe, with his matter of fact tone. "We'll move on to the happy hunting grounds whar tha mountains is full of beaver and the plains full of buffalo. Go riding with ole Kit again."

"Waugh, Ole Mule Driver, hee-haw....that'll be the day. You gonna be around forever. Okay boss, I could point the herd in your place, but where you gonna meet us?" asked Jesse.

"On the Colorado up east of Fort Concho, is my best guess, if our hunches on where the Quohadis might be are on target."

275

"That's sorta vague, boss," said Tom.

"And if you don't?" said Jesse.

"Then Tom rides scout and you point the herd up to Dodge, like you've both been training on, and trade off jobs. Ben Burnette can handle the remuda, with you watching over it. You can handle what comes, after all we've been through," said LaPoint. "We'll catch you when we catch you, about where ever you are at the time, and then it will be here and now, like here and now, except you'll able to handle more work."

"Oh, we can handle the work. Jesse's got another cousin staying with us now that's skilled with horse working and looking for a steady job. Vaqueros are always stopping by looking for work, being as it's the main ranch around friendly to Tejanos, and has got the best crew. That youngster nephew of Poncho has already worked a lot of these mounts with a gentle touch, learned real fast. But I can't figure why you'd want to risk your neck to bring in the wildest bunch of Comanches that ever chased buffalo or evaded the army," said Tom.

"Me neither. You said most of the captives have come in, which was the main danged reason you both got in it, I'm thinking. It's got something to do with Kathy's brother, doesn't it?" asked Jesse.

"Well, maybe. I think I might have seen him at the Mow-way battle on the Red River. I think he was the one who shot that arrow into Mackenzie after I startled him. He looked a lot like Kathy's brother in facial structure, and had blue eyes and the same color light hair, though it was well greased. About the right age too, and size. I think he may be with Kiwih-nai and the Quohadis. Or maybe even at Fort Sill, since pressure has brought most of the captives in. I've got a tin-type picture of the two of them, right before he was stolen. He might recognize it."

"It would be good if she could know, that's for sure," said Jesse. "I figured that's mainly what it was, because she has that sad spot in her from not knowing. Like my aunt on the Rodriguez side, who lost those boys to Lipan-Apaches. They stay busy with their lives and loved ones, but when they stop for a moment, you see that sadness reappear in their eyes, wondering what happened to their kin."

"You're right about wanting to get it resolved, that and my respect for Kiwih-nai and the Quohadis. We saw lots of buffalo bones on our ride back down here last fall, but no live animals. He's got to bring his band in or perish. The hunters are wiping out the last of the southern herd. Their time is over on the plains."

"Kiwih-nai..respect...?..who nearly killed you with a bullet, a spear, and a cottonmouth snake he threw at you!" said Jesse.

"Yeah boss, sounds like ya barely escaped with your scalp the other times yal met, with that slug in your journal..." said Jackson.

"Well, that was in battle, and we gave it our best shots. But he could have killed me and didn't later on. Maybe he was counting coup," said Josh.

"Yeah, I bet he wished he had killed you back when he saw you on the Blanco, before you led the cavalry in on those attacks," said Tom.

"Seems like you counted coup with that stone to the chest, and maybe he's pissed off about it still," said Jesse.

"Josh and Kiwih-nai are blood brothers, ya know. Me too," said Gabe.

Jesse laughed out loud and said, "Oh yeah, that time he captured the two wily always-alert scouts butchering buffalo up in the cap-rock canyons and let you go. He probably just felt sorry for the stupid white guys butchering meat for him. Maybe the slice on the palm for being blood brothers was just the first slice, eh? He'll find you before you find him, I'd bet. And yal both got famous scalps and horses, not to mention long rifles and the best repeating firearms."

"Likely," replied Gabe with a crease in his brow. "We're taking lots of white flags."

"He could have taken our horses and guns already, and he let us go," said LaPoint.

"That was before the war got hot and popping," said Tom.

"Don't go, let the army handle it. They got a lot of scouts and interpreters at Fort Sill, don't they?" said Jesse.

"We're going, plan accordingly," said Gabe, unbending as cold steel.

"We have to go. We committed," said LaPoint. "We shook on it, gave our word."

"Alright then," said Jesse. "I guess that's that. But I don't like it."

"Do you think he's still got the big gray pacer that you sold to the army for Mackenzie?" asked Tom Jackson.

"Yeah," said Josh, "...from what we heard, Mackenzie and the 4th cavalry searched for him non-stop after we left them at Tule Canyon, after the Palo Duro battle and horse slaughter, until the end of the year. Sergeant Charlton says they nearly froze to death, like some of the mules did. They will be going out after them again if we fail in this mission. The Big Gray will likely get killed in battle if that happens. And Kiwih-nai too. The Quohadis will be wiped out. I don't want that to happen. They could come in, learn to be stock-men, like us."

"Why not let it happen, you led the troopers into the two other battles already?" said Jesse.

"But boss, he shot you in the chest," said Tom. "And he would have killed you if not for that journal you carry in your inside vest pocket. We all seen that bullet hole near the book binding from his .44 Colt. How do you know he won't do it again?"

"That was in battle, like I said. He was defending his village. Later he could have shot me and didn't. It's less likely than getting assassinated by a back-alley back-shooter in Helena, or by a bush-whacking rustler. It's something I've got to do."

"Well maybe you should get another journal, for the other vest pocket, a thick one, or some of those French philosophy books in your room, that Rousseau fella maybe," said Jesse.

"Yeah, or a Bible like the Comanches use ta stuff their shields," said Tom.

"Naw, tha best be them thar 'lightenment books," said Gabe. "'Cording to Kiwih-nai, our Josh LaPoint is tha lightning cougar, I reckon that's whar he learned ' bout en-lightenin', huh?" asked Gabe with a wry look.

"Not a bad idea, just stuff my pockets with Voltaire and Rousseau, eh?" Josh replied with a chuckle, hoping to ease past Jesse's agitation. "I might even get religious too, layer in some Bibles. Not that I believe in the Israelite notion of invasion and slaughter on God's say so. We're not the chosen people, just the ones with better guns."

"Why shore, that's what the Comanche's do, stuff their bull-hide shields with Bible pages to turn bullets," said Gabe.

"That old grampa warrior in the Mow-way battle had a shield just a-littering Bible pages out a big shotgun hole in it. They like Bibles 'cause they say it's the white man's medicine talk, heap power."

"Probably the most good it ever does," said Tom.

"Now Tom, what would your sainted mother say to that?" asked Gabe.

"She'd say any God that don't get up early and git ta work better quit slacking and get out of her house," replied Tom, drawing a general chuckle. "She always said a shotgun was better than prayer."

"Or a frying pan of hot grease," said LaPoint.

"I heard them Bible-stuffed Comanche buffalo shields can turn bullets, so maybe it does work," said Jesse.

"She'd run any slacker off with a hot frying pan, just like those Comanches, huh?" asked Gabe.

"Yep, ran me off, more than once. That's why I work with you guys."

"Wal, that explains it, then," said scout McBride. "And here I thought it was tha biscuits."

"I thought it was so you could learn to rope from a real vaquero, like me," said Jesse.

"Alright. So we're going, then," said scout LaPoint. "We'll meet you somewhere along the drive if we're still alive. Most likely before you cross the Red River."

"Scouting for Comanches again. Damn! How about me going with you, boss?" asked Jesse. "They killed my horse, remember, with the Smith boy captives when you made me go to the doctor while you both trailed them. I'd still like to shoot a Comanche for that."

"No. We're not going to fight, just to talk them into surrendering. That was a Lipan-Apache that shot your horse anyway, a bunch that traded those captives off to the Comanches later on. Anyway, I've been training you to replace me when I have to go off like this. It's Gabe and I have signed on to do this, because of getting hooked into it before, starting with trailing those Smith boys, unsuccessfully. And you're right about Kathy's brother as well, I want to follow my hunch on that."

"But I would have gone with you then if you let me, you and this old hammer-man."

"You would have if you had not been wounded and half knocked out. Right now you've got to step up and help run things, manage the horse training, take some load off Poncho."

"I already got that worked out, with a new trainer, my cousin Enrique. And he's got brothers too."

"We have got to finish what we started together," said Josh in his most serious tone, " the two of us, Jesse. You have to fill the hole we leave behind."

"Yeah, we do, " said Gabe. "We're goin', so make accommodations for it, and we'll be back when we can. We aim to see it through. That's what we do, ya know. With an extra vaquero or two, Jesse and Poncho can move to full time trainin' while yal bring in mustangs. We'll find Kiwih-nai as soon as we can. I know their regular camping spots, along the Pease, at Quitaque, or the Red River canyons, or Cedar Lake. We'll find 'em or they'll spot us with white flags. We'll meet you before Fort Griffin, I reckon."

"Well alright, but don't let them finish that scalping and torture job they started on you back when, ya scar-headed old fart, we'd be wanting for biscuits and scouting, talking to Raven, buffalo jerky, all such as that..." said Tom.

"Hell, Kiwih-nai could have made jerky out of us in the cap-rock canyons, and he let us go. He's a satisfied knife customer," said Gabe. "Now that General Ord wants one."

"Hell, he wants to buy the one I stabbed McCairn with," said LaPoint.

"Yeah, satisfied horse customer too, rides the best horse we're produced so far with this outfit," said Jesse.

"Maybe you should take some extra knives along," said Tom.

"Yeah, both of you take pockets full of books and a bunch of knives to trade, so he don't stick you with the ones he's already got...take some rattlesnake belts and hat-bands too."

"Wish I could take some knives, left them at the Blanco ranch," said the blacksmith McBride. "I think Josh has some rattlesnake sashes and headbands in his saddlebags."

"I do, for gifts. I'm also carrying a notion that Kiwih-nai is as tired of this war as we are, and might see the end is near, with all the buffalo disappearing," said Josh, who had a rattlesnake hat band on his broad-brimmed tight-weave palm leaf hat.

"So Kathy's going to stay in Fredricksburg and teach while you go out and try to find her brother, huh?" said Jesse.

"Yeah, and try to bring Kiwih-nai and the Quohadis in."

"Your blood brother that shot you in the chest," Jesse replied, dissatisfied with the situation. "And your brother-in-law that shot an arrow at Mackenzie's chest, and the only reason he didn't kill him is because you startled him into shooting early, that right?"

"Pretty close," said Josh with a smile.

"Well, will you be bringing the big gray pacer back?" asked Tom. "We could breed him to the batch of nice mares we got down south."

"I doubt it," said Josh. "Though I might take it to Mackenzie if I got it. But Kiwih-nai fit the Big Gray better than Mackenzie, if the truth be said, never saw a man ride so well in battle as that day on the north Red River."

"Hey boss," said Jesse. "What about me moving up to the Blanco ranch and work horses there while you're gone, keep an eye on the place. I'm tired of the riff-raff at Helena, just like you. They want to gunfight you because you're so fast, to get a reputation and all with a quick shot while you're not looking, but they just want to bull whip me because I'm a Tejano. I want to try a new place too, just like you."

"Alright. Good idea, if Poncho can train another vaquero in the methods of starting saddle mounts I taught him."

"My cousin, Enrique, has got the touch. He could do it. We already trained him, on this remuda. He's working now with mi papa on the next bunch."

"Alright, you've earned that chance. I'll pick up some raw two-year-old stock I spotted in town here, and bring them out there for you to work into the remudas. There's still a few cows to practice cutting and roping on. You can head for the Blanco after delivering this remuda to Winger this afternoon, and Tom will head back to start the next remuda on the San Antonio. We'll take the best of this stock and some others I've seen in town for you to train while I'm gone. Oh, I forgot to mention, another rubber boat came in to my mail station at the Hotel Menger here. We can take two up the trail, in case we end up in the mountains with nice whitewater rivers to run."

They all shook hands and went to their tasks. Tom and Jesse delivered the remuda to the buyers, then Tom headed

281

south with the vaqueros towards the Eagle Ford Ranch near Helena. Jesse went with Josh and Gabe to meet Kathy at the Menger Hotel and to take Kathy to Fredricksburg. Then Jesse headed back to the Blanco River ranch they called Clear Spring to work the horses there, driving a group of seven horses down the Pedernales and then the Blanco Valley.

Gabe and Josh headed north out of Fredricksburg, where they had learned at Fort Martin Scott that Colonel Mackenzie awaited their arrival at Fort Sill, where he presided over a new military district, the entire reservation system, and a prison house full of surrendered chieftains who had come in after the Palo Duro battle. They made the long ride north in late March, with spring rains freshening the grazing for their mounts and one pack-horse. They traveled fast on a course nearly due north by Fort Griffin, passing the three hundred miles in fifteen days. The grass was still fresh and abundant near the streams from plentiful winter rains, and the stock stayed well maintained. They saw no sign of Comanches along the way, though they were checking out Quohadi haunts in the upper branches of the Pease River, and along the cap-rock canyons of red sandstone topped with crumbling limestone. What they saw was lots of buffalo bones, especially while approaching Fort Sill, where the blue skies were littered with dark circling buzzards and crows.

The Fort and reserve headquarters was busy with all the Indians who had come in recently, and they looked forlorn and discontented. Some scrawny longhorns were in the corrals near the Indian agency headquarters, apparently their only meat. There was an amazing number of Indians all around the area of the fort, their massive horse herds cropping the grass down all around the wide plains surrounding the reserve. Many were complaining of scanty rations, and murmuring in general depression with sidelong glances at the two scouts riding in.

At the fort the scouts conferred with Dr. Sturm and Colonel Mackenzie while resting their mounts and rebuilding their endurance with grain. Mackenzie thanked them again for their help in scouting the two major battles he had fought with the Comanches, and they had a good dinner with the serious officer and Dr. Sturm, followed by a long meeting.

During that informal talk they learned that the Colonel of Scottish ancestry had been particularly impressed when he had heard from Sergeant Charlton, in a heated discussion after the battle, of LaPoint dressed in buckskins and moccasins and headband with shaved face with long braid, armed with knife, bow and arrow, and hidden pistol, resembling nothing so much as an Indian brave while slipping down the trail to kill the sentries. Remembering his shock at seeing LaPoint before the battle in buckskins and rattlesnake headband, the Colonel expressed amazement that LaPoint had not been shot for an Indian during the battle. Mackenzie remarked that silencing the sentries was the most important job in the battle, and thanked the two scouts again for it.

At the meeting the two scouts learned that Mow-way, Maman-ti, Long Hungry, Lone Wolf, and Wild Horse were incarcerated in a converted ice house nearby with other chieftains. They toasted the fact that the chieftains that LaPoint and McBride has set out to capture were now incarcerated a few yards away, and they felt well satisfied that their work had been successful. The scouts congratulated the Colonel in being the first military man in a century and a half to whip the Comanches by turning their tactics against them, and Mackenzie responded by emphasizing the job was not finished until the Quohadi came in. The dedicated soldier always seemed to have a mission foremost in his mind.

LaPoint was anxious over the captives, and led the discussion there. Dr. Sturm told them that the Smith boys had been returned, along with many other white captives, so they felt some relief that their involvement in the war had been worthwhile in that regard. Josh showed Dr. Sturm the tin-types images of Kathy's brothers in hopes that he had seen some white Comanches or returned captives with similar face. He had not, but Josh was on alert for those facial features among the many Indians around the post. The several white captives at the post waiting for relocation did not fit the age, sex, nor features, so LaPoint kept the search alive, showing the images to Colonel Mackenzie in case new captives came in resembling them. Upon hearing of the fourteen years in captivity, the men from the fort and agency all remarked how hard it was to spot someone that had been that long with the tribe.

At their final meeting Mackenzie emphasized while tapping his finger stumps on the map that with only a few hostile bands remaining on the plains, bringing in the Quohadis became most important, for they were the fiercest and most respected band, the ones who had always disdained contact with the settlements and lived in their high plains kingdom of the buffalo with their horse herds. Mackenzie reasoned that if they came in, all stragglers would follow, and Kiwih-nai or Isatai were deemed as possible leaders for the Comanches on the reservation around Fort Sill. Most of the other war chieftains were being deported to the mosquito filled damp dungeons of Fort Marion in Florida after being found guilty of depredations. Mackenzie had chased Kiwih-nai for years to no avail, and was reaching for other options. He acted like he had heard or suspected somehow that scouts McBride and LaPoint knew and had known the whereabouts of Kiwih-nai, or so it seemed to Josh.

After gaining an understanding of the plan for the expedition to parley with Kiwih-nai's band of Quohadi, the scouts went to the stockade, a thick walled converted ice house with stone floor and no roof, to look at the enemies they had forced to surrender by their scouting actions at the Palo Duro Canyon and North Red River battles.

They especially wanted to see the famous medicine warrior Maman-ti, who had precipitated the Warren wagon train massacre and butchery of the freighters that had inflamed Sheridan enough to begin the Comanche campaigns. Maman-ti's likely presence at Palo Duro Canyon was a main reason the two scouts had opted for leading the 4th Cavalry there instead of into the breaks of the upper Pease where they had figured Kiwih-nai was hiding. Maman-ti's fame as a fierce warrior, inspiring orator, and uncanny medicine man with a talking owl mascot has spread throughout the plains, and they were very glad their scouting had been instrumental in bringing him in. While some Indian medicine men like Isatai were born with personalities unsuited to combat, Maman-ti was a legendary fighter who awed in battle with uncanny anticipation of the opponent's tactics. He had prophesied that the bands would be safe in the Palo Duro, and that was his only notable failure.

The ice house was under heavy guard, and full of various chieftains who had committed the worst depredations, massacres of settlers or freighters, torture of hunters, and captive taking. With about thirty warriors packed into the jail, it was hard to spot the ones they wanted to see, despite the descriptions by J.J. Sturm. They were mostly Kiowas, with only a few Comanches sitting away near the wall. Many had been tried and sentenced to prison in Florida, and were grimly awaiting deportation. Several sat in the corners, facing the walls and muttering, while others lounged around on the plank floor, their eyes dull and listless, as if they wanted to die. There were bones on the grimy flagstone floor with gnawed on hunks of raw meat on them, and flies buzzing everywhere.

The scouts stood at the door with barred window and searched the room full of warriors. They were looking for Maman-ti, whom they had led the 4th Cavalry to find at Palo Duro, and spotted a lean and muscular warrior in the corner with wide set gleaming eyes. He was bent down a little, pacing and pounding his thighs in rhythm to his chanting, while gazing out the barred side window.

"Is that Maman-ti?" Josh whispered to Gabe, not wanting to break the semi-trance that the man seemed to be in.

"That'd be my guess, from what Dr. Sturm told me. He's the Sky Walker, heap big medicine they say, the Owl Man, but he lost his owl, it appears. Good dancer, though."

While they were peering into the barred window of the ice house door, Maman-ti spotted them out of the corner of his eye and suddenly sprang up from his crouching, dancing position and approached them, talking loudly in Kiowa, pointing his finger at LaPoint and then McBride. Seeing Gabe begin to sign, he signed back in Plains hand language as he spoke.

"Oh hell, here it comes, the Kiowa are famous for speechifyin', and he's the most speechifyin' of all. And I think that is Lone Wolf behind him thar, that older one, and Mow-way turning this way, by the far wall. He's told 'em we're the scouts who led the army into the canyon."

Maman-ti started making a loud harangue, gesturing in Plains sign language as he spoke with the controlled vocal powers of a practiced orator. Gabe's face drew a frown as he tried to understand the fast-talking Kiowa. He began to sign back faster and use what few words of that language he knew. Maman-ti grew more agitated, signing and speaking fast, pointing at Josh, then the big McBride knives on their weapons belts, then at Gabe's head, motioning upwards with his long fingers, as if urging McBride to lift his hat. Gabe tipped his wide-brimmed straw hat up and revealed the scar and Maman-ti gave a startled cry when it was revealed, reeled back a step, then began a rapid chant, evolving into a long speech with the medicine man again pointing fingers at Josh and Gabe.

At one point the medicine man reached towards LaPoint's solar plexus and made a grabbing motion at the door, scratching it with long nails while babbling. Josh felt his gut churning as if the man's hand was wrenching it while the mystic warrior gestured and spoke at him, locking him in a fierce but resigned gaze. LaPoint's right hand swept in front of his chest and the feeling stopped while a surprised look crossed Mamanti's face. He lunged against the door with wide eyes and pointed at LaPoint's face through the bars while Josh stepped back, sweeping his hand back and forth in front of his chest, flashing glances at the mesmerizing eyes but not holding the gaze.

Lone Wolf was slowly stamping his feet and shaking his fist at them while muttering in Kiowa. Mow-way had started blabbering at them too. Gabe held the stolid composure he always did while conversing with Indians, with his stout arms crossing the fringed buckskin across his chest, but Josh could feel his nervousness. His own buckskins were soaking with sweat at the intensity of the encounter with a man they had heard of for years.

Maman-ti finished his speech with the word LaPoint involved, and went back to hunker down in the corner, facing towards the wall as he began a mournful chanting song, rocking on the balls of his bare feet as he squatted. Josh was somewhat unnerved by the experience, and was glad to walk away as he felt a queasy quaking experience in his solar plexus. As they walked back towards their quarters, Gabe tried to explain what the powerful medicine warrior was saying.

"Wal, I ain't up on Kiowa all that much, but what I think he said was that he has seen you in his dreams many times, and that he dreamed of this day when we three would meet in the shadow of the bars, and it marked the beginning of his death song. He knew when he saw us that the time of the Kiowa is over, and his time is over."

"Looks like he could have figured that out without seeing us."

"He's one of them misty fellas. His dreams is what rules him. He seen us in dreams."

"He looks familiar. Like he's been in mine."

"Oh yeah? Thar's more. He also said he dreamed of you leading the troops down the cliff into Palo Duro looking like an Indian with a Tonkawa bow and poisoned flint arrows to kill the sentries, on the night it happened, but it was too late. He awoke from his dream when he saw us slit the throats of the sentries, and ran to stop us, but you had just taken down the herd night-riders with the Tonkawa bow and coral snake-poisoned arrows, after we slit the sentries' throats with our knives. That's when he knew you had pierced his magic. Then the troopers charged at him, and he had to run and hide in the boulders."

"Why did he keep pointing at our knives and jabbering so fast?"

"He said he dreamed of our knives often. He said you were the point of knife blade for the whites, the only point strong enough to pierce his magic, because you were a big medicine power shape shifter who turned into an Indian when you needed to. And that I was your scar-head knife father, invulnerable to Indian weapons."

"Damn, you caught all that?"

"Yeah, I reckon, with words and signing, though I was nervous and mighta missed somethin'."

"Well, Old Coon, if I'd known you were invulnerable, I'd have hid behind you in those battles."

"Yeah, well you ain't been superstitious yet, have ya? Anyway, it's a bit uncanny he knows how you come down that tiny trail and took care of the sentries."

"Well, he could have heard through the Tonkawa scouts."

"John'son wasn't thar, remember? He's the one always spreading talk about us. We stuck him with the troopers out of the way after he bird-dogged us on that scout. Only that front patrol with Jack Charlton saw you dressed as an Indian with the bow, and they're down at Fort Concho. And Maman-ti say's you was shaved and smooth faced, how'd he know that?"

"Alright, it is strange," said the bearded LaPoint, "and I have a feeling I've seen him in my dreams too, vague images of this meeting floating around my mind. I actually think I saw his face in dreams the night before, and while I was slipping up to the horse herd I saw an image like his face again."

"Maybe he saw us. I'da shot him if I knew."

287

"Me too. He's a pretty tough looking warrior, still all muscled up, got some spirit about him, not like those others."

"He got my neck hairs bristlin', got me feelin' wrathy, blood rushing for a fight that ain't thar."

"Yeah. And I could feel some powerful waves coming from him into my chest, like he was trying to reach into me there. Same as my mother would do in a gentle way, he did it in a fierce way. He's for real a medicine man. He's got more power than the ordinary warrior. Those eyes."

"He could shore bore inta ya with 'em, couldn't he? And was the head medicine man for all the unified tribes when Isatai lost favor after the failure to take Adobe Walls. Hell, I heard the Cheyenne and Kiowa were ready to kill Isatai if Kiwih-nai had not protected him, beat him with their bows and called him skunk pussy magic."

"Maman-ti looked like a fighting medicine man, very tough looking. So did Lone Wolf, still fierce for an older man."

"Maman-ti warn't no spectator and rattle shaker like Isatai at Adobe Walls, he fought in the front-line of nearly every battle his people fought, and could prophesy better than anyone, they say. All the Indians here revere and fear him, 'cordin' ta Dr. Sturm The only prophesy of his that didn't come true was when he told 'em that they'd be safe at Palo Duro Canyon, and we led the troopers in to ruin it last fall."

"So that's why he was carrying on so, because I slipped through his magic spell, fighting as an Indian?"

"I reckon, first time somebody did. He said you didn't have hair on your face then, which is another uncanny fact. He also said you wore a rattlesnake headband."

"He's got some kind of sixth sense, that's for sure."

"Somehow he successfully called the outcome of lots of engagements, they say, down to the particulars. Said his owl spirit told him the future."

"That's the talking hand puppet we heard about for years, huh?"

"Yeah. It's for shore he had an owl puppet, a flayed owl skin with feathers and all, but plenty of solid warriors swear it started flapping and flew out of his hand and hovered there talking to him. Even lots of skeptical Comanches swear they seen it circling around in the air telling him the future."

288

"Yeah, the same ones who saw Isatai vomit up a wagon-load of ammunition, and then swallow it back down, right?"

"They all say Isatai predicted the appearance and duration of that comet, and that drought last summer. They all claim this Maman-ti knew what was comin' down tha turnpike in war after he conversed with his Owl Spirit. Then he'd predict the future, down to particulars of each battle. They say he could have called for a raid on Sheridan but held off and hit that Warren wagon train instead, for he foresaw the soldiers fighting too hard."

"Yeah, well another way of looking at it would be he attacked the wrong train, and could have gotten the leader of the white army."

"Yeah, yore right thar. But they'da just put another railroad man in there, or bumped Sherman up, and he's the worst of all. Grant mighta used it as an excuse to invade Mexico for all we know."

"And now Maman-ti's locked up at Fort Sill, magic shot to hell, but still strong enough to make my guts crawl. Was he cursing us?"

"Naw. More like grim recognition. What his long speech was about was, lets see now......he dreamed that if he saw us together, the *red bear sharp knife* with the scalpin' scar, and the one they call *LaPoint*, then his end was near, and the end of the Kiowas. He said you were like them changing lizards, a shape shifter, and that you changed into an Indian to break his magic, and when he saw you again, that was his end. Said he dreamed it all. So he went inta his death song, making ready for the next world, where he has been already many times, and makin' ready to return to."

"Well, magic or not, his raiding career has ended in an ice-house with steel bars on the openings. I figure he belongs there. That Warren wagon train massacre started off this damned war anyway."

"And he's probably on his way to prison in Florida. He was a man staring at his own death and the next world, said he was crossing over soon. The last thing he said was he will take Kicking Horse with him when he goes to the next world, for his great betrayal."

"More medicine man magic?"

289

"I reckon. Glad he was cursing Kicking Horse and not us. He rose the hair on my neck, real spooky, that fella. Gave me goose flesh."

"Me too, I've got to admit. I felt some powerful waves coming from him, shook me up some. And Lone Wolf wasn't too happy to see us either, though he wasn't as intense as Maman-ti."

"That's the last we'll see of either of those, they're taking most of that bunch to Florida real soon, and Maman-ti is headed for the spirit world. "

"You believe him"

"Durned right. That's his death song. He's goin', and he knows it. We went after him last fall, and right here and now we got him. Too bad he didn't get to die in battle, as a warrior's just desserts."

"I'd have killed him if I saw him."

"Me too, but with a gun, not a knife. He looked pretty dangerous for hand to hand, nothing but lean rippling muscle, and quick."

"Yeah. Or a poisoned arrow. You don't need to be knife fighting young bucks, remember what happened to Kit, heart burst on him."

"When yore time's up, it's up, gotta keep livin' 'til then. If somebody better suited for this job steps up, I'll retire ta poundin' hot steel instead of slingin' hot lead. Powder is dry til then."

"Was that Mow-way in the corner, facing the wall?"

"I reckon it was. He warn't at the village when we led the cavalry in though, he was in Washington with ole drunken Grant, getting a lecture. I think he may slip outta going to prison in Florida, though his band had lots of captives, including the Smith boy you nearly grabbed. He's pretty good at negotiation, the wily ole rascal."

"What about Isatai, the Comanche prophet, where is he?'

"With Kiwih-nai, I reckon, out running free. He's the peace chief for the band, while Kiwih-nai deals with strategy, according ta what I heard around the fort. But after his medicine failed at Adobe Walls, only the Quohadis listen to him. The Cheyennes call him somethin' like skunk ass dung now, or worse."

"Well, I hope he hasn't been dreaming about me. Nor Gray Blanket either. I never felt such rage and hatred from a man, though Lone Wolf was giving it a go. It's sort of strange, but I'm not nervous about seeing Kiwih-nai, just that mean sidekick of his with blond hair, that hardheaded German Comanche that wants my scalp for his lance."

"Yeah, a full lance it was too, including a scalp of long auburn hair from a woman, like them long scalps in front of Bise McCairn's lodge....and you should be wary of that guy...but not Kiwih-nai, though if we ever find him it'll be a wonder. Hell, we already checked out a lot of the Quohadi haunts coming up, with no buffalo and no Indians, just bone piles and early cattle drives."

"Gotta be further west. You think he may be friendly like he was that time in those red canyons of the cap rock near Quitaque?"

"Wal, he might be ready to come in, if approached rightly. How can they live out here without buffalo? He ain't never lost a battle nor been caught by the cavalry, but he knows it can happen with Bad Hand Mackenzie, who don't never let up. He knows they can't live out here much longer. They don't like eating horses, like Apaches."

"Well, the sooner we get it over with, the sooner my name is cleared."

"From what I gathered, Mackenzie already done cleared yore name, and it's up to us to pay him back. We'll get it done."

They left the Comanches and Kiowas grimly enduring their fate at the brig, with real hopes that the wars were over with them forever. The mournful wailing and muttering of Maman-ti was echoing across the yard as they walked away. Lone Wolf had joined him in the death chant, and it was as mournful a wailing as Josh had ever heard, so they walked quickly to get away from it. They spent the rest of the afternoon talking with post interpreter Dr. Sturm, a likeable and smart fellow, and discussing things with Mackenzie.

Mackenzie was aggravated because he could not get adequate supplies to keep everyone from being hungry at the fort, and was dictating letter after letter up the chain of command, decrying the situation of missing supplies and the Indian Ring that funneled off graft, while trying to deal with the remaining renegade bands. He complained that the government had become a huge spoils system since the war, and he didn't know if it would ever straighten out. He assured LaPoint that the warrants were past history, and was very hopeful that the two scouts would succeed in their mission, and bring in the last highly respected chieftain of the Comanches, who had so far evaded the determined colonel. He felt that he had the Kiowa situation mostly in hand, and only the renegade raiders after cattle herds remained a major problem, if the Quohadi could be brought in. His last task would be to find the hiding place of the last bands of renegades, hiding in hills to the north, and bring them in or destroy them in place. The long string of herds heading for Dodge were the constant prey of these renegades, and they had to be cleared out.

Soon there-after the Indian chieftains left under heavy guard for prisons in Florida, and Kicking Horse died suddenly a couple of days later, just as Maman-ti had declared when pointing at him and yelling a loud speech. Dr. Sturm could not figure why he died, and the army surgeons began an examination of the corpse while the Indians all nodded their heads and muttered about Maman-ti the Sky Walker. The agitated Kiowas spent the next few days in oratory while Dr. Sturm and the other post interpreters and agents tried to calm them down from their near hysteria. Already the Kiowas had nearly stampeded when simply put on a census, and it took some time to calm them down.

Mackenzie was even more anxious then for a respected chieftain to replace the powerful position held by Maman-ti and help him maintain order on the reservation, and urged the two scouts to find Kiwih-nai and bring him in, going so far as to say that Kiwih-nai could keep the big gray pacer he called Bad Hand Horse, because he was still undefeated in battle. Mackenzie seemed to hold "The Eagle" and his Quohadis with a similar measure of respect that Josh and Gabe did, and the colonel did not want to have to destroy them. Though so far every effort to even find them had been unsuccessful.

Gabe enjoyed the meal immensely, and impressed Mackenzie and Strum with how much buffalo meat, a rare treat, he could put away. Throughout the meal, the determined Scottish Colonel kept returning to the subject of where the Quohadi were hiding, of 'bringing in The Eagle', and badgering Gabe as if he suspected the old scout knew exactly where the

Quohadi hid. Gabe remained steady with his gorging on buffalo, then drank brandy and smoked his kinnickinnick in a red stone Comanche pipe, and said, "reckon they'd find 'em somewhars."

LaPoint took the time of that verbal stalemate to toast Mackenzie's two victories that had brought in most of the captives and most of the hostile bands. Then he shifted the talk to horses and the big mounts he was readying for the army, perhaps to replace the big gray pacer stolen by Kiwih-nai. Mackenzie finally seemed to mellow out and relax as Josh and Gabe carried the trail of conversation to lighter subjects. They ended the evening with more toasts, then repaired to the last indoor beds they would have for a while.

When the small negotiating party was finally ready, they left Fort Sill on an early morning near the middle of April, with Wild Horse acting as Comanche guide. Gabe and Josh trotted their horses out towards the front to ride with him, and the former chieftain spoke with Gabe about the Red River battle, where he had seen both Josh and McBride in the fighting. Their mutual participation in the battle seemed to form some kind of bond of respect, and Wild Horse was actually friendly towards them. He and Gabe did a lot of talking with hands and Comanche tongue as they rode in front, leading the small group. Soon the three of them formed into a scouting unit, riding far in the lead to search for a Quohadi village, with LaPoint in the middle, and the other two on the wings, signaling with mirrors. Wild Horse had been amazed to learn their signal system with the mirrors and binoculars and telescope, and the telescoped Whitworth and Sharps rifles, instantly grasping the advantage this and the long range guns had given the scouts.

They headed southwest for Doan's Crossing of the Red River, where drovers were scouting the crossing and pounding brush into the riverbed sand with a small herd, to stiffen the bottom for the coming procession of herds heading for Dodge City and the rail heads. From the crossing they followed a branch of the Red River that headed west into the haunts of the Quohadis, but they searched the rough headwaters in vain, finding only old campsites in the upper breaks and grassy canyons. The absence of buffalo herds and the presence of scattered bones was always striking, every day the same grim circling buzzards and littered bones. Coyotes were slinking around in broad daylight, gorging on the buffalo carcasses under swarms of black and brown birds, while the buzz of flies filled the fetid air around the waste.

After a week of riding they were together at daybreak, preparing to strike out scouting when a raven flew by, cawing. Gabe returned a few caws and the raven circled the three scouts, speaking with Gabe. Then it flew back with noisy wings in the direction it came from.

Wild Horse shook his head and gave a grim look, pulling on his horses mane as he did when worried or feeling frustrated.

"Well, what did it say?" asked LaPoint. "Buffalo herd ahead?"

"Nope. Raven said the buffalo are dead."

They pushed on as the days grew warmer, the grim notion of the end of the buffalo weighing on their minds. They often heard the rolling noise of the big guns, like thunder in the distance. Sometimes they spotted huge spirals of black buzzards circling above buffalo hunter camps where skinners worked at a frantic pace to keep up with skilled shooters booming their Sharps big-fifties in endless rolling thunder across the flat plains as they wiped out the last of the southern herd, completing the virtual extinction of a species and the people who depended on it. Gabe was particularly chagrined by the re-occurring sight, for he had grown old enough to regret his part in wiping out the beaver in his youthful days as a mountain trapper, and he saw another species on the road to extinction.

From there they ranged along the edges of the broken cap-rock cliffs, searching for signs of smoke or recent passage of horses, but were unsuccessful. Day after weary day they rode the grassy plains, hearing the constant booming of buffalo guns like distant thunder, seeing the scattered piles of buffalo bones instead of the brown running herds of several years ago. They explored all the upper branches of the Pease River watershed, moving slowly through the breaks with wary searching for ambush, but the Quohadis seemed to have abandoned their former campsites.

After about twelve days of riding southwest they came upon a group of slaughtered buffalo hunters, one shooter and two skinners, dead, mutilated, and burned in a wagon half loaded with hides after being filled with steel tipped arrows. The buzzards had gotten to the cooked carcasses, but they buried the remains and marked the graves. They rode on this way for two weeks, heading generally southwest eventually, for Wild Horse told them that Kiwih-nai went west as far as the Guadalupe Mountains to evade Mackenzie the previous winter. Every Quohadi camping spot they checked was empty. Every morning they awoke with fresh hopes and rode out scouting, but every evening they went to bed frustrated and wondering where to search next.

They had traveled over two hundred miles southwest in two weeks of steady riding through short grass and bleached bone piles, but never found the Quohadis until they came to a ridge-line the Comanches called Blowing Mountain, about fifty miles south of Blanco Canyon, where they had also searched in vain. LaPoint and McBride had seen the campground the previous year, and by process of elimination they figured it was the likely hiding spot.

Early that morning Josh had spotted the dust of a small buffalo hunt with his field glasses from a little rise. The three scouts immediately headed south to follow the Indian hunters, hoping it would lead back to a Quohadi village. By stopping to stand in his saddle stirrups, LaPoint kept the hunting party in sight with the telescope that Gabe handed him. They tried to stay far enough back while trailing the hunting party to be unobserved. Soon they came upon a few buffalo, and shot one to butcher the meat for camp, dividing it on their horses. Within an hour of riding south they saw what looked like the smoke of many small campfires. They walked their horses to keep quiet, and found cover to move in when they could.

McBride and LaPoint were walking slowly with Wild Horse when they came to the tall ridge-line of a stony butte overlooking a grassy valley to the south, and there on the edge they spotted the lodges of the Quohadis, stretched out below them on the grassy flats across the small stream at the base of the ridge. It was a breathtaking sight like overlooking the Palo Duro Canyon villages, though the solid stone butte was not as high as those canyon walls. The clear running steam below the long cliff provided water for their large horse herd of around a thousand horses, and the grassy flats ran back several miles. The village was quite large, stretching along the waterway for a mile at least, large and small buffalo hide lodges, cones with darkened tips where smoke wafted out.

Wild Horse was very nervous about riding down alone, and more nervous about bringing the whole negotiating party in unannounced, so they conferred with him on a plan. Gabe was to take the lead, with his hat off and scar exposed to be recognized, and bearing gifts. He gathered bags of that morning's leftover sourdough biscuits, the fresh buffalo meat, coffee, sugar, tobacco, and jerky, and took the lead position as they descended the butte and circled around into the camp.

LaPoint and Wild Horse rode side by side behind scout McBride on the early afternoon of April 28th, 1875, into the camp of the Quohadis, each bearing a white flag on a long cedar bough they had cut and skinned. They were quickly surrounded by yipping outriders who escorted them into the heart of the encampment, where they saw Kiwih-nai standing with his arms folded.

LaPoint had his eye out for Gray Blanket, the aggressive German Comanche who wanted to kill and scalp him. The leather loop was off his knife, for fast access, but the holster flap snapped on his big revolver, still worn backwards on his left side. LaPoint no longer carried the fast draw tie-down rig with the .36 caliber Remington, having left it with Kathy. All their rifles were in the saddle holsters, and upon arriving at the headmen lodges they stuck the white flag poles in the ground, and Gabe held the gifts up and spoke in Comanche.

"Don't dismount until he says it's okay," said McBride as he handed down bags of gifts to a warrior around his own age, who walked them to Kiwih-nai.

"Your play Gabe, I follow your lead," said LaPoint as he handed tobacco wrapped in two rattlesnake sashes to squaws standing beside his horse.

"Unha hakai nuusuka?" said Gabe to Kiwih-nai.

Under his breath he said to LaPoint, "Just say how ya doing, like I just did, in any language, and glance him in the eye, polite greeting like."

"Buenos Dias, Kiwih-nai. How are you doing?"

"Tsaatu untse?" replied Kiwih-nai.

"He said 'fine and how are you'?"

"I'm doing fine, glad to see you still alive."

"Still alive! Seguro," said Kiwih-nai, who then looked at Gabe and conversed with hand and word. Josh recognized the English word 'Smith' near the end of the speech.

"He says he's alive because you didn't shoot him at Mow-way's village in battle, so he could save the Smith boy from the pool full of blood and bodies. He said that's why he didn't kill you when he could have. He says you are brothers in spirit. He says we can dismount and parley."

"So far so good, lead on," said LaPoint.

They dismounted and strode up to Kiwih-nai in front of Wild Horse, each gripping his hand in turn. He seemed worn and gaunt but friendly towards LaPoint and McBride, gripping their hands firmly with stoic countenance and a light in his heavy-lidded eye. Wild Horse greeted Kiwih-nai, whose face had gotten stony again, then backed away as another young leader walked up.

Kiwih-nai pointed to him with one thumb while opening the gift bags. "Isatai," he said. "Coyote Rump." He pulled out a biscuit which Gabe had put honey into that morning, and nodded his head in satisfaction, then spoke to Gabe some more as he passed the bags to others. Taking a bite of the sourdough treat, Kiwih-nai's face lit up. He looked like a hungry man who had at last found something very good to eat. He looked at Gabe and swallowed.

"You make?"

"Yeah, every day," said Gabe as he nodded his head.

"Glad you didn't burn them today, huh?" said LaPoint.

"Good grub, McBride. We make coffee," the chief said, as the squaws took the ground Arbuckle coffee and poured some with sugar into a copper pot filled with simmering water over a mesquite coal fire.

Kiwih-nai kept chomping on the biscuit until it was gone, then asked for another one before the bag got away. He nibbled the second one slowly, savoring the flavor, and began speaking to Isatai, beside him, telling him to taste it.

Isatai took a taste, and then looked at Gabe and LaPoint in the eye after swallowing it, instead of the sideways glances. His eyes were very dark and shimmering, and he gave a slight shiver ever so often, despite the heat of the day. Kiwih-nai asked to see the rattlesnake sashes, and they were carried to him by a beautiful woman in a white buckskin dress. He looked them over with an appraising eye, then looked at LaPoint,

"You make?"

"No."

"Your woman make?"

"Woman of my friend."

"You kill?"

"Yes."

"This gift for Isatai, sad now," said Kiwih-nai, as he handed the sashes to the medicine man.

"Kiwih-nai talk English."

"Some English. Some Spanish. Isatai no English. Drink coffee, smoke, my home, LaPoint, McBride, you sit." They sat and enjoyed the coffee and smoke together, passing around Gabe's red-stone pipe, then Kiwih-nai's. Isatai just touched the pipe to his lips and passed it on. Josh and Gabe felt much more relaxed, and Gabe spoke in Comanche with them in a casual way.

The scouts recognized the name of the young medicine man they called Coyote Butt, who had predicted a comet and helped Kiwih-nai unify the tribes for the Adobe Walls battle, and was discredited with the other tribes there. He looked about as fierce as a hotel desk clerk or Bible salesman to them, and he was beside Kiwih-nai instead of the ominous Gray Blanket, which was an improvement. It was obvious he still held a position of respect with the Quohadis, as they deferred to him, and he walked up to stand beside Kiwih-nai in the position of peace leader. He had a dreamy look about the eyes, and seemed resigned to see them there. His eyes were red rimmed like he had been crying, with very large black pupils, and would not match gazes very long with LaPoint or Gabe. He looked at his moccasins and muttered while waving an eagle feather fan towards them. At his belt was a small gourd shaker with snake rattles on it. He took that out and began a rhythmic buzzing, while holding the rattlesnake sash in his lap.

Josh nodded towards Isatai, who gave him a sideways look and a strange smile, followed by a grimace. "Isatai, I am LaPoint. How are you doing?" Josh saw that his pupils were huge, nearly covering his eye, and he looked almost in a trance.

"Tsaatu untse, LaPoint?" The medicine man replied in a low melancholy voice.

"I'm doing fine," said LaPoint.

"LaPoint!" said Kiwih-nai, and rubbed his chest where the rock thrown by Josh in battle had bruised him.

"Kiwih-nai," said LaPoint, and touched his own chest where he also carried a sore mark of the slug from Kiwih-nai's pistol that hit his journal in his vest pocket. LaPoint pulled out his journal and showed Kiwih-nai the bullet hole partly through it. Kiwih-nai broke his stoic face into a smile, the hooded eyes crinkling, then turned to Gabe and seemed to ask a question in Comanche. Gabe replied, "good shield, paper word magic".

Kiwih-nai touched the journal. "Good shield, paper word magic. You make, LaPoint?"

"Yes, I make."

"You give me, for my shield?"

"No."

Kiwih-nai nodded and tapped the journal.

"I learn paper word magic. Squaws learn sourdough," said Kiwih-nai in halting but clear English. Then he conversed with Gabe some more in the language of the Numunu, and slowly put his hand on the journal and pulled it from LaPoint's hand, turning the pages and staring at the writing.

LaPoint looked at Gabe and the old scout spoke, "He says it is the white man's magic, the writing and passing talk a long way, like the singing wires, and he wants to learn it, the way of his mother's people."

Kiwih-nai traced his long finger along the curve of the writing, then looked at LaPoint as Josh remembered the same long fingers trailing along the top of the Red River water as Kiwih-nai rode hanging from the big gray stallion to pick up that cottonmouth from the bloody stream and hurl it at him.

"What's the word for snake, Gabe?"

"Kwasinaboo."

Josh said "Kwasinaboo" and motioned like he was grabbing a snake from below and whirling it like a lariat in the air, then throwing it. Kiwih-nai broke into the biggest merriment they had ever seen him let loose, his eyes crinkling and tearing as he laughed for a while. His laughter seemed to be infectious, for soon the surrounding group was laughing, and even the nervous Kicking Horse joined in.

"Kwasinaboo!" He imitated the fast draw motion of LaPoint and pretended to fire a pistol at the ground. "Ekakwitsubitu LaPoint!"

LaPoint smiled at his adept mimicry and Kiwih-nai continued, now animated and friendly, revealing a young man in his early twenties instead of the war-painted fierce battle leader. He bent down and picked up a stone and hurled it off in the distance, imitating the way LaPoint had hurled a stone at him in the Red River battle, then grabbed his gut and whooshed out air, making Josh laugh as he did when he was a boy. All the Comanches thought it was very funny and the excited murmur of laughter passed through the gathered tribe.

Josh pulled his straw hat off and took the diamond-backed rattlesnake hat band from it by cutting the threads holding it with the point of his razor sharp knife. He handed it to the young warrior in friendship, and the half breed Indian reached into a bag at his waist and drew out three wizened peyote buttons, which he handed LaPoint, who nodded and stuck them in the big pocket of his buckskin pants. Then the big chieftain conversed with Gabe a while more, still chuckling.

"He says thanks for the sashes and hat band, and he got the notion from when he first saw you on the Blanco and you drew down on those cottonmouths with your lightening draw. He wanted to see you dodge a cottonmouth. He said he couldn't hardly believe it when you did a backward flip off Scorpio's rump and came up hurling that rock that nailed him in the chest. Made him sore for three moons, he said. All the time he led Mackenzie on a wild goose chase that winter his chest was aching from that rock. He said you matched him move for move, but you will never have the chance again. Those days are over, but if he had to fight again, he would want to fight you."

"Tell him the same goes for me, he's the best horseback warrior I've seen." Gabe translated, and Kiwih-nai nodded in satisfaction. "Tell him I thought of our fight many times, and will always carry pictures of him in my head. Tell him I only wish I had caught the snake and thrown it back."

Gabe spoke with the big chieftain. "He says same goes for him, with the river stone. He says the peyote is for when you need to visit your spirit animal, the cougar, and ride the lightening. Also he said that your horse had better kicks than his, but his was faster."

They both smiled and nodded while LaPoint put the journal back into his pocket. Isatai stayed grim and dreamy looking, with squint-eyed glances at LaPoint without looking him in the eye. He waved a fan of eagle feathers towards Josh and muttered some incantations. Josh was wondering if Gray

Blanket would come out and join in the hostile glances, or try to kill him and take his scalp. He had decided earlier that he would only draw his knife and not his gun if attacked by the surly warrior, and ask for man to man combat in Comanche words Gabe had taught him. LaPoint figured it was better to deal head-on with someone who wanted to kill him so much. But the German Comanche was nowhere in sight.

Gabe began signing and speaking as many Comanche words as he could remember, telling Kiwih-nai of their mission. The dignified chieftain held a stoic continence and listened as Gabe tried to convince him to come in. LaPoint watched silently, occasionally sharing eye contact with Kiwih-nai as Gabe explained the situation. Isatai began weeping steadily, the tears rolling down his gaunt cheeks. Some women in the gathering crowd began to weep while men muttered darkly and low among themselves.

Gabe started a new speech with words and signs, this time using the words J.J. Sturm and Mackenzie several times. Afterward as Kiwih-nai considered what he said, Gabe told Josh. "I told him that we were on a mission from Mackenzie and Dr. Strum to bring him in voluntary like, but Dr. Sturm don't know we are here, so if he don't want ta come in, we won't tell Sturm we found him. I also told him about the papers for safe passage ta Fort Sill by Mackenzie, should he decide to bring the Quohadis in."

When Gabe was finished, Kiwih-nai nodded, held a thoughtful look on a creased brow, then looked at LaPoint. The face of the big warrior was not painted in fearsome colors, and he looked much more vulnerable since they had seen him last, much leaner, more grim than foreboding. Josh thought he saw the young man behind the warrior's mask, weary of the killing role the world had forced on him, and LaPoint understood that feeling well. Kiwih-nai lifted his chin up and opened his hands towards LaPoint, as if asking his opinion. Then he turned to Gabe and signed to him, speaking his own language as he did.

"He wants ta know what you think of this situation. He says he could hide from Mackenzie forever, like the time they led the blue-coats in circles and stole the big gray stallion, and this is Comanche land, so why should he give up the free life of the Numunu on the plains, when the whites can't live here anyway?"

Josh looked into the eyes of the Quohadi chieftain, and could see the weariness and desperation there, mixed with defiance and fierce resistance, feelings he had known. Kiwih-nai, still a proud warrior, seemed like a guy tired of running and seeing his people suffer, who just wanted to live with his horses but was forced to war, like LaPoint had been.

"Tell him we have ridden for a moon in the land of the buffalo and seen only their bones. Tell him I think going in to Fort Sill is the only way for the Quohadis to survive. Tell him Bad Hand Mackenzie will find him eventually, if he does not come in. Tell him just as the Comanches beat the Apaches for this land, now the Army is beating the Comanche. The land will go to the most powerful, no matter whose ancestors are buried here. More and more soldiers will keep coming until they win. Tell him the time of the Numunu on the plains is over, for the buffalo are disappearing forever. Tell him he fought the good fight for his country and his people, and nobody defeated him, but now he must change to survive, become a horse rancher like I did."

Gabe told all this to Kiwih-nai, whose face registered recognition and grim acceptance of the pragmatic reality it contained. Isatai sunk to his knees and hung his head down weeping, pulling out a small knife to cut his hair. Wild Horse shifted his feet and stared at the ground, grim with anticipation and foreboding. Kiwih-nai stared into the eyes of LaPoint as Gabe talked and gestured. He nodded his head at Gabe and made several hand signs, to which Gabe nodded back and made a palm down clearing sign across his chest. Kiwih-nai looked at LaPoint, and spoke to Gabe while Josh waited for translation.

"He says he knows that we led the cavalry into Mow-way's village, and into Palo Duro, and that we caused the horse herd to be slaughtered. But he says he also knows we didn't lead the cavalry to his people, that we kept our word to him. He also says that the Quohadis could have lived on the staked plains, and the whites could have lived below the cap-rock, but instead we went to war, because of angry fools who pushed too far. He said the Comanche have no big chief to stop the young men raiding, and the white soldiers just keep coming and coming. He says he has just returned from a vision quest at Blanco Canyon, where the eagle spirit told him to go to Fort Sill, and now you tell him that also, so he will go. He says you were a good enemy in battle, maybe you could be good friends in peace. He wants to raise and train horses like you, and learn to write in a magic journal, like you. He said he will give the rattlesnake sash to his son, to hold the McBride knife I gave him that time in the Cap-rock Canyons."

"Tell him the army won't stop searching until all the white captives come in, and all the bands. It's time for the war to end, for his people are hungry with no buffalo to eat, and we have seen their lean faces with sadness. His coming in will bring the other bands in, and save what is left of the Comanche."

Gabe spoke with Kiwih-nai again for quite a while, then turned to Josh. "He says there are no captives with the Quohadis, and they have killed many buffalo hunters, but more keep coming, and the buffalo are hard to find."

"The times of living with the buffalo are over," said LaPoint.

Gabe spoke more with the proud warrior, then again to Josh.

"He says he can't stand to see his people going hungry. Gray Blanket, the one that wanted yore scalp, and the other one ya think might be Kathy's brother, Red Hawk, have joined a renegade raiding band. They hide in the Wichita mountains north of Fort Sill and scrounge around for buffalo and deer, or raid the cattle herds to eat."

"Oh. Well, there's one part of the mission that won't be accomplished. Yet."

"'Fraid not," said Gabe as Kiwih-nai walked over to Scorpio and breathed into his nostrils, then rubbed his muzzle and head. He spoke to Gabe again, and he translated to Josh.

"He admires your horses, and wants to be a ranch-man and raise horse, like you. He asked if they have biscuits at the reservation like these, and I told him they got tha flour for it and I'd show his wives how to make 'em. And he wants to race horses with you, the big gray pacer against Scorpio, before we head back."

The big chieftain smiled again when he saw LaPoint understand and accept the challenge. He walked up to LaPoint and tapped his chest.

"LaPoint," he said. Then he tapped his own chest, saying, "Nu nahnia tse...Quanah. Quanah Parker."

"Waugh! World in changes. He just said 'my name is Quanah Parker'," said Gabe in a surprised tone, though he usually kept his voice calm and mono-toned when talking with Comanches. "He knows all about his mom and her folks now."

Josh frowned at him, the unbeaten war leader of the Quohadi, the one they called The Eagle, the one they could never catch. "Kiwih-nai?"

The Quohadi chieftain shook his head with a sad frown. "Waugh!," he said, in perfect imitation of Gabe, sounding like a young bear. "No, LaPoint. Quanah Parker. Fort Sill." He walked up to Gabe and tapped him on the chest, saying 'Waugh!' again in a loud voice. Gabe replied in kind, then Quanah tapped LaPoint on the chest, and he said 'Waugh', causing Quanah to laugh, then point to Gabe and say, 'wasape'.

"He says I'm a bear," said Gabe, proudly.

Then Quanah made a short but loud speech to Gabe with lots of vigorous hand signing. Isatai began sobbing and rubbing his hair in the dirt, and many squaws began crying as well. An older squaw who seemed content with the news brought them metal cups of dark steaming coffee, and Kiwih-nai called for the bag of biscuits back, pulling out the last three. He handed one each to LaPoint and McBride, and they each nibbled the biscuits and drank the coffee together on the ground, while Gabe conveyed his sourdough recipe to the squaws, and described the dutch oven, and how the mesquite or oak coals should be heaped on the lid and covered with ash.

It was like an afternoon social, a coffee break from the war, with each man examining the others' McBride knife and testing the sharpness. Gabe kept passing his red stone pipe with a recent mix of kinnickkinnick, then passed the coffeepot around after the biscuits were gone. He also showed them his green Pennsylvania sandstone sharpening stone, and when Kiwih-nai admired it, Gabe gave it to him. Kiwih-nai seemed to really love those McBride sourdoughs and coffee, and the soothing smoke was enjoyed by all as the pipe was refilled twice. Isatai seemed to calm down and sat on the ground nearby chanting in time to a small drum he tapped. Kiwih-nai spoke to Gabe about his name, Quanah Parker, some more.

Josh glanced at Gabe, who translated. "He means he's gonna go by his childhood name, Quanah, which means sweet fragrance. Says his mom gave him that name when he was born among the flowers at Cedar Lake. He's giving up his war name, Kiwih-nai, or Eagle, and the war trail. And he's taking his mother's name, Parker, to walk the white man's road. He was ready for us, says that Isatai already told him we two were coming to bring the end of their running hungry times. He's coming in, and bringing the band with him. Josh LaPoint Robinoix, meet Quanah Parker, the only Comanche who will retire from the war undefeated. He's gotta start over, like you did, make a new life as a rancher."

Josh smiled and nodded, tears forming in his eyes, then shook the strong hand of the the mixed blood warrior like himself.   "Quanah Parker, amigo, Josh LaPoint. I'm glad you agree, for it's the only way for the Quohadis to survive. Well, let's seal the deal. Ask him what he calls the big gray stallion, and what he wants to wager on the race. I will not wager my horse, let that be understood."

Gabe relayed the question, and Quanah replied. Gabe laughed as he relayed. "He says he calls it Bad Hand Horse, and he was trying to tell us that when we met that other time at the cap-rock canyons, but we were too nervous to catch on, with Gray Blanket wanting yore scalp so bad." LaPoint chuckled at the memory.

Quanah nodded smiling at that, pointing to LaPoint's weapon belt, speaking to Gabe.

"He say's you don't have your fast draw holster on, and wants to know why."

"Tell him it makes young fools want to draw down on me. And that I left it with my woman, after I taught her to shoot it well. Tell him I'm tired of war everyday."

Gabe told Quanah, who nodded with a serious look at LaPoint., then questioned Gabe again.

"He asked how many wives you have. I told him just one and he said too bad."

Kiwih-nai was watching intently with an amused look, and spoke to Gabe again.

"He asked if you would rather make war or train horses and make love to your woman."

"Train horses and make love."

305

Gabe translated to Quanah, who nodded at Gabe and touched his own chest. "Quanah, train horses, get more wives, no more war."

Josh nodded his head, remembering how he was ready to draw the small quick-shooting gun or his knife during the previous encounter, while the big chieftain had tried to explain that he had stolen the big gray pacer of Colonel Bad Hand Mackenzie, the one Josh had trained.

"And the wager?"

"Yore McBride knives and a lock of hair. Plus he wants a batch of biscuits from me first chance I get."

"He's so hungry that your sourdough biscuits are luring him to the Fort, old coon, is that it?"

"Wal, beats starvin' and searching for one buffalo at a time. Settling for rabbits and deer and snakes. And maybe he's as tired of war as you are. He mentioned he wanted one of the blond locks from the top and front thar." He started chuckling then. "Maybe he wants ta give it ta Gray Blanket. I tole ya to shear it off afore we came."

"Damn," uttered LaPoint as he saw Quanah Parker nod and grin when he touched his long hair. "Why am I not surprised? I should have cut my hair like you said."

"Josh touched the short blond beard he wore at the time and looked at Quanah inquiringly, but the chieftain shook his head and pointed to LaPoint's sun-bleached locks. Gabe broke out laughing, followed by Quanah, who spoke to Gabe.

"He says he already saved yore scalp when Gray Blanket wanted it back in the Cap-rock Canyons. He wants that long yellar lock in front thar."

"You probably arranged that part. Trouble is, I don't think Scorpio can keep up with Bad Hand on a long stretch, I need a short race on rough ground with lots of turns to beat the big gray," said Josh as he glanced at Quanah, who was smiling and stripping off his buffalo robe cape to make ready for riding. The torso of the big warrior was leaned down since they had seen him last, and his huge muscles stood out all the more over his ganted-down waist and ribs. He walked over and thumped LaPoint on the journal where his bullet had hit in battle, then touched his long blond locks and laughed. Josh made a point of ignoring him and walked over to talk softly into Scorpio's ear.

Quanah was soon talking to his own horse and rubbing it's withers, neck, and nose. For that time the war was over and they were young men racing their favorite horses. The horses were excited, as were the young men.

The Comanche camp was stretched along level ground south of the long cliff edge for two miles, and the race would be to the end of the camp and back. The whole village became excited as word of the race spread. Even Isatai seemed to recover from his grief and began to get involved in organizing the race. The big gray pacer, Bad Hand Horse, was brought forward, and Quanah stripped the small saddle off of it and took the regular snaffle bit bridle off to replace it with a rope hackamore. He walked over, stepped barefoot on LaPoint's black boot, handed a rope for Josh to make a hackamore, then gestured to his saddle and spoke to Gabe, who laughed and slapped his knee.

"This is a barefoot bareback race with hackamore bridals, no bits, down the length of the camp to a lance with a buffalo scull on it, around that lance and back past his lodge here. He says he gets yore knife and a lock of yore hair if he wins, same for you if he loses."

"A lock won't be too bad, I suppose, beats the hell out of Gray Blanket's demand for the whole scalp."

"You planning on losing both tha race and hair lock, Josh LaPoint? That'd be a first."

"No, but I've ridden both horses, and the big gray is faster in a long stretch."

"No Big Gray, LaPoint." said Kiwih-nai. "Bad Hand Horse."

"Wal, get the most out of Scorpio, don't let him think you let him win, he's got a lot of respect for you, and wants it back. He wants a real race."

"He's got it. I aim to beat him if I can. Let me use your buffalo tail quirt, I'm going to need all Scorpio's got, and Bad Hand Horse been here resting and grazing while we've been riding hard every day," said LaPoint as he stripped the saddle from Scorpio and replaced the bridal with a rope twisted and tied around his nose. All the Comanches were moving to line the course of the race, while riders carried a lance with a buffalo scull down to the other end for the racers to turn around.

"Scorpio and Bad Hand Horse, father and son race, let's do it," said Josh as he handed his weapons belt to Gabe, then slipped his tall black riding boots off to stocking feet, then peeling off his socks. Both barefoot riders in buckskin leggings mounted simultaneously by leaping onto their stallions, and the Comanches began to shout and cheer. Gabe started cheering for Josh as loud as he could, trying to shout down the whole Comanche village. Wild Horse was starting to look up and get interested as well, realizing they were to live through the parley. He began to chant for Josh along with Gabe, who had drifted into his Gaelic mumbo-jumbo wailing mixed with Comanche.

Kiwih-nai looked at Gabe and spoke, to which Gabe pulled Josh's pistol to start them off. The big Remington barked with a repeating echo booming against the cliff and the racers took off, the older stallion getting the jump on his taller offspring and acquiring a four horse-length lead within four hundred yards as they tore across the fresh grass along the stream, with dips and ravines to break the big gray's stride while Scorpio outran him. But the younger stallion hit his stride as they found level ground and began to catch up, with Kiwih-nai yelling and rhythmically flailing it with a small buffalo tail quirt. LaPoint leaned down low beside Scorpio's ear and talked him into more speed.

The big long-legged gray called Bad Hand passed Scorpio at about a mile with Quanah making his shrill eagle whistle call, and had a two horse-length lead as they came to the turn. The tall son of Scorpio could not make the turn nearly as tight as his sire, and Scorpio cut inside to take the lead again. Josh came alive with whipping and jostling his heels as he saw his chance to pull away, and had a two horse-length lead at halfway back, but Bad Hand was stretching the long legs he had acquired from his dam out of bluegrass Kentucky, and the lead slowly diminished.

Quanah edged past Josh with about two hundred yards to go, and Josh pushed Scorpio in one last desperate surge to get nose and nose for about half that distance, with Bad Hand finally pulling away and crossing the finish line a half length ahead of Scorpio. Kiwih-nai gave his eagle scream one more time in victory as he passed, his last as a Quohadi horseman of the plains.

The Comanches were exultant with shouting and cheering, and Josh quickly dismounted and went to congratulate Quanah, who shook his hand with a small dignified grin, his heavy lidded eyes sparkling with satisfaction, but then a grim look. He spoke to Gabe a few words.

"He said it's the last victory for him. Now he has to do something he never learned to do, surrender. He says he surrenders for his people, and if it was him alone he would live free out here forever, and Mackenzie would never find him. He says it makes him sick to surrender."

"Tell him it made me sick to see that horse herd slaughtered."

Gabe relayed the information to the chieftain. Josh looked at Quanah and nodded, noticing his eyes were moist, as Josh's were. They both felt all their associations had led to this moment when the Comanches must give up the ghost.

"Tell him I said he's the best warrior and horseman I ever saw," said Josh as took off his weapons belt and slipped the knife scabbard off. "Tell him I want to run a short course with lots of turns on the next race." Josh slipped the McBride knife from the scabbard and sliced a lock of his sun-bleached hair off, then handed the knife and lock of hair to Quanah, who nodded, smiled, and accepted them as Gabe relayed Josh's sentiments. He stuck the knife in his belt and tied the lock of blond hair to the mane of his big stallion. "Bad Hand, numero uno caballo, si?"

LaPoint smiled and nodded. "Tell him I said Bad Hand was maybe faster, but not better than Scorpio. Tell him next time I will win and cut some of his hair so he can wear a ranchers wide hat, like I do."

Gabe made another short speech to Quanah.

The old scout then turned to LaPoint and spoke. "He said the times have changed, from the many passing moons of the buffalo and men without hats or bridle bits, to men with hats and steel and guns."

Josh LaPoint nodded at the proud Comanche leader, and they all shook hands and departed, with agreement to parley with the full party the next day and sign the papers. Wild Horse had been on the sidelines the whole time, surrounded by squaws who occasionally kicked dust onto his leggings and scolded him. His main desire had been that the Quohadis would not kill him for leading whites into their encampment. He was elated when they rode out, and couldn't stop jabbering about it. They traveled for about five miles before finding the rest of the party stalled and wondering which way to go without scouts.

Informing Dr. Sturm of the situation, with the Quohadis ready to parley, they decided to approach the camp in the morning for formal talks. Gabe also instructed Dr. Sturm to give the small stoneware jar of sourdough starter culture on the pack mule to the wives of Quanah Parker, drawing a puzzled look from the amiable man.

The next day they had their official conference and Quanah Parker, arrayed in his finest white buckskins and breastplate, braids hung with fur and eagle feathers, the effect of royalty complete with grizzly claw and turquoise necklace, topped off by LaPoint's rattlesnake hat band wrapped around his forehead, formally agreed to take the Quohadis in to the reservation near Fort Sill, with ceremonies of the feathers and smoke, and passing the red stone pipe. The last free band of Comanches agreed to leave the plains where their people had dominated for well over a century and a half. The surrender of this final free-roaming band of aloof, fierce, and mobile buffalo hunters would largely mark the end of the major Comanche campaigns by the United States Army.

After the official signing ceremony, Josh invited Quanah to visit at his horse ranch on the Blanco when he could, guaranteeing plenty of sourdough biscuits, since Kathy had learned Gabe's recipe and borrowed starter, and Quanah asked him to visit at Fort Sill and race horses again. LaPoint pointed at Quanah's long thick braid wrapped with dark fur, then smiled and touched his own knife, nodding. Quanah laughed and shook his head in the negative. He rattled off something to Gabe with a smile.

Gabe laughed. "He said he's not giving up his horse, his five wives, nor his hair, and soon his squaws will be making biscuits and he will write a letter to LaPoint."

"Tell him he will meet Bad Hand Mackenzie there, who has my address."

"Hell, Mackenzie can't write with those stumps fer fingers, and neither can Quanah, so I wouldn't be expecting any letters except from an orderly."

"Goodbye scouts, LaPoint, McBride. War over now, but they never beat me," said Quanah with his big palm raised.

"Goodbye Quanah. War is over, and they never beat you," replied scout Josh LaPoint.

"Waugh," said McBride, as he made the flat palmed clearing sign across his chest, which Josh imitated. Quanah did likewise, and they parted with satisfaction achieved, but sadness overlaying their success.

Their scouting job done, they said goodbye to the negotiating party after Gabe gave Strum his sourdough starter and told him to save it for Quanah's wives.

"You've got to tell him he can't keep all those wives, Gabe," said Strum.

"Don't mention nothin' like that 'til ya get him ta Fort Sill," replied Gabe.

"Tell Mac we're done with our part," said LaPoint.

"That I will, with my commendations. You sure you don't want to accompany us back to Fort Sill?"

"Naw, we done what we signed on for," said Gabe.

"We've got a cattle herd to find and move to Dodge," said Josh LaPoint. "So long and best of luck."

The scouts headed southeast towards the meeting with the herd coming up from Fort Mason. Josh was elated and looking forward to telling Kathy that the warrants for him were gone, and the last of the Comanches, the terror of her childhood, were coming in peaceably. Gabe was lost in thought, remembering all his years in dealing with these hardy people of the horse and buffalo plains.

They both hoped it was to be their last brush with Comanches. Their satisfaction with the particulars of their mission was tinged with deep regret that the Comanches had lost their homeland with horse and buffalo. Searching back through their trail of involvement in the war, they didn't see how they could have handled it differently, and did not regret what they did, though it did not turn out like they hoped it would, with all the captives coming home to joyous reunions with long-grieving families, and the Quohadi remaining free to hunt the buffalo.

For days they rode through nasty stretches of littered buffalo bones and rotting carcasses alive with buzzing flies, and met the cattle herd south of Fort Griffin in late May. Jesse and

311

Tom were greatly relieved to see them ride up, as was the rest of the outfit. For after some difficult trials at all the river crossings, they then had the best scout and trail boss for the rest of the tough drive to Dodge, and the last of the Comanches were surrendering, to ease the fears of attack. The task of locating good grazing had become a difficult problem for a good scout like Gabe to solve, since several herds were in front of them, chomping down all the spring grass.

Meanwhile the Quohadis rode back with the Sturm negotiating party towards Fort Sill where they would surrender as the last free band of Comanches. They carried white flags on lances and papers from Colonel Mackenzie authorizing them safe passage, so they would not be attacked by rangers or buffalo hunters. Interpreter Sturm allowed them to move slowly through their old camping grounds, enjoying the freedom of the plains for the last time. They never spotted the southern buffalo herd in all their roaming there and back, but were able to hunt a few stragglers on horseback. Mackenzie received their surrender with dignity, and allowed Quanah to keep the big gray pacer.

After parleying with Tom and Jesse and Poncho over the turn of events, LaPoint and McBride took over the herd, and headed north for Doan's Crossing on the Red River. Jesse rode point with Miguel, Josh pointed the herd, and Tom scouted up ahead with Gabe. The Comanches wars were over, the Quohadis no longer roamed the buffalo plains, which were littered with buffalo bone piles as the time of the Numunu faded to the dust of history, and the cattle were being driven up the long trail from south Texas to replace them.

Chapter Ten: Ranching the Rockies

After passing Fort Griffin, where the chuck-wagon resupplied, they continued north with the mixed herd of around a thousand beeves, crossing the Brazos River, the Little Wichita, and the swollen stream of the Big Wichita before reaching the Red River. Some cattle were lost to the quicksand or high water in each crossing, and it took a full day to cross the Red River at Doan's Crossing, after waiting days for two other herds to cross. Fortunately there was still good grazing that spring of '75 because of passing storms, and the cattle put on weight while waiting to cross the brown torrent. Brush and tree branches had been piled in the river bed and pounded into the sand by passing herds, to keep the cattle from bogging. Nonetheless the herd lost two dozen head to the crossing of the turbid Red River, and LaPoint breathed a sigh of relief when the last of the drag was across.

Then came the chuck wagon, and E. Earl the cantankerous cook and driver wanted to drive the mules across with drovers towing, but LaPoint thought the better of it and unhooked the mules while drovers pulled in dry logs from driftwood jams miles upstream to lash on either side of the wagon. Then with a half dozen horses towing it, they floated the wagon across, and E. Earl followed swimming his mules, hanging on to the tail of the big jack when it got too deep. He came up sputtering but smiling his gap-toothed grin with his dirty glasses tied to his head along with his bowler hat. The water dripped from the side braids of his long black beard as he pulled his boots back on, laughing about the mules farting in the water in front of him. They moved north four miles to camp, to get out the way of approaching herds, for the cow traffic towards Dodge that year was immense.

Then for the next few days they followed the north fork of the Red River, the same fork on which the first Comanche battle had been fought at the villages of Mow-way, Para-coom, and Kiwih-nai, or Quanah, as he now called himself. LaPoint did well at managing the men and the herd during his long

313

waking hours, but at night his dreams were disturbed by the ghost herd of horses in his mind.

They kept to the east side of the river, where plenty of grazing was available, letting the herd string out without fear of Comanches raiders for the first time in several years of driving cattle up the Staked Plains. The river wound along in oxbow loops and they kept far enough to the east to make a beeline north, crossing the smaller branch as it veered northeast to head for a line of prominent pointed hills about four miles northwest, where the river looped back west and would be crossed again.

There were dark lines of thunderstorms approaching from about ten miles away as they hurried the crossing, hoping to get over before a freshet sent a wall of brown water down over the horns of the cattle. Rumbling thunder and lightening streaks appeared in the northwest as the blue-gray line of storms rushed towards them. The clanging of the bell on the lead longhorn bull, Old Plunger, was clanking faster than LaPoint had ever heard it. The wind was gusting from the south as the storm hurled in from the west, and the sky in front of the blue-gray wall was a strange yellow color. The cattle were restless and ready to bolt, prompting Josh to yell at E. Earl and the wranglers to drive the chuck-wagon back away from the herd along with the remuda, and cut west for the lee of a small set of hills. E. Earl started blowing his cow horn and then he turned away to the west, with Ben Burnette and another wrangler driving the remuda, leaving the volatile cattle.

At that point Josh heard three rapid gunshots and a building roar from the north where Gabe was riding scout, and spun his stallion to see a twister dropping from the front line of the oncoming gray-blue wall of the storm front. Gabe had his bugle out and was blowing it to beat all hell as he galloped on Buck in fear for his life, but LaPoint could barely hear it. The wall of clouds behind the fleeing old scout ended in a spinning hook of rapidly moving clouds in the west, and hail was spitting from the sky. Tom Jackson was racing about a half mile ahead of Gabe to help the point rider in turning the herd.

Behind the racing scout a strange group of twisting clouds coalesced, gaining a solid gray form as it came down and formed a column. The tornado hit the ground several miles behind of where he saw Gabe riding back as fast as Buck could carry him, and LaPoint pulled out his field glasses to get a better look. When he focused on Gabe he saw the dark solid twister whirling grass and dust in the background, it's gray-green funnel now in the middle of a spinning and expanding cloud of debris. LaPoint felt helpless and sat motionless on Scorpio while watching scout McBride whipping and spurring to get away from the gray whirlwind, which was growing in size and approaching at an angle from the northwest. LaPoint had seen plenty of small dust devils out west and larger twisters in the distance on the staked plains, but this one was big and making a fearsome roaring noise as it approached with a surrounding halo of dust and debris. No sooner had he thought of the smaller whirlwinds in his memory than several white ones appeared near the big dark twister, then disappeared in the dark haze. The magnificent and terrifying sight was stunning, mesmerizing to LaPoint, who sat watching in fear and awe and uncharacteristic indecision.

Suddenly hit by a bit of falling debris and snapping out of his inaction with the realization that he could not help his best friend and mentor Gabe, the trail boss LaPoint rode to turn the herd away from the twister, whistling and giving hat signals to the point riders. He saw the best safety in getting behind a cluster of small hills to the west about a mile. Jesse was on the east point and had already moved up to turn the lead to the west, away from the path of the approaching tornado. Tom was riding in front of the herd by then, helping to turn it away from the oncoming monster that whirled debris in an ever-widening pattern. The twister hit the small hill about four miles to the northeast and lost some form and power for perhaps thirty seconds, then reformed as it moved down the steep hill to the plains again. The air filled with bushes and branches of the cedar and oak foliage on the hill as the tornado grew on the downhill and picked up speed.

LaPoint had spotted a small hill about a half mile to the northeast, and directed the point riders, Jesse, Tom, and Miguel, to run the herd to the flat land behind it, away from the twister. The nervous cattle were ready to bolt anyway, so LaPoint directed the drovers to put them into a fast trot to get behind the little hill. He could see that Gabe was approaching from a quarter mile away at that time, and that the tornado was veering southeast to hit at about where he and the point of the

315

herd had been a few minutes before. He pulled out his big Remington revolver and began firing into the ground to break the cattle into a run as the twister got closer, moving at an angle to hit the rear of the herd. Tom Jackson rushed by alongside the herd and began to shoot his revolver as well as he passed by heading east and the cattle broke into an all out run. LaPoint turned with the field glasses to find Gabe again, and saw the twister closing in on him.

"Turn Gabe," said LaPoint. "It's going west, come this way. Turn, damn-it." LaPoint pulled his rifle and shot towards Gabe but to the west side, hoping he would hear the shot. Gabe instantly veered left after the shot, and Josh breathed a deep sigh of relief.

The air around the big tornado was a dark expanding cloud of whirling debris, at that time only about two miles behind Gabe, who was angling east to avoid its southwesterly path. The huge gray cloud of debris was whirling above them in a counterclockwise expanding rotation. Gabe was pushing Buck harder than Josh had ever seen, trying to outrun the monster at his back, veering hard to the west as he saw it veer southeast, laid out in a full gallop.

In past times LaPoint had pulled a rifle to shoot Gabe's pursuers, but this time he was helpless to do anything but watch from the little rise below the hill. He was not about to join the drovers running the cattle and lose sight of Gabe McBride, who had taught him since he was very young. He put his rifle back in the saddle scabbard and watched Gabe through the binoculars.

The tornado was a dark whirling pillar of wind and debris that made an intense noise as it approached with the lightening-flashing blue-black cloud-bank a couple of miles behind it with a curtain of rain and line of dust. The front of the herd had run behind the hill and the middle was following as Jesse kept turning them to the east and south, hoping to mill them behind the hill. The drag riders, seeing the funnel approaching, were firing pistols and rushing the rear of the herd to avoid it. Many of the drag animals were cows and calves or old cows that were unable to keep up with the rush.

Gabe eventually reached the edge of the middle of the herd and joined in hustling it forward as the tornado noise increased and the edge of the debris cloud approached. LaPoint kept firing his gun to run the cattle away from the deadly twister, as did other drovers. The herd was by that time into a semi-controlled stampede towards the lee of the small hills, with the point turning south into a mill under Jesse's skilled handling, with the fearless Miguel turning long-horned steers in the middle of the herd, sustaining the milling circle. Jackson had ridden over to help Ben Burnette handle the remuda, as the horses were in a near panic and beginning to scatter. Lightening began to strike nearby, with hardly a second between the flash and the boom.

LaPoint stopped shooting and rode to a higher rise ahead of him near the beginning of the little hill, to survey the scene. As soon as he got there he saw the tornado would likely hit the drag of the herd, and he pulled the Winchester '73 and shot three times to alert the drovers with the louder shots, then made signals with horse position and hat to the drag riders, about a half mile away. When they saw his signal they bolted directly east, leaving the stragglers to fend for themselves and spurring their mounts as hard as possible as the edge of the debris cloud settled onto them and the drag of the herd. Cattle panicked with wild eyes and lolling tongues as the loud roar and dust cloud engulfed the drag of the herd.

LaPoint spotted Gabe hustling towards him and waved his pale straw hat, since grass and dry leaves were filling the air by then. Gabe spotted him and rode that way as Josh holstered his rifle and returned to gauging the tornado's path.

The tornado seemed to veer off the slight rise of land around the hill in front of him and move east a bit as Gabe rode up and stopped beside LaPoint, and yelled while jamming his hat down on his head and tightening the horsehair string under his chin. The tornado moved southeast and passed in front of Gabe and LaPoint, about three quarters of a mile to the east, as the debris field dropped scattered bits of twigs and grass clumps on them. Soon they were pelted with muddy water, frogs, and even a horny toad that knocked LaPoint's hat askew, despite the strong chin strap. Lightening and thunder were flashing and booming along the line of the front.

They saw tiny white twisters spin off the same cloud-bank that spawned the big one as it rapidly approached. While they were both watching to see if the drag of the herd escaped the path of the twister, a squealing jack-rabbit came hurling out of the sky and thumped down a few yards away from them,

317

causing both of them to jolt in their saddles. The horses began whirling and straining to bolt at that point, having had enough tornado to feel their fleeing instincts urging them. The white ass of the rabbit was quivering on the ground about ten yards away as twigs and branches showered them and the wind change blew dust into their eyes as they labored to control their horses. Scattered hail and fat hurtling raindrops began to pelt them as their hats tugged on the chin strings that held them down.

"Gol-dang-it what the hell was that?" yelled Gabe in the roar of the wind as debris became thicker and larger tree branches and sticks began to fall with swirling dry leaves whipping by their faces. The wind was howling from the northwest by then, streaking lines of dust and dry grass south. The counterclockwise whirling debris cloud of the tornado was getting thicker, and more rabbits and snakes went sailing by with clumps of dry straw and branches overhead.

"A screaming jackrabbit, look there he lies," yelled LaPoint. "Look at that twister, see the path? The drag riders are out of the way if they don't get hit by debris, I think," said Josh as he moved Scorpio closer to Buck so Gabe could hear him. Gabe noticed the jackrabbit moved, jerking it's back legs, then got up and ran towards the hillside behind them, dodging into cedar brush. They laughed despite the danger, and returned to watching the twister approaching the tail of the herd.

"It's gonna miss," yelled LaPoint. Missing the main body of the drag, the twister caught the last of the weaker cattle who could not keep up with the pace, and some cow and calf pairs, lifting them easily into the swirling winds and sailing them high and counterclockwise in twirling patterns towards the south. The sight of cattle flying held both scouts in amazement as they watched them gaining altitude and tumbling head over heels in the dust.

"Dang, never thought I'd see that, flyin' fuggin' cows," yelled Gabe.

"Glad it isn't us," yelled LaPoint.

The main herd escaped and stampeded as fast as they could go away from the noise and flying debris towards the lee of the small hill. McBride and LaPoint turned towards the east and away from the swirling blast as they saw the drag move towards them. They rode down to help turn and mill the herd behind the hill as the tornado headed south to where the herd had crossed earlier, sending another burst of debris flying. The cattle were frantic and the milling was a sea of clashing horns that took every drover to contain. Slowly the energy of the stampede was contained by the milling mass, and they stopped running, from fatigue as much as anything else, and the sound of the storm moving away.

After an hour of concentrated work, the herd was bedded down and grazing, and drovers had ridden south to pick up calf carcasses to cook for an evening meal. They soon returned with several small beeves for cooking, and word of the devastation to the gallery forest along the river by the twister as it cut a swath southeast.

With all the vaqueros and drovers with good singing voices out calming the exhausted herd with their songs, Gabe and Josh decided this was a good time to relax and celebrate while the herd settled down and grazed for a day, and the Comanches out of action. LaPoint conferred with E. Earl about a feast with peach cobbler for the night camp, and a big meal was prepared. E. Earl recruited some help and put on one of his best spreads, cooking the rump roasts in Gabe's metal oven with garlic and onions slipped into cuts in the flesh, and making mushroom and wild onion gravy for the meat, cornbread, and potatoes that preceded the huge pans of cobbler.

By the time the meal was ready it was sunset and the herd had bedded down in weariness. The campfire talk was lively and excited as the rain behind the storm missed their camp and left them only a stiff northwest breeze to contend with. Every drover had a tale to tell of his adventure in the storm, several of them being pelted with frogs and snakes during the mad dash, then tales of other storms, with lightening strikes and foxfire on the horns of stampeding steers, and then songs and drinking shot-glasses of brandy poured on the wagon shelf by E. Earl, who kept track and limited it to two each, on LaPoint's orders. Gabe sneaked in some extra drinks and got lit up to start telling tales of the last trappers' rendezvous in 1831, and all his years trapping and scouting in the mountains, and the storms he had seen on the plains, and about it being so cold once up on the Gunnison that his piss froze in a golden arch and stuck him to the ground by his pecker, the yellow ice-sickle being struck by his knife to free him. Before the yarn spinning was over, Jesse asked him if he came over with Cortez and the conquistadors, to which Gabe replied that's another story, and went to playing a Jew's harp, since the drovers had hidden his trumpet.

After the life-threatening act of nature on the high plains where warm moist and cold air masses collide with fury, the campfire party was one of their best ever, despite the chilling breeze of the late spring norther. Some of the drovers found an old dead tree that had been lightening struck, and drug it to the fire with their lariats to build a big sheltered blaze. The singing went on into the night, with the clear voices of the drovers singing the songs they sang as night-riders to calm the herd. Fiddles, guitars, and guitarrons lent strings as accordions, keg-pounders, and singers filled in the rest. LaPoint even played the kegs and pots with his fast and accurate hands, amazing all at the rapid rhythms he could make. They all were celebrating being alive after that incredible storm.

A couple of hours past midnight LaPoint and E. Earl closed up the chuck-wagon and turned in after laughing about Gabe snoring in a cedar bush. Josh slept under the the back of the wagon as E. Earl snored under the front, while Scorpio rested nearby. Josh felt relieved that they had only lost a few cattle to the tornado, and didn't worry about raiders nor rattlers in the cold wind as he fell asleep. He had drank more brandy than he was used to, and felt woozy until he passed out.

With the first peach and golden light of dawn in the sky the renegade band of about two dozen rustlers came riding from where they had been hiding behind a tiny hill to the west and north. They struck the herd with skillful methods, firing guns and snapping bull whips and blankets to stampede the herd and the remuda. The four night-riders were rushed and fired upon from several angles, and two were killed outright while another was wounded. Part of the well-practiced rustling crew peppered the LaPoint outfit sleeping around the campfire with rifle fire, causing a scramble behind the big log that had been dragged up. The herd arose in an instant and took off towards the southwest, while the remuda was struck with many rustlers and driven around the tiny hill to the northwest. Ben Burnette and Miguel Cavasos went racing after the remuda into the darkness, rifles out, and within five minutes a gun battle was heard from that direction.

LaPoint and Jackson had both fled on their nearby mounts from the initial assault by rushing up onto the hill above the herd to find better firing spots with their repeating rifles. They met up near some small live oak trees, and had some luck in picking off rustlers who were shooting at the LaPoint outfit drovers, but had to let the herds go. After the stampede, they counted heads and felt lucky they had lost only two men with others wounded with flesh wounds that went through. They left a half dozen rustlers where they lay dead or dying, food for coyotes and buzzards.

"The sons o bitches meant ta kill us all, I reckon," said Gabe as he kicked the body of a rustler over to look at his face.

LaPoint stayed mounted and asked. "Can you tell anything?"

"Kiowa, I reckon," said Gabe. "But wearing a drover's vest, and a bridal with a snaffle bit on his horse thar."

"They killed two of our outfit and got the cattle, damn them."

"It ain't over."

"I know it. We'll pull back together and get the murdering thieves. I have got to ride over and get organized with the drovers, take a toll on who else is hurt."

"Go ahead on, I'll be thar directly."

"You going to scalp him?"

"Naw, need to tighten my girth strap. 'Lessin' ya want me to?"

"No, I want to get the others, and the herd. If we have enough horses left to go after them."

LaPoint noticed that Ben Burnette and Miguel had not returned from chasing the remuda, and sent Tom Jackson leading six heavily armed riders after them. They returned shortly with the wounded Ben riding between two of them, clutching a bandaged shoulder. Miguel was unhurt and reported that they lost the remuda in a gun battle and last saw it heading north towards the sharp hills there, about four miles distant. The LaPoint outfit had lost two drovers, while one had tumbled in a prairie dog hole and broken an arm, one with a slug in his thigh, and two more were gunshot with the lead gone through.

LaPoint told E. Earl to doctor and bandage the wounded, then to make a good breakfast and lots of coffee while he parlayed with Gabe, Tom Jackson, and Jesse. E. Earl

321

changed his dirty apron to a clean one and proceeded to apply long wrapping bandages on the drovers with minor wounds, the air filled with his cussing and telling them to 'shud-up and sit still'. On the broken arm he needed LaPoint and Gabe to help hold and straighten the break to set it with sticks and a plaster wrap. For the bullet wounds the experienced chuck-wagon doc used brandy water, then lemon juice, then honey and aloe vera gel on the wounds, binding them tightly. LaPoint had to wrap his strong arms around the man with the lead in his thigh as E. Earl probed for the bullet with narrow blade. Feeling the man's intense pain had a profound effect on LaPoint. When E. Earl was finally done, they had wrappings that would not come undone easily, and the wounds E. Earl dressed never infected and healed quickly. The bullet lay on a metal saucer, a misshaped .44 slug, and the drover was hobbling on a crutch made by Gabe from a tree branch.

"Just feel lucky I don't use a hot iron on ya, ya crybabies," said E. Earl as he finished up and put away his doctoring kit.

LaPoint spoke up. "They came in and killed two of our outfit in stealing the stock. This is war now, boys. Here's the plan, drink plenty of coffee and water, we're going after them. These renegade rustlers have got to be cleaned out. Tom Jackson and Gabe McBride will lead the most of you after the cattle, and shoot to kill is the password. Aim for the chest or gut, and shoot the murderers. Jesse and I will take one more drover and go after the remuda. We will meet about three miles ahead, east of that big pointed hill where we cross the river again. Check your weapons, tighten your war straps. Hell's gonna be popping."

Jesse selected Miguel, a vaquero friend of theirs from down south, to help with the horses, and the three of them took off on the trail of the remuda around nine in the morning. Instead of following directly, they headed east and then north to circle the hill they camped behind, so as to avoid ambush from back-riders lurking in cover.. Then picked up the trail of the remuda in the wet ground about a mile north of the small hills, and followed it as it headed to the row of three big pointed peaks in front of them about three miles away.

Those hills looked just under a thousand feet high to LaPoint, with his experience in the rocky mountains helping his judgment on it. Smaller rises appeared first as they rode northwest, giving rustlers lots of ambush spots, slowing down the pursuers. They began to ride from cover to cover as the small rises led to the big hills, and saw the remuda tracks circled around to the south of the tall peak there. They followed the trail around the base of the peak until it turned north and east into a hidden box canyon, where they spotted the remuda through binoculars after climbing a live oak tree on the hillside.

"I can see lots of horses back in the canyon, and two riders near this end, with the gap roped off. Probably more riders out of sight, or up on the rises of the canyon," said LaPoint while peering through field glasses.

"How we gonna get them guys, boss?" asked Jesse.

"Check your rifles, get lots of ammo, and lets stop at that little stream and hide them."

Watering their mounts at a winding little stream that came off the steep hills, they made a plan. Hiding their mounts in a clump of cedar trees with feedbags on their noses, they crept with repeaters and bags of ammo towards the canyon, slipping low from bush to bush. Both Jesse and Miguel were armed with revolvers and Spencer repeating rifles, while LaPoint carried his long range Whitworth and his new Winchester 73.

LaPoint headed away from the two vaqueros, using brush at the bottom of the draw to slip away. He crossed the small stream coming out of the box canyon and climbed the rocky hillside to the north as Jesse and Miguel made their way along the south rim. They used mirrors to signal each other as they progressed to good shooting positions. They planned to rain down fire from three positions above the rustlers, and give them pure hell for rampaging through their outfit the night before. They'd all agreed that these were ambush killers deserving no quarter.

Within an hour they were in position and signaled each other with long fluttering flashes of their mirrors. Their plan was to alternate fire from different positions to keep the rustlers confused as to their elevated positions, with Josh using the Whitworth for the furthest targets, firing first.

LaPoint took aim while resting on his folded leather glove that padded a rough boulder notch with the long Whitworth, and he took down the furthest rustler at around six hundred yards. The loud boom echoed back and forth in the canyon, making it hard to discern where it came from, and the breeze quickly dissipated the smoke. There was no return fire, nothing but the sound of frightened horses. Then Jesse and Miguel each took a shot from their separated positions on the south rim, each taking down a rustler and leaving his horse scampering off. Three shots from different locations and three rustlers were in the dirt, and LaPoint had reloaded.

The remuda horses were nervous, surging back and forth, but there was a brush and rope corral holding them in the canyon. LaPoint sighted the furthest rider and fired again as his vaqueros on the opposing rim immediately thereafter took down two more riders with four more shots from their Spencer rifles. Six rustlers had been taken down with eight shots, and just a few more were left. Those were now firing their rifles at the canyon walls near Jesse and Miguel, who were well covered and not hit.

Sighting in on a rider coming down the canyon from a small camp they had up there, LaPoint hit him in the upper chest and knocked him off his horse in a backward flip with the long rifle. Two riders following him veered off into the brush when they saw him go down. LaPoint set down the Whitworth and used the field glasses to try to spot them. Bullets started pinging around him as the rustlers below spotted his smoke. He saw the distant rustlers had light hair and sunburned faces as they turned and beat a retreat up the canyon, joined by another with dark hair. Then they stopped, dismounted, and walked their horses up a switchback trail and over the rise out of sight. Readying the big gun while they climbed, LaPoint sighted in on them near the top and let fly with another booming round that whizzed over the head of the highest man, causing him to duck. The renegade rustlers hustled over the rise and out of sight. More rifle fire struck around him, while Jesse and Miguel started laying down constant fire at the rustlers below.

Then LaPoint began to use his '73 Winchester on several renegades within a couple hundred yards and riding his way. With three shots he took two of them down, forcing the other to duck behind a boulder. Jesse and Miguel kept firing from the other side and took him down. With the rustlers in a crossfire from above, after another half hour of rifle battle, most of them were in the dust or fled over the back rise of the canyon. When all the return fire stopped, the LaPoint men carefully walked down their hillsides and checked the bodies. All were dead or dying, and they wore mixed garb of Indians and whites. Most of them looked Indian or Mexican Indian.

LaPoint used his .44 Remington revolver to finish the dying ones off with head shots. They decided to leave them for the coyotes and buzzards, and move to gathering the herd. It was the first time after years of having herds rustled that he had caught them and attacked them in their lair, and he was not regretful of it.

LaPoint directed Jesse and Miguel to round up all the horses, including the rustlers loose mounts, and drive them to the arranged meeting place at the next river crossing. They took off with the herd after a half hour of work rounding them all up, while LaPoint scouted the rustler camp and a small trail up over the rise behind it. Jesse and Miguel began to drive the remuda south and east around the base of the sharp little peak before looping north towards the river. LaPoint figured they would reappear on the plain in front of him if he headed east through the line of hills. He felt a strong hunch that he should follow the renegades who fled from the main camp up over the ridge.

After Jesse and Miguel left with the remuda he walked Scorpio up over the steep wall and saw the adjoining box canyon which opened to the west. He moved forward cautiously, wary of ambush. At one point he topped a small rise and saw them a half mile ahead of him, then pulled out his field glasses and studied the sides of their faces when he could. He recognized Gray Blanket and another sunburned blond-haired face that could have been the brave he had seen shoot Mackenzie with bow and arrow. His excitement rose at the thought of finding out about Kathy's brother, but he figured that Gray Blanket would try to kill him and would fight to the death. He pulled his fast draw rig from his saddle bag and put it back on while he rested and watered his horse. He had left his first gun with Kathy and had Gabe customize another exactly like it, which he usually left in the chuck-wagon, but had put in his saddlebags. He thought he heard the sound of distant rifle fire, southwest of there. Straining to listen, he heard lots more. A gun battle raged in the distance, too far away to be Jesse and Miguel, and LaPoint figured it was his outfit winning the herd back. The gun battle went on for ten minutes, then trailed off.

With his practiced tracker's skill, LaPoint followed a clear trail of three riders on shod horses along the high ridge until two went west into the valley and one went north towards a ridge-line. On a hunch LaPoint pursued the lone rider north, whose trail went into a small cleft in the hill, then up and over the next ridge-line into a deep valley with a tight canyon at the bottom. Josh followed the horse tracks into the deep canyon, sidestepping Scorpio in switchbacks down the steep talus slope, then turned west to trail them along the sand wash at the bottom. Because the tracks were obvious in the sandy ground with a tiny creek, LaPoint moved quickly. The canyon seemed to head straight back west out to the plains, so he urged Scorpio at a rapid walk through it, figuring the rustler would bolt for the plains out the long straight chute of the tight canyon.

When he had ridden a half mile with his eyes down on the fresh tracks in the sand he came to a small steep bluff and rise with live oaks and cedar, forcing a turn in the wash before it emptied into the plains. As he was passing under some twisting, spreading, thick oak boughs, a stout warrior dropped out of the upper branches and landed on his back, pulling him off Scorpio and onto the ground while yelling very loud. Scorpio bolted and fled from under the branches, since the weight dropping had felt like a mountain lion, and the man had snarled and bellowed as he dropped and grappled LaPoint to the ground with a thud.

LaPoint began rolling as soon as he hit the ground, tumbling the warrior in buckskins along with him to keep him from gaining a good footing. Every time the warrior landed on top LaPoint would continue the roll through the rough sandy wash. With a quick glance LaPoint saw a boulder coming and slammed the warriors body into it on the last roll. Scorpio had made his run and was returning at that point.

Then LaPoint leaped to his feet and reached for his knife as the warrior arose reaching for his about six feet way. LaPoint realized his knife was gone so he reached for his fast draw Remington, to find it had fallen from the holster in the tumble. The flap was buttoned on the reverse cavalry holster holding his big .44 long barreled Remington, but as he reached to unsnap it the warrior lunged at him with the knife, and all LaPoint could do was dodge the strike and grab the attacker's buckskin sleeve to hurl him forward in the direction he lunged as LaPoint took two strong steps to the side. Scorpio reared up and approached on his hind legs at that point, screaming a challenge at the opponent of his master.

The brave went flying with the strength and whipping speed of LaPoint's arching motion, and Josh squared off for his next attack as the fierce Comanche turned and began slashing motions while Scorpio walked up with flailing hooves. Jumping to avoid the horse, the blond warrior wielded his knife with practiced skill while LaPoint dodged.

Sidestepping and jumping back with forearm blocks as the fierce warrior slashed at him, LaPoint recognized the man he thought was Kathy's brother, Red Hawk. His face looked like the guys that Josh had drunk dark beer with at his wedding, Kathy's kin.

The husky warrior was nearly as tall as LaPoint and stouter, with thick chest and muscled arms and shoulders under his dirty buck-skins. There was a grim look of deadly intent in his pale blue eyes of this German Comanche who outweighed him by around twenty pounds. He meant to kill LaPoint, and pushed Josh back with slash after wide slash until he was pinned by oak tree trunks behind him. When Scorpio got close again he slashed at the stallion's shoulder and made him back up with blood spurting, then turned back to LaPoint, who was under oak limbs.

When Red Hawk made a wild slash at him LaPoint dodged, jumped up, grabbed a branch, and swung his boots up into the blond German warrior's solar plexus, knocking him back onto the ground, gasping for air. LaPoint immediately rushed him and got on top, pinning his arm and slugging him hard in the jaw several times, then once in the side of his head, which knocked the man unconscious and bruised LaPoint's knuckles. He motioned for Scorpio to back up at that point, and the muscular stallion took a dozen steps backward and stood.

"Damned hardheaded German Comanche," said LaPoint. "Feels like you broke my knuckle."

Catching his breath while unsnapping the Army holster over his pistol, he drew it while rising and kicking the knife away. He looked for his other pistol but could not see it in the sandy wash. Whistling for Scorpio, he pulled his canteen when the stallion came over, and poured water into the warrior's face. The man began to come to while Josh stepped over and dug into his saddlebags for a leather bag with the tintypes he had obtained from Kathy years before. He opened the bag, walked over to the man, and aimed the big revolver at his face from far enough away to avoid a kick. The warrior started to rise. LaPoint yelled at the man to hold still and jammed the gun in his chest, getting what he demanded. Then he pulled the gun back and holstered it to handle the bag of tintypes, tucking the holster flap out of the way for quick retrieval. The warrior started to rise again and LaPoint knee dropped him in the chest, knocking the wind out of him.

"Stay down, damn it, I want to show you something," said LaPoint as he pointed to the man's eyes.

Josh stood over the man and pulled out the tintype of Kathy and her little towheaded brother taken just before the boy was captured. He held it out for the man to see. The gasping man began to yell at him in Comanche and started to rise until LaPoint touched the pistol and yelled at him to hold still again, forcing him back down with a sharp knee to the chest.

Josh stuck the picture into the man's face, determined to make him look and remember. He said, "Kathy. Kathy." and saw a glimmer of light in the man's eyes. The warrior's big hands came up to take the tin-type, and Josh let him take it to examine. The blond Comanche stared at the images and traced his big finger on the faces.

"Kathy. Kathy," he said. "Kathy."

"Kathy and Rudy. Rudolph Hartman. Rudy. Kathy," said Josh, pointing at the faces with his free hand while the other touched the pistol to hold the warrior still. Seeing the man was taken aback by the tintype, with a growing glimmer of recognition in his eyes, Josh stepped back far enough to avoid a kick and pulled out two more tintypes, one of Kathy and her brothers taken at the wedding, and one of Josh and Kathy at the wedding. He showed the picture of Kathy and her brothers, who resembled Red Hawk in facial features, to the warrior with greasy blond hair and sunburned face, who was starting to bald in front, like his German brothers, and had the shadow of a beard on his jawline. He pointed to Kathy and repeated her name, then showed him the wedding couple picture, pointing to her and then him.

"Kathy. LaPoint. Kathy. LaPoint."

328

"Kathy. Wa-ipu. LaPoint. Tenahpu?" asked Red Hawk, then he put his fingers together and clasped them, looking Josh in the eye.

"Yes, Kathy is my woman. Kathy and LaPoint. Your sister is my woman. Tu hermana es mi esposa."

"Mi hermana Kathy es tu esposa?"

"Si. Yes. Su nombre is Rudy Hartman, es hermanos aqui," said Josh as he pointed to Kathy's older brothers pictures.

"No. Eka Huutsuu."

"Primero Rudy Hartman. Despues Eak Huutsuu."

The stocky warrior nodded his head while looking LaPoint in the eye, then stared at the tintype of him and his sister as children before he was captured. His eyes watered as he stared at the faded tintype, then he looked at Josh, and handed him back two of the tintypes, but clutching the one of him and Kathy. He rose to his haunches and slowly reached out for the pistol barrel, pulling it close to his chest, then stepping forward so that it touched his heart.

"LaPoint! Ekakwitsubitu Pia waooo!"

"Yes, Kiwih-nai named me Lightening Cougar. But I'm not going to shoot you," said LaPoint. "Tu es de hermano del esposa. You are the brother of my wife. Bienavides del me ranchero. You are welcome at my ranch. You can come be a drover. El vaquero, tu."

"Rudy es el nino. Yo soy bravo. Eka Huutsuu, no Rudy Hartman. Numunu, no toso taiboo. Numunu, Comanche, no white man."

In a flash Josh grabbed the buckskin pants of the warrior and tugged them down a bit to show white skin on his hip. "Rudy Hartman!" said Josh, pointing at his pale flesh under the pants. The German Comanche grabbed his pants and jerked them back up, then started stomping off, leaving Josh standing there with his gun out.

"You got a white ass, whiter than mine. Hey, where you going with my picture?"

"Mi hermana aqui. Por favor, LaPoint? Kathy and Rudy. Long time," said the renegade as he turned and locked LaPoint with an grim imploring look, as if he was ready to fight for the tintype.

"You come back, see Kathy."

329

"No come back. See picture Kathy." Josh had met the last of the stubborn Hartman brothers, it seemed.

"Alright, Rudy. You can have the Kathy picture," said Josh as he stepped over and picked up the warriors knife that had been slashing at him minutes earlier. "But look here first, mira aqui." Josh pointed with the knife-blade at the shimmering north branch of the Red River out on the plains, then holstered his pistol and drew a line on the earth. "Mira, look. Rancho LaPoint. Los Rios. Red River, Rio Rojo," said Josh, looking up to see if Red Hawk understood he was drawing a map of the rivers of Texas. The sunburned German broad face came closer and the blue eyes peered as Josh drew his map of the major watercourses, the Red River, the Colorado, the Concho, the Brazos, the Llano, the Pedernales, down to the Blanco and the Guadalupe below, the former range of the Comanche Nation. Josh named all the lines for rivers, as Red Hawk named them in Comanche, then Josh showed where the Blanco joined the San Marcos, then traced the knife point up to the location of his ranch and put an X. Clear Springs Ranch, me casa con me esposa Kathy. Rancho LaPoint."

"On Rio Blanco?"

"Si. Rancho del LaPoint. LaPoint and Kathy. La Casa del mi esposal, tu hermana, Kathy, and LaPoint."

"Et Scorpio, tu grande macho caballo, si?"

"Si, bueno, comprendo."

"Kathy Hartman. Good bye."

"Rudy Hartman. Good bye."

"Adios, LaPoint. Yo...Via con los compadres."

Josh handed him back his knife. "Por que no trabaja con LaPoint vaqueros?"

"Yo soy Comanche, Adios esposa del hermana."

"Adios Rudy Hartman."

The warrior accepted the knife and slipped it into his scabbard, then looked at LaPoint with sad longing and wistfulness in his blue eyes, followed by a grim set-jawed look of determination, then turned and paced off into the brush, where he mounted his hidden horse and rode off to the west, out the widening canyon to the plains.

LaPoint was glad he had found Kathy's brother alive, but was not surprised that he wanted to remain a Comanche, what he had grown up to become since stolen at a young age. At least he had made contact with the converted warrior, and had lit a fire in his eyes with the old tin-type. And he could tell Kathy her brother was still alive, though determined to remain a raider on the plains, and bound to be attacked by the 4th Cavalry in the near future. He had fulfilled his intentions for Kathy, anyway, and found out her brother had lived as a Comanche all those years.

LaPoint found his small pistol half buried in the sand and spent a while cleaning it out while Scorpio grazed and settled down. Scout LaPoint admonished himself for letting that German Comanche get the drop on him, a move that his ever-cautious scout mentor Gabe would have deplored. He could hear Gabe in his mind as he cleaned the sand from his gun and calmed his mount, "Careless spells disaster for a scout."

After five minutes of pistol cleaning and calming himself, LaPoint remounted and rode west out the canyon. As he did he heard gunfire out in the plains, the sound of rifles and pistols fairly close, and pounding hooves. He urged Scorpio into speed with his boot-heels and surged to the opening of the small canyon, sighting the cattle herd to the west about two miles, and the remuda rushing to join them from the south, where Jesse and Miguel had driven them around the small mountain.

Josh rushed out onto the plains and made out Jesse chasing Red Hawk in the distance while Miguel ran the remuda towards the chuck wagon beside the herd. Tom Jackson was riding left point and Gabe the other side, pushing the herd at a fast walk towards the river about three miles north. The gunfire had stopped between Jesse and Red Hawk, and Jesse was sliding his rifle back into his saddle scabbard as he chased the German Comanche on his black gelding. Jesse rode a fast horse and Josh could see him un-lash his riata as he gained on Red Hawk.

Jesse was the best of all the vaqueros at roping from a full run, and LaPoint knew what he had in mind. Too far away to shout and be heard, LaPoint laid Scorpio out into his fastest run and spoke to him as he leaned down by his right ear, gaining on Jesse as the expert young vaquero edged into position to rope the renegade. Knowing his German Comanche brother in law was about to get jerked from his horse with a tight loop, LaPoint figured that it might be good for him, get his attention, wake him up to his encirclement and eventual fate. So he just raced for

Jesse and watched as the young vaquero began twirling his loop, intending to keep everyone alive.

The strung out herd in front of Red Hawk cut off his escape to the east, and as he veered northeast towards the river, Josh could see the dust of two other riders in front of him, one in the far distance. A vaquero had replaced Tom Jackson on point of the herd, and both Tom and Gabe were rushing after those riders as the herd ambled for the river, three miles away.

Jesse had his lariat swinging when LaPoint pulled his head up to see how close he was, and from fifty yards back Josh saw Jesse sail a perfect loop onto Red Hawk and cinch it, then loop a daly on his big Spanish saddle horn and jerk him from his horse in a dusty heap, the superbly trained cow pony under Jesse keeping the rope taut on the stunned German Comanche, dragging him when he tried to rise.

LaPoint yelled at Jesse as he approached, "Don't shoot him, that's Kathy's brother!", then raced past towards the other fleeing renegades, angling north. He could see that one fleeing rustler had a long lead on the other, and might be out of reach except by stopping and shooting with the Whitworth long range rifle. He decided to keep chasing and catch the second one alive, for he had the faster horse who had spent hours grazing earlier.

On the speedy stallion Scorpio, LaPoint gained on them from the southeast while Jackson and McBride rode at them from the west. They headed due north for the river crossing, but were soon being pinched in. Scorpio steadily narrowed the gap between them.

With a hunch it was Gray Blanket, LaPoint wanted them captured alive and questioned by Gabe, but he saw Jackson pull his carbine while approaching them from the west. Gray Blanket began launching arrows at Tom as he pulled in range and raced alongside over rough ground. This caused Tom to veer away for his life and bide his time, running parallel.

In an amazing show of dexterity and horsemanship, the young muscular warrior slung his body into a loop that held him down low on the side of the racing horse while he shot arrows from above and below the surging neck. It kept Tom busy dodging the accurate shots from the running horse, which kept flying until the warrior was out of arrows. The horses were jerky in stride on the rough ground, and neither man could get off a

332

killing shot, though LaPoint knew Tom would do so soon enough, for he was a deadly shot with his new carbine from horseback. Tom began to close the gap when he saw the Comanche was out of arrows, pulling his carbine into position for firing.

Josh drew his small pistol and fired three rapid shots into the ground, drawing the attention of Tom and Gabe as he closed in on the fleeing Gray Blanket from the southwest, only fifty yards away. LaPoint fired three more rapid shots, holstered the pistol, and jerked his lariat free to swing it in the air. Tom and Gabe quit shooting, holstered their rifles, pulled their lariats, and it became a horse race to the river, with the all three drovers joining in pursuit about forty yards behind the Comanche, lariats in hand.

The sunburned Comanche showed shock in his face when he looked back and saw three riders after him with loops out. Josh could see and feel that Tom and Gabe's horses were jaded from rounding up and driving the cattle, so he urged Scorpio to pull ahead after yelling at them not to kill him.

Scorpio responded with all the speed he had, but Gray Blanket had acquired a strawberry roan stallion since they had seen him last, and it was a long-legged and fast horse. Scorpio gained on the fleeing rustler slowly on the three mile race but could not catch him until they approached the Red River, shimmering in the distance with it's meandering loops and broad turns. When the ground got rougher near the stream is when Scorpio gained distance enough for LaPoint to start whirling his lariat.

The big strawberry roan hit the water with a lunge and splashed a couple of bounds until it had to begin swimming. The loop from LaPoint's lariat landed around the rustler as the horse slowed into deep water, jerking him back into the brown sandy torrent, and LaPoint felt some satisfaction that he had finally learned to rope as good as a vaquero. He threw a couple of hitches around his saddle horn as he whirled his mount and headed upstream, which jerked the hell out of the renegade The brown current swirled over his head as he struggled against the rope, and LaPoint drug him upstream for a while, as Gabe and Tom approached.

LaPoint backed Scorpio and towed the Comanche to shore after pulling him against the brown current enough to nearly drown him. The German warrior was washed with sagging wet buckskins, revealing white skin on his hips, and sunburned skin elsewhere, with flaxen streaks in his hair. He was sputtering and coughing up water, but tried to rise and get free of the riata. Whenever he did LaPoint backed Scorpio up and tugged him to the ground, slowly dragging him across the soft wet sand. Jackson and Gabe came charging up on lathered mounts by the time the struggling rustler had left a trail in the sand of thirty yards.

"Hold him to interrogate, Gabe, while I see that Jesse doesn't kill my brother-in-law."

"What? That other one is Kathy's brother?" asked Gabe as he popped his loop off the ground and expertly snagged the renegade's feet, pulling him taut in the sand.

"Yeah, I already had a wrestling match with him and turned him loose. Then Jesse saw him coming out of that canyon and took off after him after I let him go. Roped him from his horse at full speed."

"Wal, boys will be boys, ah reckon," said Gabe. "We got this one, flip your riata to Tom and I'll hobble the mean square-head. Hell, he looks like one of those Panna Maria farmers when he's washed off. Can't ya just see him with overalls, puffing his pipe under a tree, sipping a stein o beer?"

"Well no I can't, not this one. I see him snarling for my scalp, like he was back at those Cap-Rock canyons. I need to go check the other one that he doesn't get killed."

"Go on, Jesse is still pissed off over those raiders killing his horse a while back, no telling what he'll do if his blood is up."

"Gemme the rope, boss,"said Tom. "Nice job of looping him, you done gotten better at it."

"Well, not as good as Jesse, he caught that other guy on a full run, I waited until this guy stopped at the deep water, and gave him a good dunking."

"I can see he's just happy to be on shore, rope or no. Here, gemme the rope, here's mine for now, boss."

LaPoint flipped the rope to Tom, grabbed his and tied it to his saddle loop, and headed back south to meet Jesse riding up pulling Red Hawk's horse with the German brother-in-law draped over the back and bellowing like a mule. Jesse had a wide smile and started singing a Tejano cattle song as LaPoint rode up.

"Trying to calm the savage beast, boss. He sure don't like being tied with hobbles. Did you get the other two?"

"Only one, Gray Blanket, the one we told you about with Quanah that time in the canyons, who wanted my scalp. I already wrestled with this one back in that canyon he came out of, and let him go. He's Kathy's brother, Red Hawk. Rudy Hartman."

"Oh shit, I didn't know that....glad I didn't shoot him.., well, you want me to cut him loose?"

"No, bring him for Gabe to question in Comanche. I roped the other one at the river."

"You roped him on the run with that high headed horse?"

"Well, I saw you loop this guy, thought I'd try my hand, and actually caught him when his horse slowed at deep water. Gave him a bath."

"You sure you don't want me to cut him loose, being as he's your brother in law? Kathy would get mad if she knew."

"No, maybe it will knock some of the German stubbornness out of him. I gave him a chance to come in and be a vaquero for us, and he decided to take his chances out here. Didn't get too far with that, though. You roped him like a cow."

"Hell, he came bolting out of that little canyon back there right in front of us as we rounded that little hill, so I took off after him. I tried to shoot him too. And he shot back. I liked your other in-laws, but I'm not sure you're going to tame this one."

"No problemo, amigo. You got him tamed down nicely. Bring him on to the river for questioning."

LaPoint had to chuckle at the writhing angry Red Hawk with a gag around his mouth, well secured to the saddle riggings of an ornate carved leather Spanish saddle with silver trimmings and saddle horn cover.

"Well alright, you sure did a good job trussing him up on that fancy saddle, bring him back to the river and we'll get Gabe to talk with them."

"He can't talk any English, or German?"

"Very little, some Spanish, Gabe can question both of them and explain things better."

"So you didn't get the one in the lead?"

"We got one, Gray Blanket, the German that used to be buddies with Quanah. The other got away, since he was so far ahead."

"He may bring more back. He was on a fast long legged stallion. He could have been a white guy too, judging from his sunburned skin."

"Yeah, we'll hold these as hostage while we question them, and fort up in a river loop. I doubt they will come back in force, since we shot so many of them. Walk at a fast pace but don't trot and shake him loose, let's join Gabe and see what he's finding out."

The took off towards the river at a fast walk with the captive complaining in a loud voice under his gag. LaPoint figured it might provide the stubborn German Comanche with a taste of his future, enough to make him reconsider the path he had chosen.

When they set the prisoners in the sandy river bottom, Gabe tightened their hobbles and began to question them. As soon as he pulled the gag from Gray Blanket's mouth, a stream of Comanche cussing came out. Gabe put a loop around his neck and tightened it until he stopped, then relaxed it and stepped back with the end of it at his feet. Red Hawk was silent and stiff jawed when they un-gagged him.

Gabe questioned both captives for a while with sign and words, while Jesse and Tom went to meet the herd and help with the river crossing. Within thirty minutes the lead bull was crossing the river with the others following at a steady walk. They washed a few yards downstream when they swam the middle, but made the crossing all right. LaPoint had to oversee the whole operation, leaving Gabe with the captives.

Gabe spoke with the captives the whole time the herd crossed, and then loosened their bindings, at LaPoint's insistence. As the two captives struggled free of the leather lace, LaPoint and Gabe mounted and bore down on them with rifles cocked.

"Yal made yer decision, now get. Vamos, hasta la vista con 4th cavalry e Big Chief Mackenzie. Go back where Bad Hand will wipe you out."

The warriors leaped back onto their horses and took off east towards their hideout in the Wichita mountains north of the reservations.

"Alright, give it to me," said LaPoint as they mounted up and walked towards the herd, which was grazing along the river slowly moving north.

"Alright. In a nutshell, they ain't comin' in. They was both stolen from German farm families as young kids, and had ta become Comanche braves or get beat every day, which they did. They said it was hard to do, but they adapted to it and got good at it, then the bottom fell out of that life, with the war and the buffalo slaughter. They can't go back to being German farmers any more than we could after living horseback on the range."

"Well hell, I learned to dig post-holes and build barns and corrals, why can't they?"

"'Cause they's Comanches and that's all. They ride after horses, buffalo, and booty."

"So what did they do after the cavalry raids when the bands started going in?"

"They hid in the Wichita mountains, and they hunt deer and raid cattle and horses from the herds going to Dodge. They don't believe Kiwih-nai surrendered, and they say they will never come in, for the agent will send them back to the settlers. They hate the settlers."

"They understand they're the last holdouts, surrounded now, and that they will be wiped out by Mackenzie and the 4th cavalry?"

"Yeah, they said they'd take their chances rather than get penned up like pigs on the reservation and starved to death, while listening to Bible talk of the Lord Jesus the murdered peace chief, by invaders who took their land and way of life away."

"Did you tell Red Hawk that he could come back in, learn to work stock, still live out on the range?"

"Shore did. It lit a spark in his eye, but he didn't jump at it. Said he would stay where he was, where they could at least hunt deer in the mountains as the buffalo disappear, and where he was close to the plains. He said he couldn't go back, that all his life he was taught to hate the settlers and raid them."

"And you told them we would get word back to Mackenzie about them?"

"Yep. Seems to me like they want to die in battle with the 4th under Mackenzie, as an honorable way to end it."

337

"Damn. Don't tell Kathy that. We'll just tell her he's alive and well and a full-fledged Comanche warrior, which I told her was the best she would ever hear."

"Anyway you can tell her that he's got that tintype stuffed inta his possibles bag at his waist."

"Best we can do at this point, I figure. I already wrestled him down and showed him all the pictures, but couldn't talk Comanche like you."

"Wal what good is a keen eyed scout that can't talk Comanche, pard?"

"Won't need it much longer, I think."

"Right you are. My skills are becoming useless, like tits on a boar. Maybe I ought to settle down some-whars with a fine little gal and pound steel. But first I'm gonna do what I promised them fools, send a rider back to Fort Sill with the news. They done stepped from the pan to tha fire now. Gave 'em both fair warning and they made their choice, ta live or die with."

"Right. These rustlers have got to be cleaned out of here. At least Kathy will know he lived this long and enjoyed being a Comanche until the sky fell in on them. I showed Red Hawk where our ranch on the Blanco was, tried to tell him he could join us as a drover, did you tell him that?"

"Yep, but he's a stubborn square-headed German like her other brothers that hates all Indians, and a Comanche to boot, that hates all whites. We can't change that with arguments. If he's got a practical streak like Quanah, he may think about it and try a new path."

"I hope so, for his and Kathy's sake. But Quanah came in because his people were hungry. This guy has no people other than these renegades. Mackenzie will finish what he started, and the renegade rustlers will be wiped out next, along with the Comancheros. How many did you guys take down while getting the herd back?"

"Around a half dozen, for that Tom don't do much missing with that new carbine, and he was taking 'em down from a run. How many did you and the vaqueros get?"

"We got about the same plus a few, and got nine extra saddle horses from the encounter. That leaves around ten or less rustlers, depending on how many went down in the initial raid, and the leaders with rope-burns and knowing the 4th cavalry will be after them soon. With way over a dozen rustler bodies being eaten by coyotes and buzzards while we take our leave of Texas. They picked the wrong outfit this time. Did yal get those boys buried proper like we discussed?"

"Yep, took a travois back to the river with them and marked it nice with crosses and all."

"Well, telling their folks is a job I don't look forward to."

"Yeah, ah reckon. Right when we thought the war was over, these damn renegades strike. Ya better get word ta Muldoon from Dodge, he can take a message, and a letter. He knows 'em from church at Panna Maria."

"Let's keep moving the herd slowly through the night and take a short rest before dawn, then move again, get away from this area before they regroup. If Gray Blanket hated me before, now I've roped him and drug him through the river and up the bank. He may come back to ambush me."

"Right, let's go."

They moved the herd steadily up the winding Red River North Fork, and then along the upper reaches of the Canadian, without further incident. Recent rains had freshened the grass, so the cattle and horses fared well. They arrived in Dodge with the stock in fair condition, but found the stockyards full of cattle from early herds. They also found one-armed Bill Wilson looking for them with a letter, a bank draft, and a contract sent from Charles Goodnight in Colorado, all written in a fine hand by his wife Molly. They were to count the cattle, fix the appropriate amount on the draft to Mr. Winger, deposit it in the bank at Dodge, and drive the herd west towards the Apisha ranch to winter over while they drove the herd already there into the Rocky Mountains. Wilson handed LaPoint the blank check and said, "There ain't many Mr. Goodnight would lay so much trust on, but I vouched fer ya."

"Why thanks Bill. I'd do the same for you," said LaPoint. Within an hour LaPoint had the business done and was ready to get out of Dodge.

They moved the herd twenty miles west of town to find good grazing for a few days on the Arkansas, fattening them up before heading southwest towards the Apisha to winter them over. At the Apisha ranch they were to take the herd, already there for a year, into Colorado for Charles Goodnight, who was living at the time on the Arkansas at a placed they called El Pueblo, upstream a good sixty miles from Bents Fort. The

339

wintering over was necessary to cross Texas beeves into Colorado, and the pass had been forced enough to make the passage regular by then.

The weather had turned from warm to scorching and the grass was turning from green to tan and yellow as they followed the Arkansas River towards the distant blue mountains. LaPoint kept thinking of the cool air in the high valleys of the Rockies as the sun blistered down on them.

With fresh grass and flat country to traverse, they made the trip of nearly three hundred miles in twenty five days, then took the well-fattened Goodnight herd that had wintered over at Apisha ranch up through the Trinchera Pass. The drive through the gentle pass with a spring near the crest, where they had forced their way with cocked rifles the year before, was smooth as silk, and soon they were heading for Trinidad, where Goodnight was supposed to be waiting to meet them with further instructions and the contracts he had lined up. They picked up a riverbed with good grass north of the pass in which the Pugatory River flowed. Gabe referred to it by the mountain guide name of Picketwire River, and led the way down this familiar trail to Trinidad in a few days, keeping the herd well fattened with the fresh grass on its banks. He knew the river valley well, having hunted the area during his days bringing in meat for the Sante Fe Trail caravans.

They bedded the herd in grassy flats east of town and LaPoint took Gabe and Jesse into town looking for Goodnight while Jackson stood in charge at the camp. The Spanish flavored town had been an early stop on the Sante Fe Trail and had grown to over a thousand residents with log and adobe buildings lining the main street and new stone ones being erected. They went to a hotel where they had word to meet Goodnight, and found him at the bar and grill, having a steak and potatoes. They had a friendly meeting and found out they were to deliver the herd to the interior of the mining area, across La Veta Pass and down into the broad San Luis valley, then past Blanca Peak towards the mining camps around Creede and on to Lake City and Silverton, in the heart of the soaring San Juan Mountains. With multiple contracts for beef all the way up the Rio Grande on the table, Charlie laid out the routes on a map while LaPoint took notes and drew charts in his big hard-backed pocket journal with the bullet-hole in it.

340

"How come you carry that book with a bullet hole in it?"

"Reminds me of the importance of keeping a journal in my vest pocket, Charlie. I've even got Tom and Jesse doing it now. Gabe also writes a little, claims that Alex Robinoix made him start the habit. And I have a little metal flask of brandy in the other pocket. Want some?"

"I'll take a nip. You are really gonna like running herds in the mountains, after those dusty plains and deserts, I reckon. Look here while I sketch out what I got for ya." They discussed the plan for over an hour, draining LaPoint's flask in the process.

Charlie even had a special smaller, narrow gauged chuck-wagon built and waiting for them at the livery, better able to navigate the narrow mountain trails they would deliver the cattle on. Gabe admired the reinforced wheels, heavy brakes, and scaled down rigging on the stout mountain wagon. At the livery stables, the LaPoint outfit listened to Charlie describe this trip into the unknown, delivering cattle into the Rocky Mountains, everyone thankful they had the old mountain man Gabe McBride to lead them.

"Why, this ought ta suit you to a T, LaPoint. Opening up the west, bringing cattle to hungry miners. Should be a relief after what yal been through on the plains, huh?"

"What, the Comanche wars, you mean?"

"Why hell yes, I heard all about it, from drovers coming up from Texas. Red River battle and Palo Duro battle. You heard about that ghost herd?"

"The what?"

"Drovers from the staked plains are saying there's a huge ghost herd of horses, roaming the canyons of Tule and Palo Duro, and in between. Lots of riders say they could hear a big bunch running and neighing and screaming, and some say they seen it. They say it's that bunch that got slaughtered, after the Palo Duro battle."

"The hell you say, Charlie. Gabe put you up to this?"

"I never," said Gabe.

"Naw, I'm serious. I heard it from a half dozen Texas drovers. They bring herds to my ranch up here every year. They call it the ghost herd of Tule Canyon. Over a thousand horses, they say."

"Wal, that's what ya been dreamin' about," said Gabe. "They's out thar, runnin' the plains, so ya can quit your frettin' It ain't just in yore mind."

"Hell Josh, there wasn't nothing you could do about it, once the man in charge decided. That slaughter is on Mackenzie, not you."

"No. Nothing we could do."

"Wal then, time ta let it go," said Gabe.

"You're talking true about this, Charlie? You really heard this from Texas drovers?

"Hell yes."

LaPoint, for once, was speechless. He pondered the thought of being haunted by a ghost herd of horses from that time on. He drank another brandy in silent wonderment, then went back to talking business with Goodnight and Gabe. He felt a renewed urge to leave the dust of Texas behind him, with all the memories of war and horse slaughter tied to the land in his mind and heart.

Riding back to the cow camp at twilight, they filled the rest of the drovers in on the endeavor they had contracted for, emphasizing the unknown dangers so anyone who wanted to back out could draw their wages and head back down the plains and be replaced with vaqueros hired in Trinidad. After years of facing the dangers of the plains, with Comanche and Comanchero rustlers, wild weather, and scorching heat, the thought that the Utes had just signed the Brunot treaty and were not in a fighting mood made taking the mountain changes easier. Ben Burnette, recovering from his gunshot wound, and Jesse, enthusiastic as always, led the campfire talk about staying on. Only two drovers opted out of the drive, and Gabe hired two more when he traded off the bigger chuck-wagon to Charlie the next morning on the way out, smoothing the deal with biscuits as Gabe walked away with two extra mules for the steep climbs. The new oakwood wagon was equipped with extra brakes on all the stout wheels for the mountains, and was about eighteen inches narrower than the other they had been using. Gabe had used the blacksmith shop to make an extra metal circle and shelves to hold the meat smoker, and they were set up as well as before, to the satisfaction of E. Earl, who was somewhat fussy about his kitchen rig.

Leaving early in the morning they covered the sixty miles to the pass in five days of easy trailing, with the solid misty blue-green wall of mountains getting ever closer as they ascended the high golden plains towards them. The front range still had snow along the top of the north-south wall, and they paused in their shadow to grass the herd on the fresh grass near the rushing streams that dissected the slopes. They held the herd grazing around a small adobe town for a day and night, then they took four days to make it slowly through La Veta Pass at over 9000 feet to the flat valley of the Rio Grande River behind the great wall of mountains they called the Sangre De Christos.

The cattle were strung out in a long sinuous line that snaked for miles through the winding switchbacks as they threaded the tall pass. There was plenty of grazing both up and down, so LaPoint let them move slowly until they reached the valley floor. The trees turned from cedar to pinõn pine, then ponderosa pine, then thick stands of fir on the tallest slopes before the rocky crags. The outriders were carrying carbines out, watching for mountain lions, bears, and wolves. It was slow going but they pushed through at a steady pace, losing only a half dozen cows to falling down gulches. LaPoint and Gabe were satisfied with the passage after making a count of the herd at the bottom, and rode off to scout a good bedding ground in the valley.

The route to the upper Rio Grande mining camps lay due west across the flat San Luis valley, pushing the herd south of the rearing pyramid of Blanca Peak, with its snow covered cap. They made an early camp a few miles south of the peak, as the drag of the long herd hit the valley floor, then Gabe took LaPoint out riding in the late afternoon, leaving Tom and Jesse in charge of the herd.

They rode at a gallop, west through the flat valley floor, alongside the great peak and then north until they spotted huge sand dunes nestled up against the west wall of the range, shimmering white with mirages pouring off of them. Another hour of hard riding had them at the edge of a great sea of white sand at sunset, where they made camp, ate, then walked the dunes in the long lingering twilight with the western sky pink and highlighted with purple streamers of ice clouds. It was an amazing sight to Josh, who had never imagined mountains of fine white sand in the wide alpine valley, piled up against a mountain wall. To Gabe it brought back memories of his early days as a mountain trapper when he had first seen it. Josh was intrigued at trying to figure out why the huge deposit of white sparkling sand was laid up against the towering stone wall of the Sangre de Christos.

They slept well to the faint sound of the sands shimmering in the wind, then explored the dunes in the morning. With their looking glasses, they stood on the tallest dune while Gabe pointed out the jumbled La Garita Mountains due west across the wide alpine valley, where the ill-conceived Fremont expedition, to force the peaks in winter for a railroad route, had failed in disaster. Leaving after breakfast with extra biscuits in a ready pouch, they shot an antelope within an hour and headed southwest to meet the herd with fresh meat.

They met the herd as it reached the Rio Grande River near a little Spanish town called Alamosa for all the cottonwood trees lining the river, along with willows and colorful rose hip bushes. The drovers had decided to stop and graze about twenty miles southeast, and they were bedding down the cattle and wondering where the scout and boss were. There were already cattle buyers in camp when they arrived, and LaPoint had the men cut out fifty head for them immediately for good prices.

That night around the campfire the scouts told of the amazing sand dunes, and were met with skepticism and laughing accusations that they had gotten lost or found a town and hotel to stay the night. When Jesse asked if they had found any of those camels that old Jefferson Davis had imported running around up there, they decided to quit talking about it. Gabe then switched to spinning yarns of the Yellowstone, with its steaming geysers.

Although the valley was flat and semi-arid, it was still a high alpine valley, and the men were not used to it. Some of the men had been experiencing headaches, queasy stomachs, and nosebleeds from the high altitude and dry air, so LaPoint decided to move very slowly up the Rio Grande, with it's abundant grazing, to put weight back on the herd after the climb up and down the pass.

It took three days to reach Monte Vista, a mining supply center, where LaPoint received high prices for a hundred head of cattle. From there it was another day to Del Norte, where they also sold cattle, then two days through the valley with rushing clear river and good grass to the junction of the Rio Grande South Fork, where they rested the herd in the grassy flats. The valley floor and adjacent mountains had been rising steadily, and everyone was having a struggle with the thin dry air. LaPoint met with delegations of miners who purchased another hundred head of beef. The cook, E. Earl, also purchased some burlap bags of potatoes that the farmers were growing in irrigated plots along the river, keeping them in underground storage bins during the frozen winter.

With good grass along the ice-cold and fast-running Rio Grande, LaPoint decided to slowly graze the mixed herd of 600 up the valley to Creede, arriving there in two days. They passed south of the high La Garita peaks to the north where the Fremont expedition had met disaster, which prompted some grisly mountain times tales out of Gabe around the fire in the cold night. After detailing the cannibalism that had occurred nearby in exploration days, Gabe was addressed by Jesse.

"Well you don't have to worry about anyone eating you, Biejo. You'd be too sour."

"That's right," replied Gabe. "We'd go fer you and young Burnett thar, like young mountain goats."

"Like hell," replied Burnett from warming by the campfire.

"Well, you might be alright if we stewed you in brandy," said Jesse.

"Hell, ah reckon ah'm doin' that fer ya now," said Gabe as Josh handed him another jigger.

The mountain walls surrounding the town had gotten taller and steeper as the upper canyon narrowed near the ramshackle mining camp. The air chilled quickly after dark and the mountain lions and wolves began their calls. Extra night riders rode with carbines out to protect the herd.

The mornings were white with frost, but the days warm, so Josh unpacked the rubber pontoon boat for a night-cloth over his ground tarp, and then decided to run the river, which he did in five mile stretches while the herd picked up the weight lost in the climb through the pass. When Jesse came in from leading the herd and learned Josh had done it, he wanted to try it too. The jumbled mountains to the north increased in size, and the drovers looked with field glasses to where Fremont and old Bill Williams had gotten lost.

With steep forested hills on either side, the valley tightened as they headed upstream, and it took many hours to thread the herd through a narrow pass near a place called Wagon-wheel Gap, it's steep canyon walls composed of dense pale stone with a rugged broken face. They had cattle to deliver to the miners around Creede, and looked for a spot to rest the herd near there. Past the Creede mining camp they found good grazing along the river and rested the herd while LaPoint again fulfilled beef contracts with miners. They cut out part of the herd and left them in corrals for the miners, then moved on.

They headed west up the valley with the sunrise sparkling off the river and a herd of 500 fat cattle, heading for the upper reaches of the narrowing Rio Grande Valley. The mountains lining the valley had risen to monumental size and impressive shapes, like crumbling castles and buttressed stony battlements, leaving a lot of drovers with open mouths and wide eyes as they gazed around and panted in the thin air. They stopped the herd and rested at a turn in the valley, where more miner reps came in to buy beef.

By that time word of the herd had reached beef-hungry miners all over the San Juan Mountains, and most who could pay had sent for some. Miners seeking beef had come over Wolf Creek pass up the south fork of the Rio Grande, and from the mountains to the north as well. When they left a day later, the herd had been whittled down to three hundred head.

Tom Jackson went out in the evening and shot an elk in the high meadows for some fresh meat besides cow, and all the drovers loved it smothered with mushroom,garlic and wild onion gravy whipped up by E. Earl. Gabe and Josh panned for gold in the upper Rio Grande, but said they found very little, and the water was icy cold, with the snow still melting from the tops of the mountains.

The valley narrowed and climbed as they followed the river up towards the northwest, with peaks rearing above tree-line on both sides. The herd moved slowly up the rising evergreen valley, grazing as they went. The clear river, lined with cottonwood and willows mixed with the darker conifers, was running faster in a steeper bed, with the grazing being limited by the closing walls of the valley, pinching the herd into a long struggling line. LaPoint and Jesse took the extra time to test the rubber boats in the rapids of the upper Rio Grande, running five mile sections at a time.

For three days they pushed the cattle up the valley along the cold Rio Grande, until they came to a splitting of the trail between what Gabe called Baker's Park, with a new town there called Silverton, and Lake City. Since beef was contracted for both miners' supply camps, it was agreed that Tom Jackson and Jesse would take half the herd to Lake City, while Gabe and Josh would take the more difficult climb over the Hamilton or Rio Grande Pass and into Silverton. Then they would rendezvous at the same place they parleyed, in two weeks.

Waving goodbye to Jesse and Tom as they pointed half the herd northwest, they started the climb by following the furthermost branch of the Rio Grande west up the steep mountain side. The river turned into a creek that was fed by tiny rivulets from the north and then the south as the trail got steep and began to switchback. The cattle protested in a continuous low breathless bawling moan as they strung out to climb the sharp incline. Gabe and LaPoint rode a half mile in front, at times clearing fallen trees from the path with both stallions tugging on them with straining lariats after using the bucksaw and ax.

The narrow wagon trail wound through the mountains along a tiny creek in alpine meadows to 10,000 feet elevation with peaks towering two thousand above on either side. Occasionally they came upon pegs driven in the ground, with metal tops on them marked Hayden Survey. The ruts in the wet parts of the road, especially the dozens of shallow creek crossings, indicated a lot of wagon traffic. At one point they met a wagon train of five coming towards them, and with great difficulty Gabe and Josh got them pulled aside to let the herd by, paying them some silver coin for the time lost. The freighters, glad to hear of cattle coming and beef to eat, were even happier to be paid for a rest, not knowing how long was the line of cattle. After the wagons, they ran into mule trains carrying ore, and had to negotiate a narrow passage with them.

With the cattle only traveling at most four abreast on the narrow road cut into hillside and valley, the herd was stretched back two hundred cow lengths down the trail, followed by remuda and chuck-wagon towing extra mules. Often drovers looked over falls of hundreds of feet as flatland horsemen grew accustomed to the thin air and long drops, and E. Earl more than once nearly had a conniption fit as one or the other of his wagon wheels hung out in space.

The high meadows and valleys were lush with grass and thousands of tiny alpine flowers, and LaPoint let the cattle graze as they made the long slow climb. As their lungs, livers, kidneys, and blood-steams barely acclimatized to one altitude, they rose to another. Dark forests lined the high meadows, dense with pine, fir, and spruce, spotted with mule deer and elk. Clouds rushing through the pass hung on the shoulders of the rocky ridges. From a small rise of fallen talus, LaPoint watched the herd with field glasses. It resembled a dark narrow winding snake that twisted through the wagon trail of the high passes, up and down the constant dips and rises, stretching back beyond sight. After years of trailing on flat ground, this was an amazing experience to him, and the only thing unpleasant was the thin air, causing him to pant for breath at times, and to notice Scorpio laboring after sprints.

Snow still lay on the north faces of the peaks overhead, rearing stony ramparts out past timberline to over twelve thousand feet, according to the maps carried by LaPoint. Scattered dry flakes sparkled down from passing clouds, causing the drovers to bundle in their sheepskins. They followed a wagon road that was used to haul supplies, and the climb was steep, but the descents steeper, and the only way to move the cattle was very slowly, as the thin air had all the stock weakened. When they thought they could go no higher, the road switch-backed up over a pass nearly twelve thousand feet up, which had all the men and animals reeling. Clouds filled the pass, and it was like plodding through an ice fog to get through, with several inches of snow on the ground. The view from the pass at the steep descent was daunting, frightening the men, horses, and cattle. LaPoint kept them at a steady pace.

A passing cloud sent snowflakes scattering over the stretched out herd as they plodded down towards Cunningham Gulch. A cold wind whistled through the pass as they plodded past stony peaks on both sides, their craggy heads rearing above tree line. The decent was very steep and they had to switchback down, hooking the wagon to trees to lower it with ropes and save the overheated brakes and overworked mules. Finally they saw the break in the mountain walls that signaled a turn towards a gentler incline to the west, according to Gabe, who had traveled the pass three times in earlier decades. It was at the beginning of this steep stony canyon heading west that Gabe spotted the white mountain goats in his telescope, and decided to ride up with LaPoint to check out the trail ahead with binoculars, then to take down a goat for some different meat in camp. They ran their horses ahead of the lead of the herd for several miles up the well marked roadway, to an area below the goats, who were browsing on a steep ridge-line. In the stream Gabe was elated to see beaver dams and ponds, and showed Josh the lodges and slides they used, then spotted some of them swimming to the dam with sticks in their mouths.

They rode to a high slope below the white goats and watched until they saw one that would fall in an accessible spot if shot correctly. LaPoint took him down at five hundred yards in the clear air with the big Whitworth, and they were able to ride to a talus slope to collect the body while the echoes rolled up and down the tight valley. The shot had gone through his shoulders and heart, killing him quickly. He had a nice horn rack and plenty of meat for the drovers. They took it down to a where the small stream braided in two at the bottom of the high valley to butcher the meat and salt the hide. The found a convenient branch in a grassy flat near the smaller stream to hang the carcass. The creek was babbling and giving a slight roar from small waterfalls and beaver dams as they worked with the body strung up from a Spruce tree.

It was perhaps because of this stream noise that they did not hear the grizzly bear until it was only thirty yards away, downstream and downwind, standing on his hind legs with his long nose sniffing the air at about eight feet high. It looked large enough to kill a horse with one swipe of its mighty paw, but stood there looking like a giant curious dog on its hind legs, sniffing for something good to eat. LaPoint grabbed his Winchester 73 repeater from the saddle scabbard of his nervous horse, and walked to confront the bear while Gabe hurried the last of the meat cutting and began to roll it in a canvass wrap. "Ya didn't bring the ten gauge, did ya?"

"No, didn't think to."

349

"Take a blanket and try flapping it if he comes this way, and then shooting in the ground if that doesn't work. Ohh fer some skunk potion! Shooting him may not keep him from killing us if he takes a mind to. You got to put .44 slugs in his eye sockets or his heart, and I seen 'em keep fighting with six bullets in 'em," said Gabe as he rolled the meat into a tight roll of canvass and began to do the same to the salted skin. "Forget the small pistol, except as a last resort if he's eating yore head."

"Well that's encouraging. You never told me they were so damned big!"

"Blanket might work, big or not, worth a try."

"Alright."

Josh stepped over to Scorpio and pulled the bedroll from behind his saddle, unrolling it and tossing the canvass to Gabe to wrap with the roll of meat. He hurried with the blanket and repeater to cut off the bear if he came towards them, but stopped by a small blue spruce at the edge of the shadows.

The huge bear was still standing erect and sniffing the air by the stream that was the headwaters of the Rio Grande River, and Josh stayed in the shade of the trees, watching. The great beast looked as heavy as a horse and very strong, with powerful humped withers, huge shoulder muscles and forepaws, and soon it was walking up the creek on all fours, still sniffing the upwind breeze. Another grizzle, not as big, came down to the stream from a small side creek gorge and began to follow the first.

"Damnation, Gabe, there's another one, hurry up and get that packed and let's leave them the rope and what's left of the carcass."

"Are they coming this way yet?"

"Yeah, the first one is twenty five yards away and coming slow, sniffing the air. The other is ten yards behind it, following. They've caught our scent."

"Almost done. We'll skedaddle west and up the valley to the north to get away from them, if we can, but remember, they're faster uphill than down."

"If we can?"

"Hell, they can sprint fast as a horse, even better uphill, and will trail ya for days if they take a notion. We may have to shoot to kill at some point," said Gabe as he began wrapping leather thongs around the meat package and slinging it behind the saddle.

At that point the lead grizzly picked up the pace and ran forward until he spotted them, standing up and raising his huge front paws when he did. At fifteen yards away Josh could scarcely believe how big it really was. The long-snouted grizzly began to growl and roar at them, waving his paws with claws extended, and made a short charge towards LaPoint, stopping at the edge of the stream about five yards away when Josh yelled as loud as he could and began popping the blanket in the air. At the same time Gabe threw the head of the goat at the bears, the horns twirling end over end as he lobbed it in a high arch at them. The startled bear jerked back and circled to stand and stare again as the other one bolted a few feet to avoid the goat head, then came back sniffing it.

LaPoint began a series of sharp whistles at the bear while still flapping the blanket with loud pops. The second grizzly seemed only about seven feet tall, without such a long nose, and it picked up the goat head. When it did the other became interested, and moved to take it.

"I'm ready, here's yore bull whip, throw me the blanket and pop that whip at them."

With the bull whip cracking and the blanket popping the bears were held back, then they made a short retreat and stood up to look back, growling and pawing the air with their long dark claws.

"Time to go, get mounted," said Gabe as he climbed onto Buck and pulled his rifle out. The headless carcass was mostly stripped and still strung from the tree branch. The horses were frightened and were ready to bolt at any instant. Josh ran back towards Scorpio with the bull whip draped over his shoulder and the bigger grizzly charged again, pursuing LaPoint across the stream. Josh ran as fast as he could to where Gabe had untied Scorpio and was holding the reins out. Gabe fired a shot into the ground in front of the charging grizzly and blew gravel onto his feet and legs, stopping him and causing him to rear up again.

With the bear standing again about ten yards away, LaPoint sprung onto his horse while Gabe aimed his revolver at the huge snarling beast. Then they wheeled their mounts and bolted upstream while both bears stood there and snarled with paws waving high in the air. They drove their mounts about a half mile up stream, then climbed the sloping sidewall of the valley to work their way back beyond the bears to the herd, only a couple of miles back up the trail. LaPoint rode with blanket wrapped around his shoulders, that and the bull whip ready to use it again if necessary, for the popping seemed to startle and stall the grizzlies.

The bears were engaged in stripping the goat skeleton and did not notice them pass by high above them. After they got a half mile past the bears, they watched in the binoculars a while, and it seemed like they were big fat puppies enjoying their first meat.

They rode back to the herd and told everyone of the bears ahead. Ben Burnett levered a round into the chamber of his Spencer and said, "Well, I don't think we have to worry about a stampede, since they barely got enough air to walk, and there's no place to go but up the trail. I'll pour some lead into them grizzlies if they come for these cattle. We brought these dumb beasts too far to give them up. And a bear rug would be nice."

"Might not have to, but if we do, make every shot count, for winging them will just piss them off. They weigh a thousand pounds on average, I'd say, big as a horse, covered with muscle, and a thick scull, " said LaPoint.

"It'll take everyone pouring lead into it at once, and some luck to take Ole Ephraim down, boys. This is the real thing, a monster like ya never dreamed of. Hit the heart or eyeball if we gotta shoot," said Gabe. "But try ta avoid it. I'd give 'em a cow or two to let us pass without a maulin'."

They decided to hold up and camp in the high valley, hoping the mild weather held for the evening, and let the bears finish their meal in peace. They heard wolves howling and cougars screaming in the dark, but managed to keep them away with a few shots without stampeding the weary stock. They saw no sign of grizzly bears, though Jackson and LaPoint had taken a knife and cut the lead of some bullets crosswise to make them expand and blow a bigger hole in any of the giant beasts. LaPoint had done the same to a dozen slugs he carried in the weapons belt for his big Remington .44 revolver. The night passed without attack, though they heard cougar and wolves alike. Near daylight a drover fired his carbine at some near the edge of the herd, to run them off. The cattle rose and milled, but were bottled up by the terrain and extra night riders.

The next morning was frosty, but they passed the spot of the bear encounter without seeing the grizzlies or even a trace of the goat carcass. Soon a pack train of mules came towards LaPoint, with well-armed drivers.

"Howdy, sounds like you got beeves coming," said the lead mule skinner.

"Yeah, we have a herd stretched out a long way back there, gonna make it hard on yal to get through this tight canyon. Maybe you could take a rest in a spot up the rise for a while to let us get these cattle through. I can't rightly move them all off the trail."

"Man, we was wanting to take a break anyway, that is the steepest damned climb. Glad to hear you got beef coming, those guys back in Bear Town a few miles back are about starving, too weak to dig, even though they got some good veins. Same goes for Howardsville and Silverton too, no beef, just salted pork old as your grandma's shoes. Come on ahead with those cows, pard, we'll take a danged break, just let us water the stock at the stream here and we'll move up to that ledge under them trees up there, yonder."

"Will do, how's the road on down?"

"Steep as hell, mister. A piss strainer for sure. Where yal come from?"

"Texas, originally. We drove one herd to New Mexico, then picked up one that wintered there and brought them up here."

"All that way? You gonna be a sight for sore eyes for these hungry camps, fresh beef, lawd it's gonna be alright for while, if the bears don't get 'em first. See any grizzlies up here?"

"Yeah, two big ones caught us skinning a goat yesterday, and we barely got away."

"They guard the pass. Ole Ephraim and Mary Belle. My mules are terrified of them. Mostly black bears down at Bear Town and Howardsville, though. Ole Ephraim and his mate are the ones that got us scared, though."

"Scared me too, good luck to you guys."

"The same, drover. Hey...What's the name of the man who brought the first herd of cattle over the Rio Grande Pass?"

"Name's LaPoint. Trail boss Josh LaPoint and scout Gabe McBride. Good day to you."

Josh hurried the herd through after the mule train got watered and situated up the rise. He spotted a broad meadow further on to hold them in after the drag was hurried through the pass.

Gabe rode ahead and shot an elk on a plateau above them, slowing coming down the switchback trail with it slung on Buck's rump as they entered Cunningham gulch. Gabe put the meat leftovers on a rock by the river as an offering to the bears for passing through as they moved on to a turn in the trail into a higher valley. There they found miners working in the creeks and sinking pits in veins of ore bearing quartz, and each one of them wanted to buy a cow and eat it then and there.

LaPoint arranged to sell twenty head and left them in a small improvised corral as they pushed on towards Silverton. The descent was in ways harder on the animals than the climb, and the wagon had to be strung with four ropes wrapped around tree trunks and lowered down some inclines with brakes smoking. The steep angle and constant slipping on rocks was hard on the legs and feet of all the animals, but slowly the herd trickled down like a brown bawling slug of beef. At the end of the gulch they found a miners' community of Howardsville, with lots of digging and board shacks, and they sold another fifty cattle, turning west for Silverton, with around seventy head of beef. It was a short drive down the Animas River to Silverton, past lots of placer outfits and some diggings.

They arrived at the miners' settlement that had sprung up into a sizable town in a couple of years, and settled the reduced herd outside town, grazing along the river called the Animas. The seven mile long flat valley nestled under surrounding peaks was first called Baker's Park, and the year before had changed to Silverton, a town that supplied miners in placer and digging operations all around the park.

The air in the high valley turned cold quickly as soon as the sun went down, and LaPoint rode with McBride into town. There were a lot of saloons and cafes of raw pine lumber from a small mill outside of town. The animals tied up in the streets were mostly the miners' mules and burros, and groups of big jack mules. The saloons and boardwalks were full of drunken and profane miners. Small tents lined Blair Street with women of the night sitting in front, smiling at the passing traffic. Garish music came from open doors of saloons and dance halls, where painted ladies danced with the miners. LaPoint was amazed that they had hauled heavy pianos through the pass into the miners' town.

"Why hell yeah," said Gabe. "What little wages the miner's get is shaken out of their pockets by these here dance halls and cat gal houses. I sorta figured you might want ta stop in one. End of the trail, and all."

"No, I just want to eat a good dinner, sleep, do some sight seeing, river running, and deal off these cattle, finish the job."

They pulled into the best looking place for a meal and drink, after riding through the town to look it over. They ordered elk steak with wild mushroom gravy, and ice cold beer, and found the steaks tasty and the beer perfect. They had reached the furthest point in their trek north with the cattle, and were drinking iced beer at over 11000 feet high, surrounded by mountain peaks of soaring stone. The big meal and several beers combined with the altitude to put them fast asleep in the hotel for the night.

They awoke the next day and took a ride around the flat park surrounded by the sharpest peaks above tree line, the ice-shattered upper stone in various colors, the high altitude forest dense with tightly packed fir. The peaks surround the town like a great cathedral of the sky. The smell of raw pine lumber, sawdust from the small mill, and pack animal dung filled the cool air as the frost melted in the morning sun. They rode a few miles north and sighted a huge red mountain gleaming like a scarlet pyramid, then cantered back to town.

After their ride in the incredible mountain scenery, they contacted buyers and met over lunch, sealing the deals for the rest of their beeves. The buyer for the last thirty head met with LaPoint in private and told his tale of misfortune. He said he had lost his claim and cash in a cave in, and could only offer half ownership in his freighting business as payment for the cattle. With his saddlebags already full of cash, LaPoint accepted the offer, based on his feelings about the man, and they made out the necessary papers and signed them.

With contracts fulfilled and saddlebags heavy with payment in silver, they had made a success of their first drive into the mountains. Locating the wagon with the freighting business which LaPoint was new partner in, they kept the mules for packing gear. They rode back to the herd and had it delivered to corrals outside of town by noon. The outfit spent two nights in the hell-roaring miners' town while McBride and LaPoint worked the nearby streams and the Animas Canyons south of town for color during the days, adding some dust and flakes to their pouches.

      The setting of Silverton was as beautiful as any of the LaPoint outfit had ever ridden into, the dense forest of the high mountains contrasted with soaring ridges and peaks in every direction, layered in dark evergreens and light green aspen mixed with scrub oak and meadows of grass and wildflowers. They rode down the river valley for a few miles until they reached rapids which Josh knew he could not run in the rubber boat. Then the next day Josh ran the Animas River in his inflated pontoon kayak to a spot above those rapids. Gabe was waiting with the horses, and LaPoint enjoyed it so much he did it the next day for the exhilaration of several miles of white water. They ate fresh trout every day they spent around the river. The river run was nearly all whitewater, a long steep descent, and Josh loved it.

      After a few days they felt much more acclimatized, and resupplied to begin their trip back. It was mid June and the days were warm but the nights often frosty, so they departed when things were coated in white. The six riders and three pack mules climbed the same Stony pass without cattle and made it over in two days, passing lots of wagons and pack trains going each way, carrying supplies back and forth.

      They spotted the grizzly bears fishing in a rocky stretch of rapids in the stream a dozen yards below the trail, but quietly walked by while trying to keep their horses under control, knowing that fleeing animals might provoke the giant meat-eaters into chasing. The grizzlies kept fishing after glancing up and watching the small group of riders for a few minutes. The riders felt lucky the grizzlies had not given chase, for the horses and mules were winded from the steep climb up. The climb down proved not as difficult, and they only spotted a brown bear along the way, about half the size of the grizzlies.

      The LaPoint outfit of six riders camped at the headwaters of the flat Rio Grande Valley and waited for Tom,

Jesse, and the rest of the crew. With good grazing, they fished for trout in the stream and beaver ponds, and hunted for elk and mountain goat. Gabe got a mountain goat the first twilight, and a fat elk the second, so lots of time was spent cutting and smoking meat while guards were out to run off bears with popping bull whips, blankets, banging skillets, or rifle shots into the ground, since there where no more cattle to spook into crazy runs.

The rest of the outfit showed up on the third day, well satisfied with their trip. They had easily sold the cattle for good prices, and had watched a short industrious little Russian man named Otto Mears building on the road, and were amazed at the work he was doing. With the gold and silver combined, LaPoint paid off all the hands, and everyone was ready to head back, so they joined up and retraced their trail back down from the source of the Rio Grande, aiming to go all the way to Texas, down the heart of New Mexico, following the mighty river.

Moving fast without cattle and with their bodies finally acclimatized to the thin air and cool nights, they made steady progress. When the Rio Grande had leveled out some, both Josh and Jesse ran it for a few miles in the rubber boats, enjoying the fast flow of the clear and cold water that was snow the night before, the mountain sunlight sparkling off the rolling ripples of the winding flow. They had become expert in negotiating tight rapids in the stiff pontoon kayaks with double paddles whirling, and saw canyons that nobody else did.

The trip through the high valley was leisurely, filled with hunting elk and fishing for trout. Then they picked up the pace around Del Norte, as the high San Luis valley flattened out before them, with the wall of the Sangre De Christos rearing up to the east. They made twenty miles a day on average and were approaching Taos on the west side of the river within two weeks of riding the high semi-arid valley, walled by mountains on both sides.

Small Spanish villages had been scattered along the river during their ride south, with precise irrigation canals for their crops and livestock, with some riverside pastures green for herds of sheep to graze. The feeling in the villages was different from the mining towns, peaceful and relaxed. The weather was warm in the daytime and cold at night, with plenty of grazing for the horses, and places to buy corn for them and the mules. Without fear of attack by rustlers, and confident that their arms and numbers would deter would-be bandits, they enjoyed the scenery without constantly scanning for enemies, though they did have scouts out at times.

Approaching Taos, the river fell away into the deepest of gorges, with ominous black cliffs on either side, and they headed east across the high desert towards the huge snow-capped sentinel of Taos peak, north of the village. Entering the brown adobe village from the north after passing by the massive mountain topped with snow, they rode to the square and checked into an adobe hotel to the south of the plaza, taking a whole wing with two bunking in each room. In the cafe, bar, hotel, and all the way into town they had drawn stares from the locals, nervous at seeing a band of well-armed and well-mounted riders with extra mounts and pack mules in tow. Soon they spread the word that they had delivered cattle into the mountains and were on their way home, and the smiles lit up and senoritas filled the cantina to dance with them to flamenco music.

On a small stage two gypsy looking dark haired men with twin guitars had spotted the Andalusian stallions of LaPoint and McBride, tied outside. Their names were Jorge and Ale, and they held beautiful gleaming wooden gut-string guitars of the classical, wide necked, Spanish style. They began an Andalusian gypsy improvisation as a tribute to the horses, with one strumming a perfect fast chord-ed rhythm while the other flailed the strings with high speed melodic picking in perfect time to the chord strumming. The crowd ceased talking and listened attentively, mesmerized by their fluid interplay of rhythm and melody. They played a marvelous progression of themes in a fluid melody, to the loud applause of the audience in the adobe cantina with terra cotta tile floor.

LaPoint clapped and whistled, proud of his Andalusian horse, and the guitarists spoke to him about it after they took a break. He praised their playing, and they asked him if he played, to which he replied the piano and tapped on kegs and pots at times with the drovers making music on the trail. They pointed to ceramic hand drums with goatskin heads in the corner behind the stage, so he accompanied them on a half dozen tunes, to the delight of the full cantina. When LaPoint got going the couples hit the dance-floor, and soon the crowd was twirling around the room.

After an hour of fiesta dancing and gypsy singing by a raven haired songstress, they finished and took a break while several ladies in beautiful low cut Spanish dresses flitted by to catch LaPoint's eye, but he thought of his lovely Kathy and just had a nightcap of Taos lightening before going to bed upstairs in a room where Gabe snored loud enough to rattle the wavy glass in the windows.

The plans had been set to split the outfit up in the morning, with Gabe, Jesse, and Josh staying in the mountains for a while as the others headed down to Las Vegas and the Comanchero towns south of there, to scout for herds of stolen Texas cattle. Their meeting was set for Las Vegas in several weeks, after Josh, Jesse, and Gabe visited in Taos for a while.

The next morning after parting company with the departing crew led by Tom Jackson, they went to visit Rodney Rojo, Gabe's son. The heavyset Taos blacksmith had a new sign hanging from his shop saying , Toro Rojo, and smoke curling from the chimney in back. They were greeted warmly by Rodney and his aunt Juanita who was the sister of Gabe's deceased wife, Lupita. She was there making an omelet, and added more to it when Gabe, Josh, and Jesse showed. They ate breakfast after introducing Jesse to Gabe's husky son as he stoked a coal fire with big leather bellows, heating some horse shoes to red hot.

"Looks like ya keepin' busy, huh?" asked Gabe as he sipped his coffee, happy to watch his son working.

"Too busy, Senor McBride. Wish you would take over for a while, I'm working twelve hours a day except Sundays. Why don't you work with me for a while, show me how you make those knives?" asked the thick-armed young blacksmith.

"That'd suit me fine," said Gabe, which brought a grin to Rodney's face.

So they settled into the big adobe cluster of dark rooms around a central courtyard that was the Ramirez hacienda for many decades, since the early days of the first Spanish land grants, on a stream outside of town. The square compound of adobe rooms for people, storage, and animals all formed a box around the patio with central well. They lived there for a couple of weeks, with Gabe working with his son Rodney Toro Rojo in the blacksmith shop while Josh and Jesse hunted for meat in the mountains, selling elk and mule deer to a local butcher, enjoying just being in the high alpine areas with stunning views all around. Josh and Jesse took several runs down the box canyons of the Rio Grande south of town, paying locals to bring their horses down for them.

Gabe began to get friendly with the aunt of his son, the widowed sister of his former wife. She seemed to be very receptive to his friendliness. In the evenings they would have the guitar players in the patio playing by the fountain while couples danced, with old Gabe showing some lively steps with his new flame who resembled his old one. LaPoint was tempted by one of the dark eyed cousins, but limited his contact to chatting and dancing, with images of his love Kathy always in his mind.

After the blacksmiths had caught up with the overload of waiting business, they devoted several evenings at a time to making knives of Damascus steel. They made six knives which were as fine as any Gabe had ever made, enjoying every stroke of the hammer as they folded and pounded the soft and hard steel together while it glowed red hot from the coal fired forge.

LaPoint increased his skill as a mountain hunter, and soon was commissioned by local pastores herders to hunt a cougar that had been eating their sheep. He spent four nights hunting for the mountain lion with Jesse before he shot it in the chest at sunrise near a pen of lambs in the hills south of town. He worked the skin at the patio of the blacksmith shop while Rod and Gabe worked inside.

Rodney kept stepping out and saying he wanted to go hunting with Josh, so they began to hunt together on Sundays, with Josh enjoying the gregarious company of the younger man, who was strong enough to throw game over his shoulder and hike a couple of miles with it.

They stayed in Taos for three weeks, heading south when the aspens in the mountains started turning yellow, the first week of September. Riding south thorough the San Juans as the frost turned the aspens gold was a rare beauty treat, and they made a leisurely trip, fishing and hunting along the way. They met the rest of the outfit outside Las Vegas at a pre-arranged campsite on the Gallinas River, and received information about Texas brands on the cattle herds in the area.

Leaving the outfit observing all the stolen herds in the area, LaPoint and Jesse made a hard fast ride south to meet with a delegation of Texas cattlemen at Fort Sumter. Jesse rode Buck and pulled an extra mount, as did LaPoint. They covered the rough country, a distance of over a hundred miles, in twelve hours of continuous fast travel, changing horses every two hours.

Meeting the trail bosses and drovers, they returned in two days to gather the stolen Texas herd. The trail bosses carried all kinds of powers of attorney to collect the Texas herds and sell them. The first battle was at Puerta Del Luna, where they stormed a canyon full of cattle, then a corral full of horses near the Comanchero bunkhouse. There was fierce gunfire for over an hour, with casualties on both sides, but the Comancheros taking the brunt of it, and the remaining live ones scampering for the hills to escape.

The large party of Texans drove the horses and herd of two hundred stolen cattle north towards Anton Chico, where LaPoint's men were keeping watch on a herd of three hundred beeves with Texas brands. Pausing south of town with the herd, a group of well-armed drovers rode north and struck the next Comanchero herd at daybreak, engaging in another long gun-battle with rifles, until most of the rustlers were shot full of holes or fleeing.

The herd was gathered and driven to a grassy valley with a creek flowing from the hills, just south of Las Vegas, where it was held while drovers raced to rustler ranches outside the town to strike that gang of Comancheros. Another attack and herd gathering was made there with results similar to the others, and the gathered Texas herds driven to a prearranged spot west of Las Vegas. From there they were driven north to winter just south of the Colorado line, while the LaPoint outfit headed west and slightly south to cross the staked plains.

They began their crossing of the Llano Estacado in the last week of September and spent six long days of hard riding to reach the Palo Duro Canyon. Walking their horses along the south edge, they saw no Indian lodges where the year before a battle had been fought and won. They camped in the canyon and that night LaPoint was awakened in a hot sweat from a dream of racing on Scorpio in front of the herd of horses they had captured in the Palo Duro battle, the ones he had led to

361

their eventual slaughter. He could not sleep the rest of the night and was up with a mesquite fire and hot coals ready for Gabe when he awoke to make sourdoughs.

"What the hell, ya scared me," said Gabe as he saw Josh appear. "What got ya up so early, nightmare?"

"Yeah, that horse herd again."

"I figured, find me some dry mesquite for coals. Get your mind busy."

Josh busied himself with helping the breakfast preparations, they ate, and quickly prepared to depart. They headed south and bi-passed the huge pile of horse bones from where the 4th cavalry soldiers had to shoot the Indian horse herd, riding the nearly forty miles to the Cap-rock Canyons where they had encountered the Quohadis. They neither heard nor saw any ghost herd of horses. Camping there below the stunning tall red sandstone cliffs lined with horizontal steaks of white and green gypsum, they headed south for Fort Concho and arrived in mid October to re-provision, make contracts for more army mounts, and move on. It took them another two weeks of riding to reach Fredericksburg, where Josh waited for Kathy outside the schoolroom until the bell rang and they could embrace after the kids left for home.

The rest of the LaPoint outfit headed south to begin their next horse working assignments, while Gabe and Jesse headed southeast to the Blanco ranch. After sharing the weekend time with his wife, LaPoint headed for the ranch on the Blanco to finish saddle mounts with Jesse, after purchasing stock from the Fredericksburg area and putting his gold and silver in the bank. The rest of the year Josh spent the weekdays working horses and the weekends in Fredericksburg, and whittled down the time he took to travel there and back to the ranch with two mounts. By the end of the year he could ride the fifty odd miles in six hours, changing mounts once.

In the spring of the year Josh and Jesse had nearly fifty horses trained as saddle mounts, with half of them trained at working cattle. Josh was best at starting the horses, and Jesse was best at training them to cut out cows, so they formed an effective team. Their spare hours were spent running the tumbling Blanco River in cypress and rubber boats. They headed for San Antonio with the big remuda in late March, after hiring two extra drovers to help them.

362

The meeting with General Ord was pleasant and successful. The military man offered LaPoint the last copies of the quashed warrants, and he burned them in the fireplace. They drank a toast, and LaPoint signed over the first batch of horses to the San Antonio garrison, then moved the remuda north, supplying the forts as he did so. They delivered mounts as far as Fort Concho, then returned to San Antonio and met a herd gathered by Winger and a remuda gathered and trained by Poncho Menchaca in south Texas.

The LaPoint outfit regathered and drove the herd to the Apisha ranch south of Trinchera Pass, then drove a herd that had wintered there up the face of the Rockies to the mining camps of Pike's Peak and as far as Denver. They repeated such drives the next several years, each year pushing herds further, using the streams coming down from the mountains to water the herds, helping to supply northern forts, reservations, and cattle ranches. By the forth year of driving herds north, often in partnership with Charles Goodnight, who was establishing another ranch that included the Palo Duro Canyon, they were pushing cattle into Wyoming.

Chapter Eleven: Narrow Gauge to Silverton

In 1877 LaPoint sold his remaining interest in the south Texas ranch to Pancho Menchaca and bought raw acreage with Gabe and Tom Jackson around the Chimney Rocks on the Piedra River in southern Colorado. They spent their spare time clearing the valley floor of tall trees there for the next few years, and later building a log lodge with Rumford fireplaces and chimneys of native stone. The constant work with large crosscut saw and ax kept LaPoint layered in muscle. They used mules to haul sleds of selected building stone to the jobs. Gabe set up a sawmill for the pine logs, and they then had lumber for all their needs. The huge pine logs yielded barn boards that were 16 inches wide, and the scrap was used for battens. Steep roofs were built on all the houses, for the heavy snowfalls, and the excess snow was drained to stock tanks in spring. The Andalusians fared well on the mountain grass and grew huskier with thicker coats, as Scorpio lost most of his dappled gray and turned to white.

While still teaching school in Fredricksburg, Kathy began to spend summer time there, and they acquired one more rubber boat to run that river together as it slowed to meanders in the ranch land below the deep mountain canyons. Several horse and cattle drives took stock to populate the river valley with rich grazing.

While in San Antonio dealing horses to the army, LaPoint learned that Kathy's brother had been killed in a battle with the cavalry, and had to tell her the sad news. They weathered that as best they could, and returned their focus to building a ranch home together. At least the captive issue that had bothered her for years was over with, though with the sad but long-dreaded conclusion. Kathy loved the high valley of the Piedra River as much as Josh, and said it reminded her of how her mother described Germany to her when she was small. And their new home carried no harsh memories of Comanche wars nor ghost herd of horses, so they enjoyed the fresh start, building a life together in a beautiful mountain valley of the Piedra, growing corn where the ancients had done the same, and raising cattle and horses where no one had done before.

Their ranch extended south of the canyon for ten miles, and was full of grasslands beside the river and forested hillsides. Slowly the herd there expanded to over sixty fine horses who grew thick coats in winter to stand the cold. They also raised hybrid cattle with thick furry coats, for sale and home consumption. They hired pastores from the Chama Valley to run goat and sheep herds. LaPoint became expert at hunting mountain lions and bears that threatened their stock, and shortly had several fine rugs of each. Soon other ranchers were hiring him to hunt down the predators taking their stock, as ranching pushed into the lush mountain valleys. Tom built himself a small foreman's home, and Gabe was soon ensconced in a bunkhouse that adjoined his blacksmith shop.

Each year they built another hay barn or shed, and acquired more haying equipment to carry the horses and other stock thorough the long snowy winters with feed. In summers they drove the stock to the high pastures that were lush with snow-melt water. The horses shared that high pasture with elk, so the outfit hunted for good meat while tending the herd. They had no fights with the Utes, and often supplied them with beef in the snowy winter. The rustler bands that operated south of Durango into the Chama Valley usually avoided the expert marksmen of the LaPoint spread.

There were plenty of markets for the horses, and Josh continued to prosper because of his talents with the animals. Jesse took over the ranch on the Blanco River and used it for training and gathering remudas. Several times Jesse drove Texas horses and cattle into the mountains and stayed a month or more at the mountain ranch lodge with LaPoint and Kathy, learning how to hunt in the mountains with Josh, and how to run steep rivers in the rubber boats. Together they explored the upper Piedra River canyons by taking their rubber boats down when the water was not raging, being forced to portage many times, but making the incredible trip through the steep and narrow canyons in five days. They also ran the San Juan River, and twice the steep Animas River from Silverton down to Animas Forks, being forced to portage the lightweight boats many times on that trip as well.

The Pagosa Hot Springs proved a pleasant gathering spot for soaking and meeting people from different tribes. They met and became friendly with many Ute and Apache Indians, as well as trappers and guides who frequented the soaking pools. They were always hoping that Alex Robinoix would appear at the hot springs, but they never spotted him nor heard tell of him.

After several happy and creative years of making the mountain ranch a productive and comfortable working spread selling horses and cattle throughout the southern Rockies, Josh and Kathy moved their full time home there when they found out Kathy was pregnant. She had her first boy in the fall of 1879, naming him Alexander Rudolph LaPoint. She stayed with the baby for two years until she got a good Ute babysitter housekeeper and cook, then started teaching at a school in nearby Pagosa Springs, because they were desperately in need of one.

By that time LaPoint had begun to supplement his income by working as guard for payroll shipments and agent for the Denver and Rio Grande narrow gauge railroad that was heading west for the new town of Durango, and running short spurs into the valley for timbers to make ties and mine supports. Hunting for cougar and pelts and elk hides also supplemented LaPoint's income, and he shipped them on a small narrow gauge railroad that came up Cat Creek from Pagosa junction to Pfeiffer's spread a few miles east of his. Pfeiffer was heard to be staying near Fort Garland to the east somewhere, trying to get his pension and suffering from his various ailments. They tried to find him on a horse buying trip, but could not, and returned the horses to new range they had purchased downstream. At least once a year LaPoint went panning streams in the high mountains and returned with pouches of gold dust, which helped him to expand his operations and purchase more grazing and timber land.

LaPoint worked in various ways for the emerging rail lines, from scouting for, and guarding surveyors, to guarding payroll shipments and being foreman and guard for clearing and retainer-wall crews. Several times he actually planned the small spur lines to gather timber and built masonry retainer walls to reinforce the tracks. The correct stone-laying techniques he employed in the retainer walls impressed the railroad supervisors, and word of his various skills was passed up the line to the head office.

The railroad then contracted with him as a scout surveyor, and he spent several months on scouting trips around the canyons between Silverton, Ouray, Telluride, and Lake City, finding possible rail routes to carry ore out of the high mountains. The railroad company also contracted him to run the river in his rubber boat and map it down to Animas Forks, which he did with Jesse in the summer of 1879. It was a wild ride, and they were cold and wet while paddling for their lives at times, dragging around impassable rapids at times, but they completed their mission, in secret, as directed.

They made a rough topographical map, marking all the cliffs, steep river turns, necessary crossings, and places where masonry buttressing would be practical to protect the lines from the spring floods. They made a survey of the usable timber and rock in the narrow valley, and the good camping spots and river fords. They mapped out and marked where all the mule trails would be, and selected the camp sites. Palmer and Wigglesworth were very pleased with their report, and swore them to secrecy about it.

The necessity for hard rock mining in the San Juans meant that compound ores had to be hauled to a mill and smelter for efficient processing. Roads and railroads had to be built for those endeavors, and the premier road-builder was Otto Mears, the short but incredibly strong Russian that the LaPoint drovers had met near Lake City in 1874. LaPoint was impressed with Mears and became friends with the feisty Russian, visiting with him in Silverton and scouting for him several times over the years. Some of Mears' toll road work around Telluride and Ridgeway were based on survey scouting by Josh and Jesse. The overall objective was to gather all the compound oar by rail and get it down the Animas Valley to Durango for processing.

To the west of the LaPoint spread about thirty mountainous miles, Durango was a town being built around a railroad terminus there to accommodate a smelter near the abundant coal seams along the Animus river. The older town of Animas Forks, upstream a few miles, was being abandoned as the railroad made Durango the town of the future. The rail line would reach there in late summer of 1881, and at that time

LaPoint signed on to foreman crews building a line up the Animus River canyon to Silverton.

The contract signing was done on August 5 in the private car of General William J. Palmer, the man behind the railroad, with LaPoint, the General, and Colonel Wigglesworth, the capable engineer who ran the job. The officials wanted to keep the construction as much of a secret as possible, and allowed no photographers to record the progress. After Josh engaged with the company, the young couple bought a small home in Durango, and Kathy helped begin the school system there while having a place to enter her precocious youngster in child-care as her husband helped build the mountain railway up the Animus, a river he was quite familiar with, having run his rubber boat or ridden down it several times.

A narrow gauge railroad, only three feet wide, was being built from Durango to Silverton to haul the complex ores back to a huge smelter being erected there near the river. It was a private enterprise pushed by the visionary entrepreneur General Palmer, an experienced railroad man who was setting up the narrow gauge railroad all over the southern San Juans and calling it the Denver & Rio Grande Railroad. After their scouting report, Colonel Wigglesworth was ready to send surveyors to mark the line, based on LaPoint's sketches and detailed descriptions. It was nearly fifty miles up the twisting, steep canyon, with the only early access by mule train.

LaPoint made another extensive scouting trip with surveyors and engineers in mid-summer, accompanied by Jesse as scout and helper for the transit surveyors. Both of them had previously run the river several times, and hunted the nearby mountains for elk, so they were familiar with the terrain, and easily sketched in all the side streams. Although the rails were only three feet wide, the river valley tightened to canyon walls north of Animas Forks, sometimes coming directly down to the raging torrents in straight stony drops and steep cliff faces. The river raged high in spring snow-melt time and would tend to wipe out tracks built along the shore, so the task presented formidable challenges. For the first few miles the incline was gradual, but then they had to climb tall cliffs.

"Look at it down there, that's some serious white water. How we gonna get that train past this narrow gap, boss?" asked Jesse.

368

"All we need is a ledge for a three foot wide track and a little more for the train, eh? We'll have to set it up to lower men down to blast a ledge off. It's way too high up here for the engines to make the grade, according to what I've been told. We need to string our lariats together, plus that other rope I brought, and take a look at that cliff face, see if two men can punch a hole in it."

"Punch a hole? That why you brought that long star drill and that short-handled heavy hammer on the mule?"

"Yeah. I told you we were going to do some more cliff climbing."

"Okay, I'm gonna change to the camp moccasins my girl made for me, better for climbing."

"Good idea, I have some too. Give me your rope."

Fastening the lariat with two half hitches to a ponderosa pine on top the cliff while Jesse readied the gear, Josh looped his rope to the first, then added another long rope he had brought on the mules, pitching the coil over the sheer drop. He then united two other long ropes and did the same with that line, while Jesse stepped to the edge with hammer and drill. With short pieces of rope he made double slings for them to wear and fasten to the line when they reached the place to drill. The river was roaring through a narrow gap of perhaps twenty feet, hundreds of feet below them.

"You take the drill, tie it on your belt. I'll do the same with the hammer. Stay close together all the way down, so we don't dislodge stuff on each other."

"Alright, let's get it happening before my hands start shaking any more," said Jesse as he pulled his gloves on. "We've climbed some cliffs, but just one lariat high. This is three. And then a long drop and a tumble down ice-water rapids. You think there will be ledges?"

"No. It's exactly the same deal as those short cliffs. Rely on the ropes, they will hold. Those tree trunks aren't going anywhere. Just keep away from the wall by using your feet, like we've done before. Don't look down at the drop, just the wall you're dealing with. And no, from what I could see with the field glasses, there won't be ledges."

"You a bit scared, boss?"

"Yeah, enough to be damned alert, make sure that drill is well tied so you won't have to mess with it until you get down there."

"It is. How far we have to drill this hole?"

"Just a few inches, enough to see it can be done. They will have to drill a lot deeper to blast. We just need a test now."

"I hold it and you hammer it, just like on the ground at Clear Spring, building corrals in stone, huh?"

"Yeah, except on a vertical, and it's a lot harder than that limestone. Let's go, slow and easy, keep facing the wall and walking down," as he gripped the strong rope with his gloved hand and stepped backwards into the abyss, facing the cliff and edging down. Jesse did the same, stayed beside LaPoint as they slowly walked backwards down the ropes, facing the rough gray stony wall while listening to the roar of the white torrent below.

"Damn that's a long way down, boss. Feel that cold rush of air down in here?"

"Don't look at the drop, just look at where you have to step," said Josh. The roar of the Animas River below was much louder as they descended like spiders into the narrow canyon. Step after step they backed down, their leather gloves helping to grip the ropes that dangled down between their widespread legs. They went down for about five minutes, past the joins in the rope.

"We don't have much rope left, boss, maybe twenty feet." LaPoint looked down and saw Jesse was right, and shuddered at the sight of the drop down the rough cliff into the river. He quickly returned his focus to the convoluted wall in front of him.

"Alright, this is far enough. Let's hook our slings on with bowlines."

They tied on, got the tools tied to their belts, and set up to drill a test hole. With years of practice doing the same job together on level ground, they soon found a rhythm, with Josh slowly pounding as Jesse turned the drill a tiny bit each time. Within fifteen minutes they had a hole several inches deep.

"Hell, it works Jesse, that's deep enough. Let's take a rest, then tie the tools back on and climb up."

"Climb up. Shit. I've been thinking about that. Take a rest is right. Hard to get my wind, like the river's sucking all the

370

air out of this canyon. Look at it rushing through that gap. We shot that gap at lower water, but it'd be hard to do now."

"I told you not to look down."

"I couldn't resist, now that I'm more used to it. Doing the work made me forget to be afraid so much."

"It's a sight that not too many men will ever see, eh?" asked Josh as he looked down at the rush of ice-water below. "Tie that drill on tight and let's stay right together so we don't drop rocks on each other," said Josh as he fastened the short hammer to his belt.

"I'm ready when you are, boss. You the one doing the pounding."

"I've been sawing trees and carrying stones at high altitude. I'm okay, but we'll have to stop and rest going up. Ready? Let's go."

They walked themselves back up the cliff, hand over hand up the lines, with the long ropes trailing between their widespread legs. It took twice as long as coming down, and their legs were trembling with fatigue, requiring several rest stops near the top, where they tied on and hung in the slings to ease their aching legs. Finally they crept over the rim.

"Whew," said Jesse at the top. "My legs are give out. That was the hardest climb I ever made. How we gonna get Chinese and Irish to do that?"

"We will lower two guys down in slings already made up, then pull them up with mules and pulleys later. They'll drill enough holes to set charges for a good blast, then come up and blow off a section a day. Bit by bit a ledge will appear. About where we were drilling."

"Alright. We should get a bonus for that climb. You're getting a bit old to be doing stuff like that, I thought. Aren't you around forty now?"

"You're not the teenage kid I met after entering Texas on the run either, are you? If I'm near forty, you're near thirty, eh?"

"My legs sure feel thirty, and then some. They're shaking. Let's ride and let the horses do the work for a while."

"It's still a long way to Silverton."

"How far you figure?"

"Maybe forty miles. But no more cliffs to climb, just lay out some mule trails and do a general survey and description, then come back with the information to the head office on that

371

railroad car at the bottom of the track. It'll take a couple of weeks, I imagine."

"Well, it can't be worse than hanging over that cliff. I like running that river in our boats, but that cliff hanging is for somebody else."

"Yeah, that's why we get the big bucks, for the hard jobs. I told you learning to run white water and climb cliffs would come in handy some day."

After the surveyor-scouts made it to Silverton and returned, they presented their route descriptions and sketches, as well as the drilling report, to the engineer Colonel Wigglesworth, and got his approval. Trail-making crews were then dispatched to make paths for the mule trains, under LaPoint's direction. The project was still secretive, and no photographers or reporters were allowed access. Construction crews and mule trains were readied to head north in mid September of 1881. The first work would be clearing trails and campsites, then building masonry abutments and retainer walls to shore up tracks in many places along the river. The cliff area where the scouts climbed for the drill test would require long-term blasting efforts to make a ledge, but it was the most feasible way to enter the fifty-mile canyon that followed the snaking river to Silverton.

In addition to supervising the placing of the masonry work according to the surveyors directions, Josh and Jesse were given the tasks of laying out the mule trails, hunting for fresh meat, leading the advance parties up the line by reading the map and finding the surveyors points, setting up the camp sites, and overlooking the first crews that would be cliff-hanging and punching holes in the stone cliffs for blasting with the new dynamite sticks. The necessity to hunt and supply meat gave the scouts a break from the heavy responsibilities of the construction work, and they learned the mountain terrain around the deep Animas Valley while bringing in elk and mountain goat for the camp fare. Their most successful hunts brought in young elk from the Needles Creek valley that ran east from the canyon of the Animas River.

Both Josh and Jesse spent plenty of time dangling from lines over the cliffs, setting up a safe system for the men holding chisels and the men swinging the hammers while hanging like spiders on the stony cliff faces over the raging white ice-water below. Sometimes when they could finish their work early, they would run the river down to base camp in their rubber boats, meeting with engineers and riding mules back at night. Some of the workers lived in rail cars, while some lived in tents and sod-log shelters near the cutting edge of the work.

Adding to the cliff blasting danger, bringing in mule trains with supplies, as well as dynamite for blasting the cliffs, proved a challenge even to LaPoint's stock handling expertise. They had several incidents of mule trains bolting around the area they called the high line. Just a few miles north of Durango the river was pinched by cliffs coming down to waterline, and the first major dynamiting would begin there, to blast a ledge for the tracks. The first cliff-hangers were strung from big ponderosa pine tree trunks on long lines that hung them a few hundred feet above the white water of the narrow canyon below. A pulley system was set up with the steadiest mules to raise and lower them. Although it took men of raw courage to do the work, the only way to proceed was to avoid looking down at the raging white foam and ice water far below, and slowly pound a star bit chisel into the stone to set the blast deep enough to blow off a ledge to place a narrow rail line on. The work was very slow, requiring hundreds of slowly pounded holes, but proceeded at a steady pace as the men gained skill at the difficult task, and soon a pile of blasted rubble lined the bottom of the cliff as a ledge was made in the solid stone. The boom and crash of dynamite punctuated each day as the stone shelf for the tracks was punched forward through the solid rock. Eventually the mules and men became more used to it.

At times the scouts and surveyors worked a few miles ahead of the blasting crews, who had to spend weeks on certain spots to build a ledge in the solid cliffs of flinty stone. LaPoint and Jesse also began the masonry retainer walls that would reinforce the shoreline where the tracks ran right beside the rushing river. The mules would pack in the mortar, and then they would lower it in buckets and use the available nearby stone to shore up the route. Their progress was steady, and they drew bonuses for keeping ahead of schedule.

The weather grew colder as the aspen and cottonwoods turned golden and bright yellow in October. Every daybreak would reveal a white frosting over the tools as they went to work, and passing clouds dropped snowflakes and pellets of

373

whirling ice on them as they dangled over the cliffs and pounded the ringing steel. Josh took to arising early and making big breakfast fires of scrub oak, and trying his hand at sourdough biscuits for the crew. The Chinese were wizards at combining various herbs into the meat and rice dishes, flavoring it with a rich brown soy sauce. The Irish put oats in their drinking water and worked like mules on it. Steady progress was the rule, pushing the leading edge up nearly halfway to Silverton in the narrow valley.

By mid November they had worked their way north up the canyon for twenty five tough miles until it became too cold to work, and headed back to the ranch for Christmas at home. They had left timber cutting crews behind, to work at clearing mule paths until the snow got too deep. Satisfied with their achievements and pay for the fall, they rode the railroad on their free pass to Pagosa Junction, and cantered their horses back from there, after they were unloaded from stock cars.

"That horse is as white as this snow now, boss. I remember he was dappled gray when I first saw him as a teenager. He's carried you a long way and turned white in the doing."

"He's the reason I'm still alive," said Josh as he let Scorpio have his head to canter through the foot of snow that sparkled in the winter sunlight. "Sure going to be fine to see smoke coming from that ranch chimney, eh?"

"Yeah, a warm house and a warm gal with a warm meal."

"Let's get there, Kathy and Feather should be glad to see us."

When they arrived they found Gabe and his wife Juanita there waiting by a roaring fire. Jesse's sweetheart, a lovely Ute maiden named Quaking Feather, hugged him at the door. LaPoint and Kathy hugged in the kitchen where she had a meal going. After unsaddling their horses, rubbing them down, and shaking the snow from their boots, Josh and Jesse parleyed with the old mountain man and spent hours smoking his special blend of kinnickinnick, drinking the double distilled Taos lightening he had in a stoneware jug, and exchanging tales. Tom Jackson was there with a gal named Laura from around Pagosa, and they had several days of Christmas celebration, with the men hunting together to bring in fresh elk and mountain goat. Jesse and Feather announced their engagement, at which point the lovely girl broke into tears of joy. She attended with her mother, who cooked native Ute dishes and stayed in the kitchen or squatting near the great reflective Rumford fireplaces, marveling at the heat they threw off. A blizzard hit on Christmas night, and they awoke to a fresh white topping of two feet of powder everywhere. It was a memorable holiday season, with so many main men of the LaPoint outfit gathered around the fire with their women.

It was a very snowy winter, and they passed it caring for the horses and training when they could, while improving the insides of the barns and blacksmith shops. They built stone well-houses half underground with cisterns on top to collect the runoff from the roofs. Josh ordered books sent in on the railroad, and they had a special pass to ride wherever they liked on the Denver and Rio Grande. Gabe built a sleigh with metal runners for Kathy to ride to her teaching job during the winter, a few miles east where Josh had organized a schoolhouse building for the local rancher's children, so they wouldn't have to go all the way to Pagosa Springs to school, down the often icy hill into town.

When the snow was too deep or blizzards howling with white-out she would stay at a small place they rented near the schoolhouse. The winter passed in white peacefulness, with only the lonely howling of wolves to worry the horses, who ate the hay stored in the barns during the previous summer and fall. When notified of the time by a messenger from the telegraph, Josh and Jesse departed for Durango by catching a train down at Pagosa Junction and heading west near the end of March of '82. Work on the railroad to Silverton was being pressed by General Palmer, and he wanted to begin as soon as conditions permitted. They acquired snowshoes in Durango, and vests of goose down and oiled canvass. By then they had rigged their rubber boats to make effective one man tents in wet weather as well, so they were equipped fairly well as they rode up to scout the last of the route on May 3, 1882.

The shady side of the tight valley was loaded with snow crusted with ice, making travel difficult even up the mule trails. Several times they had to dismount and batter down a trail in the snow and ice with branches. The river was still lined with ice in shady spots, but starting its annual rise with the snow-melt of spring. Several snow laden trees had fallen across the trail, necessitating cutting and hauling with the powerful mules they towed. They pushed to the first camp for land clearing and cliff scaling, and built huge bonfires to clear the snow. Then they set up tents for the surveyors, who arrived several days later, and started working with them setting up the route.

Many places in the line required shoring up along the bottom with stonework, so Josh built huge fires there to heat the stone and the ground, then laid retainer walls of double stone facings with plenty of weep-holes to release the hydrostatic pressure. The supplies for these were brought in with mules and the mortar lowered in metal tubs, while the rocks were found along the canyon. With fires set in front of the work to smolder all night, the work was covered with blankets and tarps, insured from freeze damage until it cured, and they moved upstream putting in retainer stone when necessary as the drilling and blasting resumed on the cliffs. Work crews followed the masons to fill the abutments with rip-rap and gravel, providing solid footings for the narrow rails to follow. The cliff hanging drillers and blasting continued unabated, slowly cutting down the cliff into a ledge the engines could reach.

For seven days a week, LaPoint and Jesse pushed the front of the line and the crews supplied by Wigglesworth built track behind them. As the spring floods receded, LaPoint set masonry crews building stone retaining walls all along the lower tracks, and both he and Jesse ran the river in their rubber boats to check the progress of the masons, riding mules back to the leading edge at twilight. This section of high canyon valley was less than thirty miles long, but it took another spring and early summer of steady work to push it through. The first train pushed through to Silverton in July, and hauled multiple millions in gold and silver ore, passengers, and payroll from then on.

When their job was over, LaPoint and Jesse left Durango heading east after one last river run in the rubber pontoon boats, and spent the autumn and winter training new mounts at the Piedra River spread. When the snow was melting they were herding stock south a few miles from the lodge along the meanders of the river when they spotted smoke from the plateau below the rocky spires they called the Chimney Rocks. It looked like a small campfire. Curious, they rode up the south side of mesa, following tracks of a rider with a loaded mule. It took two hours of hard climbing to reach the top, and when they did they found the campsite of a solitary traveler. They hailed the camp and rode in.

Warming himself in front of a small fire was Joshua's father, Alexandre Robinoix, with a full graying beard, but recognizable to Josh by his piercing blue-gray eyes. His mount was a small jenny mule, and he was dressed in buckskins and moccasins, with headband.

"Hello Mr. Alexandre. I'm Joshua, under this beard and hair. I'm surprised and glad to see you here."

"Josh. My son. So it's true. You have a ranch near here?"

"Yes. How did you know?"

"A friend passed a camping night with me a few days ride west of here. I've been with some ancient healers there. He told me he visited with Gabe McBride in Taos and learned you were here, ranching in the mountains. I decided to find you, but wanted to see these ruins I had heard about first, and sort of prepare myself."

"Well, we have some catching up to do, I guess, sir."

"That we do. I'm glad you're alive and well. I heard everyone was killed on the Teche, your mother."

"I could say the same, glad to see you alive. My mother was killed, but I killed the men who did it. We've looked for you all along our trails, from south Texas to Silverton. Gabe and I built the south Texas ranch up pretty well, and one on the Blanco, and this one as well."

"I'm proud of all that, but mainly glad you're alive. You and Gabe. Well, let's visit here by my fire while the stars rise above this magic place. I feel the ancient ones here. Do you have bedrolls?"

"Yes."

"And this young man with you is?"

"Jesse Menchaca, Pancho's son, expert vaquero, like his papa. He and I have been helping push a narrow gauge railroad up the Animas Valley."

"Glad to meet you, Jesse. I know your father well."

"And you, con mucho gusto. I've heard about you for years from mi papa, Josh and that old hammer man McBride."

"Well join me for supper and let's get caught up. Tell me about this railroad, for the Animas is a steep and narrow valley."

They squatted around his fire in a rock circle of old ruins and ate elk with beans, rice, piñon nuts, and wild onion with Alex Robinoix. They talked until early dawn, each filling the other in on their activities since 1863 when Alex had disappeared. He told of being bushwhacked twice, being captured by Federals and put in prison camp, escaping and going to the mountains to hide in the stone houses built in cliffs to the west of there, and being shot by Kiowas near Fort Union while on his way to visit Ceran St. Vrain, and spending years recovering.

Not knowing if he was on a wanted list, Alex asked them to keep all his activities private and not to mention his real name to strangers when they asked him to come stay at the ranch the next morning. Accepting those conditions, they rode down to the ranch to be greeted by a worried Kathy at the front porch. A big reunion dinner was soon underway and celebrations lasted into the night.

They had a pleasant few weeks of visiting while Alex got to know his grandson, his daughter-in-law, and the man his son has become. When not outside working with the men, Alex was playing on the floor in front of the fireplace and carrying his grandson Alexe on his back everywhere to keep his feet out of the mud of spring. Josh was happy to see his father playing with the sturdy precocious youngster, as it was something that both he and Alex had missed in his upbringing at the mission school.

After a week there Alex asked Josh to use the Robinoix name, and signed papers acknowledging him as his son and sole heir. Without being able to speak, Josh nodded his head in acceptance, and joined his own family with his father's, adding Robinoix to their names. Kathy wept in the kitchen for joy as she made cornbread, her tears of joy seasoning the yellow dough. Jackson bolted out the door to tell Gabe out at the anvil, who trailed a couple of salty tears but kept hammering the red hot steel, saying he'd been waiting for that, between strokes. Tom got the jug and poured them both a drink to celebrate Gabe finding his son and Josh finding his father, and all of them finding good women and good land to ranch on.

Alex was eager to pitch in and lend a hand with the busy start of summer activities at the ranch, and was a quick study on every task, with clever solutions to difficult problems. It wasn't long before he presented a drawing for a mill utilizing the river's power for sawmill and grain grinding, as well as ore crushing. Soon he discovered veins of coal up the Yellow-jacket creek, that could be utilized in the forge. He was glad to help Tom Jackson run the summer operations when LaPoint and Jesse met a herd coming up from the Trinchera and La Veta Pass cattle trail at South Fork to scout and point it up the Rio Grande Valley to Silverton. Like his son, he was an excellent shot with a flawless memory, and liked to work.

Since they were familiar with the route, the drive went without hitch, and many cattle were sold along the way at the various diggings and mining camps. The only difficulty was heavy rains making the trail over the pass a quagmire, but they pushed through, glad it wasn't sleet. They arrived at the grassy flats outside Silverton with four hundred cattle in early August of 1883. The town had exploded in growth after the railroad had reached it in '81, with thousands of miners pouring in to work the deep mines of the surrounding peaks. These drives into the mountains was a surefire way for the outfit to earn extra money, for the miners were hungry for beef.

Selling most of the herd easily, LaPoint and Jesse celebrated with a hot bath at their hotel, then watched a stage variety show put on by an enterprising woman named Jane Bowens, who spoke with a British accent and called her saloon the Westminster Hall. After enjoying the show and a little gambling on Blair street, they ate dinner with Otto Mears and Jack O'Sullivan at the Grand Imperial Hotel dining room. The gregarious O'Sullivan offered to buy the remaining cattle and buy out LaPoint in their freighting business partnership, which Josh accepted, since he had only taken the partnership to get O'Sullivan out of a jam a few years before.

It was after dinner of elk steak while they sipped drinks at their hotel, the Walker House, that the messenger from the rail office came to the hotel and told them that the Silverton train had been robbed, and LaPoint was requested to appear as soon as possible. Josh rode with Jesse to the railroad offices on the gravel river flats south of town. The official there was named Sam Waterston, and asked to confer with LaPoint alone. They talked in his office for an hour while Jesse waited by the window and watched the light snow falling from a passing cloud in late summer, a sign of approaching fall. He resented being left out of the meeting, since he knew the Animus River valley as well

379

as Josh, having paddled it with him several times and hunted the high mountains around it.

Josh came out of the office grim-faced and walked to the door, motioning Jesse to follow. He saddled up and Jesse followed him back to the Walker Hotel, where they conferred in their double room as they packed gear.

"I got us a scouting job, a man hunting job, if you want it. We have to pack, if you're going, " said Josh as he checked his big Whitworth rifle. "I'm going, whether you chose to or not."

"What's it all about, boss?"

"For me it's about the money, and being in the right place at the right time. I'm in a bind right now, trying to pay off that new section I bought three years ago. A payment is coming due and I need money to hold on to what I've got. There's a big reward offered for these train robbers, dead or alive."

"Alright. If you're going I'm going. So what are we packing for, exactly?"

"We are going to run the boats down the river to meet a posse coming up from Durango. Somebody robbed a payroll train coming up from there yesterday around noon. They killed the conductor and a passenger, robbed everybody, and got lots of gold and silver payroll. We're to help track them into the mountains, catch them, bring them in."

"Good pay?"

"Hell yes, a tidy sum for both of us, even split. The pay is double our normal scouting pay for a month, with a thousand bucks bonus for return of the money, and a thousand reward for each man involved in the killing, dead or alive. Also I wrangled a free railroad pass on the Rio Grande lines, for life, for us and our wives, just for taking the job."

"Alright, Let's go. I guess we wear wool and mackinaws with the rubber pants because the river is up from these passing storms, eh?"

"Yeah, it'll be a heck of a ride, lots of splash and bump, get the cork life jackets too."

"But we won't have horses when we get there."

"No, but there's mules down at the work station. We'll go there, pick up some good ones, ride the last few miles down to meet them."

"Those pack mules don't ride too well, most of them."

"They have the ones that carry riders well waiting for us."

"Why don't they just send a train with one car down and drop us off to meet the posse."

"Because the gang sent rock-slides over the track at both ends to prevent it. The posse has to come up the mule trails about a mile after the high line cliffs, or that toll road maybe. And there's at least two slides on the line at this end. They sent a hand car to check the line, and found that out."

"So that's why they came to us, because they know we ran it and scouted it, and your shooting and tracking reputation?"

"Yes. That's why we're being offered as much as we each made the first fall of railroad work, plus a bonus."

"What about supplies? We just going to live on what we carry in and hunt?"

"They're bringing extra."

"Sounds like it would work. We know those mountain passes and valleys as well as any white men. I bet they went east up Needles Creek."

"Good guess, that's around where they hit the train. They're bringing a Ute tracker too. There's a hitch, maybe. The railroad suspects its the work of Mike Stockdale and that rustler bunch posing as cattlemen, with the butcher shop in Durango. The trouble is, Mike's brother is the sheriff, so the railroad doesn't have much faith in this posse coming up. They think it might be sent to *not find* the rest of the gang. The posse doesn't know we're coming, and I'm carrying authorization to join them, from the railroad and the sheriff here. The railroad officials down there insisted on sending the Ute scout, over the objections of Sheriff Paul Stockdale of Durango, who might be in on the whole deal. The manager up here who was waiting for the payroll tried to wire back just to send the Ute scout, but the telegraph wires were cut, on down the line."

"Hell, why not take the Ute and just leave them wandering around in the high valleys, dodging lightening?"

"We might. I've heard plenty about this bunch. They're like the Comancheros and rustler gangs we helped clean out down south, except they raid in northern New Mexico and escape over the line to ranches on the mesa southeast of Durango. They've been rustling and killing and running bold

381

around here for years, driving honest ranchers out of business in the Chama valley and elsewhere south of the line. We're taking the weapons in greased canvass bags, lots of ammo, field glasses, extra clothes and jerky in greased parfleches, knives and fire starters. Let's get going as soon as we can, so we can run it past those heavy rapids before dark."

The beginning of the run was not difficult, with enough space in the stream to dodge boulders, and they made good time, moving as fast as a swift pacing horse, until they heard the roar of the oncoming rapids and falls. Straining to paddle their rubber boats laden with heavy weapons and gear through the foaming breaks where the water was half air and did not offer much purchase to the paddle, they made it to an eddy behind a rough black boulder right before the first heavy rapids thundered into a series of drops with boulders gardens to dodge through.

The rapids and boulder garden below were as difficult to traverse as either of them had ever done. Recent rains had made the water cloudy, and both of them were constantly breaking through standing waves over their heads as they fought their way down the twisting currents with double paddles flailing white foam. The canyons deepened and the shadows grew dark around each corner as they followed the fast dropping current around boulder after boulder, the turbidity blocking a clear view of the underwater boulders. Within another furious twenty minutes of paddling while gasping for air, they had made it without injury to Ten Mile Creek, and they knew the worst rapids were coming from the sound echoing out of the rocky walls ahead. Finding an eddy, they tugged their boats out of the current onto the rocky shore alongside the narrow gauge tracks.

The canyon was tight and the roar intense as they drug their boats and then their gear down the hundred yards it took to get past the heavy rapids of No Name Slide. Putting in and paddling below there, they saw the rock-slide that had stopped the train, but had to keep paddling for their lives in the rapids, and did not stop. The river was constant white water at a very steep incline, and they paddled harder than ever to manage it. It was boulder after boulder, turn after turn, with sucking holes behind each big stone, trying to stay aligned with the current with constant turning and paddling as hard as possible to stay upright. Then they heard a greater roar ahead, and made for the side, finding an eddy behind a great boulder.

That waterfall caused them to portage for thirty yards, pulling the boats through thick trees and berry bushes where bears had been, with plenty of scat on the rocks and torn bark on the trees. They saw no bears and put in below the tumbling white water of the falls, their hearts pounding.

Soon after putting in Jesse passed LaPoint while they took separate routes through some braided rapids, and Josh watched as Jesse took the wrong route through a falls and hit a boulder below it. The nose of the rubber boat bent against the boulder as water pounded against it, pinning it to the smooth rock. In an instant the boat turned and dumped Jesse into the cold flow of the whitewater, and LaPoint watched him get swept away, paddle in hand, followed by the boat, which popped free without his weight in it.

Josh paddled as hard as he could to hit the falls a couple of yards to the right of where Jesse went down, clearing his boat through a gap and into the backwash, then past the wall of foam and downstream after Jesse. Paddling hard through a long boulder garden, LaPoint was able to pass Jesse's boat and finally catch him. He was floating on his back with legs out, looking very cold. He tried to yell but the sound came out like a little duck squawk, his chest was so tight with the icy water. Passing Jesse with furious paddling, Josh yelled at him to grab the stern line, which the struggling Jesse did. Quickly Josh found an eddy behind a boulder and they struggled to shore. Jesse's upturned boat floated past them and Josh took to paddling after it, catching it within twenty yards as Jesse ran down the shoreline after him.

"Try to jump around and warm up while I fetch your boat to shore. You've got to get back in and paddle hard to stay warm."

"I'm okay. Thanks for saving my life, boss. Again." Josh grabbed the stern line of Jesse's craft and towed it into an eddy behind a boulder, where Jesse grabbed it. He jumped in, shivering from cold, and they quickly embarked into the white rush. Jesse paddled as hard as he could to try to warm up, and LaPoint kept up with him, then passed him to lead the way.

After that they paddled another lively stretch of boulder gardens to Needleton siding, where a big wooden water tank rested on the rise above the track, and the stables for the railway crew sat on a narrow ledge. They found mules waiting, with a stove going in the work shack, and a man attending to a pot of stew. They dried Jesse out by the stove, ate some stew, and took the best four mules, riding two big jacks and pulling two more. They headed south along the west side of the cold white water, following the mule trails they had blazed for construction a short time earlier.

From a high point LaPoint saw coal smoke from the idling engine of the train that was stalled at another slide and track dislocation a few miles south. The train had tried to return to Durango after crews dug out the slide behind it and cleared a return path, but it ran into slides above the high line cliffs and was stuck between slides.

After riding a mile and a half down the narrow Animus valley they met the posse in a wide area across from the Needle Creek entrance to the Animas Valley. There were four white men and a Ute tracker, not a very big crew to go after six train robbers. LaPoint held a parley with the leader and then the Ute scout, who could speak English well enough, and called himself Standing Bear.

The tracks of three riders with two mules crossed the river, while an equal number of tracks headed south along the old Animas Forks toll road. After studying signs for a hour, they held a parley on the ground a few yards back from the river so they could talk without shouting over the roar of the rapids. The posse wanted to follow the trail south, and were dead set on doing that, so LaPoint agreed, and told them to go on, while he scouted out other possibilities. After the posse left with disgruntled airs, they set out with the Ute scout on a slow trailing walk up Needles Creek and into the high mountains, where they had hunted for meat before. The sparse ponderosa pine gave way to thick fir and aspen forests as the three scouts gained altitude in a slow walk with the steady mules.

The Animas River Valley at that point was around 8000 feet in altitude, but the mules were used to it, being worked daily clearing and hauling around the narrow gauge tracks, so they made the long climb without complaining. The creek was full of white water tumbling over rounded rocks and twisted its whitewater way up the valley. They found enough sign to know the trail went up the valley and they climbed as fast as they could to catch up with the train robbers. The strong mules had no trouble picking up the pace, and they followed the trail of disturbed rocks and creek bank for several miles up the valley.

"What are we gonna do if we catch up to them, boss?" Jesse asked at a break for grazing and water.

"They killed already to steal the loot. They'll kill us if they get the chance. I'd just as soon shoot with the Whitworth long rifle and wing them, knock them down. And if they keep trying to kill us, kill them. That's what the railroad folks want, to end the work of this crew, all around. They've played havoc with honest folk trying to raise stock."

"That's what I'm thinking too. Why let them shoot at us when we can take them down long distance, eh?"

"Let's take it slow and careful then. Don't let them get wind of us."

At around three miles up, after a half hour of tracking, LaPoint called a rest break on a spot where there were hoof marks circled in the gravel and mud bank of a curve in the stream. While having a smoke, some elk jerky carried by Standing Bear, and a rest on his back, LaPoint noticed a possible trail out of the valley up a small valley to the south. He decided to check it out on foot, and walked several hundred yards up it while studying the ground closely. He made a methodical sweep back and forth until he was thinking that the riders had split up with a pack-mule each and mounted this rise, but the signs were so uncertain because of all the elk and mule deer tracks, he wasn't sure. When he rose from his haunches to return back down the hill, he turned and saw a large golden tan mountain lion with big yellow eyes, staring at him from a crouch, about twenty yards down the hill.

Armed with only knife and revolver in a holster on his left with a buttoned flap, LaPoint froze into position and looked at the cat. The cougar stared mildly at him, then put his big head down and slowly approached while calmly gazing at LaPoint, who stared back and unbuttoned his army holster flap with a quick movement of his left hand. He began to draw the gun with his right hand as the cat began it's acceleration, but the mountain lion sprung to LaPoint in one pounce and past him with another, before he could aim the pistol. He spun and watched the cat scamper up the tiny valley full of spruce and fir trees, and soon saw the last flicker of his black tipped long tail.

With his blood rushing LaPoint rushed back down the hill and mounted up, leading Jesse and Standing Bear up the tiny steep valley as it climbed up the mountain to the south. The slope was sharp, and they had to dismount and walk their mules, but they progressed and spotted tracks further up. They followed the winding creek as it tumbled from above, and within a hour of hard climbing had reached the crest of the slope, which led to a high valley with tracks heading into it. They trailed the robbers up over a ridge to the southeast, where a herd of elks was scattered out grazing. They saw and heard a pack of wolves hanging in the forest near the elk, awaiting their chance for fresh meat. There was good grass along braided tiny streams there, so they rested their horses and scanned the area.

Ahead of them was another dip into a treeless high valley, followed by a ridge and a similar high bowl as they headed east on the trail. Jesse and Josh had hunted the area before for elk and mountain goats, and they guessed the train robbers were heading for a deep valley a few miles to the east, which bore directly south to the Los Pinos River Valley, which then fed south to the mesa below Durango where the outlaw headquarters was situated. After trailing over another ridge they came to a steep valley with a small creek, heading southeast, and recognized it as a trail to the deep valley to the east. At the head of the valley in some fir and pine trees they found a camp with fresh ashes and signs of two horses, two mules, and two men.

They found a clear trail in this valley, where the robbers thought they were beyond trackers, and followed it quickly to the bottom, where it turned and joined a very deep valley heading south. With the surefooted mule under him, LaPoint decided to seek a high viewpoint on the ridge above, and slowly angled the strong jack up the steep incline. It took ten minutes to climb to the ridge, but then the way was smooth and clear, and Josh ranged ahead of the riders below.

After a half hour of cantering on top of the mesa, Josh spotted a glint of light in the valley to the south. From an accessible high viewpoint LaPoint pulled his field glasses in a bit of shade and spotted the two train robbers plodding along. He urged his mule along the ridge-line while Jesse and Standing Bear followed the trail in the valley floor, a long way below.

From the ridge-line LaPoint could move quickly instead of following the twisting stream bed as the riders below had to, and soon he was within a thousand yards of the slowly moving robbers and their pack-mules of payroll silver and gold. He raced his mule along the flat top mesa, searching for a good perch, trying to narrow the gap, for a few minutes more.

Then LaPoint found a good shooting spot in a cleft in the cap-rock, dismounted, and pulled out the long-range Whitworth. Loading the long heavy rifle, he set it on a clean rest with a leather glove for a pad, and sighted his quarry with the field glasses. They were stopped and dismounted on a gravel bar in a meandering turn in the creek, drinking from a whiskey bottle. One of them had a rifle out and was standing on a rock, looking back towards Jesse and Standing Bear with a telescope. The opening of the tall mountain walls of the narrow valley into the wider Los Pinos River Valley was about two miles distant.

With the field glasses LaPoint studied the heads of the bandits until he recognized Mike Stockdale from seeing him at the butcher shop in Durango and the recent likeness he had seen in the rail office. At that moment Stockdale aimed his rifle towards Jesse and Standing Bear. LaPoint drew a bead on the man with the Whitworth, using a V notch in a boulder for his rest, slowly sighting his chest in the long brass telescope, then squeezing the trigger, seeing the flash of fire followed by the cracking boom of the exploding powder, and waiting to see the man spin around and fly back with a splash into the creek, his back exploded and draining blood. The sound of the boom rolled down the canyons in crescendos of echoes that slowly died out as small rocks tumbled down the cliff below LaPoint. Jesse and the Ute quickly dismounted and took cover behind trees. LaPoint reloaded and took aim at the other bandit, who had mounted and was trying unsuccessfully to pull both mules away. With a clump of ponderosa pine trees just in front of the train robber, LaPoint aimed for the upper middle of his back and hit the moving target cleanly, knocking the dead body from his horse in a cloud of dust beside a cone shaped blue spruce tree.

LaPoint studied the scene with his field glasses. He detected no movement but the horses and mules on a slow lope down the river gravel bars and through the shallow water. Sighting Jesse and the Ute below him, he signaled Jesse with his hat to hurry and catch them, then mounted and hustled down the ridge-line until he found a place to descend a small wash leading to a talus slope. He gave the surefooted beast his head at the steepest places on the rocky cliff trail, then guided him down the scree slopes to angle south towards Jesse and the other scout. Soon he met them, and Jesse left the spare mules with Standing Bear and hustled with LaPoint after the loose pack-mules laden with the loot from the train robbery.

They found the horses and mules grazing in fresh grass at the joining of one creek with another below, where the wider stream turned west and south. They gathered all the mounts, found the bags of gold and silver from the payroll delivery, then rode back to check the bodies of the outlaws. Both men had died before bleeding much, but already wolves were lurking near the bodies.

"Damn, boss. Look, the wolves are already on the prowl for their carcasses. Let's haul them in and collect the reward, eh?"

"Yeah, I'll put a few shots near the wolves and scare them off, I hope, while you get ready to lash them on." LaPoint drove them away with shots that blew rock chips over them.

They loaded the bodies onto the mules after wrapping them in their ground tarps, and rode the outlaws horses, pulling the mules with bodies. They headed south with the heavy-laden mules, then west towards the grassy valley of the Los Pinos River. They camped in a hidden spot and fished for trout, which they cooked for supper, then moved to another spot to hide the stock and sleep. Lurking wolves tried to come in for the bodies that night, but a few well aimed shots drove them away. They howled on the ridge for hours after that, keeping LaPoint and Jesse awake, while the Ute slept soundly. The next day they rode to Durango and collected their rewards after turning in the two mules laden with gold and silver, and the dead train robbers. They paid Standing Bear what he had been promised, with a bonus, and found out where to contact him for future scouting work, as he had showed a keen eye for cutting sign in the rocky stretches.

Riding over the hills back towards the ranch on the Piedra, Jesse told Josh that he wanted to buy a part of the ranch south of the chimney rocks, marry his Ute sweetheart Quaking Feather, and build a cabin there with his share of the earnings added to his savings.

Josh agreed with enthusiasm to have so many of his family around him, and they spent the rest of the year felling logs on the hills above the river to build Jesse and his new Ute bride a log cabin with fireplace. LaPoint finished the Rumford fireplace of bricks hauled in on the railroad on November 22, 1883, and a month later they made a small fire in it which they slowly built for three days, for slow curing of the dense masonry mass. He added another fireplace to the large den addition to the main lodge at that time, wrapping and placing several well-filled journals into a sealed stoneware jar and then securing them in the space between the firewall and the stone.

On Christmas the happy young couple had a house warming party and Tom Jackson announced his upcoming marriage on New Years day to his sweetheart from Pagosa Springs, a Miss Rosalee Archeleta. All the bachelors of the original LaPoint outfit were now settling down with their sweethearts, working the big spread together. Gabe and Juanita spent a long Christmas visit with them, joined by Rodney Rojo after the new year. The snowfall was extra heavy that year, promising good grass and high water in spring. By that time Scorpio had turned a brilliant snowy white, and blended in beautifully with the snowy fields of the Piedras Valley.

The three married couples and their visitors spent a happy winter snuggled in their warm ranch houses in the mountains, with Alex Robinoix playing with his grandsons on the floor in front of the fire while LaPoint, Jackson, and Jesse hunted mountain lions, and Gabe pounded hot steel in the blacksmith shop out back with his son Rodney Rojo. The next spring the women planted a huge vegetable garden near the river, with irrigated rows, and the LaPoint outfit continued doing what they did best, raising good stock and building the ranch, utilizing a valley that had first been farmed by the ancient ones of Chimney Rock, the first people on the land. And the seasons tumbled in their changing colors as the LaPoint outfit prospered in the shining mountains, each with their loved ones, raising livestock and children in the sunshine and the snow.

389